THE LIVING NIGHT

Volume One

THE LIVING NIGHT:

Volume One

Jack Conner

For Buddy.

Chapter 1

When the sun went down over the Sahara, Ruegger stuck his head above the sand and scanned the horizon for assassins.

Clear. For the moment.

He stood, dusted himself off and lit a cigarette, feeling the cooling desert wind against his neck. It was so peaceful here. So hot during the day, but when the sun disappeared the land cooled rapidly. As a vampire, Ruegger was only able to enjoy the last of the day's heat before the cold of night took over, and he relished it.

Sand stirred. He turned to see Danielle emerging from the ground and brushed at some of the sand around her lips.

"We survived another day," she said, and kissed him.

"Now to start running again."

She shook an arm, and sand spilled out of her sleeve. "At least it's better than tunneling through dirt."

Too true. Tunneling didn't afford much sleep, whereas some rest could be had sitting on a camel—not much, but some. He could see the exhaustion in her beautiful face, and the fear. Though also a vampire, Danielle was much younger and therefore more vulnerable than he was.

"The hunt ends tonight," he promised. "One way or another."

As they checked their weapons for sand clogs, Danielle swore.

"What is it?" he asked.

She pointed. A sandstorm boiled up from the south, blotting out the stars. Before it moved a string of dark figures—the death-squad, surely, ready to continue the pursuit across land.

"Damn," Ruegger said. "Let's hurry."

They picked their way over to the camels, which they'd led along by psychic means during the day while the two vampires tunneled. He helped her mount, then climbed astride his own camel. "Ra," he said, and the animal set out. Danielle rode at his side, looking half ready to slide out of her saddle.

"Want some more blood?" he said.

"You don't have any left to spare, babe."

He bit back a curse. "I'm sorry I got you into this.'

"Hell with that. *I'm* the one that wanted to come."

But I'm the one that let you. When she'd learned of his habit of going on a vision quest every decade or so in the Sahara and asked him why he hadn't gone on one since they'd been together, he hadn't known what to say. Under the premise of their anniversary, she'd demanded to go with him on one. Now here they were.

"You couldn't have known the abunka would show up," Danielle said. "Besides, if there's a hit out on us, they would go after us anywhere. Hell, coming all the way out here to get us probably slowed them down."

"Maybe," he said. "But why are they after us in the first place?" It had been a strange hunt, with the abunka (a race of immortal distinct from vampires) and their abilities to tunnel through sand at speed. It had certainly kept Ruegger and Danielle busy.

"We've made plenty of enemies," she reminded him.

Too true. "They must be renegade." Traditional abunka lived only in the ground, but these only went below during day. Neither race, abunka nor vampire, could survive the sun.

"They're pretty handy underground, though," Danielle said. "Anyway, tonight we reach the pillar."

"And Triboli, if he's there. Are you strong enough to face him?'

"Like a bull."

Frowning, Ruegger watched Danielle. Sand plastered her face and tangled her hair. Her lips were dry and cracked and parted slightly as if she didn't have the strength to keep them closed, and he was sure he looked just as bad. They required human blood on a regular basis, sometimes feeding more than once a night when they were in a city (only small sips, never a kill . . . unless the person deserved it), but it had been too long now and, in heading toward one of the twenty or so sacred pillars scattered throughout the desert, they hoped to find a source of blood. And cigarettes.

"That the last one?" he said.

She nodded, the dark-stemmed clove crackling between her lips. She corkscrewed atop her bumpy perch to catch a glimpse of their pursuers less than a mile behind and slapped the flank of her camel to make it go faster.

He glanced up at the moon, half full and waltzing across the clear sky, a hot wind having blown up from the equator. He focused on the wasteland before them, trying to sort through the billowings of the sandstorm ...

"Bingo!" called Danielle. "I see it."

A sudden clearing of the storm had revealed the pillar, about a hundred yards ahead.

"Is that what I think it is?" she said.

He examined the structure more closely. Three camels were tied to a post outside it. Probably one rider, he thought—one animal to ride and two reserves. Ruegger and Danielle kept reserves, as well.

"Looks that way," he said.

"Think ..." She swallowed. "Think it's Triboli?"

He heard the fear in her voice. If Triboli had reached the pillar ahead of them—if he'd fed ...

"We'll be all right," he told her, hoping it wasn't a lie.

They drew near the pillar and he hopped off his exhausted mount, then helped Danielle out of her stirrups.

"I hope this place has got some cigarettes," she said.

"Don't count on it." He wondered at the reliability of the *suka*, the tribe of humans that worshipped immortals, then looked back one last time at the hunters. It would be some time before the death-squad arrived.

Ruegger stepped forward alone, moving past the generator half buried by sand, and stopped before the pillar. About five feet in diameter and fifteen high, with exotic sculptural embellishments at the top (just below the satellite dish) reflecting its African roots, the moon glinted on strange bas-reliefs and sand raged like a screen in front of it.

A small hole opened at waist level, just big enough to put one's hand in, but deep. Mortals who wished to be admitted were supposed to prick their fingers on some unseen spikes at the back of the recess; if the hole decided to admit them, a panel would fall back and reveal a narrow stone staircase leading below the sand, but if for some reason (maybe if it sensed some duplicity) the hole took a disliking to the supplicant's blood, a rusty blade would descend and slice off the part of their forearm in its grasp, leaving them to bleed to death in the desert.

Having lived for hundreds of years and having learned to use some of the powers immortality had given him, Ruegger used his mind to *push* the panel in; it opened slowly, sand scattering about, moonlight illuminating a few slivers of time-worn steps, bowed in the center, that disappeared around the twist of a bend.

"You sure you're ready?" Ruegger asked.

Danielle hesitated, but only an instant. "Let's do it."

Ruegger crossed into the pillar and edged down the staircase, Danielle just behind. Both drew their pistols.

At the bottom, they emerged into the sanctuary. Torches flared along the walls in different-colored gouts of flame—blue, red, green—casting dream-like hues across the chamber, which was low and wide, the floor and walls of stone, most of the cabinets of wood, probably built in more modern times. Blankets arranged loosely on the floor, as if to give the room a warmer appearance, and a great four-poster bed loomed at the far end. A computer with a modem hunched on a desk in a corner, and Ruegger thought how bizarre it was that this symbol of modern technology had invaded even this most ancient and sacred of places. There were several pantries, some oil paintings on the walls along with decorative curtains and crossed swords, and a basin had been carved into the floor, half-full of water. Rafters that looked semi-petrified arched over the room.

The vampire Triboli occupied the center of the chamber, naked and covered in blood. He stared at the vampires expectantly.

"Good evening," he said, his English inflected with a South African lilt.

Ruegger stared at the object that hung from the rafters—no, he saw. *Objects.*

Two humans, a man and woman, both naked, had been bound in razor wire and suspended in a cocoon made from the wire. Though both were clearly dead, blood, not quite coagulated yet, continued to drip down on Triboli. A vampire could not drink corpse-blood, but he seemed to be enjoying the tactile sensation.

"Bastard," hissed Danielle, and started forward.

Ruegger pulled her back.

Triboli smiled. "I'm honored, really. To merit the attention of two such notorious shades. The Marshals, is it? Ruegger and Danielle?"

"You better believe it, motherfucker," Danielle said. Anger burned in her eyes, and Ruegger feared that she might try to leap at Triboli without him to back her up. Ruegger could feel the power coming off the other immortal and knew it would take both of them to kill him—if they were even enough together.

Ruegger indicated the bodies. "Why? Did they offend you somehow?"

Triboli wiped a bit of blood off his chest and sucked on his fingers. "They're sacrifices," he said. "What else was I to do?"

Ruegger knew that the suka often selected, either by lottery or with the aid of volunteers, people to go into the sanctuaries and sate the hunger of their gods. Most immortal races fed off humans one way or another—vampires with blood, werewolves flesh, morbines brain fluid and so on. It was an awful custom and unique to the peoples of the Sahara, who alone among humanity knew of the immortal community—*the* Community.

"Accepting their sacrifice is one thing, terrible though it is," Ruegger said, watching the way the razor wire dug into the mortals' flesh. "Sadism is something else."

Triboli lifted his lips. Blood coated his fangs. "That's right," he said. "I've heard you two only feed off of those you feel deserve it—murderers, rapists and so on."

"And wicked shades," Danielle added.

Triboli spread his arms. "Take me if you think you can."

"Well?" she said to Ruegger.

He shoved his pistols away and drew out his curved dagger. She did the same.

"Are you up to it?" Ruegger asked her.

"Hell yeah," Danielle said.

"Then I find this vampire guilty of the murder and torture of innocents."

"I concur."

"Then let's do it."

Without another word, they moved in.

* * *

Jarvick frowned as he chased Ruegger and Danielle across the desert. The hunt had lasted eleven days and nights and he was beginning to feel a weariness in his bones, as well as a twinge of something he hadn't felt in a long time. Fear. He turned to Sasha, second-in-command of the death-squad, and said, "There it is."

Sasha squinted into the wasteland until he saw the pillar, then yelled to the men, "Faster!"

Jarvick studied the pillar with detachment. Erected by the ancients long ago, it marked the presence of one of the several dozen sanctuaries scattered throughout the desert. Often called "resting places" by those who used them, they'd been built to ensure the safety of any immortal crossing these bleak regions. The suka kept the sanctuaries stocked with foodstuffs, booze, fresh sheets and the occasional human sacrifice.

Jarvick hungered.

The hunt had gone on too long, and the immortals of his squad needed blood and flesh. Without it, they would die. It was this threat of imminent death, at least in part, that sobered Jarvick. Mainly, though, his small-but-growing feeling of apprehension stemmed from the threat of Ruegger and Danielle themselves. Ruegger especially had a savage history, and he was very strong—much stronger than a two-hundred-year-old shade had any right to be, thanks to his friendship with the werewolf Lord Kharker. Danielle was reportedly quite fierce, as well, but she was young and posed a much lesser threat. Hunting those two—who, together, were known sometimes as the Marshals, sometimes as the odd flock—had been a sleepless endeavor, and if the vampires lived up to only a fraction of their reputation, violence would be the inevitable outcome.

As the abunka drew closer to the pillar, two black-clad figures with livid black eyes emerged from the sanctuary, a corpse in their arms. Ruegger and Danielle flung the blood-drained carcass of a tall, dark-skinned immortal to the ground, then withdrew into the pillar.

"Impossible!" hissed Sasha. "They couldn't have killed him in the sanctuary!"

"Is that where your thoughts are, Sasha?"

Sasha's gaze moved to the corpse. "Triboli," he said. "They killed *Triboli*."

The vampire was ancient and well-known in the area.

"That means they'll be strong," Jarvick said. "And we're not."

They traded grim looks.

"What now?" said Sasha.

"There may be another way," Jarvick said. "I'll go in alone."

"They could kill you, too. To them, you're no better than Triboli was. Why don't we all go in together?"

"We'd only make them nervous. Then they'd be in no mood to bargain."

"Fear is persuasive."

"Prudence is required, Sasha. Right now they're stronger than any one of us and perhaps all of us together. They've had blood—immortal blood—when we haven't had even a sacrifice in weeks."

"They're trapped."

Jarvick gave him a hard look. Sasha backed down, turning to his men and twirling a finger. Together, they started riding in a circle around the pillar, shouting obscenities and firing the occasional gun.

Jarvick entered the pillar. He paused at the bottom of the staircase, staring out from the passageway he occupied into the room, trying to locate the vampires. Ruegger and Danielle were nowhere to be seen.

Reluctantly, Jarvick stepped from the bottom step into the room. Instantly he was seized—the vampires had been waiting to either side of the stairwell opening—and flung to the ground.

Ruegger shoved a foot on his chest and aimed a .45 at his face, while Danielle held a sawed-off, pistol-gripped shotgun in her hands. None of the guns could kill Jarvick, but they could prove painful and maybe incapacitating. The best way to kill an immortal, any immortal, was dismemberment, sometimes burning. Crosses, garlic and holy symbols were only for the movies. Sunlight worked, too, but only for certain species.

Jarvick studied Ruegger and Danielle. Both had black hair, dark eyes, and smooth, pale skin, an appearance which made them surreally picturesque as far as vampire lore was concerned.

"You know who we are," Ruegger said. "Please, introduce yourself."

"I'm Jarvick, leader of the abunka who've been following you. Can I have a cigarette?"

Danielle threw him a pack, along with a lighter. Awkwardly, he lit it, feeling the weight of Ruegger's foot on his chest. He could feel the vampire's strength and knew that, although he was only half Jarvick's age, Ruegger was the stronger.

"Are you working independently or is there a general hit out on us?" Danielle said. Her lithe attractiveness piqued Jarvick's interest.

"General," he said.

"Whose black list are we on?" asked Ruegger. He was tall, though not as tall as Jarvick—probably a couple inches over six feet, something like that. Lean and sinewy, with capable hands, he moved with the sharp grace of someone who had lived through many battles.

"It's not my policy to ask," said Jarvick. "I'm always hired by anonymous employers. Some of my boys figure it has something to do with the Scouring, but I don't think so."

"The Scouring?"

"You've been out here too long. It's been going on, what, the last few weeks, I guess. High-profile shades all around the world are biting it. No one knows who's taking them out or why. Anyway, I don't think that's who hired us—whoever's behind it, I mean. You don't fit the pattern." He waved the subject away. "I didn't come here to kill you."

"I suppose not. Otherwise you wouldn't be down here alone."

"It occurred to me and my associates that you might pay more to be rid of us than our employer had paid to be rid of *you*. If you see what I mean."

"You won't stay in business long with that attitude," Danielle said.

"Yes. Well. Being rich is better than being dead, and we hadn't counted on you feeding first … and on an immortal." Such would make them immeasurably stronger, at least for however long Triboli's blood burned in their veins.

"At the last pillar, we heard from the suka about Triboli coming through," Danielle said. Darkly, she added, "We saw what he left behind. The blood … We'd been on our anniversary vacation, but after that …"

"How about this?" Ruegger said. "We *will* pay you—"

"Excellent," said Jarvick.

"—with your life."

"My associates will not like that bargain." Jarvick tilted his head, and the sound of gunfire and hooting drifted down.

"That's your problem," Danielle said. "Hell, I'd *rather* kill you—all of you. You're killers. Murderers."

"Immortals kill humans, girl—that's the way of things," Jarvick said. "Immortals killing other immortals—that is a sin, and to do so here, in the sanctuary, is blasphemy."

"We don't worship your gods," Danielle said.

"Go," Ruegger said. "Now, before we change our minds. If you and your people are still out there in five minutes, we're coming out, and I don't think you'll enjoy the experience."

Jarvick swallowed. "Fine. But …" He started to say *watch your back*, but then he realized that it was better to go while he could. "Let me up."

When he returned to Sasha and the others, they drew around him, hopeful that he had bargained a good sum for them.

"We have five minutes and then they kill us," he said. It would have to do.

* * *

Ruegger waited at the head of the stairwell until he was sure Jarvick and his people were gone, then released his telekinetic hold on the entrance panel and descended into the sanctuary, where Danielle had already laid the mortal man and woman on the bed.

She stared sadly down at them. "I know they believed they were destined to die," she said. "But like *this*?"

"I know." He squeezed her shoulder. "If nothing else, we avenged them."

Tears spilled down her cheeks as she nodded. Silently, they carried the bodies upstairs and buried them in the sand. Danielle said a short piece over their graves, and the two vampires stood silent vigil for a time. As they started to go back inside, Ruegger sniffed the air.

"Blood." He moved into the wastes, then swore at what he saw, half hidden by a dune. Their camels had been led off and killed, but Ruegger had been too distracted to notice their absence till now.

"Jarvick did this," Danielle said.

"He and his people will be stronger." Ruegger scanned the dunes around them. "Let's get back inside."

They backed down the stairs and sealed the door after them.

"Why *is* there a hit out on us?" she asked.

To that there was no answer. They moved to the water basin, which was the size of a hot tub, and splashed their faces. Danielle's pale cheeks were shot through with pink, water dripping down from her eyebrows to her lips.

"Look, there's bottles down there." She reached into the water and pulled one out—fat, long, dark and frosty. "Chardonnay." She stared at it, sighed, then lowered the bottle back in the basin. "I'm no longer in the mood."

She was still grieving over the mortals, he knew. It didn't surprise him. Her compassion was one of the reasons why he loved her so. She started going through the pantry, finding various foodstuffs and things, a radio and some batteries—and cigarettes. Apparently the pack of cloves she'd found earlier had been the only one of its kind, so she grabbed a carton and lit up.

"Dorals?" he sighed.

"It's what they've got." She threw him a cigarette and turned her attention back to the room.

He lit it, grimacing. She moved over to the bed. Its cream-colored sheets were splotched in several places with something that had taken on the color of rust and, to Ruegger, still carried a heady fragrance.

"I guess our vision quest is over," she said.

"We can't continue it with death-squads after us. Besides, it's almost time for the sled race."

"We wouldn't want to disappoint Ludwig."

She sat down around a large blackened pit, which looked to be a sort of fireplace, and Ruegger joined her. Immediately, a flame came to life, and lusty smoke billowed from the fire. There didn't seem to be a vent anywhere, but then the pit was mystical. The vampires stared into the fire. The world grew red and violent for a while, but the odd flock stayed that way, holding hands and taking comfort in each other.

"We need to leave," Ruegger said. "Jarvick could gather reinforcements or alert a more motivated team to our whereabouts—that's if he's not out there right now, waiting for us."

She glared at the door. "I guess we can call a helicopter to get home—I mean, without the camels, and with Jarvick …"

She crossed over to the computer in the corner, booted it up and accessed the internet, which was surreal to have out here, but the suka didn't skimp on providing for their gods. After she digitally summoned a helicopter, she checked their email.

"There's a message from Ludwig," she said, referring to Ruegger's oldest friend. Ruegger and Ludwig had met while still human and crossed over into immortality within a month of each other. Now Ludwig lived with his wife in their ice-encrusted compound in Northern Alaska.

"What's he say?" Ruegger asked.

"He says ..." Danielle made a face "... there's a hit out on us and for us to get our asses up to Alaska for his annual winter solstice dog-sled race."

"We should check our email more often."

She considered. "The solstice is only a few days away."

"He knows we'll be there. We always are."

"How does he know we're on a black list, though? This message is three weeks old!"

"Strange. Maybe ..." He frowned. "Could Ludwig know who's after us?"

Chapter 2

Ruegger stared out into the pulsating violet that surrounded them, sitting with Danielle on the floor of the plane that they'd sent for in Anchorage. Wrapped up in an orange patchwork quilt, the vampires jounced to the small plane's rhythm as it tore its way north during the middle of Alaska's annual three-month night. Lightning flickered below.

"Don't you love the storm?" Danielle said, exhaling spicy clove smoke.

"Always."

Mardi Gras jazz knocked its way up from the dusty speakers of the private room, mixing with the swirl of incense, hash, and cloves. Multi-colored lava lamps (red, orange, blue and green) swelled luminously from different pockets of the compartment, the only light except for a Chinese paper lantern that rocked from the ceiling. The lights cast strange and comforting hues across the interior of the plane as the vampires shared the cigarette and let their sweat mingle beneath the patchwork quilt.

Danielle sucked in another clove-flavored hit as she moved to the window and peered out, and the cigarette crackled as she inhaled. How she could tolerate those things Ruegger didn't know, but he pretended to enjoy them for her benefit.

He watched as she made her way back to him, seeing her lean nude body, small firm breasts, ribs just visible, pubic hair damp and soft below her skinny stomach and the gentle slope south of her navel, where a single silver loop gleamed.

He held the quilt aloft and she slid smoothly in, her lips brushing his shoulder.

"Ahh," she sighed, tilting her head to better listen to Frankie Ford's fast-paced, steam-whistle-blowing rendition of "Sea Cruise".

"Reminds me of New Orleans," she said. Turning to Ruegger, she said, "I bet you can't wait to see Ludwig."

"Good bet." With every mile that took him closer to his old friend, the memories of their times together grew in him.

"Go on," she said. "Tell me. You've told me so little about your past."

And for good reason. "Well, we were joined at the hip for years, you know. Ludwig and I. I've told you that much. Back in the old days, we'd spend all our time together, just knocking about Europe without a care in the world, except what to fill our stomachs with. Mostly beer, as it turned out."

"You've changed so much it's eerie."

He laughed. "We were vagabonds, wanderers, both still mortal at the time. Until we wound up in the French Revolution ..."

"Yeah?"

In his mind's eye he saw blood, and lots of it. A limp form dangled from long arms, and a cold face stared at him, blood dripping from its mouth.

"Another time," he said.

She seemed about to protest when the cockpit door opened and a man wearing a snake-skin jacket stepped out. He didn't seem bothered by the fact that the vampires were naked.

"We're beginning our descent," he said, then hesitated.

"Yes?"

"It's just . . . I don't know. We're getting some weird readings on the instruments . . . and the weather reports don't make any sense. Strange cloud formations and wind patterns." He shrugged and returned to the cockpit.

"What do you think it means?" Danielle said.

"I don't know."

Wanting to see the odd cloud formations, Ruegger moved to the window. She joined him, and they watched the clouds give way to an all-consuming whiteness. Soon Ruegger could distinguish land features, then Ludwig's compound itself, an arc of large buildings against a very white nowhere; Ludwig called it Liberty.

"Damn," Danielle whispered. "Do you see that?"

One of the main buildings along the arc appeared burned, almost as if it had exploded, and its debris was scattered over the snow. Ruegger had no idea what to make of it. Maybe some drunk revelers had bombed the building.

"Think it can have anything to do with us?" Danielle said. "That we're wanted dead?"

"I don't know, but keep an eye out."

The float-plane dove for the iced-over lake as the vampires threw on clothes. Engines screamed and the winds howled. The aircraft shuddered to a stop near the pier.

A man on the outside helped Ruegger and Danielle open the door. They stepped down onto the wooden planks, where they were given snow-shoes. The ice-cold temperature didn't bother Ruegger much, but he knew Danielle must be freezing, and he caught her checking the buttons on her coat. She said nothing about it.

"Some welcoming party," she said, only stuttering slightly.

Those who'd come to greet them included five baggage-carriers, ten armed (but casually-dressed) shades whose postures were so straight they had to be soldiers, a werewolf named Damaini, who was the Chief-of-Security for and third-in-command of the compound; and Maleasoel, Ludwig's wife and vice-president of Liberty.

She belonged to the immortal race of the jandrow—winged creatures that fed off of human hearts, though another animal could do in a pinch. Long black hair cascaded down her back, and bright green eyes blazed from her beautiful face under a sharp black beret. Her wings were hidden within the thick folds of her coat, which was part of a clothing line designed and tailored especially for jandrows. Of course, she didn't need to hide her true nature here of all places, but the outfit kept her wings warm.

She embraced Ruegger and Danielle both. "Welcome back to Liberty, my friends. Come with me. My associates will get your bags and Damaini will accompany us. Would you like your old room?"

"That would be great," Ruegger said.

They all followed her as she set off, moving between two buildings and emerging on the inside of the arc, an area referred to as the Commons. Soldiers patrolled in large numbers, and a well-organized crew tended to the remains of the gutted building, apparently trying to repair the extensive damage. Burn marks stained the walls of the buildings to either side.

"Dear gods," Danielle said, and pointed.

A line of ten or so immortals lay on the cold ground, stripped naked and bound by heavy titanium chains. Various spears and blades stuck through their midsections, making the victims writhe in pain.

Ruegger suppressed a shudder. "What's with the Inquisition?"

"Dissidents," Maleasoel said.

Ruegger frowned, prompting her to continue.

"They destroyed that building over there, one of our barracks," she said. "It's disrupted some of our activities and made sleeping accommodations rather awkward. Also .

. ." Her voice lowered. "Some of them were involved in a plot to kill me a few days ago. I took it personally."

Danielle indicated several shades that sat on stools beside the dissidents. "Who're they?"

"Our strongest mindthrusters. They make sure that the dissidents aren't able to use their telekinetic abilities to get free."

"Right." Danielle arched her eyebrows at Ruegger.

He shook his head, trying to light a cigarette against the wind. Now wasn't the time to talk.

"Where's Ludwig?" he said.

"Attending to something of vital interest, I'm sure." Maleasoel laughed. "This whole place has gone to hell. I remember twenty years ago when we had it built, we were so full of shit then."

Ruegger had thought so, too, but at least their intentions had been noble. The dissidents and something about Malie's tone suggested something had gone terribly wrong, however.

"What's happened?" he said.

"Well, you know," she said. Her wings ruffled under her jacket. "We wanted to raise an army of immortals and take over the world, 'not to enslave humanity but to set it free'. Ludwig's words, not mine. Thought mortals were destroying the world and themselves in the bargain, and we could do a better job of it, help them out." She sniffed. "Shades taking over the world! It's been tried before, I guess, and it'll be tried again. Well, we've got over two hundred soldiers now in this compound alone. There's three smaller compounds you may not know about; two in Europe and one in Antarctica. Just enough Libertarians to set some of our plans in motion. And now, when we're finally ready to do something, Ludwig's starting to falter— not that I blame him, really. My enthusiasm's diminished, too."

Her face flushed with anger. "What right do *we* have to enslave humanity? For God's sakes, we're just as human as they are, in our own way. This whole compound was built on arrogance and it needs to be destroyed. But these dissidents . . . they're mad at Ludwig for not wanting to go through with his plans, for *remembering* his humanity. They'd like to depose him and continue on with his plan. They constitute a large faction, and their numbers are swelling."

Ruegger won his battle with the wind and lit his cigarette. "Doesn't sound good," he admitted.

"What're you going to do about it?" said Danielle.

"I don't know," Malie said. "It's up to Ludwig. All he really wants, you know, is to fight the system. Not even that. He just likes to *talk* about it. When it comes to bloodshed, his enthusiasm dries out in a hurry. Me, too, for that matter."

Ruegger nodded. "The happiest I remember him being was back during the French Revolution. He loved the energy, the conspiracy, the *aura*. That's what he was trying to get back when he started this place. He's always held a special place in his heart for anarchists, you know."

"Oh, I do." Maleasoel's hardness cracked a little. "Sometimes he asks me to wear my beret to bed."

Danielle laughed. They made their way through the Commons toward the smallest building along the arc, a four-story bar and nightclub that ran twenty-four hours a day during the three-month winter night. Here they could see more of the "civilian" element of the immortals here, those shades who'd come a long way for Ludwig's annual dog-sled race, which historically was one of the wildest party-going activities in recent times. Hard rock blasted from the building amid screams and shouts, and Ruegger could see a few shades already passed-out in the snow, where the faint smell of vomit hung in the air. *So much for Gothic.*

Maleasoel stopped before the bar's entrance. "Well, I'm afraid I must leave you here, for now. Things to see and people to do. Ludwig said he'd meet you here when his chores were done. Half of these guards will stay with you at all times; the rest are mine. I hope you don't mind the inconvenience." She turned on her heel and marched off, Damaini and five soldiers right behind her. The other five stayed with the two vampires.

Danielle looked at Ruegger skeptically.

He gestured toward the entrance. "After you."

They squeezed into the nightclub's main room, a large, buzzing place, escorts at their heels. After unfastening their snow shoes, Ruegger and Danielle moved to the bar, and it wasn't long before he recognized a familiar woman fending off admirers.

Sophia—the so-called Ice Queen—had won the sled race seven years in a row and was expected to win this one, too. Supposedly her title had sprung up long before her mastery of sled-racing, though. Still, she was the immortal daughter of one of Ruegger's friends, and he figured he should say hello.

"It's good to see you," he said, giving her a hug, which she shrank from.

"Too good, possibly," she said.

"Evening," said Danielle.

"Yes," the Ice Queen said dryly. "It is."

Ruegger hid a sigh. "How's your mother?"

"She lives in New York. Ask her yourself. Oh, that's right. You two can't really *return* there, can you?"

"We can go anywhere we want," Danielle said.

"Bullshit. You're wanted dead, and guess what nice death squad lives in New York?"

Ruegger spotted another familiar figure sitting alone at a booth, drinking a Bloody Mary.

"Hauswell!"

Ruegger bid goodbye to Sophia, who was only too happy to see him go, and, with Danielle, moved over toward the Vampire Hauswell, one of the most powerful crime lords in America, basing most of his operations out of Las Vegas. At one time, he and Ruegger had been very close. Now, only decades later, they weren't much more than casual acquaintances. *Even for us, time is the enemy.*

Hauswell smiled at Ruegger and Danielle and invited them to take a seat. "I was wondering when you'd spot me," he said. In a tailored suit, he looked to be a sixtyish gentleman, hair mostly gray but showing some faded red in his sideburns and at the edges of his medium-sized mustache. His English sounded very American, but he was a German from way back.

"Why didn't you come over, then?" Ruegger asked, sitting down.

"I'm trying to keep a low profile, not attract any more attention than I have to. I'm glad I found you two, though; you're one of the reasons I've come here."

"Where're your guards?" Danielle said.

"Oh, don't worry, they're around. Can I buy you a drink?" He lifted a finger, and a waiter approached. Danielle ordered a Ramos Gin Fizz and Ruegger a martini.

"So what brings you to Liberty?" Ruegger said.

Hauswell sipped his drink, waving his other hand impatiently. "I wanted to see this place while it lasts. The dog-sled race has become legendary among the Community. Sadly, rumor has it that things aren't going so well in fair Liberty."

"So we've heard."

"I'm going back to Vegas after the race. Truth be told, I'm not looking forward to it. I wanted to get away for awhile. Every shade in the world who holds a position of power seems to be in jeopardy, lad. We're being systematically killed off."

Ruegger remembered what Jarvick had told them. "The Scouring."

"That's right. I've heard that even Vistrot's gone underground to avoid it. Though still in New York, of course. He and that city are symbiotically linked, I think." He paused. "Word has it that you were off in the desert again. Remind me, what is the purpose?"

"Vision quests are supposed to bring one closer to wisdom," Ruegger said.

"So what've you learned?"

"Wisdom is elusive."

To Danielle, Hauswell said, "And how are you doing, dear?"

"I could be better. There's a price on our heads, too."

"So I've heard."

"Don't suppose you know anything about it?"

"I wish I did, my girl. I will tell you that you don't fit the profile of the victims of the Scouring. All the shades being Scoured are either religious or criminal leaders of some sort. Whoever wants you dead has another agenda." He lowered his voice. "I've given serious thought to going into hiding, myself. You might, as well."

"We'll think it over."

Hauswell looked around. "I'll tell you another thing; I'll be glad when this fucking race is over—pardon the vulgarity, but this place ... disturbs me. Ever since I got here, maybe before, strange things have been happening, and an odd tension's in the air. Someone saw a pair of wolves streak through here last night—big ones, not sled dogs. I heard them howling myself, and they weren't were. Do wild wolves live this far north? And the explosion, and the execution—"

"Execution?"

"Apparently one of the idiots who attacked Maleasoel the other day stabbed her. Ludwig had him slowly tortured, beheaded and hung by his toes."

"Gods," Ruegger said. "That's not like Ludwig at all."

"He's changed, lad. They just took the body down a few hours ago. Probably, Ludwig didn't want you to see it. Of course, the assault on Maleasoel had a precedent. It seems that one of the higher-ups, a man named Gleason, a personal friend of Ludwig, was killed two weeks ago. His killer hasn't been found."

"What do you think happened?"

"I have no idea, although I think some of this strangeness might have something to do with a mysterious visitor Ludwig had about a month ago. Not that I was here, but I heard about it. They kept his identity secret, but that itself was conspicuous, so the gossips have been running wild with improbable theories. But back to the more supernatural aspects of the madness here. For example, the bat."

"Bat?" said Danielle.

"A giant bat, larger than a man, was seen perched on a rooftop more than once, and there have been a few disappearances connected to it. Tell me, are there such things as shapeshifting vampires?"

"Not that I know of," Ruegger said slowly. "Unless . . . but no, the Balaklava aren't around anymore. And they're not strictly vampires."

"Well, all this, plus the War of the Dark Council ..." Hauswell gestured vaguely. "It's a strange time to be a shade."

He glanced up as a girl approached, smiling when she sat down beside him. Gaudily but seductively dressed, she was a ghensiv, a race of female immortal that thrived off of semen and sometimes procreative tissues. To accommodate this dependency, many of the succubae became prostitutes.

She grinned, wrapping an arm about Hauswell. "Ready, darling?"

"Sorry, guys, but I've got a date," he said. "See you around, okay?"

"Later," Ruegger said.

"Oh, and good luck during the race." Hauswell and the ghensiv vanished down a hall. A few shades who must be Hauswell's security people followed in his wake.

"Cute couple," said Danielle. She killed her drink and flagged down their waiter for another.

"I've never seen Hauswell spooked before," Ruegger said. "And what was that about giant bats?"

"Just nerves. I bet people are getting jumpy around here with the execution and all."

He finished his martini, and when the waiter brought out Danielle's second round, he asked for his.

"What do you think about Ludwig closing this place down?" she said.

"Well, we knew he'd come to that conclusion eventually."

"Speak for yourself."

"I never thought he'd go this far," Ruegger said. "I never thought Liberty would last five years, much less this long. The last thing I want is to have to act against Ludwig."

"*I* can't believe he made it work. A modern Marx with an army. Until his crisis of conscious, anyway."

"A crisis with bad timing. It sounds like even if he decided to abandon the compound, others would take his place, and with more sincerity. Or at least with a greater appetite for power."

Danielle's face clouded. "I don't want them to take over the world, babe."

There was little doubt in either of their minds that a few hundred powerful immortals could, if placed in the right positions at the right time, seize control of all humanity. One immortal alone could slip into the White House and take over the President's mind. Of course, the President had a few secretly on the payroll to prevent this, but only a few. All it would take was enough to overwhelm them. A half dozen, tops.

"The Libertarians would have to move fast," Ruegger said. "If they gave humans enough time to mobilize, to discover our weaknesses, all would be lost. But if they struck swift and sure, they could do it."

Her eyes bored into his. "We have to prevent that. You know that."

Grimly, he nodded. "If it comes to that, we'll act."

After a moment, he nodded. "The attentions of the Marshals may be required again."

"They say absolute power corrupts absolutely," she said. "I believe it. In my opinion, shades have too much power not to be corrupted at least a little. Most of the people we know are evil to a point, and maybe we are, too." She winced. "I didn't mean *you*, you know that. But . . . sometimes I feel less than wholesome."

"I do, too," he admitted. "Morality is a sticky thing when you've got to kill intelligent living creatures to stay alive."

She sniffed. "Speaking of which, you hungry?"

"I guess."

"Well, we can't wait here for Ludwig all day. He'll find us when he's ready."

They finished their drinks and moved to the door, replaced their snow-shoes and returned outside, where (trailed by their guards) they made their way to the last building in the arc—a well-disguised barn—and paid five hundred dollars for admission. There they were given their choice of cattle, selected one and drained it dry. It wasn't as satisfying as a human would be and wouldn't last as long, but afterwards the vampires were reasonably sated, at least for the moment.

They relocated to the main building of the arc, the central one, where Ludwig and Maleasoel lived, as did all the chieftains of the compound. Ruegger and Danielle had a room on the third story, in the same wing and hall as Ludwig's. Entering their suite, they left their guards outside.

"So what've we learned?" Danielle said, looking out the window.

Ruegger flung himself on the bed. "Someone wants us dead, Hauswell may go into hiding because of some weird systematic execution of power-wielding shades known as the Scouring, and Ludwig's about to be overthrown."

"Sounds like we picked the wrong month to go on a vision quest."

"And don't forget the War of the Dark Council."

They had only heard vague rumors about the conflict the Dark Lord Roche Sarnova was engulfed in and had no clear understanding of what it meant, only that shades were killing shades in large numbers, mainly in Europe. Such wanton violence could easily spill over into the human world.

"Do you think that has anything to do with what's going on here?" Danielle said.

"I don't know. Perhaps it's all connected somehow. Perhaps not."

She drew the drapes shut, slipped her shoes off and lay down beside him.

He started unbuttoning his shirt, taking off his various holsters. He traced her jawbone, running his hand through her hair, and she gave a small smile, coming in closer to him. Their mouths met.

Afterwards, Ruegger kissed her and said, "I'm going for a walk, okay?"

She nodded, saying nothing.

He ducked out into the night, refreshed by the cold. Darkness fell about him, but he enjoyed that too. He set off. Seeing Hauswell had stirred up memories in him, and he needed to be alone for a moment. He thought of whom he had once been, what he had once done. Most of all he thought of World War II.

Was I really that man? My gods. Kharker ...

A throat cleared behind him. He spun to see a shape there, framed against the lights of the compound.

"I thought that was you," said the figure. "Off brooding, as usual."

"Ludwig! It's so good to see you."

"You too, my friend. Come. I have something to show you."

*   *   *

Smoking a joint, Danielle listened to jazz and thought briefly about inviting her guards in for a toke. She didn't have but about a penner left, though, and Ruegger would probably want some. This was one of the few times during the year that he would allow himself to indulge in such things (vision quests notwithstanding), but Danielle had no such qualms. She was a punk from way back, and though her hair was less spiky these days some things never changed.

Was he celebrating now? She thought not. She knew seeing Hauswell brought up bad memories for him—why, she didn't exactly know. She only knew it had to do with him being evil once, long, long ago. She knew it had to do with Lord Kharker. She wanted him to talk to her, tell her his troubles. She knew he thought she'd stop loving him if she knew the details of the thing he had been, but he couldn't be more wrong.

He knew all about her. He knew what had happened between her and the werewolf Jean-Pierre at Kharker' Lodge. He knew how her mother was a heroin junkie and died of an overdose while driving to the supermarket with seven-year-old Danielle in the car. He knew how Danielle's father had fallen off the wagon and stuck the wrong end of a shotgun in his mouth three months later, leaving Danielle an orphan. Knew about Danielle's days of wandering the streets before she'd admitted herself into an orphanage. And about Malcolm Verger, her foster brother and the leader of the gang that had beaten and raped her and left her for dead . . .

The gang of seven, now reduced to two. And, very shortly, zero. *You know everything, Ruegger. Now open up to me.*

Smoke swirled through the room, and her mind reeled pleasantly. The jazz reminded her of New York, although most of the music she'd listened to there had been punk or heavy metal, which she still loved. Supposedly, she was more "cultured" now, thanks to Ruegger, who had been alive during the time of some of the greatest classical composers and still loved them, but the truth was her first musical love was rock. She hoped it always would be.

Sometimes she wondered if she would've ever left New York if not for him. Would she still be headbanging every night, speeding off her ass, slashing her wrists and screwing anyone that came along? No, she decided. She'd probably be dead. Before Ruegger, death was what she'd really wanted. But she was wild, in love with life at the same time it disgusted her, so it was a toss up. Strange to think that she'd look like an adult now—well, an older adult; Ruegger had turned her at age nineteen—if still mortal, her girlish figure slipping away, her smooth skin growing tougher, wrinkled.

She told herself that in a hundred years it wouldn't seem so strange, her unchanging appearance. Maybe once it was certain that if she'd remained a mortal she'd be dead and buried the thought of being beyond those laws would be more appealing, whereas now she couldn't help but to think she was missing out on something. A real life. A *normal* life. She could have kids by now. *Grandkids.*

She lit a cigarette and stared out the window at the falling snow. Where was Ruegger?

* * *

"Don't you love it?" Ludwig said.

Ruegger regarded his oldest friend, a tall, gangly man with curly brown hair and the kindest, most animated face Ruegger had ever seen. He looked like a court jester, even though here he was king. Ludwig had pioneered the Beat movement in the fifties, helped lead the masses in the Hip movement in the sixties and seventies, and had really never come out of it. Behind the act of this would-be ruler of the world lurked a long-haired hippie.

When he had originally founded Liberty, his idea had been to take over the planet in order to make it a better place. Ruegger had always known he would snap out of it sooner or later, but over the years Ruegger had begun to wonder. Now, his suspicions confirmed, Ruegger was relieved. *I wouldn't have wanted to have to kill you, Ludwig, you wonderful fool.*

Ludwig hunched over a large table in his study, a surface overflowing with blueprints, carving instruments and blocks of wood. There his latest project rested: a chess board. As both he and Ruegger were ardent players, this did not surprise the vampire.

"Remember my dream?" Ludwig asked.

"Remind me."

"Oh, you were always the better player, I'll grant you, but I was the one who wanted something new. Remember that night, we both agreed that traditional chess boards reinforced the class system? The whole object is to protect the *king*. Not only is it inherently elitist, but sexist, too."

"The queen's the most powerful player."

"She's expendable. The pawns, presumably just poor schmucks drafted by the king to fight a war, don't even get a horse. No wealth, no power. The first to die. Then the rooks, the knights, the holy men, the queen and, finally, the king. Sexist and classist and religion-ist. Well, I've just finished the prototype for my new chess board. No peons, no royalty. You'll love it."

Ruegger inspected the board. He laughed. "They're animals!"

Ludwig grinned. "Well, to make the game work right, I had to have *some* sort of class system. But see, now the pawns are the small bugs. Rooks are birds. Bishops are deer. Knights are lions. Queens are humans. And the king ..."

"Is that the big bug?"

"That's right. The whole cycle. From bugs and back to bugs again. See, the pawns are beetles and the king is a maggot."

"You should have been a toy maker, not a revolutionary, though I pity the dreams you'd inspire in children."

"Can't wait to play it, can you?"

The truth was that Ruegger was far from in the mood to play a game of chess. Yet seeing Ludwig's enthusiasm kindled some familiar spirit in him. Before he could accept the invitation, though, the door burst open and both men looked up as a messenger approached. He whispered in Ludwig's ear, and Ludwig's face dropped.

"What is it?" Ruegger said.

Ludwig visibly gathered himself. "There's . . . there's a situation developing in Barrow, my friend. Just north of here. It ..." He cleared his throat. "It concerns you and Danielle."

"I don't understand."

"I think you should get her. We leave immediately."

*   *   *

"So what's going on?" Ruegger asked, once they were in the helicopter and en route to the small town of Barrow.

Ludwig's face darkened. "Junger and Jagoda."

Ruegger blinked. "The Last of the Roving Balaklava? I ... I thought they'd given up and gone to Jamaica long ago."

"They're back."

"What're you talking about?" Danielle said. "Who are Junger and Jagoda, and what are Balaklava?"

"A race of immortal," Ruegger said. "Very strong. Brutal. Their method of feeding requires them to rip open living humans. They're called Bone Crushers."

"Damn."

"Luckily, there aren't many left in the world. The other immortal races banished them to the West Indies four hundred years ago. We haven't heard much from them since."

"They're the second strongest race of known immortal," Ludwig added. "Shapeshifters. They feed off of living human bone marrow. To get to the marrow, they have to tear open humans while they're still breathing— break open their bones. Hence the name. Junger and Jagoda, two of the most violent creatures ever to walk the earth, assassins on a global level, were also Balaklavian artists, sculptors, known to incorporate their victims into their work, and they refused to settle down until the 1800s, when they realized that the island homes of their immortal brethren were by then largely vacant of their kind—they have a tendency to kill each other off for territory—and prime to be exploited. Since then, they've fashioned themselves into Jamaican myth and folklore, becoming voodoo-gods of the islands."

"So what are they doing in Barrow?"

Ludwig passed a hand across his face. "I'm not sure, but I think they're the end result of a deal that I made not too long ago."

"What sort of deal?"

"A very bad one that I had to go back on. There was no choice, really, and now I have to pay the price. The problem's that I've endangered you two as well, and Malie."

"Tell us," Ruegger said.

"No," said Ludwig. "I can't, not yet. Please understand."

"This is bullshit," said Danielle. "This has something to do with the hit that's out on us, doesn't it? Is *that* the deal you made?"

Ludwig covered his face with his hands. "You'll find out soon enough, my friends. But please believe me, I'd never do anything to hurt you unless there was no choice in the matter."

Ruegger seized Ludwig by the lapels of his jacket. Immediately, guards shot to their feet, crouching in the shuddering helicopter, but Ludwig waved them away.

"*Trust me*," said Ludwig. "We've been friends too long."

"I don't know what's going on," Ruegger said, "but you haven't just put me in jeopardy. You've endangered Danielle, and I won't tolerate that. You owe us an explanation."

Ludwig glanced at the guards, then back to Ruegger. "You're right, but not now, not here. I'll tell you after the sled race tomorrow. Let me go."

Ruegger released him and sat back down. Danielle reached for his hand. They spoke little after that, and shortly the craft landed. Several trucks waited for them, and they piled in and set out for downtown Barrow. To Ruegger's horror, almost every building in the heart of the city burned or had at least been touched by flame. Fire trucks choked the main street, and corpses littered the ground—many of them police officers.

"*This* is the end result of the deal you made?" Ruegger said.

Ludwig's face twitched. "Actually, I think this is only the beginning of the end result."

Danielle tensed. "Why did we come here, Ludwig? You could've sent others to scout out the damage. You didn't need to come here yourself, and you didn't need to bring us."

"What are you trying to say?"

"I think you were hoping to meet with the ones who did this. Junger and Jagoda. That's the only reason you would've come yourself."

"If they're strong enough to destroy an entire town, Danielle, why would I want to put myself in the danger required to meet them?"

"Because you're not in jeopardy, are you?"

Ludwig said nothing.

"Jesus," said Ruegger. "You're not, are you? Did you bring us out here to hand us over to the Balaklava? Is that it? Why else would we be invited?"

"Of course not," Ludwig said. "It's just . . . you're going to meet them soon. I wanted you to have the proper appreciation of them first. Don't fight them. I'll take care of the rest."

"What are you talking about?"

"Here," Ludwig said to the driver. "Stop the truck."

The vehicle braked and Ludwig bailed out, the odd flock behind him. The other truck, the one bringing up the rear, halted and disgorged Ludwig's troops. The revolutionary leader glanced up at the building they stood before, a structure untouched by fire but surrounded by a dense layer of bodies, both living and dead.

"This was the mayor's house," Ludwig said, marching up to a few cops who stood on the stairs leading into the small mansion. Ruegger and Danielle followed.

"You can't come in," one police officer said. He looked wretched, sickened and saddened.

"I'm Ludwig Keaton. You're familiar with my name. I probably put both your kids through college, and I own most of this town."

The cops straightened. "What can we do for you?"

"Tell us what happened here."

"I don't know, not really. Everyone's dead, sir. *Everyone*. If we'd been on duty at the time we would be, too."

"Did you see who did this?"

"I'm not a religious man, but they were demons. Had to be. The ones who saw them say they were foreigners, big black fellows, two of them. They killed and torched everything. Shot, stabbed, raped, whatever, they kept going . . . left some witnesses just to have witnesses, I guess. But that's not all. Here," he said, his voice curdling with hate, "look at this." He led the way inside, Ludwig and the odd flock following through halls strewn with the bodies of domestic servants and personal guards, their blood arcing across the walls in gruesome abstraction.

They passed a bench where an Inuit woman sat sobbing, her shoulders sunken and her face hidden by her hands. A man tried to comfort her.

"She's the mayor," the officer explained as they walked on, up the stairs and down another hall into a large, windowed room, the focus of much official attention.

When Ruegger and Danielle crossed the threshold, Danielle stopped and braced herself against the doorjamb. Ruegger stared. Blood and various body parts lay strewn throughout the room, but this was second to the vision that looked down from the ceiling, where intricate patterns of bones were spun in surreal, nightmarish configurations, connected by rotting flesh and grayish tissues. At the center of the pattern hung two pale wisps, the remains of what used to be the torsos of two young girls, identical twins with wide dark eyes and hair that fanned about their lifeless faces. Very few bones of the girls' bodies were left below their arched necks, and their sinewy bodies disappeared in a ragged fashion just above their navels. Their arms stretched out pleadingly, but they too disappeared before the girls' elbows. The rest of their bodies were woven into the overall fabric of the tapestry at different and symmetrical intervals. A quick glance at the pelvic areas revealed that the girls had been more than killed.

Danielle slammed an elbow against the wall. "What creatures could *do* this? Destroy a town … kill children … fashion their bodies into … God, some *art* …"

"It's terrible," Ruegger agreed. The thing that bothered him the most was the gruesome appreciation he had of the art itself.

Danielle balled her hands into quaking fists until the worst of the shaking had subsided, then went about the empty motions of lighting a cigarette. Ruegger wrapped an arm about her, glanced at Ludwig and led the way out.

"Why did you show us this?" Ruegger said.

"You know why," Ludwig said.

"We're to meet them soon."

"Yes. And it's important you know who they are before you do."

Danielle spat. "Well, we fucking know now, don't we?"

It occurred to Ruegger that all this action seemed centered around the winter solstice, by chance or design, and the climax of the winter solstice was the dog-sled race.

Tomorrow.

Chapter 3

Danielle woke up half a day later with a blood-wringing hangover, propped herself up in bed next to Ruegger, squinted her eyes, and vomited onto the floor.

It took a lot of alcohol to give a vampire a hangover, but it hadn't been enough to erase the memory of the Balaklava's art. She had only to close her eyes to see the horror imprinted on the back of her eyelids. The bones stretching across the ceiling in some deathly spider-web, the faces of those two girls, whom she had learned were the mayor's daughters, and the burning of a town. But this latter was, disgustingly, secondary, because the destruction of Barrow could be seen as calculated—maybe it was a message to Ludwig—but the Tapestry of Death (as they were now calling it) was a creative effort, and obviously the artists had enjoyed its creation. That was something else altogether.

The noise of Danielle throwing up woke Ruegger, and he silently massaged her shoulders and poured her a glass of milk from the mini-fridge—not that any fridges were really need out here; it was *cold*. Noticing that Ruegger was on his second smoke of the day, she started her first and moved to the balcony, after first wrapping a jacket tight about herself. She looked down on the snow-laden trees and iced-over lake. Distantly, she could hear the swarm of voices coming from the Commons, where the party-goers had gathered for the dog-sled race. Slowly, she could feel their energy and enthusiasm affect her and undo some of the horror.

Ruegger brought her a hot black cup of coffee after diluting his own with sugar and cream. They drank without speaking, and she realized that if they didn't talk about it they might just go on not talking.

"So—you think we'll meet Junger and Jagoda today?" she said.

His face clouded. "What ..." He cleared his throat. "What could they possibly have to do with Ludwig?"

"I don't know, but it helps answer a few questions. The Balaklava are often shapeshifters, you said, so they were probably the wolves and bat Hauswell talked about."

"They've been terrorizing the compound, or that's what makes the most sense based on what we know."

"Why, though? As part of the deal Ludwig was telling us about?"

"If that's the way it is, then it looks like Ludwig's bit off more than he can chew. He may be the leader of over two hundred immortals, but the Balaklava are stronger than any of us. So as long as they're careful, they could stick around for awhile."

"But that's it!" she said. "Why are they hanging around *here?*"

"I don't know."

"Maybe they're trying to intimidate Ludwig. Remember, Hauswell said Ludwig's friend Gleason was killed."

"You think Junger and Jagoda did that?" Ruegger said.

"Who else? Maybe that's why we've got five guards on us. Could be that's the number it would take to kill the bastards. Plus us, of course."

"Perhaps. If the guards were very good. But Ludwig said that we would *meet* them, not confront them. Actually, he said that he would take care of us, or something like that, which implies that the Balaklava might not be so friendly. Why would we meet them in the first place?"

Danielle shrugged. "Like I said, they're trying to intimidate Ludwig, and what better way than to attack his closest friend—you. And, of course, his best friend's wife, or whatever I am."

He kissed her forehead. "Wife sounds fine to me."

"The dissidents attacked Maleasoel, right? So she's protected by guards, like us. The dissidents seem to be trying to intimidate Ludwig, too. So they're behind *that* plot . . ."

"That might explain the death of Gleason. But, if the dissidents compose as large a faction as Maleasoel hinted, they would be strong enough to operate independently. So—"

"Why would they employ the Balaklava?"

Ruegger nodded. "A very good question. Therefore the Balaklava represent a different party entirely, assuming they're not acting on their own. Which means that in meeting them we'll be dealing with the emissaries of someone else . . ."

"Perhaps the mysterious visitor that came to Ludwig."

"Ah. That. I wonder ... could any of this have something to do with the Castle?"

She looked at him. "You mean Roche Sarnova? God, I hope not."

"He is the most powerful shade in the world, and if Ludwig, or at least his people, are planning to act after all these years, he might have grown nervous ..."

She crossed herself. "If he's involved, this whole thing could explode into open warfare." She didn't have to say that a war between two armies of immortals could prove devastating to the entire world.

"Okay," said Ruegger, "so where does that leave us?"

"The sled race." She sipped her coffee, watching its steam rise into the night.

"Which should be kicking off here shortly."

They finished their morning rituals and made their way downstairs to the Commons, which buzzed with the activities of hung-over immortals. Everywhere dogs were being fastened to sleds. The animals' barking and the party-goers mad whoops lifted Danielle's spirits, and she actually smiled when Ludwig spotted her and Ruegger and made his way over to them. He clapped Ruegger on the back and kissed Danielle's hand. He could be very charming when he wanted to be.

"Looking forward to the race, I hope," he said and led them to their respective sleds. "Good luck. Just remember that I'm looking out for you, okay? You'll be fine."

He vanished into the crowd. Danielle shot a glance at Ruegger, but he appeared solemn.

Five minutes later, the racers lined up at the starting line, talking and chuckling, some finishing joints or beer cans or sniffing a few quick lines. Danielle could tell by experience that these were the lightest of the drugs involved. She switched on the radio fastened to her sled—she and Ruegger occupied different vehicles—then deliberated on the choice of music.

"How about Wagner?" said Ruegger, his sled alongside hers. "Seems fittingly grand and energetic for a sled race."

She smiled. Their tastes in music varied widely, she was all too aware. She and Ruegger had actually met in the New York punk scene, where he had been attempting, without much success, to learn the intricacies of the new sound.

She punched a button, and heavy metal flooded out. Ruegger sighed.

"Sorry," she said, "but *Wagner*?" She made a face. "A sled race of shades in the heart of darkness of northern Alaska earns a little Metallica, if you ask me."

"If you insist."

A gun blasted, and the racers lurched off in a confused flurry of dogs and shades, snow kicking up in all directions. The Ice Queen Sophia leapt into the lead at once.

Danielle kept her stance firm, maintaining a tight rein on the ten dogs at all times. Still, the sled bucked and rolled, and more than once she felt her position shift precariously. Her blood started to rush. Despite her best efforts, she laughed, then yelled defiantly at the other contestants, who laughed and yelled back. She tried to pretend that Barrow had only been a nightmare.

Casting frequent glances at Ruegger, she could tell that, after some time, he was getting into it as well, making his dogs go as fast as he could, trying to stay just a few strides ahead of her. Sticking her tongue out at him, she prodded her animals on and screamed in exaltation when her lead dog breasted his.

The competition proved determined, and Danielle tried to extend her mind into those of her dogs. Never very good at the whole psychic thing, she nevertheless knew instantly that her dogs couldn't be controlled by her—because they were being controlled by someone else. A quick look at Ruegger's grimace revealed that he wasn't that one. He was having trouble with his dogs, too.

"Fuck," she said.

Their sled dogs started to veer off, cutting across the tide of the other racers and into the more deeply forested regions surrounding the main racing grounds. The boisterous cries of the racers receded, replaced by the stirring of the wind, which swept through the white trees and tickled at Danielle's ear.

She ripped out a gun from beneath her jacket. For his part, Ruegger pointed up through the trees at something. Twisting, she saw a winged figure, barely discernable against the stars. Maleasoel. What could she be doing up there—

following Ruegger and Danielle? The jandrow's speed lagged suddenly and she swooped in a tight arc off in the direction she'd come from.

Ruegger withdrew a gun of his own.

Their dogs went mad, deliberately charging close to shrubbery or low branches, forcing the sleds to smack against trees or knock into stubs or small rises. Ruegger jumped off his perch and Danielle followed, embedding herself in the snow.

Slowly, she rose on her snow-shoes, turning to locate him. For a wild moment she couldn't see Ruegger, but he was there, dusting himself off and shaking his head. He glanced up, saw her, and they trudged toward each other, embracing quickly and checking one another for wounds.

"It's them," he said.

"Junger and Jagoda," she nodded, and fired off a round to make sure her gun wasn't jammed. He did the same. They each retrieved another gun and merged back-to-back. They watched the twenty sled-dogs—wolves, really—bite through their harnesses and assemble around the vampires in a bristling circle. The creatures were no longer operating under their own wills—rather, they had to be under the mind control of someone else. Two Jamaican assassins, most likely.

The wolves leapt.

Danielle fired. She blew apart the head of one wolf, then another, shooting into their trunks and throats, too, not taking time to aim. They swarmed her, biting, biting, their bodies heavy and rough. Beside her, Ruegger fired, too, sometimes clubbing the beasts over the head with his pistols. Bone broke loudly.

When her guns clicked empty, Danielle started to go for another pistol, but there was no time. The wolves were all over her, ripping and tearing. She bit back, elongating her fangs, and used her vampire strength to hurl furry bodies against trees, where they broke open in red showers.

Ruegger flung his spent guns away and went to work with a blade, but it got stuck in the ribcage of the first wolf he stuck it in. Danielle heard him swear.

The wolves forced the vampires to the ground.

Danielle fought on with her fingers, teeth and feet. A scrawny dark-haired thing burst at her, a knife (Ruegger's) stuck through its chest, but still it tore at her. Danielle grabbed it by the mouth, ignoring the pain, and ripped out its throat with her fangs. Several other wolves gnawed at her legs and chest.

Their bites were calculated, teeth locating her arteries. She could feel herself growing weak and knew that much of the blood that stained the snow around her was her own. It wouldn't be long before she was dead.

At last all the wolves lay in bloody chunks on the ground, their blood soaking the snow in bright crimson, and in the middle of it sprawled Ruegger and Danielle, their clothes and flesh torn. Too weak to move much, they reached out their arms and held hands.

Footsteps approached, and the vampires propped themselves up against each other to face whatever was coming.

The Balaklava stepped forward slowly, letting themselves be examined. They seemed to enjoy the attention. They were very tall, their skin nearly sheer ebony. Both of them were completely naked.

"Good to see you," one said, boasting a thick Jamaican accent. "I'm Junger." Bald from head to toe, his flesh was so covered by twisting, intricate tattoos that his actual skin was hard to see. Very small thin bones that were likely supposed to resemble tusks stuck out of his skin in twin arcs along his cheeks. *Dear God*, Danielle thought. *Are those . . . ?*

The bones looked very much like the ribs of an infant human.

I'm going to be sick, Danielle thought.

"I'm Jagoda," the other said, his accent equally as thick. He wore expensive sunglasses and his face, framed by long dreadlocks, was masked by a heavy, unkempt beard. A gold ring gleamed at his lip, one through his nose, and several accentuated his right ear. "Sorry about your clothes."

"Grant me a last smoke?" Ruegger said. "I'm afraid your wolves tore all mine to pieces."

Junger laughed. "We're almost out as it is."

"Then could you please find our radio and bring it over. I'd hate to die to silence."

Danielle knew what he was doing—separate them, for all the good that could do.

"Well, mon, Bob Marley does go well with rape," Junger told his partner, and marched off to find the sled and the radio.

"Why kill us?" Danielle asked Jagoda. *Did he just say what I think he did?*

"We're not going to kill you," Jagoda said. "We could have—there was a certain party that wanted us to, and would have paid well for it—but we've chosen another route. Ultimately, this line of action will be the most rewarding."

"What do you mean?" Ruegger said.

"This is only our first visit to you. Before we can see you again, though, we've got a grand opening to attend in Europe at the Castle."

"You're working for Roche Sarnova?"

"We never limit our fun to one possibility," Jagoda said.

"Is that what destroying Barrow was?" Danielle said. "*Fun?*"

He smiled, revealing his large and seemingly malformed teeth. "That was very entertaining—our coming-out party, you could say. It's been some time since we'd access to that much . . . skin. And I think we did some good work there, too, although I doubt the police photographers will give it the treatment it deserves." He seemed absorbed in thought for a moment. "Today we won't kill you. But we will rape you both, oh yes." He started to advance.

Danielle looked around desperately.

Just then, sounds of alarm issued from the south.

"Seems Ludwig and the rest of the cavalry are on their way," Jagoda said, disappointed.

"We've accomplished what we intended," Junger said, returning.

"Next time, then."

"Next time," Jagoda agreed, and flicked away his cigarette.

They jumped to all fours, changing from men to the shape of great wolves in less than a second and running off into the forest just as the first sounds of rifle fire erupted behind them.

Ruegger dragged himself over toward Danielle, who felt herself dying. She'd lost too much blood. Cradling her in his lap, he bent his head to kiss her bloody mouth. She opened her eyes and tried to smile.

Ruegger's strength gave out, and he toppled face-first into the snow. After a moment, darkness filled Danielle's vision, and she fell back into it, too.

*   *   *

Ludwig, rifle gripped smartly, fired off his last shot at the retreating demons, then turned to the other snipers that lined this brittle ridge of snow.

"Let's go."

Covered by more snipers, his crew moved swiftly down the ridge toward the bloody snow where once-beautiful wolves littered the scene, and for a second only Ludwig allowed himself to lament their loss, then he knelt next to Ruegger and examined him. Maleasoel, kneeling over Danielle, looked at him questioningly.

"Alive, thank God," said Ludwig. "How's she?"

Maleasoel shook her head. "Bad."

"Let's get them out of here, sir," he heard one of the others say. "They could come back."

Ludwig rose to stare in the direction in which the Balaklava had vanished. His gaze lingered. He didn't know when, or how, but he knew beyond question that he'd have hell to pay. And hell was not forgiving.

*   *   *

The first thing Danielle wanted when she woke up was a cigarette. A nice, fat, hand-rolled one, made out of that wonderful tobacco Ludwig kept. She lay sprawled in the absurdly large four-poster bed in her room on the top floor of Ludwig's villa. The view was grand, if only she had the energy to go to the window to see it. At least she still smelled and felt clean from all the doctoring and bathing she'd been treated to.

When he heard her request, Ruegger gladly retrieved the tobacco for her and rolled the cigarette himself. He'd been up and about not more than an hour after the attack, as his age enhanced his recuperative abilities, and he'd doted on her constantly.

"Better than cloves," she said softly, once he lit it for her.

"How do you feel?"

"Great." She reached for his hand. "You're cold, baby. Come here."

He obeyed. "We've been out searching for them—Junger and Jagoda. Unfortunately, the snow's erased what tracks there were. During the search, though, we came across something else—a mass grave of shades."

"Damn."

"It explains all the disappearances lately."

"You're sure it's the work of the Balaklava?"

"No, that's the worst part. The bodies were intact and drained of blood, as only a kavasari could do."

"What's a kavasari?"

A dark light settled in his eyes, and when he answered, his voice was bitter: "A type of immortal that feeds only off of other shades—a vampire's vampire. They're the strongest race of known immortal, and they're very rare."

"You're kidding me. There's something that can feed on *us*?" When he nodded, she said, "Holy shit. Why didn't you ever tell me?"

"They're very rare, and I didn't want to worry you."

There was something in his face as he said it, though, that made her think there was more to it than that. She decided not to press him. He would tell her when he wanted to.

"Why would one be hanging around Liberty?" She paused. "Well, the high concentration of shades here, I guess. A perfect feeding ground. But you've gotta admit, what with all the other strange things going on here, it makes you wonder. What did Ludwig say about it?"

"Nothing, really."

"Damn, but he is acting suspicious. What do you think? You know more about the kavasari than I do."

"They . . ." He passed a hand across his face. "One killed someone I loved very much, a long time ago. But as to their role in the greater picture, I haven't a clue. Could Junger and Jagoda be involved with a kavasari? I don't know."

"The most powerful immortal involved with two of the second most powerful? God help us."

"I'll drink to that."

She breathed in a long draught of smoke. Softly, she said, "Who did you lose?"

He looked at her. "I ... don't want to talk about it."

She waited a beat, then nodded. "Well, I've been doing some thinking. Jagoda said something about more than one possibility, and he said that in connection with the subject of his employment. I think maybe the Balaklava are working for at least two employers. Or at least two different people approached them."

"I've had similar thoughts. It seems likely that one of those employers was the same one who hired Jarvick. But Junger and Jagoda had something else going, perhaps a deal from this second person, and it's that that they carried through today, neglecting the contract from the first one, the one who hired Jarvick. That one wanted us dead and the Balaklava didn't. If that's true, then someone wants us six feet under and someone wants us . . . harassed, or something. Whatever the Balaklava intended to do."

She suppressed a shudder. "Maybe to put pressure on Ludwig."

"Maybe. That leads back to the question of the dissidents."

"Not necessarily. Maybe there's more than one entity that wants to pressure Ludwig. Maybe for different reasons."

"Maybe one wants him to continue leading Liberty and the other wants him to step down. And both are using the same method—threatening those Ludwig's close to."

"It explains why he's been acting so weird," she said.

Ruegger lit a cigarette. "The Balaklava mentioned Roche Sarnova. It's possible both they and Jarvick were hired by the Castle."

"Jarvick didn't seem as if he was getting paid enough. The Castle could have paid him whatever he wanted."

"Unless they *wanted* him to bargain with us instead of kill us."

"That's a reach. Anyway, so where does the kavasari fit in? And what's with the Scouring? And the War?"

"Well—"

Someone knocked on the door. At Ruegger's invitation, one of Ludwig's many servants entered. "Master Ludwig is having dinner prepared. If you're feeling well enough to attend, he'll expect you on his private terrace in half an hour."

Danielle smiled. "We'll be there. Count on it." When the man had gone, she said, "*Now* we'll get some damned answers."

Chapter 4

Francois Mauchlery looked down from the helicopter as it swept just above the Carpathians past an outcropping of rock. Crevices, fissures, sheer facades and crumbling ruins dotted the ragged mountains which rose like rotting fangs from the jawbone of a monster. He knew each rise and bump by heart, and loved them all.

Keeping one leather-gloved hand on his black attaché case, Francois smiled. Blackout curtains, drawn tightly over the compartment's windows, prevented him from peering directly into the gaping void below, so he watched the sinking sun through the pilot's eyes; it disappeared and reappeared sporadically between the mountains.

Slowly, the light drained from the Dark Country as night sank its teeth into the hard Transylvanian hide. Villagers and gypsies, those that believed, would be retreating to their homes and cowering behind doors and crucifixes, but some, believers or nonbelievers, would be corpses in the morning.

Francois lost the sun as it sank below Carpathia. Only then did he raise the blackout curtains to watch the frozen tumult of twilight. The new dark sent his hairs on end and a shiver up from the base of his spine.

His companion in the passenger compartment of the helicopter, Victoria Lisaund, removed her sunglasses, then uncrossed and recrossed her legs.

Sitting opposite her, he regarded her in silence for a moment. She had dark red hair and muddy brown eyes, was wearing a navy blue suit-dress and long combat boots that emphasized the shapeliness of her legs. They were nice, and Francois remembered they tasted quite good, too. Full lips, turned up at the corners, grinned at him.

"First time in Transylvania?" he asked in well-etched English, as he knew her to be a Brit.

"Of course not," she said. "But it *is* my first visit to the Castle."

He nodded. He'd met her two days ago in Paris on his way home from the front lines in London. She was the representative of a group in Wales that had been forced to flee the island, and now she was making the journey to the Castle in order to request aid on their behalf from Roche Sarnova, the Dark Lord, the most powerful immortal in the East, if not the world.

She leaned forward and placed a hand on Francois's knee. He'd been her escort since they had met in France, and they'd grown close.

"Will *he* help me out?" she said in an excellent Romanian accent. "If anyone could know, it's you."

Francois ignored her hand. "I can't answer for him."

She slowly sat back. "Something wrong, lover?"

"Don't," he said.

"Don't what?"

"Call me lover."

She sulked, or pretended to.

That was the thing that bothered him; she wasn't half as ingenuous as she pretended. Somehow she had her own secret agenda, but what that was, or how she was going to go about it, was something she kept guarded, even pretending at its nonexistence.

The helicopter blasted between twin snow-capped alps, and a rough gust shook the craft rudely. Rocky outcroppings challenged the skids as the machine cleared the crest of the next mountain and snow swirled thicker as the ship flew on, ice and wind whipping madly against the thin walls. Neither moon nor stars could be seen. The dark heart of the Carpathians loomed ahead, hidden in the spinning night.

"How old are you?" she asked suddenly.

He paused. Few were brave enough to ask the question, though he was sure all wondered. He couldn't tell if she actually expected him to answer, but he thought courage should be rewarded.

"I . . . to give you some idea . . . was quite old when Caesar wept at the feet of the statue of Alexander the Great."

"You're that old?"

"Older."

"So Christ has nothing to do with us? I heard rumors that shades were mixed up with the early Christians and got damned somehow."

"Every culture has its creation myth. We've got reams of them."

"So God had nothing to do with us?"

"Which god?"

She nodded. "I'm sorry, Ambassador. You understand, I had to ask. I'm not yet a hundred years old and I still think about these things."

He softened. "We all do."

Silent again, she turned her face to the bleak nightscape.

"We're approaching my home," he said.

Using one of his mental powers, he merged his mind with that of the pilot, making sure the mortal didn't crash the helicopter. Francois preferred a shade to pilot these things, but most of the immortal fliers were in London or thereabouts, engaged in the war, and the ones that were available couldn't fly in the daytime.

In the pilot's mind, Francois felt Victoria's psychic presence brush up against his own. She, too, kept tabs on the human. Frowning slightly, he turned to her and saw her brown eyes fixed on him with some awe.

"Such control," she said, to answer his question. "What I mean to say—"

He waved her off.

"We've arrived," he said.

The helicopter swept past its last ice-covered summit and plunged down toward an immense stone structure whose great towers and bulwarks burned with light from within. The castle sat embedded in the side of the approaching mountain like an iron thorn. Like a torch blazing on a catacomb wall.

"My God," she whispered. "It's beautiful ..."

Francois smiled as he watched the looming castle from the eyes of the human pilot. Coldly grandiose, his home looked. Mysterious in its bed of stone.

They approached it cautiously. From a distance it really did look like a cluster of sharp iron thorns embedded in the mountain's side, but as they drew nearer it seemed more like a flower, the cold battlements rising like deceptively delicate-looking stems into the freezing, snow-blasted night. Landing wasn't going to be much fun under these conditions, but a visit to Roche Sarnova always tended to be dramatic.

Tensely, under partial mind-control from Francois Mauchlery, the pilot approached a battlement that doubled as a helipad and landed. The machine rocked back and forth on the icy surface.

The deafening roar of the rotors wound down as three figures on the stone platform ran carefully toward the black helicopter and accepted the emerging couple as the doors were flung wide and Francois and Victoria stepped down. Wind blasted them without mercy.

"Ambassador Mauchlery!" shouted a ranking general and member of the Dark Council, the leader of the welcoming party. "Wonderful to have you back! Welcome home!"

The Councilman led the way toward the battlement doorway and out of the freezing snow. The cold didn't disturb Francois, but he respected the needs of the others.

Inside, he was made to feel at home (which it was) as he was courteously led to his chamber. He looked fondly around as he went—the wide crimson drapes, the flinging snow against the courtyard windows, the warm torchlight along open halls. The comforts of the modern world too nestled snugly amidst the splendor of the old ways: the electric elevators, indoor saunas, and cellular phones against the backdrop of stone and tapestries.

He found himself running his hands along the familiar walls and smiling to himself as his manservant led the way.

Finally, they arrived at his suite, and the servant opened the thick mahogany door and showed the way in. Francois followed the young one into his room and turned to dismiss him.

Once alone, Francois saw the cart of champagne in its silver bowl of ice. The accompanying meal could be smelled from the bedroom. He laid his attaché case on his dresser and followed the smell down a short hallway into his bedchamber.

Tied in white silk bonds to his bed, a beautiful young woman struggled on his satin mattress.

The girl couldn't be eighteen, and her flesh was warm and supple. Her luscious figure, bursting from silk panties and brassiere, was emphasized even more by her thrashings. Golden hair fell about her head and over her wide blue eyes. Caucasian, Francois mused; some length must have gone into fetching her. Her breasts rose and fell quickly with her frightened gasps. Her long legs squirmed to and fro. Sweat glistened on her thighs. The smell of life rose from her sweetly and Francois inhaled it with a sad smile.

His fangs lengthened.

"Ah," he said. "It's good to be home."

*   *   *

The dining hall was immense, all mahogany walls and burning incense. The seemingly endless dining table stretched on forever in the grand hall. In its life the table had risen heavenward from its soft bed in the redwood forest of northern California, but, like everything else in this room, the table had moved beyond mere life. It was law that nothing mortal should pass into this room, except the food.

Dozens of beautifully bound mortals wriggled hysterically along the redwood table, their young skins rubbing delightfully against the dark and polished wood. Several scores of vampires and other assorted immortals hunched at the table, which had only one head; the other end was rounded off.

Francois had the guest position (his usual) at the left hand of the head of the table, which was vacant. Roche Sarnova would make an entrance when he chose. Then the festivities would begin.

Mauchlery lifted a large wine-filled goblet to his lips and drank as his eyes scanned the familiar faces—many tried to catch his eye, but he pretended not to notice—until he lit upon Victoria Lisaund, the beautiful representative of the fugitive Wales faction, who it seemed had been watching him for some time; when his eyes met hers, she quickly looked away, then slowly back. Coy.

Finally, the host of the evening appeared, making his way down a lavish staircase which branched off at the middle to disappear upward in two opposite directions. Dressed in carefully-embroidered black garments, the host smiled at his guests as he descended the last stair. Simultaneously, the meals ceased writhing and grew quiet.

Mauchlery appreciated Roche Sarnova's understated entrance. No thronging escort, blaring music or superfluous attire. Not even a crown or cape. Simple and dark and smiling.

All the guests were on their feet in deference, as if they were the host and Roche Sarnova their honored guest. His half Anglo, half Egyptian face radiated warmth and friendship, and—in his characteristically understated way— absolute command.

"Sit, sit," he beckoned in Romanian, and his guests took their places while he remained standing. "Thank you all for coming. I know the difficulty of a great meeting such as this in these chaotic times and appreciate the sacrifices you've all made to get here. I won't bore you with a speech. I dare say you'll hear enough of my voice in the days to come. Now, a warm welcome to a newcomer to our home, Ms. Victoria Lisaund."

She stood briefly to scattered applause.

Roche turned elegantly toward Francois and smiled deeply. "Now with great affection we welcome home our best friend, Ambassador Mauchlery!"

The Ambassador rose and grinned as they applauded him, then sat back down.

Roche Sarnova continued. "I've met with many of you today and will continue the meetings throughout the week— business unfortunately taking precedence over pleasure when our brothers and sisters are dying on the front lines. For now, let us enjoy each other without the stresses of war intruding and enjoy the life of these beautiful mortals." He smiled at his company and lifted a crystal glass of red wine in the air. "To the night!" he cried and drank deeply.

"To the night," Francois muttered and did the same.

Later, while Sarnova and Francois were trying to converse between the host's many visitors and between Roche's sips from the gypsy-girl's big toe (he was trying to make her last), Sarnova said, smiling, "So you and the dear Ms. Lisaund know each other well?"

"I took her on the scenic route from Paris."

The Dark Lord convulsed with laughter. "I'm glad someone's having fun these days."

Francois made a face. "There's something . . . not quite right . . . about her."

"What race is she?"

"A Finnish werewolf."

"Finnish, really. I always did like the Finland girls."

"Roche . . ."

"I know, I know. Did I ever tell you that you take things too seriously?"

Francois pretended to count on his fingers.

"Just enjoy her," said the Dark Lord. "These may be the last days of my empire and do you see me complaining? No, you do not. Why? Because—"

"You live in the moment, right."

Sarnova grinned. "Have you heard any news not related to the war, something to take my mind off it?"

"Yes, actually. The odd flock, Ruegger and Danielle—you've heard of them, the American vampires, they go around saving humans and killing shades—"

"Oh, yes. Very amusing. I had them here once. What are they up to now? Don't tell me they've died. They may be a pain in the ass, but they are fun to have around."

"No, no. They're fine. In fact, I heard they just returned from a vacation in the Sahara—during which they took another one of their 'police actions'."

Roche rolled his eyes. "Who did they kill this time?"

"A vampire named Triboli."

Roche shrugged. "Good riddance. Is it true people are calling them the Marshals?"

"People are foolish. Ruegger and Danielle are getting to be celebrities." He frowned, genuinely offended. "They go around helping our prey and killing us, Roche. I don't think it's as amusing as you do. I'm not saying we should kill them—I've been around too long to discount colorful characters—but they are quite anti-establishment, Roche, and, my friend, *we* are the establishment."

"So we are. But they can't touch us, and we've got bigger fish to fry. Subaire, for one, and the rest of her Half."

Francois nodded grimly. Ever since half of Roche's cabinet had sided with the Lady Subaire, she who had declared war on the Dark Lord, things had gone to hell. And if Roche, a man of never-ending enthusiasm, was joking that these were the last days of his reign, Francois knew even more dire events were ahead.

"I think Ruegger and Danielle have the right idea," said the Ambassador. "A vacation is just what you need."

"Right, and who'd manage the war while I was gone? You? You'd just nuke London and get it over with, probably. Who cares if humans discover our existence when we're in the middle of a civil war and in the weakest position we could possibly be in? Who cares if they hunt us down like dogs when we're too busy fighting to state our position, defend ourselves, make our peace . . . ? No, my friend, you don't like humans enough to manage a war taking place in a human city."

Francois rolled a shoulder. "All I'm saying is you should take it easy, Roche. It's not going to help the cause if you get an ulcer."

"I'll get an ulcer from friends as much as from enemies these days. And don't give me that look, I'm not talking about you. Spies, Francois. *This* is what I'm worried about."

"What are you saying?"

The lord of the castle swished the girl's blood back and forth in his mouth. "Intelligence has it that they're here. *In my home.*" His voice nearly choked with rage as he said this. He glanced quietly around his beloved castle.

The Ambassador was about to respond, but just then a familiar figure approached and he smiled.

Victoria Lisaund bowed politely toward the seated figures as she approached; for a moment, she looked uncertain, as if she wasn't sure whether to kiss Sarnova's ring or hand before speaking with him, but when Roche Sarnova gestured to an empty chair, she accepted gratefully.

"Thank you."

"No, thank *you* for coming to my home, young Victoria. We're most delighted to have you. You're British, correct?"

"Welsh. I represent the *Laegstrom*, a small faction fighting within the front lines."

"I understand you've got a special petition," Sarnova said, casting a glance at Francois. "As well as an intimacy with our shared friend."

Her cheeks colored, contrasting with the strange look of determination on her face. "Well . . . yes. He was very helpful."

Roche lowered his head to the dying gypsy. Lisaund knitted her brows in consternation. Mauchlery would remember this later and draw conclusions.

As Roche bit into the gypsy's big toe for the final time, the girl jerked suddenly and fell still. With a start, as he felt the psychic scream of Lisaund via the last dim thoughts of the gypsy, Sarnova jerked up and stared at Victoria, clutching at his throat and slipping from his chair. Lisaund flew over onto the ground with him, the heavy chair toppling to the floor.

As Francois looked on in horror, the woman *changed*. Her clothes shredded about her and through the ripped garments he saw dark flesh and her face twisting outward. The snout slashed into the Dark Lord, teeth flashing and blood spraying.

Assassin!

Mauchlery leapt into the brawl. Bones fragmented in a chaos of sweat and blood, the ancient carpet sopping with red. In a moment, guards seized Lisaund, apparently some sort of werewolf-vampire hybrid, a strong and hairy demon-thing, and without pause dismembered her. They butchered her swiftly and efficiently, even cleaving in her beautiful skull.

A clawed foot kicked a few times and was still.

Sarnova's living remains dragged itself away a few feet and collapsed. His body was ripped open from throat to crotch and little remained of him that was recognizable; but he lived.

Mauchlery himself had taken his share of the werewolf's fury and was savagely slashed and bitten in places too many to name, but he remained conscious long enough to pull the ruin of his friend into his arms and think, *The revolution has begun,* before he too collapsed and fell into blackness.

Chapter 5

Ludwig and Maleasoel waited at a circular glass-topped table on his enclosed veranda. He had a goblet of red wine to his lips and a hunk of beef Wellington on his plate. Bloody, of course. Maleasoel, the dark angel, with black hair, subtle fangs, and graceful wings tucked behind her, looked disconcerted, possibly at something Ludwig had just said, as Ruegger and Danielle entered the room.

Beaming, Ludwig gestured toward facing chairs, which some helpful attendants held for them. A well-dressed young shade approached and placed generous portions of beef Wellington in front of the vampires, and Danielle had to smile at his unconscious hypocrisy; for a man devoted to stamping out class consciousness, Ludwig certainly employed enough servants and ate enough fine food.

"Sorry we didn't wait for you to start," said Ludwig.

"I'm glad you didn't," Ruegger said, and dug in.

"Fabulous, isn't it?"

"Sure is," Danielle said. Then, to Maleasoel: "Thanks for following us today."

"Ludwig's idea. I was supposed to keep an eye on you and let him know when I saw the Balaklava."

Ruegger didn't waste time. "What the hell happened this morning?"

Smooth, Danielle thought.

Ludwig pursed his lips and glanced at his wife. "It was a trap. Allow me to explain."

"Please do," said Danielle.

After a few false starts, he began: "The dissidents are trying to blackmail me into staying here at the compound as Liberty's leader, but I'm tired of this excuse for megalomania and want to tear it down. Unfortunately, that's not really much of an alternative, because the dissident faction is large and would prevent me from doing so. They want me to stay on because they know that if I stepped down at least half the population would leave with me. So the dissidents want me to remain, but they want me to advance my original plan, to start taking over the world. They feel Barrow would be the first logical target, just to hone their skills. I said no. Under the leadership of a man named Captain Raulf D'Aguila, the dissidents killed a close friend of mine. Gleason."

"You can't prove it was Raulf," Maleasoel said.

Ludwig and his wife exchanged a glance. Malie's cheeks flushed and she stared down at the table as if to look up from it would make her sick.

"Why'd they kill Gleason?" Danielle said.

After a ragged breath, Ludwig said, "To prove they were serious. Then, when I still made no advancements, they attacked Malie and blew up a building—killing several loyalists, I might add. Next we got wind that they'd hired the Balaklava—so we set a trap for them this morning. I'm very sorry that I had to use you as bait, my friends, but you understand that if I followed the orders of the dissidents I would—God!—be forced to enslave humanity! Unfortunately the Balaklava escaped." He raised his goblet and toasted, "To my courageous friends, and to better times."

They drank. Danielle drained her glass and poured herself some more, then turned to Ludwig. "So you're saying that the death-squad that attacked us in the desert was hired by the dissidents in order to put pressure on you."

"Maybe. I don't know much about the assassins in the desert, to be honest. I just knew there was a contract out on you, and I assumed it originated here."

"Why wouldn't the dissidents simply wait until we arrived? Killing us here would've been more affecting to you. And once we were here why would they bother to confuse the issue by hiring the Balaklava?"

Ludwig tugged on his lips. "I suppose that by hiring Junger and Jagoda they were trying to make the point that they were connected with powerful elements—yet another way of threatening me. As for why they sent someone to kill you in the desert—well, I have reason to believe that the dissidents themselves are divided into at least two factions: the more conservative and the more extreme. I suppose the more extreme wanted you killed in a hurry so as to make their point before the winter solstice, by which time north Alaska's three-month night is officially halfway over. They wanted me to seize Barrow while we still had time to expand our operations. If we could take the town and keep it secret, we could refine our techniques."

"Use the people of Barrow as guinea pigs," Danielle said. "Fucking great, Lud. I'm so glad I know you."

"When the days get longer—and most of us must hide during that time—the task of organizing a force that could take over the world would be more difficult. That's why we founded Liberty where we did, so that we would have this extended darkness. In the summers, as you probably know, we go to Antarctica." He took a breath. "So now would you both please forgive me for being a self-centered jackass and putting you in peril?"

"Not by a long shot," Danielle said.

He nodded sadly. "What else can I tell you?"

"The Castle. Roche Sarnova. We have reason to believe the Dark Lord is mixed up in this."

"Why would Blackie care?"

"Because Liberty's gotten strong."

"He'd want it crushed," Ruegger agreed. "It's the only army that poses a threat to him. Except for the one that's warring with him, of course. Which would make it even more important to stamp out Liberty; he's got enough troubles without worrying about you."

"Really, I know nothing about it," Ludwig said.

Even Danielle could tell that he was lying. "So what of this mysterious visitor we've heard about?"

"What visitor?" Ludwig said it a little too quickly. Seeming to realize his error, he immediately added, "I receive visitors all the time—some wish me to keep their identities secret. It's no big deal, just a symptom of being a movement's leader, I guess."

"And the Scouring?" Ruegger pushed. "The War?"

"I know nothing about either."

Danielle could sense Ruegger's blood rise, could feel that old dark streak blossom within him. He would want to lash out and beat Ludwig to a bloody pulp until he spilled the truth. But Ludwig was Ruegger's oldest, dearest friend, and with visible effort he held himself back.

"So," Ludwig said brightly, "how about a game of pool after dinner?"

"You still owe me five hundred bucks from last time," Danielle said. She shot a look at Ruegger, and he nodded. They would play along, for now.

*　　*　　*

The dinner continued on a more pleasant note, but Ruegger couldn't help picturing their confrontation with Junger and Jagoda. Things had almost gone very, very bad. *What are you hiding, Ludwig?*

When dinner ended, they moved to the pool room and the couples paired up. Ludwig opened with his own special cue and declared stripes. Ruegger played, mentally counseling himself to be patient. From time to time he looked out the enormous windows that faced out onto another terrace, this one running the length of the house on this side. In the distance, clouds gathered.

Maleasoel, Ludwig's partner, gripped her cue delicately and leaned over the table. The dark flesh of her wings quivered slightly, as a muscle clenched and unclenched there—a nervous habit of hers. She missed the shot.

Danielle smiled at Ruegger as he passed her his cue.

She sunk three balls and scratched on the fourth. In a normal game, of course, immortals would have no trouble winning because of their sharper reflexes and more able strength, but tables could be custom-made for shades, as this was. Its balls and cues were heavier—no human could play with them—lending the game a proportionate degree of difficulty. The use of telekinesis was considered poor form.

The game progressed, Danielle eventually sinking the eight ball with a triumphant yell, but as they began setting up the next game, Maleasoel smiled politely. "You'll have to play this one without me, guys. I think I'll get some fresh air." She cracked a sliding glass door and walked out onto the terrace, blue light falling about her and filtering through the tops of her wings. Before she slid the door closed, a gust of cold air briefly filled the room.

Ruegger also declined to play, leaning against a wall and watching Ludwig and Danielle go at it. He was vaguely amused by some of the other tables in the room, namely a snooker and a billiards table. He thought it odd that Ludwig would spend so much money on games he couldn't even play. Most shades had large stashes of money and properties they'd taken off their victims, but not all were . . . as *materialistic* as Ludwig was, as strange as that sounded.

Leaving the players to their own devices, Ruegger joined Maleasoel on the terrace. The frigid air gusted forcefully, and it felt wonderful to his flushed skin.

"Invigorating," he said, then noticed, with some surprise, that Malie was crying. The wind played among the dark downy hair on her wings and blew her tears in a gentle stream downward toward the arching curve of her jaw.

He laid a hand on her shoulder, but she shook it off. With an apologetic smile, she turned to watch the rolling clouds and the lightning that flashed down.

"I love storms," she said.

"Especially here. The Northern Lights ..."

"Beautiful, aren't they?"

"Very." He leaned out over the railing to peer into the dark tangle of the forest. Waited.

"Ludwig—" she started.

"What about him?"

"He . . . we . . . never meant for you to get hurt."

"I know."

Her forehead furrowed. "It wasn't the dissidents that hired Junger and Jagoda, but I'm sure you've probably guessed that."

"Who did?"

"I don't know. Truly. Ludwig does, though. And he knows more about the kavasari than he's saying." She turned to him. "This may be the last time I see you, at least for some time. Things will be different from now on."

"How?"

She placed the back of her hand to her nose and shook her head. Suddenly, she smiled. "I love to fly before the storm. Ludwig is always afraid I'll get struck by lightning or something, but it's so beautiful up there. Like a dream."

She began to undress, folding her blouse and skirt into a neat wad and handing them to Ruegger for safe-keeping. He couldn't help but notice that she had a very nice figure.

Her wings fanned out in anticipation. With sublime gracefulness, she mounted the railing and leapt into the abyss. Ruegger feared for a moment she wouldn't open her wings in time, but they fanned out gloriously and caught her above the frozen treetops, and the wind carried her away on the tails of the storm.

*   *   *

Later that night, when the couples had retired to their nightly activities, and Ruegger and Danielle were lying on the bed, she said, "Ludwig's a prick."

"Did he ever beat you?"

"Not really."

"How much does he owe you now?"

"Who counts?" Danielle said.

"So what do you think's going on, here? Maleasoel was in tears, and Ludwig's acting strange." He saw her frown. "What's wrong?"

"I don't know. They're so goddamned quiet about this morning. Do you think they were in on it somehow?"

He shook his head. "High-profile shades are being killed in the Scouring, the Dark Lord is engaged in some mysterious war, Liberty's in chaos and Ludwig knows something about what's going on. The whole *Community* is in crisis. Add to that two sociopathic Balaklava and a kavasari, and what have you got?"

"A mess and a half."

"Ludwig would never do anything to harm us. I know that much."

She let out a breath. "I know. He's got his faults, but he's a good man in his own way. But what's the big mystery? Why won't he tell us what he knows? We can take care of ourselves."

"Not against Junger and Jagoda."

She touched an eye fleetingly. He could see the moisture there, and raised a hand to trace her jaw. He brought her closer to him and kissed her. She broke the kiss and laid her head on his chest. He could smell the sweetness of her hair.

"I thought we were dead this morning," she said.

"So did I."

Her lithe body trembled against him, trying to avoid an attack of tears. Tough as nails, she was.

"Somehow we've gotta beat them," she said. "The Balaklava. They may be stronger than us, but I bet we could figure out a way to trap 'em."

He said nothing, but he knew from legend that Junger and Jagoda, as well as being extremely brutal, were quite intelligent, too.

"The question is what they have to gain by all this," he said. "Surely more than money's at stake."

She rose from the bed and walked naked to the sliding glass door, which led to the bedroom's terrace, and flung open the door. The wind whipped her sweaty hair, and she paused on the threshold. Becoming accustomed to the chill, she stepped outside. The storm thundered and crashed about the compound, and the rain flung its icy self down on her exposed skin. The rain mixed with her recent sweat and washed it away. She opened her mouth playfully and let the rain attempt to drown her.

Lightning cracked close by, and she laughed. The stark light caressed her glistening body, and Ruegger felt himself aroused again. Slipping from the clammy sheets, he followed Danielle onto the terrace. Thunder smashed against the house, and she spit her water out so she could growl into the storm. It didn't scare easily, however, and the thunder sounded again, more loudly.

"Oh, yeah?" she roared. "Come and get me if you can!"

Lightning blew open a nearby pine. The crack echoed against the walls and the smell of charred wood wafted through the choppy night.

"So you wanna play rough," she said and began yelling obscenities into the storm.

A blast struck down another pine, this one even closer.

"I think you're losing," Ruegger said.

Thunder roared again, but seemingly from within the house. Then it roared again, only it wasn't thunder.

Suddenly, the terrace was empty, save for the whipping of the wind. The vampires chased the screams down the hall toward Ludwig's and Malie's bedroom chamber, also in this wing of the house.

They rounded a corner and burst into the room of their friends; the door was splintered and partially torn from its hinges. Five dead and butchered Libertarian guards lay outside.

Blood spattered the room, as well as fragments of bone and flesh. The central remains of Ludwig lay on his bed, his sundered carcass partially hidden by the gusting satin curtains of his four-poster bed, but twisted limbs and shards of gleaming bone and muscle covered the room. One of the wooden columns that held up the canopy to his bed had been snapped off and mounted by Ludwig's severed head.

"*No*," Ruegger said, going toward it. "Gods, no."

There was no sign of Maleasoel.

Frozen rain and wind blew into the gore-haunted room through the one great bay window, now fragmented. Most of the glass had blown outward with the impact, but the force of the wind had swept several glistening shards back in to mingle with the still-wet blood and viscera.

The moonstruck curtains blew like ghosts, and Ruegger and Danielle approached the hole in the bay window slowly. Ruegger leaned out over the icy abyss and strained his eyes to search the gloom. There, on the outskirts of the estate, ran the demons, currently wearing the shapes of great black wolves. The Balaklava vanished into the night.

* * *

The next day, Capt. Raulf D'Aguila was elected leader of Liberty, at least until Maleasoel returned. Whether or not it had orchestrated Ludwig's death, the dissident faction had gained control; Damaini, who would have been Ludwig's choice for leader after Maleasoel, was now relegated to second-in-command. Neither Ruegger nor Danielle saw the coronation ceremony or the Captain himself; they were getting drunk in their room, trying to get themselves together and figure out what to do next.

Danielle was concerned for Ruegger. He didn't even cry, just stared. A great sadness had obviously overwhelmed him and he couldn't shake it, but he couldn't seem to release his feelings, either. He'd seen so much of blood and tragedy that his heart had hardened—but, Danielle hoped, not beyond repair.

Why had Junger and Jagoda killed Ludwig? None could say. But, if the assassins had spoken the truth, Danielle supposed they would be headed for the Castle soon. Leaving Ruegger and Danielle a trail to follow, should they choose to do so. However, if the Dark Lord was sponsoring the actions of Junger and Jagoda, then he would be far less likely to admit the odd flock to his home. And, if he did, he would surely kill them.

Ruegger and Danielle headed south after the funeral, toward their estate in the wilds of Canada. Of course, the funeral was supposed to be a party of sorts, because that was Ludwig's wish; he'd wanted a celebration of his life, not a lamentation of his passing. His meager remains were burned and scattered over the frozen wasteland by Maleasoel's two winged companions, jandrows like herself but with fair hair and brighter wings. They looked quite heavenly flying above the trees in the shining night, ash falling in a gentle cloud beneath.

Maleasoel had seemingly disappeared. It was widely speculated that the Balaklava must have dragged her off into the wasteland to perform unspeakable acts upon her before rending her limb from limb as they were surely wont to do, but if so neither Ruegger nor Danielle had seen any evidence of it. In any case, she was gone.

Damaini smiled once, only briefly, as Ruegger and Danielle packed their bags.

"Where are you going?" he said.

Danielle closed her eyes, glanced at Ruegger, and sighed.

"Home," she said.

They departed in the same plane they'd arrived in. Damaini waved at the vampire couple as they climbed into the aircraft, which started with a roar and took off at speed into the clouds.

Chapter 6

Six nights later, Danielle was drinking a beer in the hedge maze out back of their estate, her potbellied pig Cerberus beside her, when the parrot called Elvis landed on her arm.

"What the hell?"

"You have visitors in the lobby," he squawked.

"Van Reisser, it that you?" Normally the bird was controlled either by Ruegger or herself, but sometimes their manservant Van Reisser would send messages through it. All three immortals could control it with their minds.

"Visitors in the lobby," the bird said again and flew off.

Danielle drained her beer, made her way out of the hedge maze and approached the old mansion. Occasionally she would ask Ruegger about its founding, but he would shrug and grow taciturn, so she'd learned not to ask. There were many things about him she didn't know, and it was infuriating because she knew many shades dramatically older than herself, and these people, she was certain, knew all about him and his past. Yet when she prodded them they invariably said that he should be the one to tell her. Danielle agreed. *So I wait.* She was tired of waiting.

Once, under his breath, he'd referred to this estate as *Casa de Amelia*, and she recognized the name of Ruegger's long-dead lover. Otherwise, he wouldn't talk about her.

In any case, the mansion was home, though they only stayed at it a month or so every year. They lived on the road mostly. Danielle called it Mount Vapor because of all the mist shrouding it the first night she'd seen it, and the nickname had stuck.

As she entered the manse through its rear entrance, she wondered where Ruegger was. He'd been brooding since their arrival. Alone, Danielle pushed on through wide stone corridors into the foyer, where a group of soldiers waited impatiently. At their head stood Maleasoel.

Danielle gasped. The jandrow's wings *had been ripped off.*

"Dear God," she heard herself say. "Malie, what *happened* to you?"

"Later."

Despite her injury, Maleasoel seemed very much in control of herself, with only her lack of humor confirming that she was even aware of her husband's death.

Danielle crossed to the dour Van Reisser, who looked greatly annoyed.

"Where's Ruegger?" Danielle asked.

"Indisposed, I believe."

She knew what that meant. "Have him meet us in the private conference room upstairs in ten minutes."

"If you insist."

"I do." She turned to Maleasoel. "Please, invite your soldiers inside."

Ludwig's widow glanced over her shoulder at her men, and this drew Danielle's attention to them for the first time. They seemed to affect a certain look of . . . was it disdain?

"I don't think they'd come," Maleasoel said frankly.

"Why?"

"Because you have humans living here with you as equals."

"We have some small staff, and friends that visit from time to time . . ."

"My people feel offended and I can't help but feel a little uneasy myself—it's almost unheard of, you know."

"Will *you*, at least, come in?" When Malie, nodded, Danielle led her upstairs to the conference room. Ruegger was already there, rooting through the cabinets and the mini-refrigerator of the private bar. He came up with salt, limes, a shot glass and a bottle of Cuervo Gold. His eyes stared out, blood-shot and crazed, and dark stubble covered his face.

"Want a—?" he started, then noted Maleasoel's absence of wings. "Dear gods."

The trio sat down at the large table and stared at each other in silence.

"Okay," Danielle said finally. "What happened?"

Maleasoel downed a shot, then told her story. "Ludwig sensed danger coming and sent me away to a little cabin outside of Barrow just before he was murdered. Later, the Balaklava found me, beat me, raped me, and tore off my wings. They laughed and said for me to never try to fool them again—they would always find me, no matter where I went. I believe them. They probably know where I am right now. They could be outside watching."

After Ludwig's murder, she said, she'd gathered some loyal troops and gone searching for Junger and Jagoda, but to no avail. She intended to scour the world for them and for answers to his death. Not even she knew why he'd been killed, and she was sure it wasn't just a random act of violence on the part of the Balaklava. With her soldiers, she would find who had hired Junger and Jagoda and rip them limb from limb.

"So what's our involvement in all this?" Ruegger said, after expressing horror at what had happened to her.

"You're involved the same way I am," she said. "The dissidents were using us as blackmail against Ludwig— either he advanced the movement or we would die, one by one. I would be last. I *was* his wife. Honestly, though, I think he loved you, Ruegger, more than me. That was a miscalculation on the part of the dissidents."

"But he didn't advance."

"No. There was someone else who wanted him to step down, someone who was even more powerful than the dissidents. He employed the same methods as they did, though, using us against Ludwig. This is the one who hired Junger and Jagoda, as well as those sand-rats who attacked you in the desert."

"So Ludwig was stuck between two bad choices and did nothing," Danielle said. "Who was this someone else?"

Malie downed another shot. "I'm not sure. Ludwig tried to keep me in the dark as much as he could, saying that the less I knew the safer I'd be. I wish I'd known even less."

"Who *was* it?"

Malie let out a breath. "Roche Sarnova. He, or one of his emissaries, was the mysterious visitor you were asking about."

The room fell silent.

"I'm not saying that it was Sarnova who killed him," Malie added, "although I'm not saying that it wasn't. But it makes sense, doesn't it? Liberty has the second highest concentration of shades ever—Ludwig almost had more direct followers under him than Sarnova himself. So it would follow that Blackie would want Liberty disbanded."

"We think the Balaklava were employed by two people, or at least approached by two," Ruegger said. "Based on your information, it seems that one of them was Roche Sarnova. Who was the other?"

"Does it matter?"

"Very much. If Junger and Jagoda had followed the orders of Sarnova—if it was he—who seems to have meant to kill us to add further gravity to the threat of killing you next—we'd be dead now. Instead, they followed the instructions of another employer—they hinted as much—

for another purpose entirely. And it was for this employer that they killed Ludwig."

"How do you figure?"

"The dissidents and Sarnova apparently had opposite aims, but neither would be served by Ludwig's death. If he died, the dissidents were afraid of half of Liberty getting up and walking away—besides, the others would know that it was the dissidents who killed him and the compound would be in chaos. If Sarnova wanted Liberty disbanded, he wouldn't have killed Ludwig. No offense, but Ludwig was a weak leader. A stronger leader would only replace him. Therefore, it must be another entity that hired the Balaklava to do Ludwig in and harass us. Tell me, did Junger or Jagoda say anything about coming to visit you again?"

"They said never to hide from them because it only made it more fun to find me."

"But nothing direct?"

"No."

"Then perhaps it's only Danielle and I that are involved. Somehow, the fact that the Balaklava intend to further harm us is connected to Ludwig's death." He raised his eyebrows at Danielle, and she was surprised to see that he looked lucid. "It's up to us to find out why. And who."

"Gimme a shot," she said. It was all she had to say. He knew she would do whatever needed to be done.

Malie took a long breath. "There's another problem."

"What's that?"

"My people, many of them, want to *act*. They're afraid that if they delay our resolve will weaken."

"By 'act'," Danielle said. "You mean ... ?"

"That's right. They want to move against the world *now*."

Ruegger and Danielle glanced at each other.

Cautiously, Ruegger said, "What's your plan for dealing with Roche Sarnova?"

"That was always a problem. I think we've solved it, though. Some of my people have found a supplier of stolen tactical nuclear warheads."

"Shit!" said Danielle.

"The weapons should put quite a dent in the Castle. Combined with Sarnova having most of his resources tied up in his war, he could, in theory, be dealt with."

Danielle put a hand to her forehead. "That's insane."

Grimly, Malie said, "The only way I've found to keep my people occupied and focused elsewhere is by finding Ludwig's killer. If we can find him or her and punish them, that will go a long way to ensuring it's *Ludwig's* legacy that prevails among my people. Not ... anyone else's. A legacy of peace and responsibility. Also, once he's been avenged, I think the half of Liberty that was ready to leave if he stepped down will do just that. The other half, the dissidents, won't be able to carry out their plans without the full army. Until he's avenged, though, the army will stay together and the dissidents will only grow in power."

Ruegger's face had gone rigid. "You're saying if we don't find Ludwig's killer, your army will take over the world."

"That's about the size of it. And I'll need your help to do it."

*   *   *

"What of the Scouring?" Ruegger asked, when he and Danielle had absorbed this new development. "Have you found anything out about it?"

"No," Malie said. "Do you think it had something to do with Ludwig's death?"

"No idea, but I'm beginning to think it's related somehow."

"What about the war?" Danielle said.

"It's a very secret war," Malie said. "That's about all I know. They call it the War of the Dark Council, but I'm not really sure what that means."

After the three shot back a last round of whiskey, Malie said, "I have to go."

"But you just showed up!"

"I just came by to assure you I was alive and to recruit you for the hunt. Until next time, friends."

When she left, Ruegger slunk off to, presumably, continue getting drunk, while Danielle made her way to the library, selected a work by Joe Lansdale and read for some time, but her mind drifted to other matters. Ruegger had skipped a significant question, she thought: why had the Balaklava chosen to follow the orders of their enigmatic "second employer" instead of those of Roche Sarnova, who had more clout and prestige than most world leaders? And that was assuming that the Dark Lord was their original employer in the first place.

Her mind buzzing, she decided to take a walk in the large green maze outside. The moment she stepped into the first dark corridor, she could hear some urgent, rhythmic sound that only grew louder the further she pressed into the labyrinth. Just before she got to the clearing with the gazebo, she recognized it as crying.

She rounded the final corner to see Ruegger and Maleasoel curled up with each other on a bench in the gazebo. At first Danielle had the horrible notion that something sexual was going on, but no. Ruegger and Malie were embracing tightly and tears were flowing from both their eyes. Their backs arching and convulsing, they looked perfectly wretched, and Danielle realized they were mourning the loss of Ludwig together, privately, in their own way. Although she felt a twinge of sadness that Ruegger hadn't come to her to cry on, she knew that Malie was really the only one that could fully share his feelings, and that Ruegger was perhaps the only one Malie could turn to as well. They'd been the two closest people in Ludwig's life and it was fitting that they mourn together.

Danielle felt her heart swell with relief; if Ruegger couldn't open up to her, she was glad he could open up to someone. Hoping that the mourners hadn't seen her, she crept back out of the labyrinth.

And stopped cold.

For there, at the mouth of the labyrinth, stood two big black wolf-like creatures. Similar to werewolves, but larger, more demonic, with long, broad snouts, horn-like ears and thick coats of black fur. From the cheeks of one sprouted symmetrical rows of small tusks. The creatures smiled at her. The smiles were eerily human.

"We've always loved labyrinths," said the one that must be Junger. The one with the tusks.

Trembling, she reached for a Colt .45—she never went anywhere unarmed these days—and pointed it at the assassin's head.

"Why did you kill Ludwig?"

Jagoda lowered his horn-like ears. "It is not for us to tell."

Junger ran his slavering tongue across his teeth and laughed.

Danielle cocked the revolver. "What did you come here for?"

"We came because of your maze, of course," Jagoda said.

"And to show that we could," added the other.

"And . . . another reason."

She fired, sending a bullet through Junger's brain, but it did no more than temporarily irritate the Balaklava. Harming the bastard hadn't been her reason for firing.

Within seconds, Ruegger and Malie arrived at her side.

"*You*," said Maleasoel. "Be gone from here!"

"Our business is only beginning," said Jagoda. "Ruegger, Danielle—we will hunt you till the end of the earth. Your life will be a hell. And then . . . death."

"But why?" asked Ruegger. "Why all this? Ludwig, Barrow? What do you have to gain?"

"You'll find out," said Junger. "In time."

"What do you want?"

"We're here to help you," said Jagoda, with that maddening sense of calm. "With incentive . . . and information."

"Get to the fucking point," Danielle said. "We already know that you're working for Roche Sarnova, and maybe someone else."

"Then you don't know anything, because we're not working for Roche Sarnova."

"Don't believe a word they say," Malie said.

"But you are working for two employers?" Ruegger asked.

The Junger-wolf turned to the Jagoda-wolf. "I don't think they're ready for our information, do you?"

"What do you get out of helping us?" Danielle said.

"The same thing you get: answers. You see, child, we know more than you do, but we know very little of the big picture. Which is unfortunate for us—fortunate for you, though, in that you're still here. We very much want to see the big picture, which we think will be very interesting indeed, and we need you two to find it for us. You have the right connections, we don't. It's that simple."

"This is all bullshit," Malie said.

"We're interested in your fate—not that we care one way or another about your deaths, but we think the circumstances surrounding them will be, as I've said, interesting."

"What's this big picture?" Ruegger said.

"The war in Europe, the murders all over the world, Ludwig's death—they're all part of a whole," Jagoda said, "We're sure of it, but we need to figure it all out so that . . ."

"Yes?"

"So that we can be in on the ground floor of the New World Order."

Danielle blinked.

"Speak plainly," Ruegger said.

"The meaning is for you to find out. There is still a hit out on you both. Someone's hired Vistrot to arrange your death and we want to know why. So we come to you. Legwork is not our forte—but, as it is your life in peril, I suggest it become yours."

"They're lying," Malie said.

"If you want us to find information for you, we'd better know what you do," Ruegger said. "Why kill Ludwig?"

The assassins remained silent.

"At least tell us who your middleman is," Danielle pressed.

"Did you think we'd come out of retirement to work for a faceless employer?" Junger said. "Do you think we're doing this for *money?*"

"Give us something!"

"We have. Vistrot."

"Something more."

Smiling their infuriating smiles, Junger and Jagoda disappeared into the darkness.

* * *

The next night, the odd flock packed their bags, said their good-byes and made their way to the enormous garage, where Ruegger kept his ever-growing automobile collection. In Danielle's opinion, the perfect road vehicle was the blue convertible '72 Cadillac El Dorado, but it wouldn't serve the vampires' needs as adequately as the van they chose. After fitting it with what they needed, they set out for the highway. Danielle brought her potbelly pig Cerberus, who was a faithful friend at the estate but rarely left its grounds. This time, Danielle felt she needed the reassurance of its presence on the road.

Last night, they had drawn up loose plans. Maleasoel would lead her army in search for the answers to Ludwig's murder in one direction, while Ruegger and Danielle would follow another path.

"You sure about this?" Danielle asked when they were driving, letting the breeze run through her hair. She could feel the old juices pumping through her veins. Back on the road again. "I mean, going to New York's where the order to kill us came from!"

"Yes, so there might also be information about where the order originated there, too. Plus I have contacts there that don't use phones or have internet service."

"You're thinking of Harry."

"He is remarkably plugged-in to the New York immortal scene."

"But Vistrot ... the most powerful shade in America ... will be *right there*. And Jean-Pierre ... that's who the Titan will send after us."

"Then we'd better step lively then, hadn't we?" He paused, casting her a sidelong glance. More softly, he said, "You know, Dani, you don't *have* to come. Ludwig was *my* friend, after all."

"Yeah, but this is *my* world." Throwing her feet up on the dashboard, she lit her first cigarette of the journey. "Step on the gas, ace. New York it is."

Chapter 7

The Carpathians weren't as impressive as Lord Kharker had hoped they'd be. He'd seen them before, of course, many times, but somehow he always managed to convince himself afterward that they had been more dramatic. Ah, well. He hadn't come here for the view.

The helicopter rattled around him, and Kharker frowned. Known as the Great White Hunter, straight from the hot killing grounds of Africa, Kharker was a werewolf, and he enjoyed the sunlight on his skin, something most of his immortal friends could never experience, but he did not enjoy the altitude or the turbulence. To calm himself, he rolled a cigarette, licked the paper to seal it, and lit up.

Smiling, he turned to his companion, the werewolf Jean-Pierre, now soundly asleep.

Jean-Pierre wore a lot of black leather and boasted a series of silver studs and loops angling along the upper ridge of his right ear—silver to spite the gods, of course. Not that silver posed any real threat to the lycans. Jean-Pierre's skin was colorless, almost translucent, his hair a spiky whitish-blond, but his eyes, closed now, were a luminous, angelic green. Light flickered in them strangely, and sometimes they looked like swimming emeralds. He was known throughout the world as the "albino", even though he was not completely without pigmentation.

Kharker, who looked to be a robust fifty-five, was coming up on his thousandth birthday tomorrow, hence the reason for his visit to the Dark Lord. Jean-Pierre probably would've been placed in his early thirties, when the truth was that he was a sinewy two-hundred and sixty.

He looks like a baby when he sleeps, though. A baby who needs a shave, maybe, but a baby nonetheless. A bit different from the waking animal.

Jean-Pierre cracked an eye.

"It's snowing," he observed, his voice characteristically empty. His wet green eyes acknowledged Kharker, then settled back on the window. "I hate snow."

"Then you should move. Running your death-squad out of New York was poor planning for a fan of warm weather."

"You know very well why I live there."

Kharker let out a breath. Jean-Pierre worked exclusively for Vistrot, the Titan, and Vistrot (it rhymed with "bistro") rarely left in New York.

"We there yet?" Jean-Pierre said.

"Yes. That's why we're still in the helicopter."

Jean-Pierre grunted and closed his eyes again.

Kharker had to smile. Though the former Parisian's ruthlessness was legendary, he often adopted the demeanor of a child when around Kharker. They weren't lovers—not now, anyway—but they'd been off-and-on companions since the early sixties. *Quite a change from Ruegger,* Kharker thought.

The albino whipped out a pack of Pall-Malls. He was just striking the match when he caught a glimpse of something outside, just visible through the storm. "We're almost there," he said. Then, almost as an aside: "The place where it all began."

Kharker grimaced. Of course returning to the Castle would stir memories in Jean-Pierre. This was where he had met Danielle, after all. Where he had *abducted* her. Kharker knew all too well that he was still obsessed with the girl.

"There's nothing to fear," Kharker said.

"Did I say there was?"

Kharker slipped on his cream-colored canvas hat. "I wonder if Blackie will have any surprises planned for my birthday."

Dryly, Jean-Pierre said, "I can't wait."

Rocked by winds, the helicopter took its time getting to the helipad that erupted from the top of the castle, but when it saw its chance the craft dove down, landing with a start that unsettled Kharker's stomach. The Hunter and the albino clambered out, Kharker shivering at the snap of the cold air, and followed their welcoming party, a single high-ranking werewolf, indoors.

"It is an honor to have you here," the fellow said. "Please, come with me."

After the outside door was closed, an inside door was opened, protecting any sun-sensitive immortal that happened to be walking around. All windows were covered, and a few shades did indeed prowl the halls, but the castle seemed largely deserted at the moment. Kharker had to fight the urge to keep glancing over his shoulders as he made his way through the narrow stone passageways. He liked the outdoors, open spaces, and grew anxious surrounded by so much stone.

The three rode an elevator to the lowest floor above the level of the dungeons and catacombs, marched down another network of corridors until they found themselves in a cold but well-furnished room. The shade who'd greeted them nodded at a man behind a desk, and this man pressed a button on a console. Shortly, a line of tired shades stumbled through the room's second door and sat down in some seats along the walls. They looked as if they'd been in conference for days. Kharker and Jean-Pierre were shown into the next room, and the door closed swiftly behind them.

Roche Sarnova hunched behind a large desk, with Francois Mauchlery not too far away, slightly behind him, in a comfortable chair. The Dark Lord smiled and motioned his guests to sit.

"Thanks," Kharker said, noting that Sarnova appeared terrible, his hands shaking slightly, sweat beading his skin ... which was rent in countless places. *Dear gods.* A black patch covered one eye.

Mauchlery didn't look much better.

"Damn it all," breathed Kharker. "What happened, Roche? Who did this to you? What the hell's going on?"

Sarnova held up his hands, warding off questions. He gave a sick cough, which took longer than it should have, and smiled. "In time," he said. "All questions will be answered. So how are you doing, my friend?"

"Wonderful, comparatively."

"And you, Jean-Pierre?"

The albino said nothing.

"How was your safari? I'd been keeping track of your progress until recently."

"Fabulous," Kharker said. "We brought down some elephants, and you should see Jean-Pierre handle a rifle. I'm afraid he'll be better than I am before too long. Perhaps next time you could join us."

"I'd love that. And much congratulations on your birthday, Kharker. Unfortunately, due to circumstances not immediately in my control, the grand celebration we'd planned for your millennium will have to be delayed, I don't know how long. I'd love for you to stay awhile in the hopes that there would be a break in my schedule, but I don't foresee one and I could never put you in the jeopardy that living here might entail. Other than the Ambassador here, you are my oldest friend, Kharker, and I hope that sooner or later I can make amends for my lack of hospitality."

"What on earth are you talking about?"

Sarnova coughed again, then looked apologetic. "I'm sorry, Jean-Pierre, but could you please give us some time? I mean no disrespect, but your friend and I must talk privately."

The albino shrugged and rose. "Anywhere I can get some coffee in this dump?"

Roche remained pleasant. "Just ask Ivan, my receptionist."

The albino left, not closing the door as delicately as he could have on the way.

"Well," said Kharker.

"Indeed," said Sarnova, and turned to nod at Francois. "Ambassador, would you care to bring Lord Kharker up to speed on recent events?"

*   *   *

Jean-Pierre stalked the shadows, wishing they'd never come here. The Castle! Gods, what a bore. A great big lump of old stone in the mountains. So what if it was the seat of all immortal activity in the world, or that it was hallowed and sacred to many, as was its lord? It meant nothing to Jean-Pierre. Though French by birth, he was a New Yorker now, a product of the New World, and the Old held little interest for him. Also, he admitted, he was jealous of the friendship between Kharker and Sarnova. If only that were all.

He glanced around the dark halls, barely suppressing a wave of mixed longing and sorrow.

Danielle, where are you?

Years ago, on one of his frequent meccas to the Dark Country with Kharker, back when the albino had found it less repellent, Jean-Pierre had seen the young vampiress for the first time. She'd been staying with Ruegger at the Castle for a few weeks. At the time, the Dark Lord had wanted to meet the notorious vigilante vampires. Roche Sarnova could have put them to death for their murderous actions (indeed, Jean-Pierre had heard that he'd intended to), but had been persuaded by Kharker into sparing Ruegger's life. And Blackie would not kill Danielle unless he could execute Ruegger, too. The issue was dropped, but it had brought great attention upon the odd flock, and Jean-Pierre had become enamored of the so-called Waif.

Calling on some favors, the albino had separated the vampires and convinced Danielle that Ruegger had been killed and that his murderers wanted her dead, too. The odd flock's enemies had decided to move against them, he said. He'd even produced a corpse resembling Ruegger, with the face unrecognizable. Thinking she had no choice, Danielle had allowed him to take her away to Kharker's vine-covered Congo estate, where they had holed up for months before Ruegger, alive and well, had tracked them down and released Danielle. Upon discovering that Jean-Pierre had lied to her, she'd attempted to kill the albino, who was saved by none other than the Darkling.

Looking around at the stone and torches now, Jean-Pierre swore. *We never should have come here.*

*   *   *

Kharker thought it amazing how synchronized the Ambassador and Sarnova were, almost as if they were part of the same organism. Mauchlery moved out from behind Sarnova's desk and started pacing the room in an organized fashion, talking as he did.

Eventually, he came to the part about Roche being wounded. "I was sent to the front lines a month or so ago to check up on our troops," continued Francois, "and I returned with a werewolf named Victoria Lisaund. She accompanied me back under the guise of petitioning Roche for protection of her clan, who she said supported our cause. In truth she was a spy. Worse, she had skills we weren't prepared for. She'd been trained to kill mortals with her mind, and she killed one that Roche was feeding from, causing him to drink dead blood. She attacked Roche when he was down, and she was stronger than she should've been. It took both me and Roche to destroy her."

"How could she have been so powerful?" asked Kharker.

Francois looked uneasy. "We think that maybe she had gotten hold of the blood of a kavasari. That would've made her very strong indeed."

Kharker's voice lowered. "That's bad. Yes, indeed. So ... all this is why the immortal world is in turmoil?"

Roche Sarnova sat up slowly. "Not quite. But I'm afraid that I can't . . . *speculate* on the reasons why things are the way they are. My war in Europe isn't at all responsible for the Scouring."

"But they are related?"

Sarnova coughed again. "Perhaps," he said. "Perhaps."

Kharker replaced his hat on his head. "So that's that, is it?"

"No, no. Please, don't take offense. You know I'd never want to slight you in any way. Here, take your hat off, let's invite Jean-Pierre in and enjoy each other's company for a while. If we've got enough time, I have a special treat for you. Then we'll feed you both and you can return to the Congo, where you'll be safe. I'm sorry you came all this way for nothing, but don't worry, I'll make it up to you sooner or later."

Kharker snorted but pulled off his hat. He knew Sarnova was being sincere, but he didn't like anything being kept from him. Still, he understood that during wartime, secrets were sacred. He leaned forward and stubbed his cigarette out in an ashtray as Jean-Pierre entered the room and sat down again.

"Enjoy the coffee?" Sarnova asked.

"You're out of cream."

Wine was poured and they talked awkwardly for awhile until the tension was broken, then Sarnova said, "Before you go, let me show you something." He moved toward the door, and the others followed.

"Weren't you in the middle of a meeting?" Kharker said, as they pushed into the next room. Many of the shades who had been sitting in the reception area slouched noticeably, either asleep or getting there.

"Let them rest," Sarnova said, talking as he led them down a hall. Escorts hovered at his sides. "Have you ever heard of Junger and Jagoda?"

"The Last of the Roving Balaklava?" Jean-Pierre said. "I'd thought they'd gone to Jamaica long ago."

"They did, but they've been wanting to come out of isolation for some time, so I contracted them to do some art for me. They finished a few weeks ago but just returned yesterday to celebrate the grand opening of their new exhibit. It's only one piece, but it's quite large. I must admit that I'm pleased." He turned to a servant. "Would you go fetch them for me?"

The servant vanished. The Dark Lord led his guests down another few corridors, then took a stairwell into the catacombs, where they followed another series of rat-tunnels. Kharker could feel hairs prickling along his spine. Finally, Sarnova ushered them into a large, domed room.

"Behold."

"Goddamn," said Kharker.

Open coffins, standing vertically, lined the earthen walls of the circular room, with about five feet of space separating each one. Formally dressed corpses, their flesh splotched and decaying, stood stiffly in their coffins staring on the world with dead eyes. From the feet of each one, human bones (held together with carefully-concealed wire and cobwebs) sprouted, snaking across the floor to converge on the center of the circle. Here the strings of bone met and rose into the air, some bleached and white, some gray and rotting. A tree of bones emerged from the chaos, towering over everything in the room, its stark and lifeless branches arching high and long in dense, thorny, crystalline clusters.

A stained-glass window with lights behind it, built into the ceiling directly above the tree, cast a strange green glow on the branches, giving the sculpture the eerie, deathly glow it needed.

"Beautiful, isn't it?" said Roche Sarnova.

"It is," said Jean-Pierre.

Kharker heard a noise behind him and turned in time to see the Balaklava enter. They were very tall, and their skin was black on black.

"Glad you like it," said the bald one with the tusks. "I'm Junger."

"And I'm Jagoda," the other said. He wore sunglasses and his face, framed by long dreadlocks, was masked by a heavy, unkempt beard. "We call it the Tree *la Morte.*"

"It's marvelous," said Kharker. "A shame we missed the grand opening. Maybe I could hire you to do something for me sometime."

Junger shrugged. "If we're inspired, we'll give you a call. Now, if you'll excuse us, we were just preparing to rape and kill a few people. Ta-ta." They bowed and left.

"I love their art," said Sarnova, "but sometimes their artistic temperaments are a little much." He shook Kharker's hand. "Now, friend, I'm really afraid I've got to get back to work. Forgive me?"

"Of course. Be sure to get some sleep soon."

An escort led Kharker and Jean-Pierre into separate rooms, where they fed. An hour later, they flew high over the snow-whipped mountains toward the lush tangles of the

Congo, away from the ice-bound halls of stone and the warlord in black.

"Well," said Jean-Pierre, over the roar of the helicopter. "Was it interesting, what he said?"

"Very."

"Care to discuss it?"

"Later," Kharker said. "When I find out more."

The albino looked amused. "So he's holding out on you?"

Kharker didn't answer.

Jean-Pierre glanced out the window. Lounging back in his seat, he closed his eyes, and it was like the sun disappearing.

"Happy Birthday," he muttered.

*   *   *

The helicopter dropped them off in Bucharest, where Kharker's personal plane waited, and they set out again for his palatial Congo estate, flying over vast ocean, never-ending desert, and a jungle that had driven an infinite number of men mad. A little dirt airstrip stretched before the manse itself, and they landed hard, dust throwing up in geysers behind the plane, which shuddered as the engine died.

"Great landing," Jean-Pierre said. He tore open the door and dropped down, then helped Kharker, not out of any infirmity on the latter's part but out of respect.

The Hunter cast a glance at the sunset, took a deep breath and smiled. "There's nothing like home."

"Don't start clicking your heels together yet."

Kharker laughed, turning his eyes toward his immense estate, built many years ago by natives who Kharker had later trained to be his personal army and grounds keeping taskforce. Their offspring had continued the tradition. He thought he treated them well, having even gone to the trouble of hiring a small faculty of English professors to educate them. Of course, he didn't hold himself responsible if he was particularly hungry or desirous one day and one of his following glanced at him wrong. He was, after all, the Great White Hunter, and he had certain needs—entitlements.

Jean-Pierre studied the trucks, parked close to the main building.

"It looks like our trophies have arrived," he said. The game they'd killed on safari had been bundled up and sent here directly.

"Good."

"What are we gonna do with more elephant hide?" Jean-Pierre said. "Make another Elephant Room?"

"We've got more than elephant hide, but I see your point. Maybe we could hire Junger and Jagoda to make some arrangement with the corpses themselves."

"Sure, why not? Maybe a necrotic Renaissance is in the works."

A man approached. He was a tall and muscular Greek-Indian mix, with black hair going gray at the fringes. Gavin had been Kharker's bum-boy when he was young, but had proven himself competent at a range of things and was now the Chief of Security for Kharker's estate. Kharker had transformed Gavin and nine other loyalists into immortals so they could better protect his grounds.

"Welcome home," Gavin said. "Too bad Sarnova couldn't celebrate with you like you wanted, but we've got a little something to make up for it—although we weren't expecting you back so soon. Anyway, they're getting ready up in the Elephant Room. It's not much, but it's all we could do on the spur of the moment. Please, at least pretend you like it; they've been practicing for weeks . . . Oh, and on that other matter, we've prepared everything the way you instructed."

Jean-Pierre raised his transparent eyebrows, but Kharker just smiled.

"I'm sure I'll love whatever it is you've prepared for me, Gavin. And thanks for attending to the other matter. Please, lead on."

He followed Gavin inside. Jean-Pierre flicked his cigarette away and trailed along behind. The inside of the Lodge was spacious and masculine, adorned with expensive rugs, paintings, antiques, and an afterlife-full of dead animals, hides and heads and all. The Elephant Room, located on the second story and overlooking the encroaching forest that surrounded them, was a testament to lavishness and decadence; entering it was like stepping into another world.

All six sides of the room (floor and ceiling included) were covered with elephant hide. The head of an enormous bull elephant dominated one wall, its long trunk arched in challenge, and on the opposite wall, the animal's scrotum (fully erect) jutted out. Tusks sprouted from its balls. Countless animal heads, hides, legs, tongues, trunks and other appendages stuck out or hung from the walls, floors and ceiling, as well as several elephant livers, hearts, stomachs, and never-ending loops of intestines, which were painted different colors. And, of course, the room was fully furnished with its share of rugs and paintings, chandeliers hanging from the ceiling. A group of comfortable chairs arranged around a large coffee table (propped up by elephant feet) not too far from the large, unlit fireplace. It was Kharker's favorite room.

Several Africans stood in front of the fireplace holding an assortment of musical instruments. Smiling, they greeted Kharker affectionately. *They're going to play for me, how nice.*

Jean-Pierre and Kharker made themselves comfortable in the chairs facing the musicians.

Jean-Pierre glanced at Kharker, who winked. Waving a servant for a beer, the albino drank as the music started. Kharker winced. It was bad. Just the same, he was impressed by Jean-Pierre's patience. The albino endured it for half an hour until the humans were through. He even clapped for them.

When they were gone, the albino said, "You need to spend more money on the music department." He crossed to the window and lit a cigarette. The night grew dark outside, and Kharker could feel its temptations in his gut.

He sparked a cigar. "You know," he said, puffing, "I've never met a shade who didn't smoke."

"Kilian doesn't smoke. Insolent bastard."

"The member of your death-squad?"

"Probably afraid it will make his clothes smell."

Kharker laughed. "That's better. You're lightening up."

"Enough of that."

"Seriously. You unwound so much on the safari. You actually *enjoyed* yourself, and you can't know how much that warmed my heart. But the moment you saw Roche's castle, you stiffened up again."

The albino shrugged. "You know why."

"It's where you met Danielle. I thought maybe you were over her by now. I remember before we went on safari, you'd pulled out the projector from my basement and were watching the old reels we shot back when she was staying with us. But once we left, you never mentioned her once."

"She was in love with me for awhile."

"When she thought Ruegger was dead."

"Maybe." Jean-Pierre didn't sound convinced. "My crew still gives me hell about it."

I imagine. Kharker knew that during the time she'd spent at the Lodge, Danielle and Jean-Pierre had become lovers. Kharker had not interfered, though he'd wanted to. Still, Ruegger had abandoned him long ago, and Kharker's loyalty belonged to Jean-Pierre now.

Instead of addressing any of this, Kharker said, "How are they?"

"The squad? Belligerent as always. And you? Don't you still love Ruegger?"

Kharker had been willing to let it go, but it seemed Jean-Pierre wasn't. Kharker didn't answer

"You know," Jean-Pierre said, "many say I replaced him in your affections."

Kharker studied the end of his cigar. "I love you as much as I loved him once."

Jean-Pierre's face was still. "You don't anymore?"

Changing the subject, Kharker said, "I think you'll appreciate my gift to you. But I can't talk about it yet—it's a surprise."

"Why'd you get me a gift? It's *your* birthday."

"Your happiness makes me happy, so it's a gift to both of us."

"I haven't even given you my gift. Hang on." Jean-Pierre left the room for a few minutes, returning with a small, flat package, wrapped in canvas.

Kharker smiled. "I'm honored, really."

"You can't open it until after the Hunt, okay? I think you'll want to take some time to . . . look it over." The albino placed it on a stand near Kharker's chair.

"I'm hungry, too."

Together, they left. Once outside, Kharker turned to Jean-Pierre. It was Kharker's custom to go down into the holds before a hunt and stare his prey in the eye, arming them and releasing them personally, often giving them a head start. Jean-Pierre, however, preferred to kill with detachment.

"Good hunting," Jean-Pierre said.

"You, as well."

Kharker had had a system of tunnels built beneath his estate, and he took a stairway down. Mostly he used them as a wine cellar—he was quite a connoisseur—but a portion of the tunnels had been converted into a type of prison for his prey, where they lived semi-comfortably until it was their time to be hunted.

Servants greeted him, bringing several wheeled tables that carried an assortment of blades and firearms.

Kharker unlocked the door of the first cage and stepped inside. Ten minutes later he'd chosen and armed the fifteen mortals he wanted. His estate had been erected on a small rise, so that this end of the catacombs opened directly into the forest. He released his prisoners, most of them collected on the white slavery market, and watched them scatter into the darkness.

When his cigar was halfway smoked, he followed.

*   *   *

Jean-Pierre wandered through the sultry Congo, smoking Pall Malls and searching for a glimpse of the moon through the tangled trees that arched like half-gnawed ribs overhead. It slivered as the nights went by; soon there'd nothing left. He remembered Danielle telling him of Ruegger's theory that all shades were strongest on the new moon, because it was the time when the world was the darkest. The albino knew darkness was a state of mind, though, not something nature could inflict upon you. Of course, Ruegger should know that too.

Jean-Pierre tugged off his clothes and let the night change him into its own image: a beast, somewhere between wolf and man, his coat almost translucent, with a hint of yellow. It wasn't true that werewolves needed a full moon to transform; all they needed was the night. Transforming under the sun would get you burned, though. He loped through the forest, between trees and along muddy ravines, howling and running as fast as his four legs would take him.

After a while, he could hear the screams of Kharker's victims ... but not Kharker himself. *As always.* The Great White Hunter was as silent and insidious as death itself. Jean-Pierre remembered once during their safari when they'd slipped into beast form and brought down an elephant together. They'd wallowed in its steaming carcass, burrowing down into its guts and rutting as if they were possessed. It was the first time they'd fucked in years, and the albino didn't like it. With Kharker, emotions were involved, even in animal form, and emotions were too much for Jean-Pierre. Life should be still, calm.

Jean-Pierre allowed himself to become a man again. Ahead moved prey. The albino followed, and the forest thickened. The human stopped, and Jean-Pierre could hear him checking his weapons. *The final sta—*

Bullets tore into Jean-Pierre, drilling his head and shoulders and torso, knocking him to the ground. A half dozen mortals dropped onto him from overhanging trees, covered in mud to mask their smell, shooting him with automatic rifles and sticking him with lances. Blades and rounds ripped into his flesh. He struggled, trying to escape, but he couldn't even get off the fucking ground.

Without conscious thought, he shifted back into a beast and lunged at the nearest attacker. Blood flew, and bones cracked. He moved to the second one.

In seconds, corpses and soon-to-be corpses littered the ground, writhing in their own entrails. The battle was over. Jean-Pierre lowered his head over one and began feeding. When he was done, he searched through the clothes of the dead until he found some cigarettes and lit up. He sprawled on the ground, naked and covered in blood, and stared up through the trees.

Someone was still hiding up there, he saw, huddled against the trunk.

"Come down," he said.

"No!"

"Then I'll just come and get you."

He closed his eyes and exerted his psychic influence (an ability he was quite strong in) on the girl. Against her will, he made her descend the trunk until she was standing before him.

"Jesus," he said. The likeness wasn't exact, but it was close enough. A dark waif, with black hair framing a pale face and deep dark eyes. Like Danielle. Amid a stream of curses, he remembered Gavin mentioning `that other matter' to Kharker. He remembered the Hunter's sly smile. *This is my present.*

The girl drew herself up against the tree. "Don't hurt me. Haven't you done enough?"

He slapped her. She crumpled to the ground, whimpering.

"Goddamnit!" He slammed his fists into the tree. Breathed. "Go on, get up!"

She stood shakily.

"Go," he said. "You'll probably get eaten by cannibals, but at least you won't be contributing to this farce any longer."

"You're ... not going to kill me?"

"Please don't thank me. You're not out of the woods, yet."

He picked his way back to where he'd left his clothes, dressed and returned to the Lodge. He found Kharker in the Elephant Room. Kharker's hair hung wetly, the man having just come out of the shower, and he was dressed in a burgundy bathrobe, smoking a cigar. By contrast, Jean-Pierre knew that dirt covered his clothes, his hair stuck up in wild tangles, and blood caked him.

He grabbed Kharker by the lapels and threw him to the ground.

"How *dare* you! How could you mock me like that? *How?* Out of all the people I know, I'd never have thought *you'd* betray me. How could you?"

Kharker looked stunned.

"Well, if you wanted to hurt me, I can play that game, too," Jean-Pierre said. He grabbed the canvas-wrapped package from off the stand and held his cigarette lighter up to it. "You know what this is? This is an original poem by your beloved Ruegger, over two hundred years old, back when he was still mortal. It took me a lot of time to find this for you."

Kharker's eyes softened, then widened in alarm as the albino set the package on fire. The Hunter leapt to his feet.

"Don't," he said. "I didn't mean to hurt you, I swear. I thought you were almost over her and this would give you the opportunity to exorcise your demons on someone who looks like her, nothing else. I never meant you to think I was mocking you. I wasn't."

The albino sucked in a ragged breath. "Do you swear?"

"I swear."

Jean-Pierre threw the package down and stomped on it until the fire was out. Kharker lovingly unwrapped it. Jean-Pierre had had each page (there were four) vacuum-sealed and bound in an expensive leather jacket. Damage to the pages themselves appeared minimal, but they'd have to be re-sealed.

Kharker rose, leaving the poem on the floor. He embraced Jean-Pierre, and, after a moment, Jean-Pierre hugged him back. The embrace was short, but it was sincere.

"Why do we insist on hurting each other?" Kharker said.

"I don't know. I'm ... sorry."

"Don't be. Maybe my gift was more thoughtless than I realized." Kharker picked up the poem. "Thank you."

"Sure."

Kharker smiled. Jean-Pierre smiled, too, and slowly they began to chuckle. Kharker waved a servant over and ordered the best wine in the cellar. He clapped Jean-Pierre on the shoulder.

"My friend, what do you say to getting stinking drunk tonight?"

Jean-Pierre laughed, the rage draining from him.

"You only turn a thousand once," he said.

* * *

Jean-Pierre departed for New York two days later. At his leaving, Kharker considered a visit to London, where Roche's little war was taking place, to see what all the fuss was about. But, before he was able to go, he received a very strange group of visitors indeed.

They were unexpected and uninvited, but they offered him a proposition that he could in no way afford to refuse.

Chapter 8

The screaming trumpet of hard rock announced the presence of Ruegger and Danielle to Manhattan. Dark and glittering spires rose around them, black monoliths with teeth for windows, to welcome the vampires beneath the eye of the winter moon. They didn't see it, but they felt it: when they crossed into the city, certain shadows moved faster, certain grins grew tighter.

"Despite it all, I do love New York," Danielle said, adjusting the radio volume.

"It doesn't love us." Ruegger stared at the grim monoliths, subdued but made colder by a skin of snow. "Not tonight."

At one time he'd hated this city because of what it represented to him, and because it was here that he'd lost the second great love of his life. He tried not to think about that. New York hadn't changed, really, but his attitude towards it had; he had friends here now, as well as enemies, but he no longer thought of the city with enmity. In fact, he'd grown to like it in some ways. To appreciate it.

"How does it feel to be home?" he asked, then thought: *Malcolm. Malcolm's here. And the other one. Locke.* The idea had plagued him all the length of their journey. Danielle's two surviving rapists, doomed to die. Waiting for her.

"Strange," she said. "I guess if I could revisit the old neighborhoods . . . but there's nothing I want to remember from back then."

They switched vehicles in a private parking garage on the edge of the city, out from the bulk of their van and into the sleeker and blacker 1969 Mustang they had stashed away for urban (and southern) driving. It had been custom-refitted so that a tiny coffin was camouflaged in the rear compartment, seemingly part of the car. If the vampires were caught in the open during daylight, it might save their lives, though given its cramped quarters they both hoped this would never prove necessary. The vehicle was cozy, and they sped from the garage feeling refreshed.

Needing a place to crash while they began their investigations, they struck out for the residence of the Ghensiv Veliswa. The ghensivs were a race of night creature composed completely of females; a second set of teeth resided within their womanhoods. Some ghensivs, like Veliswa, had a taste for blood as well. The succubi dwelt mainly in large cities. Veliswa worked as a call-girl for the rich and secretive.

Ruegger and Danielle slipped past the mortals prowling the corridors of the Cardeux Building, where she'd lived for decades, and rode the express elevator up to Veliswa's penthouse, using an electronic key to get in. They didn't know when the ghensiv would be back and weren't prepared to guess, so waiting seemed like the best option. Ruegger pressed a button on the wall next to the sliding-glass doors to the balcony and prettily-decorated blackout curtains swished down from a tasteful, even stylish mechanism set above the glass portals. It probably closed the drapes automatically at a certain time, but he didn't know that for certain. Better safe than toast.

Heady, feminine aromas flooded the spacious rooms. Rich artwork decorated the walls.

Danielle consulted a watch; often she wore two or three, and today was no exception. "Veliswa's got just over an hour if she's coming back today, taking into account that we'll see the sun here before the street will."

It was odd that a being of the night like Veliswa would brave the upper reaches of the sky, tempting the sun with all its fury, but height meant power and that is something Veliswa would never be without. She would have the biggest and best or nothing at all.

Ruegger stayed in the living area while Danielle inspected the bedrooms.

"She's still got the waterbed!"

Smiling, he entered the bedroom and found her flung comfortably across the gigantic black-silk waterbed. An immense wrought-iron headboard rose above her; stained handcuffs dangled from its dully gleaming bars. Whips and chains and oils and blades and harnesses and sadomasochistic articles of every description littered the room and hung from the walls. A large mirror provided a ceiling to the bed's canopy. Veliswa often said that the Marquis de Sade's *120 Days of Sodom* was her bible, and Ruegger had never doubted her.

Danielle fingered a handcuff. "Maybe we should . . . ?"

"Don't you dare," said a voice from the doorway, and they turned.

A raving beauty, with rich blond hair cascading down to partially hide her blue eyes, Veliswa possessed tender red lips and a strong feminine chin. Her young face had lived too much perhaps, but she was enchanting. Tall, she stood maybe an inch under six feet without high heels on.

"I like my kink," she said, "but my toys are mine. You're wanted, by the way," she added, beginning to slip off her clothes without thought to the vampires watching. "There's a nice little price on your heads."

"How nice?" Danielle asked.

Veliswa smiled. "Very nice."

"Well," Ruegger said, "if we die, at least we'll make somebody happy. Never let it be said that we were uncharitable."

"So is this a social visit?" Her panties fell in a puddle at her feet.

"Tea and crumpets, don'tcha know?" said Danielle.

"Jesus, you two. What could you have done?"

"We were hoping you could tell us something," Ruegger said.

"I don't have a clue. Honest to fucking God. I just don't know. Vistrot . . . I know the order came from Vistrot. Why, or if he's doing a favor for somebody else, I don't know."

"You think he was hired by someone? I didn't think he took orders from anyone."

"If the price is high enough—or if he can garner a large enough favor in return—he can be persuaded."

"Couldn't it be Vistrot himself? Perhaps he's mad at us for some reason."

"Vistrot, mad? At you? No. He's too entrenched in his own little criminal world. He may've even forgotten you, Darkling. And he's never heard of you, Danielle, except maybe through Jean-Pierre. The albino is his pet psychopath, one of his highest-ranking assassins here and off the island."

Danielle smiled. "Vistrot and Kharker. What a pair of god-parents."

"You're right, Dani—don't kill that fucker. If Jean-Pierre dies, you'll have to deal with the wrath of Lord Kharker, not to mention the Titan. Christ, you'll be, well . . . very, very dead." She reached out a gentle hand and poked Ruegger affectionately in the belly. "I'm sorry, love. I heard about Ludwig. I know how much he meant to you."

Ruegger nodded. "I always thought he'd outlive me."

"Me too, *mon ami*. You were the warrior, the blood-drenched poet off fighting demons wherever you found them. He was the dreamer. Wanted the world to be a better place, poor misguided bastard." She slid beneath her silken sheets, covering up her long legs, but her breasts, full and high, were still quite visible. "So what was meeting Junger and Jagoda like?"

"You know of that?"

"It's the latest gossip. Everyone's talking about how the Balaklava are going to pursue you till the end of the world or until you die, whichever comes first."

"Well," Danielle said to Veliswa, or at least her breasts. "It's sun-up and we should really let you sleep. Thanks for everything."

The ghensiv yawned gracefully and slid down, tucking the sheets up to her chin.

"Thank you, *mon amis*. Please feel free to use the guest room or, if you'd be more comfortable, in the coffins in the secret chamber. You remember where it is—behind the left wall of the walk-in pantry. *Oui?*" She smiled sleepily. "Oh, and I like your pig, but, ah, it's on the sofa."

"Her name's Cerberus," Danielle said.

"Very cute."

Off Veliswa's expression, Danielle said, "Don't worry, we'll get her off." Taking Ruegger by the hand, she led him away from the ghensiv's bedroom, and together they found the guestroom.

Quietly, Danielle, "I, uh, have a question. I've always wondered."

"Yes?" Ruegger said.

She looked sheepish. "Do ghensivs completely, er, you know . . . do they *take it?*"

He grimaced. "Depends on the ghensiv. If she's hungry and has a dark bent, she may drain the man completely. But regardless of their disposition, every now and then, just like we need to feed on blood, they must, ah, bite it off."

"With their *teeth* . . ."

He didn't have to pretend to shudder. "Right."

* * *

They woke at dusk to find Veliswa yawning and ordering from room service. The staff was well acquainted with her evening breakfasts. Dressed in a cream-colored robe, her long blond hair whirled about her head. "Where's Cerberus?" was the first thing she said after seeing the vampires.

"Ah, hell," said Danielle.

"*Guys.*"

"Sorry, Veli. We're not used to having a pet. Van Reisser usually takes care of her."

"You're forgiven, but don't make me replace the carpet." Veliswa stepped into the walk-in pantry and triggered the hidden wall. The vampires heard her move around in there, then the sound of bottles clinking. She emerged triumphantly with a musty bottle of champagne. They ate Edam Cheese on Triscuits and chased it down with cool bubbly while they waited for room service.

"Awesome," said Danielle.

"Not enough," said Veliswa. "I'm—"

Something knocked against the glass beyond the blackout curtains.

"Hide in the cellar," Veliswa whispered, referring to the hidden area behind the fold-away wall in the pantry.

The vampires, having stayed with their hostess before, scuttled swiftly into the pantry, located the trigger, and followed the swinging wall into the secret chamber. Ruegger thought he knew who the sudden visitor might be: for the last five years, a young, well-dressed jandrow by the name of

David had acted as an agent for her. Not a pimp, really, although he did find her clients and would organize help for her if needed, but he worked for her, not the other way around.

"David!" Veliswa exclaimed from the other room, and Ruegger and Danielle breathed easier.

"Good morning, Veliswa," they heard David say in his usual lawyerly tone. He would be dressed neatly, and standing very erect, wings folded and arched politely, on the large white balcony. Most immortals had talents for concealing themselves from humans, but jandrows, who are so physically deviant, have even stronger powers that allow them to (as long as they're not too flagrant about it) fly unseen.

"You, too, David. Have anything for me?"

"Certainly. Provided you haven't arranged too many dates tomorrow on your own, I've a client lined up if you're interested."

"Go on."

He gave her a name, a time, and a place. "Is that satisfactory?"

"Yes, David, thank you. Have a good evening." She started to slide the door closed.

"Hey . . . is that your pig?"

"My—? Oh, yes. That's Cerberus. Isn't he lovely?"

"Yeah, he . . . *she* . . . is quite interesting."

"Well, be off," said the ghensiv, and closed the door audibly, letting the blackout curtain fall in its place with a swish.

"Jesus," she sighed, as Ruegger and Danielle emerged. "That was beastly."

"He didn't buy it," commented Ruegger.

Veliswa shook her head. "I don't know. I thought Cerberus was male. Wasn't he?"

Danielle crouched and called to her pig. "Not *our* Cerberus. Not our girl."

"I'm really sorry, guys. But David doesn't know. He *can't.* And besides, he's really not a bad sort. Not really."

"It's okay," Ruegger said, but still he moved toward the living room phone and flipped through the Rolodex that lay near it.

"What're you doin'?" Danielle said.

"Committing David's number and address to memory."

He tensed as more knocking sounded.

Veliswa smiled nervously. "This should be room service." She turned the knob, flung it open and jumped back.

"You okay, ma'am?" asked the young man on the other side. His eyes were wide and adoring. When she affirmed that she was, he and an assistant wheeled in small tables with big domes of silver which covered about a dozen different breakfast entrees. The mortals seemed intrigued by Ruegger and Danielle, these two pale things dressed in black leather and denim, with unkempt black hair and too-dark eyes. They accepted a generous tip and left.

"Aren't mortals fun?" Danielle mused as she lifted a gleaming lid clear from a plate of Denver omelet.

Veliswa crinkled her eyes. "I may be biased, dear. Most of my clients are a repeat business, I'm afraid. Actually, a lot of them know what I am—and they *like* it. All S & M freaks, naturally, not that I mind, but to tell you the truth, I'm tired of playing dominatrix. But no; once they learn about my teeth, they want them harder, deeper, more blood, more blood—that's what they ask for. And once they build up a tolerance for pain, they want it even worse. Tighter, tighter. Grip me tighter. Tighter, for God's sakes! Teeth like sharks' teeth, rows and rows."

Ruegger made a face as he lifted a plate of *huevos rancheros* and brought it to Veliswa's long, glass-topped breakfast table.

"Sorry," she said.

He shrugged and sat down. "Hey, no skin off my—well, actually, I can see the thrill. I mean, knowing you could be, well, severed, at any moment. Plus the pleasure-pain thing. I can see it." He exchanged glances with the ghensiv, their words unspoken and unnecessary.

"That turns you on?" Danielle asked.

He lifted a glass of champagne to his lips. "Hmm, this is great, Velis. But ah, no, it doesn't turn me on, but I can see the thrill. That said, I'm not sure nowadays if I could stay, well, *focused*, with all those teeth pressing against me. But I've tried a few times, and I can't say I didn't—"

"You never told me."

"You would like to know?"

Sharing her attention between the omelet and Belgium pecan waffles, Danielle said, "Maybe not." She chewed a big, syrupy bite of waffle. "Well, maybe."

Veliswa laughed and picked at her plate of brightly-colored fruit. "You two are so cute it's almost insufferable."

After breakfast had been heartily consumed, she informed the vampires that she had to attend to a client, but she would just love to meet Ruegger and Danielle later on if they were free, maybe sometime after midnight.

"How about *Rocky Horror*?" asked Ruegger. Though he was anxious to begin investigating Ludwig's death, he knew he should spend some time with his hostess and friend. "New York always has a good show."

"Groovy," said Danielle. "I haven't seen that in ages."

"Great," said Veliswa. "Meet you at the usual place for the two o'clock, okay? There's a double feature all this week, I think. *Rocky* and its spin-off."

"See you then," said Ruegger.

"Catcha later," called Danielle liltingly, clicking her tongue. Then softly, "I didn't know there was a spin-off."

"*Shock Treatment.* It's technically a sequel, but with different actors playing Brad and Janet."

Veliswa dressed quickly and departed, leaving the vampires with the run of the house.

"I'm still hungry," Danielle said.

"Oh, really?"

"For love."

He grinned. "You're just in love with the idea of those handcuffs, aren't you?"

"The cold steel against my wrists, the warm you against the rest of me. What's not to love?"

Some time later, when he and Danielle were curled up in each other's arms in exhaustion, his mind caught hold of something and wouldn't let go. He eased himself gently from Danielle's embrace, dressed in silence, and left, patting Cerberus on the head as he went. He found his car and headed away from Manhattan.

* * *

Ruegger hoisted himself onto the alley dumpster and leapt for the nearby fire-escape, which he caught neatly and climbed until he reached the fourth floor. He stepped up onto the railing and jumped a few feet over to clutch the cheap metal bars of the adjacent balcony. Then one more over to land on the brick and cement of the balcony there, his mind moving fast to open the balcony door with his telekinetic abilities, wondering at the same time if he was being watched, if the man inside was being protected by unseen guardians. If so, they would recognize Ruegger and know why he was here.

He shoved open the door and slid inside. He felt the hunger in him as he sensed a mortal in the next room, and he moved quietly through to the comfortable living room, the colors dark and somber.

Several antique treasures lined the walls or perched on mantelpieces: a full, standing suit of twelfth century armor, complete with shield and sword; two ancient samurai swords, crossed in battle as if their wielders gripped them fiercely and invisibly; the very sword, stolen, that was reported to have cut off Vlad Tepes's head. Here a blood-rusted mace, there an early, Mid-English Christian Bible— the list went on.

The owner of these treasures, a former antique dealer, lay asleep on the sofa, head thrown back, the TV glowing softly in front of him. The man's features seemed to shift with each flickering frame, the television casting strange hues across his countenance.

Ruegger slid onto the sofa beside him. The man wore a dark green bathrobe, perhaps a little tight around his middle, and course black hair topped his head. Black stubble furred his cheeks and throat. The throat ...

Ruegger eyed it, feeling the pulse in his ears and tongue.

He craned his head down, lips parting as they drew near the arched neck. Just when he could feel the heat clearly on his lips, the man rammed a pistol to his jaw and pulled away, lightning-quick. For a mortal.

They leapt to their feet and faced each other.

The man breathed raggedly and uncocked the pistol. "Knock next time, okay? It's not a difficult concept." He lowered the gun.

"Hell of a pistol, there," Ruegger said.

"Tell me about it. I had to hock a few priceless objects to get it, thank you very much." After laying it down, Harry Lavaca walked over to his refrigerator and rooted around, coming up with two Guiness Extra-Stouts, one of which he tossed to Ruegger. "It's even got silver bullets," Harry added.

Ruegger smiled. "Why?"

"Same reason you have your silver knives. Werewolves are superstitious, sometimes. If they get separated from their makers before they learn the rules, they get to believe their own publicity. Same for all of you, I suppose, but werewolves are the most expensive. Silver, of all things. And I have to worry about them twenty-four hours a day, a *day*—when my good friends like you aren't out there to protect me." He made his way back to the couch, where he and Ruegger sat down together like the old friends they were.

Ruegger looked at the wall furnace, which blazed warmth into the room, and then not too far away, to a dreamy oil painting mounted on the wall that captured the haunting face of Marcela, the young and beautiful Spanish bride of Harry Lavaca. She'd given birth to their two children and died protecting them, in vain, many years ago, before Harry's paunch expanded, before he lived surrounded by this squalor, before his soul had all but quivered to a stop. Marcela had died at the hands of several jandrows in a painful and ritualized proceeding involving the unwilling participation of her children. It had been a slow death, apparently—at least as the dark angels told it. They'd been afraid to go after Harry himself because of his immortal friends, but they had made their displeasure with him excessively clear, as if anything needed be explained.

Of course, it wasn't only jandrows that disliked him; if it hadn't been them to act, it would have eventually been some other group. Harry had few friends, but they were well-chosen and loyal. He never seemed a hundred percent sure *why* they liked him—after all, he did kill wicked immortals as a hobby; the Slayer, they called him, partly as a joke, partly not—but they did. They appreciated his honesty, his persistence, his mind, and his tragedy—this last he seemed particularly aware of. They became even more protective after his wife and children had been killed, going so far as to retaliate in kind against the offending jandrows.

Ruegger was an early friend, one of the original company who had known of Marcela as something beyond the myth that Harry had made her into. Lavaca was a man possessed by a memory, and he had lived very little, these past ten or so years, other than to wreak vengeance and to relive that memory, those images of remembered happiness and peace. Marcela had died over a decade ago, but Ruegger knew that her laugh, her face, were more clear in Harry's mind than the day he'd found her mutilated corpse and those of their children, ages three and four.

"How's Danielle these days?" Harry said.

"Better than you, thank the gods. You look like hell."

"That's the nicest thing anyone's said to me all day."

Ruegger lifted his bottle to clink necks with Harry's. "Here's to being alive."

"In a manner of speaking." Harry sipped the black beer and grimaced. "Fucking Irish horse-piss, don't you just love it." He started to walk into the next room. "Let's finish that chess game, ace. I've been studying the situation for six months—the last time you were here, if you can remember that far back—and although I think you've got me whipped, I have a sneak move I've gotta try."

The vampire followed him into the dining room, where he had a long wooden picnic table occupying most of the available space, with eight sets of chairs sitting opposite each other, lengthwise, and no chairs at either end. Between each set of facing chairs lay a chessboard, each one in various states of battle. Every time a friend visited, one of the games would progress a little farther. Some games lasted indefinitely. Their present match had lasted two years; Lavaca evidently was ready to finish it.

"You look ill," Ruegger commented as they sat.

"I wouldn't be so lucky."

"Are you spending the money we send you?"

"No, I'm putting it in my college fund. Of course I'm spending it. Don't you see my new Blu-ray?"

"Have you converted your videotapes of Marcela to disc?"

"Need you ask?" Harry tapped the board. "Move, compadre."

Ruegger studied the board and slid his bishop forward. "Check."

"Cheap shot." Harry shielded his king.

Ruegger placed a finger on his queen. Paused. "What's your secret move, buddy? I can see your rook lurking over there in the shadows. Don't try to fool me."

"Guess again."

"You're bluffing."

The mortal shrugged. "Move and find out." He leaned back in his seat and crossed his arms. "'Thank the gods'", he repeated softly. "Why don't you believe in God, anyway? I mean, you *are* living proof that superstition isn't all horseshit, right? Religion is superstition, on that we're agreed, but if God is superstition, so are you. You're real, so why not Him?"

"By that logic you would have to agree that if one mythical entity exists, than all of them should." Ruegger could feel a philosophical discussion coming on, but he didn't mind.

"Not necessarily," Lavaca said. "After all, you call yourself damned, thereby implying the presence of a higher being to damn you. And how do you rationally, scientifically explain a creature that lives forever on the condition that it drinks human blood and avoids the sun? How do you explain that without God?"

"How do you explain it with God?"

"Much easier." He tapped the board again. "You keep forgetting."

Ruegger smiled. Moved. "Check again."

"Jesus, you're a pain in the ass. Well, take this."

The vampire cringed.

"So why don't you believe in God?" Harry asked. Obviously, theology was heavy on his mind.

"All I know is that churches don't scare me, crosses nor holy water scare me, and the thought of a god that would throw me into eternal pain for not believing in it actually terrifies me. And not in the way that makes me want to convert."

"All right, so if God didn't create you, what did? I've heard your origin myths, but what's the truth?"

Ruegger shrugged. "How would I know? I was made by the same thing that made you, I suppose."

"What, spite? Alright, enough talk about God. It's your move again, maestro. I believe I left myself open for checkmate."

"You did, didn't you. Why?"

"I'm leaving town, Darkling. I'm going to burn that fucking picture of Marcela and move far, far away."

"That's great, Harry. It really is."

"I'm trying to finish all my chess games before I go, because who knows when I'll be back again, *if* I'll be back again. Don't worry, your kind will forget about me. I was a novelty for a while, but that's over now. Besides, I'm too well known here. There's no way I can hunt you bastards down."

"That must gall you. I'm sorry to see you leave. We'll have to come see you sometime. Where are you moving?"

"The same could be asked of you, you know. You could checkmate me and be done with it, but no."

"Is that your sneak move, Harry? Suicide?"

"Are we still talking about chess?"

"I don't know. Are we?"

Harry sighed. "I'm moving to Swakashani, okay? An island paradise, or so I've heard. But thanks for the concern."

"Since you're asking for it so badly ..." Ruegger moved. "Checkmate."

Harry toppled his king. "Thanks for the game. It's been stimulating." He studied Ruegger. "So what's going on, buddy? Why the hell is Vistrot salivating over you?"

"I was hoping you'd know. You hear more gossip than I do."

"Did you know that just three nights ago Vistrot had one of his own men killed? One of the higher-ups, too."

"Why?"

"Couldn't tell you," Harry said. "No one knows. Some say he was an informant or something, but that's just conjecture. To make matters more interesting, did you know a certain pair of Balaklava are in town? Junger and Jagoda, I think they're called. I hear you've met them. They killed a bunch of people last night in Queens. Close to a hundred, I think. Some sort of feeding frenzy." He grinned. "Maybe I should pay them a visit."

"No. They'll rip you limb from limb, Harry, sun or no sun. Even I don't stand a chance against them. Your interference won't do any good, you understand? Go to Swakashani like you planned. It's beautiful. Meet some native girl and go scuba every day. Drink coconut milk and martinis—I know they're your favorite—but do not go visit Junger and Jagoda. They're more dangerous than just about anything."

"Is that a fact?"

"Just promise me you won't fuck with them."

"Alright, alright."

"Is that a promise?"

"Sure. But I'll keep an ear out, tell you anything if I hear anything, for as long as I'm in town. Come by whenever you want."

"Are you kicking me out?" Ruegger said.

"Yes, but first I've got something you'll be interested in hearing. Someone knows who hired Junger and Jagoda to kill Ludwig."

Ruegger leaned forward. "Who?"

Harry smiled. "I *thought* that would get your attention."

"Well?"

Harry rolled a shoulder. "I didn't say I knew. *Someone* knows. One of my friends sleeps around a lot. Well, she found herself with an immortal assassin last night, a vampire. He claims he was just hired to take out a very important target. He wouldn't say who, only that the target had found out who ordered Ludwig's murder and needed to be silenced."

"Who's hired the assassin?"

"I don't know that, either. But the assassin is going under the name Vincent Greggs, and apparently he's leaving tomorrow night to go after his target."

"That doesn't give us much time. Where's he staying?"

"The Clearglass Inn, just outside of town."

*　　*　　*

David didn't have to think too long. Not at all, really. Loyalty to Veliswa or loyalty to Vistrot? Not too complicated a question. Besides, he'd already chosen his style of life: the underworld, outside both law and mortality. To rise in the ranks of the underworld meant Vistrot's favor; if this were to cause Veliswa some misfortune, so be it. She was just a stepping stone to his greatness.

He wasn't well liked or well known among the mob, so he went to the most powerful figure he knew that was friendly at all toward him: a werewolf named Loirot. Wings stroking the brisk night air, David flew toward Loirot's modest three-storied manse. Landing on the roof would be rude, so he used the backdoor.

The mortal butler opened the door and waved the jandrow in with distaste. He was a stocky and impeccably-dressed old man with a square jaw and steel-gray hair.

"Sir Loirot is not expecting you."

"Oh, but he will be," David said. "Tell him it's urgent."

The butler didn't have to say anything of the sort; like many shades, the Werewolf Loirot could perform a type of telepathy with humans whom he had "formatted" to his taste—and he always kept a phantasmagorical finger in his manservant's head.

"This way," the human said, after a moment. He led David to the plush staircase, with expensive carpeting that was perhaps a touch too old. Some of the gold threads interwoven with the rich crimson ones were coming undone. The butler moved swiftly, almost faster than David could catch up with him; there must be more of Loirot in the man than there was of the man himself. He marched stiffly up to the last story and down a dark corridor to the last door on the left, right near a stained-glass window that let in a twisted version of the moon.

The mahogany door swung open on a great room with more dark paneling and rich carpeting. Heavily shadowed, the chamber seemed thick with age and dust.

The Werewolf Loirot lounged at a table some distance away from the four-postered bed, dressed only in cream silk pants, deep shadows covering his face and torso. A shock of unruly dark brown hair stuck up from his head. Calm, he sipped red wine from a large goblet with one hand and stuck a sweet-smelling cigar to his dark, ruddy lips with the other. His gaze kept drifting to the bed.

David wasn't shocked or saddened by what lay there; it did make him hungry, though, and jandrows traditionally fed off of only hearts.

A dark-haired girl, Asian perhaps, had been tied at the hands and feet by black silk ribbons bound to the four thick posts of the bed. She was very still, dead quite obviously, with several areas of dark moistness at her chest, her thighs, her abdomen, where her flesh had been tugged away; ragged muscle and bone gleamed wetly, and dark blood had splattered the sheets, the curtains flying from the bedposts and the carpet near the bed. *It looks as though she exploded*, David thought. He realized it wasn't just shadow covering Loirot, but drying crimson.

"Yes?" said Loirot.

"Um. I heard about the vampires Ruegger and Danielle being wanted."

"And?"

"You're still working for Jean-Pierre?"

"I don't work *for* anyone, David. But yes, I am a member of the team of which the albino is the head. What's your information?"

"I heard a rumor that they had a pig. Ruegger and Danielle, I mean." He expected a response from the werewolf, but Loirot just stared at him. "Yes, and . . . I saw the pig. I think. It was at the Ghensiv Veliswa's penthouse, at the Cardeux Building. It was just sundown, so it couldn't have been the animal of a customer of hers—and I know she lives with no one, and she dates no one that I know of. She'd certainly refuse to go out with anyone who had an animal like that."

"Not what I heard."

"Yes, well. I've worked for . . . *with* her a long time, almost since the day I crossed over, and I know she has no pig and doesn't know anyone with a pig, and this one had a spiked collar and an earring. Can you imagine?" He looked at Loirot, who was very still indeed, and ruffled an uncomfortable wing.

"Is that all?"

"Um . . . yes. I felt I should tell you."

Loirot shoved the cigar between his lips. "Vistrot will be pleased."

"You'll make sure he knows it was me who—?"

"Get out of my sight."

The manservant led the way.

*   *   *

As the door clanged shut on them, Loirot lifted the goblet to his lips and sipped. A grin worked its way across his handsome face, and his eyes turned once more to the girl on the bed.

"And now," he said, "the Darkling."

Chapter 9

Ruegger and Danielle were back in each other's arms when suddenly she jerked up from sleep. Almost frantic, she put a hand to her forehead, feeling sweat stand out on her brow.

Dark shapes over me, laughing ... thrusting ... cutting ... Malcolm ...

Panting, Danielle rolled over to the edge of the bed and reached for the pocket of her jeans. With shaking fingers, she pulled the last clove out of its box and lit it. *Just a nightmare, Danielle.* But it wasn't. She shook the hair out of her eyes and moved into the bathroom. Staring at herself in the mirror, it was not the Danielle of today she saw, but the scarred and desperate fourteen-year-old girl she'd once been.

She switched on the shower. *Must get clean.*

Ruegger must have heard the shower start up, as she caught the sounds of him climbing out of bed.

"Want the last half of the clove?" she called.

"I'm okay."

Twenty minutes later, after they had dried off and Ruegger had told her what he'd learned from Lavaca, she said, "So I guess we need to pay a visit to the Clearglass Inn."

"Looks like. Someone knows who ordered Ludwig's death, and we need to find out who before they're murdered."

"Fine." She paused, picturing black shapes moving above her. "Listen, I've some . . . business to attend to."

He seemed to understand. Sadly, he nodded. "Then we hunt alone tonight."

She reached a trembling hand to his face. Something in her dissolved, and she felt tears rise behind her eyes. She embraced him tight, then broke away.

"I'll be fine," she said. "This is almost the last one."

He nodded. "Yes," he said. "Almost the last one."

*   *   *

Jean-Pierre didn't smile when he heard the news. He didn't grin, or smirk, or bat an eye. He looked as if he had known it all along, as if he had heard it from other sources as well, which perhaps he had. Finally, after maybe five complete minutes of silence, the werewolf nodded to himself as if he understood the implications, but that the implications just served to confirm some defeatist theory of his own. His luminous green eyes—the only color anywhere on him—dimmed just a little.

He slumped in an uncomfortable steel chair in what was meant to be the dining room of his apartment. The entire eight-storied apartment building, situated as it was in a seedy pocket of the city, had been condemned long ago, but with Jean-Pierre's well-hidden fortune he managed to grease the right wheels to prevent its destruction. He lived in only one apartment on the eighth story and left the rest of the building to the vagrants and wanderers who dwelt here. The most unhinged of the homeless population gravitated to him. On occasion, they acted as his servants, and he could control them psychically. It was like a small, less ambitious version of hell, and Jean-Pierre was the devil.

His rooms were barren if one neglected to count the few scattered chairs, the table, and the countless blades and hooks that rose from the floor, sprouted from the wall or hung by rusty chains from the ceiling. He had an entire hall devoted to the chains, which fell to about waist-level from a barely-visible ceiling and held at their ends all variations of sharp and painful instruments. Jean-Pierre ran through the gauntlet whenever the demons closed in. The pain drove them away.

He studied Loirot. Loirot had always been the flamboyant one. He seemed to want recognition for bringing what he surely thought of as good news, but Jean-Pierre would deny him any satisfaction.

Byron cleared his throat in an attempt to prompt some response out of Jean-Pierre. A large Australian werewolf, he stood nearly six-five and probably over two hundred and fifty pounds, all muscle.

Jean-Pierre turned to Kilian, his lieutenant. "Well?"

"Well what?" Kilian snapped. "You're the fucking leader of this outfit. You're not on vacation anymore."

Jean-Pierre often had the urge to kill the insubordinate toad, but restrained himself when he thought of Vistrot. The Titan had no hand in Jean-Pierre's movements other than assigning the tasks themselves, but he had insisted that he be allowed to appoint one member of the death-squad, and Kilian was that man. It would not go well to kill him. Besides, Kilian was right. Jean-Pierre was back now and it was time to act like it. Still …

The albino lifted a flaming Pall Mall to his lips. "Do you vouch for this information?"

"*I* vouch for it," Loirot said.

Kilian said nothing. He had been the one to insist on calling this meeting, and Jean-Pierre held him responsible for its outcome.

The albino turned to the final member of the death-squad, Cloire, the only female present and the crew's technical wizard. Small, with short died hair and mismatched eyes (one green, one amber), a neurotic energy seemed to fill her.

"The van good to go?"

"Get as it gets," she said.

He stared at the fading end of his cigarette, then glanced up at the four expectant werewolves. His team.

"Then let's go," he said.

He saw them to the door and told them he'd be down in a minute, then turned and re-entered the Hooked Hall. Moving to a corner hidden by blades and spikes, he rapped on a section of wall. The wall bucked, and with a billow of dusty plaster someone shoved the section away.

Coughing, the Ghensiv Veliswa emerged from the hollow space between walls.

"Well, well," Jean-Pierre said. "It seems as though you've had some interesting houseguests."

"So it would seem, lover. What of it?"

"You've been a bad girl. Do you know what I do with bad girls?"

"I've an idea, yes." Veliswa laughed.

He struck her, hard, sending her back into the shadows of the hidden room. "I'll deal with you later. Don't leave, Veli. I'll go much easier on you if you stay. And . . . well, I really would prefer that. You've been good to me, you know. You're almost like a sister, really."

"If I'm a sister, Jean-Pierre, then—"

"Enough! We go back a long way, Veli. Don't make me come after you."

She wiped at her eyes. "We go back even more than you know."

"What do you mean?"

"I'll make sure you find out one day. But go on, *mon ami*. Just remember that if you kill my friends and don't kill me . . . well, sleep lightly, dear."

He spun and walked away, disappearing through the chains.

When he was gone, she slunk over to the fire escape and descended. She didn't hear Jean-Pierre make a phone call then, and she never noticed the motorcycle that stayed behind her all the way.

*   *   *

Danielle waited in the dark. She gripped a blade in her right hand, a long and severely-curving instrument more scythe than knife, and in her left hand she held a lit clove, one she'd found in her jacket pocket.

A blue-collar wasteland stretched around her. It was the type of place Danielle had been raised in before she lived on the streets. Cigarette butts, crumpled beer cans, and other familiar assorted trash littered the dusty one-story house, was strewn across the ugly sofa in the living room (where Danielle now stood), was carelessly flicked over the cheap coffee table/leg rest and hunched forgotten atop the TV that, though not large, dominated the room.

Jason Locke lived here. Long ago, Locke had taken part in Danielle's gang rape and mutilation. Of course, Locke wasn't what he called himself these days; he'd changed his name and moved to a different pocket of town, but he could never escape her. Try as he might, he would be the sixth to die. She'd saved her foster-brother Malcolm Verger for last. He had been the leader of the gang that had raped her repeatedly, then taken a razor blade to her adolescent face and body and left her for dead.

What happens when I finally kill Malcolm? she wondered. *After he's dead, will I still carry this hate—or will the nightmares go away?*

Light pierced the dusty drapes and bathed the living room with brutally-honest light, transforming what was almost nostalgic for Danielle into an ugly nightmare pinned in by four walls. The headlights cut off. The car engine sputtered and died.

The vampiress crossed over to Locke's ash-covered CD player and inserted Mussorgsky's "Night on Bald Mountain", which she'd brought with her, and with the first reverberations of the chords she felt a smile spread across her face.

*   *   *

With a jingle of keys, the door swung open and Locke crossed its threshold for the last time. Not registering the music until it was too late and the door was irrevocably shut, he stiffened in fear.

He'd heard the tale from witnesses—two girlfriends, one wife—of Danielle's previous revenge-based bloodlettings. She never killed the witnesses, but she always played a piece of classical music which was more or less alien to her victims' ears but was presumably the same piece every time. That's what the cops had suggested, and one witness (a rapist's girlfriend) had been able to identify the song as the one that always played on the Fourth of July.

There were numerous articles written about Danielle in the papers, most notably the tabloids, who called her the Gutter Angel. Most people thought of her as a serial killer, but at least one guilty rapist had confessed the story of Danielle's rape and attempted murder to his wife after several of his friends had died, and the wife later told the police and some reporters the story. So the public knew, and many considered Danielle a sort of folk hero.

Thus Jason knew what was in store.

His eyes flicked from one shadow to another, but she was nowhere to be found. He pulled out a cigarette as the music built up around him.

"O-one last smoke?" he said.

Silence answered.

Then, from a shadow he must have overlooked, stepped the girl, as young and beautiful as he'd heard she was, many years ago. Her eyes sparkled against her too-ivory skin and her winedark lips were hooked in a toothless smile. *How can she be so young? And her skin ... uncut ...*

"The song's over ten minutes long," she said. "And yes, you will live that long, not that you'll enjoy it."

He stared, transfixed. "What they said, they were right. The ones you spared, I mean. You're not . . . human, are you?"

When she smiled, her fangs caught the light.

He pressed himself tight against the door. "My God, it's true! You're—"

She descended, and his screams rose from his rapidly-diminishing body until the thunder of Mussorgsky's melody ceased in time to his heart.

*   *   *

Guards escorted Kilian through the several checkpoints that led to Vistrot's den, located in the subbasement of a subbasement of a skyscraper downtown. Rumor was he owned half the building. Either way, he'd officed in this granite cellar for the better part of three decades. People called it The Titanic. Kilian personally believed that Vistrot owned many such basements throughout the city and off the island and switched headquarters every night. This would explain the deeply impersonal nature of the large, echoing hall that he was being led through, which terminated in a door flanked by two more immortal guards.

One held the door for him.

Kilian stepped into a large and sparsely decorated chamber. Plastic covered the floor in as tasteful a way as possible—in case any blood was shed in the room, Kilian was all too aware.

He stopped before the great ebony desk, polished and gleaming, cluttered by papers and scented by spices that rose from the old-fashioned box of Cuban cigars, and waited for the Titan to look up. It never failed to amaze him how *vast* Vistrot was, an immense man both of bone and flesh—absurdly obese yet impossibly strong. When he stood he reached almost seven feet, which made his mostly bald head harder to see than now. The big man's girth strained against a rumpled but immaculately tailored dark blue suit. His chair supported his four hundred pounds admirably as he leaned back, phone to his pale, scaly head.

"Have it fixed by midnight tomorrow," he was saying into it. "You know the consequences if you fail." He had a cold, guttural voice. Even as his finger pressed the button to disconnect the call, his massive head was tilting up to stare at Kilian. "Sit down."

Kilian obeyed, adjusting himself with what he took to be the appropriate body language: relaxed, but not too.

"Now what is this bullshit about having to see me in person?" Vistrot demanded. "I haven't seen you in the flesh in years, and could do without it now."

"Yes," Kilian said, careful to keep his voice low, "but I needed to see you in person myself, to confirm that you're still alive and that I wasn't receiving my instructions through an impersonator." He leaned over, stretched his arm ever so slightly, and plucked a cigar from its varnished case. He put it to his nose, breathed in its odor with his eyes closed, then smiled. "Nice."

"Jesus," swore the Titan. "I should have you killed. I value your ear in the albino's squad, but ears are cheap."

Kilian swallowed. "There's something I wanted to talk to you about."

Vistrot arched his great white eyebrows, his death-blue eyes almost lethal by themselves. He waited.

"I think Jean-Pierre needs to go," Kilian said. "He's become an impediment to his own team."

Vistrot steepled his gold-ringed fingers to his most prominent chin. "He's having difficulty about Danielle," the Titan said. Was there *sadness* in his voice?

"Yes. I believe he heard from several sources about her arrival in town but only acted when one of our own brought the news to his attention."

Vistrot inhaled deeply. "I knew this day might come. I'd hoped by giving him this assignment that he would prove himself to be above such concerns."

"I don't mean to say that that was a mistake," Kilian said carefully, "but the arrangement doesn't seem to be working."

Vistrot tilted his face upward. Oddly, it looked as though he were praying. "What do you suggest?"

"Either Jean-Pierre's squad needs to be disbanded . . . or a new leader needs to be elected."

The Titan gave a closemouthed smile. "Ah."

"I'm only saying."

"You want to replace Jean-Pierre."

"I don't recall saying anything of the kind."

"Good. You won't do. You won't do at all. So go. Now, while the plastic at your feet is still clean."

"You won't do anything about Jean-Pierre?"

"His test has just begun, and you're not part of my plan," Vistrot said pointedly, and Kilian realized there was more at stake here than himself.

"What do you mean?"

The Titan shook his head. "*I* will deal with Jean-Pierre, if it comes to that. As for yourself, we'll talk later. Go."

Kilian rose, hearing the plastic crackle, and in silence crossed to the door, which he realized was knobless and could not be opened from the inside. Surely Vistrot's minions kept a tight telekinetic hold on it, too; unless the Titan so desired, the portal would not open. For a moment Kilian feared he had gone too far, that the door would stay shut, that he would be butchered here like so many others. Then, mercifully, the door swung to and Kilian, taking a deep breath, stepped across the threshold, leaving the Titan to his solitude.

Just as he returned to street-level, his phone rang.

"Yes?"

"It's Jean-Pierre. It's time."

*   *   *

Byron and Cloire rutted in the back of the van. Curtains covered the tiny windows at the rear, but several of the small slide-away panels along the van's flanks opened to reveal what could be seen through the tinted, one-way glass windows that were built in to allow easy surveillance.

The werewolves used what talents they hadn't devoted to copulation to insure that the van didn't rock too much, and to keep an eye out. The Cardeux Building stood just across the way, the obvious place to acquire Ruegger and Danielle. Kilian had already been inside and verified no one was home.

Byron tweaked Cloire's nipples. She growled, pressing her hips against him as hard as she could, bestial face locked, every fiber of muscle in her straining to sustain that intimacy. Eyes mashed shut, she let loose one long, low moan as she came, then drew closer to him and kissed his hairy chest. He continued to thrust, slicing into her now-hairless mound again and again and again, until he too let loose with a gasp, but still thrust reflexively for several moments. Sated, they collapsed.

"That was great," murmured Cloire, reaching for a cigarette.

Byron, still panting, grunted assent.

Cloire lit the Camel, took a hit, then passed it to him, who, like her, was slipping slowly back from beast to human, his fur disintegrating, his ribs and pecs sliding into place once more, his snout leveling off, his teeth losing their bite.

"Why don't you go to sleep?" Byron said. "I'll keep an eye out, wake you if I need to."

"You're cute, you know. I hope you're not falling in love or anything."

"Of course not."

"Good." She blew a perfect ring of smoke. "A big fat zero," she said. "Wreathed in smoke. I think that's symbolic."

"How?"

"Jean-Pierre's taking this whole thing way too personally. It's not professional."

He accepted the cigarette from her. "He needs this. Remember how we all cavorted around Danielle when she was one of us and the albino was staying with Lord Kharker? Have you ever seen him so happy?"

"*Cavorting's* a little strong."

"He wants that back."

"It can never be. Doesn't he understand that?"

"No," the Australian said. "But by the end of the night I think he will."

"Then what?"

He passed her back the cigarette and lit one for himself. "Then I suppose they die."

"You don't seem too happy about it."

He took a long time to answer. "I'm not like you, Cloire. I take no pleasure in killing. And Danielle . . . I taught her how to play *chess*, for fuck's sake. Jean-Pierre and

Lord Kharker would be off stomping around the jungle, and Danielle would come up to me and say she had to prepare for a chess match against Kharker the next night, and would I please refresh her on the steps and the pieces."

"You wanted her."

"Maybe," he admitted. "Does that upset you?"

"No. I actually like the thought of you fucking other women. Just don't ever try it, if you value your cock." Her mind drifted back to their days in the Congo, lounging around Lord Kharker's jungle palace; the bugs, the trees, the blazing sun, the sweaty twilight, the bloody nights.

"I remember Loirot always trying to court her while Jean-Pierre was away," she said. "I often thought of informing on him."

"Why didn't you?"

"Loirot and Kilian hate each other, you know that. Better to have Loirot around to combat that fucking asshole, right?"

One of their phones rang.

"Yeah?" Byron said into the receiver. "Sure. We're on our way."

"Well?" Cloire said.

"Jean-Pierre. He says he had Loirot tail Veliswa, and she led him to Ruegger. They're at a *Rocky Horror Picture Show* screening. Jean-Pierre's sending someone over to replace us."

"Then let's snap to it, lover."

*   *   *

"Where is she?" Veliswa asked, watching the colorful crowd pouring into the theater.

"We hunted separately tonight," Ruegger said.

Veliswa let out a breath. "Another one bites the dust, eh?"

"Only one more left. With him, the tradition ends."

"It's a dark thing, what she does."

"I know," he said.

"I mean, we all must kill to live, and you two always pick worthy targets. Rapists and killers, all of them. The world is a better place without them. But usually you do it without emotion. When she goes after those bastards, she uses a *lot* of emotion."

"I know. I don't like it either. Of course, they have it coming. Hell, I'd help if she asked. But . . . well, it takes a lot out of her. I guess that's the part I don't like. I'll be glad when it's over."

The ghensiv grew silent for a moment, then: "Does she know about us, about how we were, after Amelia—?"

"No."

"It would be okay to tell her, you know. She wouldn't be hurt, I don't think . . . although we should have told her long ago. But she *might* be hurt if she finds out years from now. Then it would be as if we'd kept something from her."

"I have."

"Does she know anything about you yet, Ruegger? About Amelia, the wars, about Kharker?"

"Bits and pieces. Here and there."

"Dear-heart, I know what you think: that she'll stop loving you if she knows, but she's stronger than that. I'm sure she suspects already, knows more than you think she does. How could she not, after having spent so much time around Kharker and Jean-Pierre? You think Kharker never talked about you? That's one thing that man never was— closemouthed. And to this day do you think he'd choose the albino over you? Of course not. So sure he told Danielle— some of it, anyway."

"You talk like you've met him. The albino."

"Well, I haven't."

He raised his eyebrows.

"I hear things," she said. "But you changed the subject, didn't you? Hey, wait. Hear that? Show's starting."

"I think I should wait here for her."

"Come on," she coaxed. "Maybe she didn't locate him right away—maybe she still hasn't. When she's ready, she'll find us; she knows where we are. Okay?"

Ruegger paused, then acquiesced.

The odd assortment of people who gathered for *The Rocky Horror Picture Show* never failed to intrigue Ruegger. Straights, gays, lesbians, transvestites, transsexuals—they all thronged to watch the horror musical and even interact with it in their own way, performing the movie scene by scene up near the silver screen. As the show began, he realized he was enjoying himself, but soon thoughts of Danielle disturbed him. *I should be there for her.*

When *Rocky* ended, many of the congregation departed, but most stayed for the second feature. Towards the end, Ruegger frowned, turned to Veli and said, "I think she's here."

"If she's here, she'll come in."

He frowned. "No," he said. "Not this time. I … feel something else, too."

*   *   *

After avenging herself, Danielle felt oddly refreshed. Burnt clean, even. She paused in the glowing lights outside the theater to stare up at what sky refused to be drowned out by the metropolis—not much, as it turned out. A picture of Jason Locke swam before her, but she was able to face it now without flinching. *You can never terrorize me anymore.*

"You *are* beautiful," said a voice from the shadows.

She spun. "Who . . . ?"

Jean-Pierre emerged from the blackness, green eye shining. "What I feel, just looking at you, Danielle—words fail me."

"Then there is a God." Ever since Ruegger had talked her into returning to New York, she'd dreaded this moment. She held her ground, but it was an effort.

"Not scared of the big bad wolf?" he said.

"Is this business or social?"

He stepped closer. "We both know that if this were business you'd be dead."

"What do you want?"

Another step closer. "You. Only you."

"Too bad."

Within touching distance now, the albino extended an arm towards her face, the colorless hairs of his fingers just brushing her cheek.

"Oh, really?" he said. "Oh, *really*. . .?"

Chapter 10

Ruegger found the aisle and flew up it too fast for a mortal to clearly see. It was a trick not feasible outside the darkened room, so at normal speed he pushed out the theater door—and froze.

"Dear gods."

A small crowd encircled a bloody mass of human wreckage lying gutted and decapitated on the asphalt. It was a man, or had been. His blood pooled around him to encompass the quizzically-expressioned head nearby. He looked as if he were floating on a red sea. The crowd muttered. Some talked on cell phones, summoning the police.

Ruegger staggered up the sidewalk, dismayed, not just for the dead man, but what it meant about Danielle. *Jean-Pierre has her,* he realized. *This is his way of thumbing his nose at me.*

Several shapes emerged from an alley. Before he knew it, they had surrounded him.

"Ruegger," said a voice, and the vampire wheeled to see a dour man with dark hair.

"Kilian. *You* did that." Ruegger gestured toward the dead man.

"Actually, I did this," Kilian said, and with one hand lifted the bloody remains of Danielle's little black pig, Cerberus.

"Bastard!"

"*I* killed the man over there," said another shape. Loirot.

Ruegger bared his fangs. "And now you'll kill me, is that it?"

"That's the idea," another shape, huge and with an Australian accent.

Ruegger braced himself. "Come, then."

The werewolves crouched, ready to tear him apart. Suddenly, a gun cracked, loud and close, and one of them reeled back. Then another. Before he knew what was happening, Ruegger was jerked by the arm and found himself running up the sidewalk side by side with Veliswa.

"*Mon ami!*" Veliswa said. "What's happening?"

"David betrayed us," he panted. "Luckily you go armed."

"I'm a New York girl. The bullets are coated in poison."

"They've been to your apartment," he said. "They know you've been helping us."

She hissed out a breath. "Then my time in the city is done. But where's Danielle?"

"With Jean-Pierre," Ruegger said. "If only I knew where he lived ..."

Veliswa fell silent, then: "Actually, I have an idea."

* * *

Danielle fingered the rusted, blood-stained end of a hooked chain that dangled like so many others from the ceiling of Jean-Pierre's apartment. *This is his living room.* She'd struggled against him, but he was just too strong, and now she was in his lair. *Great.* She stared up at all the long, black chains that swayed, just slightly, to and fro, the gentle motion making her think of some nightmare anemone that shifted to a rhythm all its own. Jean-Pierre watched her with all the patience of a cat.

"I just love what you've done to the place," she said.

He seemed neither amused nor offended.

"You're beautiful," he said.

"You've said that already."

"Don't be flip."

Angrily, she spun away from him. "Goddamnit, Jean-Pierre, this is too much. You've actually stooped to kidnapping now? At least last time I was willing."

"You were . . . in love with me."

She crossed to the one open window, the source of the breeze stirring the chains.

"I was afraid," she said, the wounds opening again. She didn't want to play games with him. "You showed me Ruegger's body, or one that looked like it. You said you'd protect me. Took me away. All lies, Jean-Pierre. Everything you told me, lies. You wanted me for yourself."

"You *loved* me," he repeated.

She paused. "Maybe I came to be fond of you. I envied your nothingness." When he winced, she added, "I'm sorry. I was crushed when I thought Ruegger was dead."

She heard him fumbling with one of his Pall Malls, clicking on his silver cigarette lighter—silver to spite the gods, of course—and breathed the acrid stench deep into his lungs.

"I *need* you."

Frustration crept back into her voice. "I can't, Jean-Pierre. I love Ruegger—not for any other reason than he's who he is. We're a part of each other, as inseparable as flesh and bone."

"Flesh and bone can part, Danielle. Flesh and bone can part."

She half wanted to hug him and tell him it would be all right and half wanted to gouge out his fucking eyes. She settled for turning back to gaze out the window.

She remembered the faces of the vagrants that roamed the halls as Jean-Pierre had led her to his rooms; adulation and loyalty had swept their faces at the sight of their overlord. She thought to herself that he was a god here. He was the pied piper of the insane, his void drawing them in like flies to a carcass.

"You belong here," she said. "You and your hooks and chains. I don't."

She turned to catch him with his eyes averted; she saw what looked like a tear in his eye, but it must not have been because he glanced up in the coldest manner he could, and that was very cold indeed.

"Is that it?" he said. "Your final word? Because not even I can save you both, and if you leave right now I won't want to."

"Fuck off."

"Just so you understand the terms. What I'm offering you."

"Either death or life with you?"

He let the cigarette spark between his lips a moment, threw his gaze to a ceiling barely visible through the chains.

"That seems to be the situation," he said.

They watched each other, each waiting for the other to speak or move. The nightmare sea festered hypnotically.

Finally, Danielle broke the spell. Her eyes still locked on his, she drifted through the rusted metal towards the door, where she could already hear mortals shuffling by the scores: the albino summoning his flock. Too cowardly to kill her himself, he would use them. She could just imagine the tormented faces of those souls who hovered on the other side, puppets to his abilities, ready to tear her apart.

"Good-bye, Jean-Pierre," she said, and opened the door.

There they waited, pinched and filthy, with lips of tanned hide and unblinking vacant eyes, all trained on her. They stood unnaturally still, a legion awaiting the fatal order. Eight stories worth of the mentally disturbed, now all zombies to the albino's will.

"Yes," he whispered. "*Au revoir.*"

She entered the hall, where she could feel the hot ragged breaths of the figures pressing in on her from every side. She shoved her way through them toward a stairwell that she couldn't even see they were so many. It seemed very far away.

She ran into a man who would not be moved, a towering, unshaven creature with lice crawling through his hair and human feces smeared across his skeletal chest. Flies buzzed about his head.

"Out of my way, asshole."

He leered down at her, and she wondered whether this man was strong enough to retain his own presence of mind despite Jean-Pierre's influence. Or maybe the albino was choosing to represent himself through him.

Either way, Danielle could tear off his head and be feeding on his heart before he could even register what she was doing, but his murder would incite a riot. The other mortals couldn't be connected to Jean-Pierre by more than a tenuous link at best. There were just too many of them for even him to control in more than a nebulous fashion.

The mortal with the crown of flies spoke: "*Kiernevar.*"

Was that his name? "Fuck you, Kiernevar."

She pressed her hands into the crusty feces that covered his chest and *shoved*, sending the mortal and all his merry lice into the mass ahead, creating a corridor for Danielle to pass through, which she did, step by careful step. The minions' eyes jittered back and forth. Spittle dribbled from cracked lips.

The hand of one woman clutched at Danielle's elbow. She swiped it away. Unease seemed to be spreading.

Shit. If these mortals started attacking her, she would have to defend herself. If that happened, she would likely kill some of them. Most were too far gone and probably wouldn't notice the difference, but she would. She did not kill innocents. Ever. Then there was the disturbing possibility that their sheer numbers were actually capable of overpowering her.

"You're a coward, Jean-Pierre!"

The mortals started to grab at her, tear at her clothes, her hair, long nails scrabbling toward her eyes. The stairwell was so close she could taste its vomit-tinged smell at the tip of her tongue. She lunged for it. The action was too much. The puppets surged toward her.

Hurry. They ripped at her, but she shrugged them off. Plucking the stairwell door from its rotted hinges, she discovered that the minions waited here too. They surrounded her, raking and biting. With a growl, she beat them back, but still they came.

She grasped what would be her last hope: the stairwell itself. It wasn't circular, and therefore she couldn't simply drop the eight floors to safety; she would have to ricochet off the balustrades themselves—painful but . . .

She rose from beneath the swarm and threw herself over the edge. Her body crashed into each and every rusting balustrade. She shoved herself on, downwards, feeling at the same time hands from mortals that lined the stairs ripping at her, sometimes digging into her with broken glass or razors.

Her head crashed into something hard, and her mind flickered, though her body still fell . . . and fell . . .

She landed on them. Their faces upturned, their arms outstretched, waiting for her. When they tore away her jacket, she woke up. She defended herself as best she could, but there were too many.

"Jean-Pierre!" she said, when she could get a breath. "Call them off!"

Their hands and fingers and limbs and teeth and bodies slashed her, pulled her and tore at her. She was going to die. She knew it. There was no way—

Crunch.

The minions fell back. The floor disappeared below her as something hoisted her into what seemed like a different realm. The hallway and the faces of the minions slipped by her as everything faded away . . .

*   *   *

Danielle cradled in his arms, Ruegger plowed through the humans to either side of him, here and there a mortal that he'd missed on his way in standing defiantly in his path only to be flung aside. Unlike Danielle, he felt no moral compunction to restrain himself. Tragic though it was, these humans were merely the will of the albino made flesh.

Ruegger burst from Jean-Pierre's little hell into the warmth of the moonlight and carried Danielle to Veliswa's waiting limousine.

A rear door flung open. "Get in, damnit!" Veliswa said. "Get in!"

Ruegger lowered his precious burden onto the leather seat and slid in himself. With one last look up to Jean-Pierre's wrought-iron balcony—actually seeing the Frenchman staring down at him from the balustrade, cigarette held close to his lips, its smoke wrapping his pale head—Ruegger slammed the door and said, "Let's get the hell out of here."

As the limo shot off, he turned his attention to the semi-conscious Danielle and stroked her bloody black hair.

She opened her eyes a fraction and raised a hand to trace his jaw. "Rueg," she whispered. Her eyes closed and her hand fell away.

"Is she all right?" Veliswa said.

"She needs blood."

"She'll be all right, *mon ami*."

"She'd better be." He bent to kiss Danielle's cold lips.

* * *

Expelling smoke from his mouth, Jean-Pierre watched the limousine pull away. When it was gone, he turned to the mortal that stood quiet and erect at the other end of the Hooked Room. Chains rattled, flies buzzed, but the mortal didn't seem to care. Tall, maybe seven or eight inches the albino's senior, with lice-ridden hair and his own excrement smeared across his bare, hairy chest, a stupid, maniacal grin had plastered itself across his sharply-angled face, but his solemn eyes belied some sort of intelligence.

"You withstood me," Jean-Pierre said. "I've never had a mortal withstand my will before."

The man just grinned, his yellowed teeth bared profanely.

"I can't let that go unpunished," the albino said. "But your death would be too much a waste, I think. You're more insane than Laslo, I'd wager. A competitor, at least."

The man watched a fly move from its orbit around his head to his chest.

"What's your name?"

"Kiernevar." The man's eyes never left the fly.

"Ke*i*nev*a*r," the albino pronounced. "Russian?"

"Kiernevar," the man repeated.

Jean-Pierre brought the cigarette to his lips and held it there a moment. He hated stupidity; it was the trait that annoyed him above all others. This one wasn't stupid, though, just deranged. Insanity was a trait the albino tended to romanticize. The shit made it hard.

"I won't kill you, yet," he said. "But I can't let you persist in your present state, knowing you're strong enough to resist my pull." He paused. "Did you know that immortal blood can cure many diseases, even erase scars sometimes? Maybe once you have my blood you'll regain your wits. Your power could be harnessed."

Kiernevar started laughing. And continued laughing. The albino frowned.

"Kiernevar!" he snapped, and the man smiled. "Kiernevar—I'm going to make you one of *us*. I'm going to let you cross over."

"Cross over," the human said. "Become an albino." He scraped at his chest, then flung the excrement at Jean-Pierre. "I don't *want* to be a werewolf!"

Some sanity, then. Jean-Pierre wiped at himself. "Now that's something *I* couldn't give a shit about."

He stepped closer. The man screamed.

$$* \quad * \quad *$$

The limousine thumped along the slickened streets, a getaway car without a destination. Danielle had roused at a few sips of Ruegger's blood and nestled tightly in his black leather jacket, drinking some coffee Veliswa had brewed for her in the car's maker. Danielle felt sick. The horrible thing was that, although she detested him utterly, she couldn't bring herself to hate Jean-Pierre. He was too miserable for that.

"I guess your investigation in New York is over," Veliswa said. "Thanks to David. And it *had* to be him."

"We found out one thing," Ruegger said. "We're going to the Clearglass Inn to follow up on it."

"I think we should split up."

"*No*," said Danielle reflexively, reaching for Ruegger's hand.

Veliswa smiled. "No, I meant that *I* would split away from you two. If I stayed with you, I'd only be dragging you down, and I know someone I think can help us—if only I can get to her."

"But Veli," said Ruegger, "and I mean no offense by this, but you haven't been on the run in years. It's just not something you're used to. You'd be too vulnerable."

"That can't be helped. And I think I could do us more good if I branched off."

"Who's this friend?" Danielle said.

"Well, here's my plan. I know it may sound far-fetched, but I can't think of anything better. The order to kill you came from Vistrot, this much we know, but Vistrot doesn't seem to have any particular motive to want you dead. So he's acting on behalf of someone else. What we need to do is *infiltrate* his organization, find out who gave Vistrot the order—find out who wants you dead. Then maybe we can do something about it. Until then, we're just going to be dodging Jean-Pierre and whoever else they send to kill you."

"You too," Ruegger said. "Don't forget that. You harbored us, knowing Vistrot had a hit out on us. He's not going to forgive that."

"I know."

"So who's this friend?" Danielle repeated.

The ghensiv turned to her. "Her name is Sophia, and she may just be our salvation."

Sophia, Danielle thought. The name sounded familiar . . .

"Shit!" she said. "You don't mean *the Ice Queen*?"

"She could just be our salvation."

*　　*　　*

At that moment, it was late in the evening in Los Angeles, California, where Sophia was staring up at the smog-shrouded stars from the veranda of a Spanish-style mansion, nestled safely in Beverly Hills and wrapped lovingly by endless vines.

Long and sleek, Sophia sipped red wine with a faint smile, and she would be the first to tell you she wasn't anybody's salvation. With long dark hair, she boasted clean white skin and an expression that seemed eternally mocking. She wore a tight black leather bikini, which clashed with her moonly pallor; from a distance she looked like some severed fragment of an old black-and-white movie, cast here in the world of color for the amusement of the gods.

Except for her eyes. They were a livid violet.

Unlike most shades, she'd been born immortal, and she wore it arrogantly. Nearly horizontal now in her reclining deck chair, she set her wine glass down on the Spanish tile, picked up a double-edged razor blade that lay nearby and distracted herself by carving bleeding hearts across the flesh of her tight stomach.

Delighting in the slow, glistening crawl of her blood, the ghensiv watched it run like warm molasses down her belly. It hurt, and her face grew very still as it washed over her; she dug deeper, and, with a quavering gasp, deeper still. She moaned as her fingers dipped in her essence, this sticky crimson that flowed through her veins. A scream threatened, as the pain built to a crescendo, but Sophia suppressed it with a ragged exhalation that ended in a smile.

She raised her hands from the blood and ran them south, the red spreading down from her navel to what lay under the black leather thong. She let go the razor (she wasn't *that* much of a masochist), and let her fingers explore. Running them over the dark mound and then inserting them in the crevice, the hole that had stole many a man's offspring and pride, the hole that was lined in the fluid that gave her immortality, the hole that even now grew tighter, the countless gleaming teeth in its folds squirming eagerly. The ghensiv writhed, wasting little time in bringing herself to climax.

She had things to do.

The Ice Queen released a long low sigh. Weary of pain and sex and stars, she went inside, the blood dried on her belly and the cuts healed. She'd a meeting that needed some preparation, so she strolled in to her long walk-in closet and examined her clothes. Selecting something properly garish, she dressed.

"You like?" she asked her cat, who sat watching her with detached interest. Anubis was a black, wretched-looking thing with three legs and one eye, but for all his handicaps he got around just fine. Sophia liked to think that in one of his nine lives he was the familiar of some witch or other.

Anubis yawned and slunk away.

"Smart cat." Sophia moved to the kitchen, picked a banana and a beer, and departed for her execution.

She drove her thirty-year-old yellow convertible Corvette Stingray—the wind a chorus of cat-calls about her, tossing her hair and teasing her eyes. She smoked a Black Death cigarette on a cigarette holder, peering out at the Los Angeles nighttime landscape through wraparound Ray Bans. She smiled as the car roared beneath her, and the gas petal grew steadily closer to the floor.

She finished her banana and beer and tossed them both overboard. She was late for her rendezvous, but that wasn't unnatural. Today her would-be lover wanted to meet her somewhere reclusive, which was as it should be for this part of the operation. The scam was almost concluded. The ending was her favorite part.

By the time she'd finished her second cigarette, she was in the hills. The moon looked gray and unhealthy above.

She took the car down a gear as she rounded a corner and spotted the big stone mailbox of her lover. Shooting down the tree-flanked driveway, she hit the horn as she screeched to a halt. She was out of the car in a slash, sweeping up the wide staircase in time to see Robert's gloomy expression as he exited his house. His face brightened artificially when he saw her.

"Well, dear, how nice to see you," he said.

She gave him a big hug, staying in character. Robert's manservant stood only a few feet behind his master, eyeing her severely.

"Well, *baby*, it's only *been* a few days," she sighed into Robert's ear. "You look as if it's been forever!"

He separated himself from her, coldly, and she could see the depth of his hurt. She had won his affection, then betrayed him. But he would still be uncertain.

"Come, dear," he said. "Follow me inside."

She did, wearing a slight pout that was to be read as *Oh, poo.* She ripped off her oversized hat, hearing the door close—and lock—behind her. She supposed this was the point at which she should start acting nervous. It took a lot of concentration on her part to play a mortal, and a scared one at that, but she was an accomplished actress of sorts, though her performances were mainly viewed in private.

"Kind of cold in here," she murmured, and affected a small shiver.

Robert led her past the rough wood walls and mounted heads of animals, from deer to alligator, past grand windows, drapes pulled, and up a polished wooden staircase, then up another. In all honesty, she did feel a draft.

"Robert," she said, "why don't you say something? You're so silent! Heavens, is something wrong?"

He scowled back at her and continued their little journey until he came to a closed door, which he opened almost ceremoniously and beckoned her to enter: his office, she knew, where he attended to his shady business when required. He was quite evil for a mortal, and though this was a trait that Sophia was inclined to admire at times, she had taken special delight in winning this bastard's affections and then crushing him.

He liked to dominate people, women especially, but the ghensiv had been able to read him, as she always could, and knew that beneath that power-hungry exterior lay a core that was afraid: a pinprick of self-doubt that craved to be told what to do, and how to do it. And though the exterior could never slip (he was far too controlled for that), she had found the chink in his armor and had penetrated deep. She'd bent him and pulped him, playing dominatrix in the bedroom, knocking him to his knees in release so that he could shed his responsibilities for the few precious moments they were alone—and in public she played every bit as submissive as he could have wanted. And then, after she'd discovered his weaknesses and exploited them, she robbed him of every penny he had available and sent rumors through his employees (rumors that were sure to come back to him) that she had been having an affair on the side, wrecking him emotionally, too.

There was no way he could touch her, though. He didn't know her real name or residence (she'd used an anonymous apartment during most of the operation), or race of being. She'd pulled this scam many times before, and it nearly always ended the same way. The boyfriend, or girlfriend as the case may be, eventually rounded the ghensiv up and demanded retribution. This was when she observed their grief personally, and this was often the time when they subjected her to tortures in an attempt to relocate their lost capital. She liked pain, so this was usually the most eagerly anticipated part of the operation, and she hoped it would begin soon.

Robert perched behind his desk, brooding and staring at her until he had to avert his eyes.

"You took something from me," he said.

"What are you talking about?" She tried not to sound too innocent because, she realized, he was confused and not a hundred percent certain that she was in fact guilty.

"I know what you did, you little bitch. You used me. The whole time, you were using me . . . and then what you took . . ." He closed his eyes, and the Ice Queen was amused to see tears spilling down his cheeks. A part of her almost felt guilty for causing him pain (she'd enjoyed her moments with him), but this was a small part and easily silenced.

Robert shook his head. "You filthy little whore. You nearly ruined me, you know. If not for my off-shore accounts . . ."

"So fucking what?" she said, surprised at the emotion rising in her. She took a step closer, all pretense at vulnerability dissolved. "I do this sort of thing for fun, Robert. To pass the time. I destroy people like you for sport. Usually that's all it is. But I'll tell you something, Bob. This time there was a small personal motive as well. You see, I'd made friends with this girl, a club-hopping little witch hooked on crack and god knows what else. You pimped her, or one of your franchises did. You strung her out and used her until she died. She weighed sixty-five pounds when she died, Robert. *Sixty-five pounds.*" Sophia's voice lowered. "She had a nice smile."

Robert pushed his chair back from his desk, more in surprise than fear, although some small tick had tugged at his face when he saw her step forward, as if he'd seen something ghastly. A glimpse of inhumanity, perhaps, but then why should this shock *him* of all people, he who profited from the weaknesses of others?

"So why didn't *you* save her?" he said. "Why single me out? I fucking loved you, you bitch. Why did you ruin that?"

Why hadn't Sophia saved the girl? Was it because she had not known, not completely, that the girl was as bad as she'd really been—or that the girl had refused Sophia's help? Maybe. Maybe that was a part of it. But mainly it was because Sophia felt that to be strong one must reject all emotion. A heart was a fragile thing. But keep it small and hard enough, and maybe it just might be safe. That's why she hadn't saved Gilly: because the Ice Queen hadn't allowed herself to know her well enough to be aware of the girl's destructive streak.

"I feel dizzy," she said.

Robert sat back down with a grunt. "I can't do this. You won't beg forgiveness, will you, and give me back the money? You wouldn't be so kind."

"No."

He nodded sadly. "I can't hurt you, you know. But I've brought someone who could." He motioned to the shadows and a figure stepped forward, tall and hard. "I'll give you one more chance. If you don't speak now, you'll die."

"You'll beg before it comes, though," the figure said, and Sophia started. She studied the man silently, and he returned the stare. His face registered subtle shock.

"Christ," Sophia said. She hadn't counted on this; often the wronged lover hired someone to do the torturing and killing, but Robert in his ignorance had hired another immortal, who apparently used this job as a guise for gathering food.

"What's going on?" Robert demanded, seeing the expressions on their faces. "Do you two know each other?"

The strange vampire remained still; perhaps Sophia intimidated him. She could feel the blood rush through her body and intuitively knew she was the stronger of the two. She was older. This new one was probably very young, some Hollywood thug that had irresponsibly been brought over. He was big, though, and hungry, she could feel it, and he would be a match for her yet.

"No," the other breathed. "Never."

"Then take her out of my sight."

The vampire moved toward her.

Sophia jumped over Robert's desk. She grabbed him by the throat and maneuvered him so as to keep him between her and the vampire. Robert struggled, but his efforts were fruitless and after a few moments he grew still, fighting for breath.

"Come for me and kill your master," Sophia said.

The vampire narrowed his eyes.

"Go on!" the ghensiv roared. "You'll get no food from me."

Although the fanger remained motionless, his discomfiture was obvious.

"Who are you?" he said.

"Who are *you*?"

He frowned and nodded again. Both of them would refuse identification.

"Why do you do this?" the vampire asked.

"There's more to life than food. There's destruction, and vengeance, and needless waste. That's where Robert comes in."

"I don't understand."

"Not my problem. What *is* my problem is that you're here, and you don't know what to do. Well, I'll tell you. Leave."

"No."

"Listen, I know you still feel tied to the living; that's why you exist in the human mob. *Get over it.* Go work for Hauswell in Vegas, or one of his rivals if you must, and join others of your kind. *Now go.* I'll take care of Robert."

The vampire's brow furrowed, then his eyes grew brighter as if to lunge for Sophia at the last second. He seemed to lose confidence, though, and a beaten look crossed his face. He edged back, his eyes never leaving her, and disappeared out a window.

Sophia waited until she was satisfied that the young one had gone, then released Robert. She could feel it in her veins: the Ice Queen was back. This man was a coward, a killer—and would die.

He sank to the ground, one hand to his throat, massaging it.

"What are you?" he said.

"I wonder about that too, sometimes." She took a step closer to him. "Want to make love to me, Robert?"

"What?"

She smiled at him, and her smile was menacing. "In a very real way, and pardon the vulgarity, I'm hungry for your cock."

She pulled off her blouse. Her nipples grew erect at contact with the cool air of the room. She descended on him, taking off her clothes as she went.

First Robert's screams were almost pleasurable, though confused—and then they were just screams.

She was used to that.

* * *

A face flashing past caught Danielle's attention as Veliswa's limo roared by; it was staring out of an office building, pale and vacant, but when the eyes lit on the car something changed. "Shit," she said. "I think Jean-Pierre's watching us still."

"He can't be," Veliswa said. "We're too far away, and his minions ..."

"He's watching through others' eyes."

Veliswa blinked. "You mean … ?"

"If that's true, then he's grown very powerful indeed," Ruegger said.

"Here's your car," Veliswa said, as the limo slowed. "If Jean-Pierre is watching, I think he'll follow you, not me, though he may come for me later. Be quick. And farewell. We probably won't meet again for awhile."

They climbed out of the limousine and dove into their black Mustang, parallel-parked between two sedans, as Veli's limo shot away. Danielle caught Ruegger scanning the windows of the buildings around. Several faces stared blankly back, office workers whose minds had been co-opted by a greater power. Danielle shivered.

"This is bad," Ruegger said, as he climbed behind the wheel. Danielle lowered herself into the passenger seat. Ruegger shoved the car into gear and shot it out into traffic. "I think that—hell!"

"What?" she said.

"Jean-Pierre and his pack have found us."

Danielle faced the rear. Sure enough, a van had just rounded the corner. It barreled straight for them. "Jesus! They're driving badly."

"Is Jean-Pierre behind the wheel?"

"Too far away to tell, but I bet he is." She turned around. "We have enough gas?"

"To get us clear of the Clearglass Inn, but not much more. The trick's going to be dodging the traffic."

"And losing *them*."

"Our car's faster."

"And older."

"Buckle up."

Chapter 11

"Launch the bikes," Jean-Pierre said.

Byron flung open the rear doors and Cloire lowered the wooden ramp. Byron hopped on a black Honda and Kilian took his Harley. The engines screamed in the close confines, then the bikes were away, sliding backwards down the ramp. Once on the street, they tore forwards along both sides of the van.

"Get 'em!" Cloire said.

Loirot groaned from the back. He'd been shot by Veliswa and was still bleeding. "I need food, or at least some blood. Cloire, would you?"

"Fuck off, asshole. My blood's my own."

"Bitch," he said.

"Goddamned right."

It was a moment before she realized that the albino was cursing something at her.

"What's it now, Frenchie?"

"Cops."

"What'd you expect, asshole? Drive better! Or do you *want* Danielle to go free?"

He bared his teeth. "Get the grenades."

*   *   *

"They've sent bikes to catch up with us," Danielle said.

"Who?"

"Kilian and someone else, a big guy . . . Byron."

"Weapons?"

"Can't tell. They're both wearing trench coats. Probably shotguns."

"Enough to take out our wheels, then." They had armored flaps that dangled behind their wheels for just such occasions, but they wouldn't be strong enough to resist sustained assault, especially by shotgun.

"Cops," she said suddenly.

"For us or them?"

"Them. Two cruisers. They must've gotten reports on Jean-Pierre's driving."

"Think it was intentional?"

"Maybe. The bikes are coming fast."

"Break out the guns."

She grimaced. "What's your pleasure?"

"Berretta nine. You shoot, I drive."

She kissed him on the temple, then hopped in the cramped rear compartment, on top of their last-ditch coffin. Reached to the floor, removed the flap (made to resemble a floor mat) that disguised their stash of weapons, and selected one of their two briefcases (one contained their clothes, the other their weapons) and a double-barreled semi-automatic shotgun designed to fit a double-magazine of rounds.

She tossed the Beretta forward, then punched out the disposable rear window, swivel-connected at the bottom so that it swung out and down. Feeling the breeze in her air, she stuck her head out the rear, keeping her weapon (already loaded) out of sight until the bikes came within range.

Kilian, on the Harley, narrowed in on their car at speed, while Byron roared in behind. Danielle's mind flashed back to Byron playing chess with her, many years ago, and she grew cold. When Kilian got within a hundred feet, she brought out the rifle and took aim.

A hole erupted in the car beside her.

"Shit!"

Byron fired openly at her, regardless of whatever cars or people divided them.

Before she could take aim at either of them, Kilian fired, as well, letting loose with a stumpy automatic weapon. Bullets punched into her, and she tried not to scream. She felt her gristle and muscle giving way as her blood warmed her clothes. Holes drilled the trunk lid, some were passing inside.

Danielle fired, and fired, and fired. Blood mushroomed on Kilian's clothes as he drew near, but he still closed in. Danielle lowered her aim and squeezed off several shots. Kilian's bike broke apart beneath him, crunching and whirring. His face flashed anger, then he was skidding under his heavy bike along the crowded street—which had grown substantially less crowded in the last few moments—and was lost to sight.

Before she could even swivel, she was thrown backwards in a bloody arc to crash against the back of the front passenger seat. *Damnit.* She hated being shot. She leapt up and fired back at the other one, Byron, who had grown eerily near while her attention had been on Kilian.

They exchanged volleys. Danielle aimed at the werewolf's bike. At last it blew apart beneath him and Danielle was slammed back in her seat again, gun forgotten, her blood spraying the rear compartment. Her chest was a painful disaster, and in her largely unfed and already traumatized state, she was in danger.

"Rueg," she whispered, and reached a hand for him. He squeezed back.

She latched onto him and dragged herself bloodily forward, slithering into the front compartment, where she lay backwards in a pitiful slump, blood soaking the seat beneath her.

"Damn," he said, seeing her broken chest, the splintered ribs, the pumping blood. He stuck his wrist in front of her face. "Here, drink."

She rocked her head back and forth. "No more. You need strength to drive."

"Take some," he demanded. "You're so young. You could be dying."

"No."

"Take some!"

She bent her face forward to where her lips touched the flesh of his wrist, and kissed him, her eyes closed. Then she collapsed back into her seat.

*   *   *

Kilian scowled as he pulled himself out from under his bike. Totaled, of course. He picked himself up and scanned downstream to see Byron moving over to the right side of the road so the van could pick him up. Kilian, being on the right, just waited.

As it came upon him, the side door slid open and Cloire reached for him. He leapt aboard without her help, even though the van was going at a considerable speed, and without a word of thanks dropped beside Jean-Pierre.

Byron scrabbled aboard next, nearly falling on top of Cloire, she having pulled him so hard. He panted and reclined next to Loirot, who seemed to be healing slowly for some reason. Had Veliswa coated her bullets with something?

"Give me a drink?" the wounded man said.

Byron frowned but stuck out his arm anyway. "Drink away," he invited, and turned to Cloire. "I hurt Danielle," he said. "Her blood was everywhere."

"*Such* concern," Cloire said. "You did fuck her. Either that or baby's developing a conscience." She ran her fingernails along his cheek, scraping his skin. "Which is it?"

"Well, I didn't fuck her," he said. "Whether or not that means I've a conscience is debatable." He jerked his arm away from Loirot. "Enough."

"Thanks, By."

Jean-Pierre yelled to the back, "The cops are on us. Cloire, you got the grenades?"

"As you requested."

"Bombs away."

Byron and Cloire moved to the extreme rear, dragging their box of explosives with them, and popped open the rear doors with a bang.

Two police cruisers followed immediately behind, lights flashing and alarms wailing. One cop had some sort of megaphone to his mouth and was shouting through it. When he saw the van's doors fly open, he quit the megaphone and reached for a gun.

Too late.

Cloire ripped the pin off one grenade and threw it through the cops' windshield. It detonated a split-second after it had passed into the driving compartment, the windshield bursting outward in a million pieces of charred glass. The cruiser scraped to a smoking halt, almost colliding with the one behind it, which swerved recklessly around and shot forward to get to the side of the van.

The passenger cop was in such a panic he fired his shotgun twice through the glass of his own windshield. The second blast caught Byron in the chest, but not before he'd lobbed two grenades—one in each hand—at the cruiser, which burst into double flames and rolled to a flaming halt.

"God I love roasting pork," Cloire said. She turned to watch the blood spreading across Byron's chest. The wound itself was closing before her eyes. "My, my, aren't we manly tonight."

He slammed the rear doors closed. "You ain't seen nothin' yet."

"Cloire!" came a shout from the front. With grumbling obedience, Cloire moved forward and blew in Jean-Pierre's ear.

"What can I do for you, sunshine?"

"We're going to need another car here soon: the cops have identified this one. Take a bike ahead and knock us off another van. A new one preferably, something very unlike what we're in now."

"What about our guns? We just going to leave them here in the fucking van for anyone to find? Some of this stuff can be traced, you know."

He grabbed her face with one hand and drew it near his own. Staring into her different-colored eyes, he said, "Just do it."

"Say please, J-P."

He shoved her backwards, and she fell down laughing.

"Please," he spat. He turned his attention back to the road.

Cloire busied herself with the task of readying a bike as Byron approached her.

"Care to lower the ramp, light-of-my-life?"

He popped open the doors and threw down a ramp, then stepped back as she roared away without so much as a nod good-bye.

* * *

Danielle woke to the taste of blood in her mouth. She wiped it from her fingers and licked it gratefully.

"Thanks," she said.

"How are you?"

She examined her chest, trying for detachment but failing. Ruegger had stanched her bleeding with a white shirt from their second suitcase, which he'd managed to hoist into the front seat with one hand. The shirt was soaked through, but the bleeding seemed to have stopped. She was hurt badly and needed sustenance. Shaking her head, she said, "I'll live. We just need a place to crash for a while, if we can get the albino off our backs."

"I'm trying."

"What happened to the cops?" she asked.

"Dead, damn it. Jean-Pierre's crew used grenades."

She fell silent. Then: "How long until we're out of town?"

"Too long. Another half hour."

She glanced at one of her watches. "It's going to be close. Sunrise in under an hour." She craned her head to see out the back. There seemed to be gallons of blood back there, but it didn't interfere with the view.

"They're way back there," she said. "But they're there."

He nodded. "Every time I try to lose him, he's right there with me. Wonder if he's still looking through others' eyes."

"Think he knows where we're going?"

"He can't. I think he's tapping into your head."

"He can do that with humans, yeah. But not with shades. Plus, he just used up all his psychic energy on his homeless guys and his other watchers. Otherwise he wouldn't have had to kill the cops."

"Right. But for a time you two were very close. You developed a tight bond: maybe he's able to use that to a psychic advantage. And in your weakened condition . . ."

"Maybe."

He passed her a cigarette and his Beretta.

"More cops," he said.

She groaned. "No rest for the weary."

She leaned out the window, squinted one eye and fired low. The cruiser's wheel blew out and the vehicle started into a dangerously fast spin, finally flipping over and skidding to a halt upside-down.

"They alive?" Ruegger said.

"Yeah, but it was close." She tried to block out the thought that she might've hurt the two in the cruiser. "Hope they don't find us again. If they only knew we were cops of a sort, maybe they'd ease off a bit."

She lit her cigarette and leaned her head back out the window, her hair stirring in the breeze.

Traffic, as the sun's advances on the horizon grew more persistent, became thicker and more purposeful, and the albino's ebony van vanished into it so that it was nowhere to be found; when the albino reappeared, it was behind the wheel of a different van, newer than the first.

Ruegger and Danielle's spirits sank. Finally, the city of New York began to dissipate, its massive concentration of steel and humanity unraveling to give way to open road and emptier skylines.

"Almost sunrise," she said. One of her worst fears was now making itself realized: being trapped in open country with the sun coming up and sun-resistant killers just behind them, preventing them from finding some place to hole up for the day. If they hid too soon, the killers would catch them and expose them to the sun . . . and if they didn't hole up soon enough, the sun would get them anyway.

Their Mustang rattled and groaned around them. The endless highway stretched ahead as they blew past the outskirts of the sprawling metropolis. They headed west, away from the sun.

"We're not gonna make it," she said. "Under nine minutes till sunrise."

He laid a hand on the back of her neck and massaged the tense muscles there. "We'll look back on this and laugh."

"From our graves, yeah. You want a tombstone or a crypt?"

"Oh, crypt, most definitely." He checked the rear-view. "Still behind us."

She grunted and tried to throw her legs up on the dashboard, but she was too weak and her legs slid off and thudded to the floor.

"Death sucks," she said.

He reached a hand to the backseat and pulled out the other suitcase—the heavy one. Both were densely packed: one with clothes, one with weapons. The arms ranged from the exotic to the mundane, tools Ruegger had collected over the years; when one got too old, he'd replace it. After a while, Danielle had gotten into it, and the guns became sleeker and more powerful. Anything that could fit, fit. Not just guns—bombs, too, from plastique to grenades.

Ruegger was probably thinking of throwing a timed device onto the road behind them, but those things were so uncertain …

He shook her gently, and Danielle cracked an eye. She must have passed out. "What?" she groaned, looking around and closing her eye again.

"We're there."

He swerved onto the exit ramp. She felt the grating of metal on concrete as their hurtling black contraption smashed against a pockmarked wall.

"What?" She leaned into him, putting both arms around him, letting the blood drip from her chest.

He glanced at the rear-view mirror. "No sign of our pursuers. We're almost to the Inn."

"*No*," she warned, her voice cracking. "Motels are death-traps, baby. All they've got to do is go room-to-room until—"

He pressed his chin against her head. "That's not going to happen, and we have something to do," he said, swerving into the parking lot of the little hide-away motel, the CLEARGLASS INN, just as advertised. He screeched to a halt in front of the lobby doors, and the car shuddered and died. The vampires bailed out of the car, suitcases in tow, and Danielle was almost to the lobby when Ruegger shouted, "Wait!"

She spun. "What?" She looked at a watch. "Under three minutes."

"We're just paying a visit, not checking in."

"Okay ..."

"What's the one thing we learned on our anniversary?"

Comprehension dawned. She swore.

"It's the best way out of this," he said.

"But—"

Not bothering to argue about it, he moved into the lobby.

"Where's Vincent Greggs?" he asked the man behind the counter. "He's a guest of yours."

"I can't give out that—"

Ruegger extended his powers; Danielle could sense it. He wasn't a strong psychic manipulator like Jean-Pierre, but he could handle one human for a brief time. "Where is Vincent Greggs?"

The registrar blinked. "Let me check." He typed into his computer, then glanced up. "Room 314."

Ruegger marched up the stairs to the third floor, Danielle immediately behind. They found Room 314 and Ruegger kicked in the door. Greggs, a prudent vampire, was just checking the windows to make sure his personal blackout curtains had been installed properly. He whirled, anger mixed with fear in his face, as Ruegger and Danielle barged in.

"What the hell—?"

Ruegger grabbed him by the throat and hefted him off the ground. "You were hired to take out someone—

someone who knows who killed Ludwig Gleason. Who's your target?"

The man tried to talk, couldn't. Ruegger eased up.

"Will you let me go if I tell you?" Greggs said.

"No. But I won't torture you, either."

Grimness settled over the other's features. "You're the Marshals, aren't you?"

"That's right. Now talk."

"Hauswell," Vincent said. "I was hired to kill Hauswell. I was just on my way to—"

Ruegger tore off his head. Even as the blood spurted, Ruegger turned, wearily, and offered the body, and blood, to Danielle.

"Drink," he said. "Go on."

She hesitated. "You … you didn't even give him a chance."

He let out a breath. "I know, but he was a hired assassin, a killer without conscience or mercy. There's no difference between him and any other shade we've taken out before. The sun is almost up."

Slowly, she nodded, and took the body in her arms.

* * *

The van jerked to a smoldering stop yards from the vampires' Mustang, and Jean-Pierre clambered from the overheated hulk to stare at the rising sun. He heard doors opening and closing behind him, but his gaze was unwavering. If Danielle wasn't in stasis by now, she'd be dead.

"The car's empty!" Loirot shouted. He'd recovered more quickly after imbibing what Byron had given him, and he was up and moving—but still not at peak health.

"Trunk?" Jean-Pierre said.

"Working on it," came the reply.

Jean-Pierre waited, breathless.

"Trunk's empty!"

"Go search the dumpster and outer perimeter of the building," he instructed Loirot. "Keep an eye out for sewer grates and air shafts. If you find them alive don't stay to fight."

Loirot stalked away.

"Check the hollow beneath the back compartment," Jean-Pierre said.

With the help of Cloire, Kilian found the catch and removed it. A metal door lay there, the lid of the vampires' last-ditch coffin.

"Waste of time," said Byron. "Vampires're paranoid about being trapped in their coffins. They'll've gotten as far away as possible by now."

"We've got to open it," Kilian said. "Just to be sure."

Byron shrugged. "I don't get paid by the hour . . ."

"It'll be booby-trapped," Cloire said. "Be sure of that."

Jean-Pierre nodded. "Can you open it?"

"Anything for you, lovey." Quietly, she set to work, and the crew waited tensely. Loirot returned, shaking his head. At last Cloire looked up. "Done," she said. "Shall I open it?"

The entire crew watched their leader. This was a decisive moment. If the coffin was opened and occupied, the vampires would be struck by the sun and become flaming husks that would blow away in the wind, dead to all the world. Or Jean-Pierre would refuse to open it.

The albino lowered his head, took the last drag on the last cigarette of the pack, and flung it to the ground. When he looked back up at his crew, his face betrayed his thoughts.

"Fuck," said Cloire. "You goddamned pussy-whipped *bastard*." She turned her back to him and walked away, casting a malicious, if conspiratorial, glance at Kilian.

"We'll wait till nightfall to open the chamber," Jean-Pierre said

"Fuck that," said Cloire, coming back, with a scowling Kilian by her side. Loirot was with them, too. "We're opening the coffin *now*."

"Get away from there!" Jean-Pierre shouted, stepping forward, but Loirot and Kilian blocked him off.

"Now now, whitey," said Cloire. "It's my turn now. Are you with us or against us?"

Jean-Pierre saw he had no choice, not if he wanted to stay leader of this crew. "You ... you've removed all the booby-traps?"

"No promises. They had it rigged pretty tight."

He flicked his wrist in disgust. "Do it."

She grinned and hopped into the back compartment. After fiddling with the coffin's catch for a moment, she turned toward the others dramatically, a showman's pause, then threw off the lid and leapt back. There was an audible creaking of leather as those assembled leaned forward to peer into the shallow recess.

The explosion sent roaring flame and twisted metal to wash over asphalt and werewolf alike. When the heat died away, it left only wreckage in its wake, with smoke billowing from nearby cars (including the werewolves' new van) and drifting through the shattered glass of the lobby. Charred rubble lay strewn across the ground, and cries of alarm could be heard from inside.

Smoking, Jean-Pierre raised his head from the pavement, searching for the others; in turn, they rose and did the same. Jean-Pierre could hear Loirot muttering, "Fucking ruined my suit, the bastards."

Despite it all, Jean-Pierre felt pleased. *Run, Danielle.*

"More cops are going to come," Byron said.

The albino nodded, watching the others gather around.

"Brilliant disarming," Kilian said to Cloire.

"Fuck off and go to hell," she snarled.

"Knock it off," Jean-Pierre said.

Loirot snorted. "Don't order them around. Not unless you're going to act like a leader, Jean-Pierre."

"That's right," Cloire said. "You're slipping, whitey."

The albino's lip curled down. "Is there a point to this, Cloire?"

Her eyes blazed. "Shape up or ship out. You're utterly fucked-up, you know, completely eaten up by someone you're supposed to be killing. In fact, I think the only reason you haven't flat out told us to pack up and go home is that you figure the best way to keep dear Danielle alive is to head the team that's sent to kill her."

They glared at each other, both spoiling for a fight.

Loirot cleared his throat. "I hear sirens."

* * *

What Ruegger and Danielle had learned on their anniversary was the importance of tunneling. So, after swearing profusely, the odd flock took to the dirt, hollowing out what little space they could as deep and dark as they could reasonably want to go.

Ruegger dug deep, reaching the cool moistness of the hidden earth, maybe forty feet down. With Danielle's help, he tunneled sideways, putting some distance between the fugitives and the motel. The dirt was cold, hard, wet, and endless, and Ruegger's telekinetic abilities weren't strong enough to eliminate the need for physical labor.

They hit an underground river and plunged into it unexpectedly. They allowed it to sweep them along. The river brought them into a network of natural caverns, which were very dark indeed. Ruegger helped Danielle out of the water and they lay along the rocky shore in silence, dripping wet, catching their breath.

Danielle laughed. "We should do that more often."

Ruegger moved their two briefcases out of the way and threw his arm around her. "I'm glad you feel that way. It's gonna be hell getting out of here."

He lay down, feeling the smooth stone against his back, and Danielle rested her head on his chest. It was so peaceful down here, if dark. He wondered when and if he'd ever be able to return to New York, but found to his surprise that he didn't care. New York had haunted his dreams for too long.

"You *know*," she said, and there was a thoughtful quality in her voice that made him wary.

"Yes?" he said.

"Well, we're in the dark, underground, with only the babble of a subterranean river for sound ..."

"So?"

"Now might be the *perfect* time for you to tell me your story."

"My story?"

"Don't be dense. Your past. Your history. Everyone else knows so much about it—Veliswa, Hauswell, Ludwig, Malie—but I don't know anything. I'm tired of not knowing about you, babe. About what you've been through, who you are. Your famous dark period. Everything."

He heard the sincerity in her voice, and the pain. He sympathized. Still ...

"I'm sorry, Dani, but ... I'm not ready," he said.

In the background, the river babbled. Danielle let out a long breath.

"So, what now?" she said.

"On to Las Vegas," he said. Both knew that's where Hauswell would be. It's where the old vampire based his criminal operations out of. "Time to find out who killed Ludwig."

Chapter 12

Bastard!

Kristen skulked past Vistrot's many guards and soldiers. For their part, they took little notice of her; as the Titan's concubine, she was as common a sight to them as they were to her.

She flew past them, this little blond girl in a tight T-shirt and miniskirt by Gianni Versace, until she reached the end of the corridor, where one of the two doormen opened the door for her, and stormed into Vistrot's office.

He was on the phone, of course. He was always on the phone.

Before she could get a word out, he lifted a finger to command her silence. God, she hated that. Early on, though, he'd instilled in her a respect for his powers. If she interrupted him now, he'd only use his psychic abilities to silence her. She didn't like that at all—drifting in your own consciousness while someone else controlled your body. It was a terrible feeling, a violation. And she was only human (more or less), after all. She could not counter his psychic abilities with her own. She had other abilities, though.

She folded her arms across her skinny chest and tapped a foot incessantly. He shifted uncomfortably under her glare. *Good.*

She and Vistrot had been lovers since the 1950s. Back then he'd had a regular harem, and when he'd seen her—a little pouting fifteen-year-old with a bow in her hair—sipping on a cream soda alone (dejected would be a better word) in an ice-cream parlor, he'd known he must add her to his collection.

So, in typical Titan sensitivity, he'd kidnapped her. He thrust all those old lavish gifts upon her, clothes and cars and jewels and servants, in an attempt to sooth her, not that it had worked. But a strange thing occurred during her first month of imprisonment. She and Vistrot, all four hundred pounds of him, had fallen in love—and, after a year, he'd disbanded his harem at her request.

She'd demanded that he send money to her grief-stricken parents and he'd done it. She'd demanded an apartment for herself and a checking account and he'd done it. He'd done everything she asked him to do and more.

One thing she'd never asked for was a taste of his immortal blood; she hadn't wanted that gift. He would just have to live with her aging self. Then the second strange thing developed. It turned out that by taking his juices into her on a regular basis, she'd become somewhat immortal herself. She didn't have his telekinesis, amazing strength or recuperative abilities, but she did not age. She still looked to be the fifteen-year-old girl he'd fallen for all those years ago, even if she was now ancient. God alone knew how old Vistrot was; it was not something he spoke of.

Sometimes she craved for her old mortal life back, even cried over it, but she loved him too much and couldn't bear the thought of leaving him. Every now and then, in the early years, he'd had his little indiscretions, but she'd put an end to that.

And that's what she would do now.

Into the phone, Vistrot was saying, "Now, listen, Junger. It's a shame about your tomb . . . sarcastic? . . . yes, that was . . . now shut up . . .you left the bodies—you killed them in the first place!—and you deserved punishment, both of you . . . Yes, so I commanded the massacres. I wasn't going to tell Jean-Pierre that. So *what* that he thought

you were supposed to kill Ruegger and Danielle? It was a
necessary lie. Do you want him to know the truth? Yes, I'm
quite aware you don't know it, either . . . Is that a threat? I'd
have you killed before you got to the first sub-level and you
know it . . . No, there's no general contract out on them.
That was just a rumor that I spread to ease suspicion. Jean-
Pierre is the only one assigned to kill them, just as you are
the only ones assigned to do what you're doing. Now do it."

He slammed the phone down, shook his head as if the
conversation had made him nauseous, and took a sip of the
sherry on his desk. He glanced up at Kristen and smiled.
How adorable he looked with that big cunning baby-face
and those bright eyes and that cruel, sensuous mouth.

"It's an unexpected pleasure to see you at work at this
time of night, darling," he said in his rich baritone voice.
"You should visit more often, really. Please, take a seat, my
dear."

"I don't think so. How can you look so smug! You're
cheating on me, Augustine Michael Vistrot, I know you are,
you bastard."

"Nonsense. Now calm down and be rational. You have
such a temper. Please, would you like me to send for a drink
or something? Care for a cigar?"

She grabbed the big cigar-box and hurled it to the
floor, then flew over the desk, wrapped her arms about him
and kissed him square on the lips, darting her tongue into
his age-old mouth. She teased at his lips a little, tugged on
the lower one, then bit it. Then bit it *hard*, drawing blood.
Before he could react, she was back on the other side of the
massive desk, glaring at him.

"I can taste her in your mouth, Auggie-dear."

He put a handkerchief to his lip and sighed, his great
shoulders rising up and down slowly. He looked so
incredibly guilty and hurt she just wanted to sweep it all

under the rug and embrace him. She held herself back with difficulty.

"You're cheating on me," she repeated.

"Never. How can you even think that?"

"It's true, isn't it? I thought all that was over years ago! How *could* you?"

"But I never—"

"You fucking *liar*! You never spend any time with me anymore, Auggie. Never. Not since that damn war in Europe began and that . . . that Scouring! And now that we're in hiding from the Scourer—I never get to go anywhere with you."

She stared into his big blue eyes and weakened a little. He looked so hurt and so sincere in his own condescending way. As she watched, the cut on his lip healed and he licked the blood away. Oh, what he could do with that tongue!

"We haven't . . . made love . . . not like we used to, in six weeks!" she said. "I'm going out of my mind. And if you weren't sleeping with some *slut* you would be too! How can you say nothing's wrong?"

He focused his mind on the toppled cigar box, lifted it and the scattered cigars with his mindthrust and placed them back on the desk.

"You're so sweet," he said. "So pure. You're the purest thing in my life. I hate to see you upset. Please . . . oh, don't cry. Please don't cry. Oh, baby, come here."

She came to him, hating the tears that welled up in her, and sat in his lap while he put his big warm arms around her. "Don't do this to me," she sobbed. "I love you."

"You know I love you, too, baby."

She balled her fists and beat at his chest. "You love your work more than you could ever love me! You're always promising we'll take a vacation . . . go to Hawaii like we used to . . . but we never do." She collapsed against him.

"We never do. You never have time for me anymore. *Never*."

He stroked her cheeks, his hands so excruciatingly tender, and ran a strong hand through her golden hair. "You know I love you more than my work, but these are times of great peril—*great* peril. Soon things will be different, you'll see. Very different. The whole structure of our world will change, and, if we play our cards right, we'll come out on top and never have a care in the world again. Don't you see? I'm doing this for *us*. It'll be wonderful, every day a delight, and we'll spend all the time in the world together. How would you like to get *married*?"

She gasped. She so wanted to believe what he was saying, but how could she? He was such an adept liar.

"Do you mean it?" she said.

"Of course I do." He kissed her forehead.

At his touch, she could feel the stirring in her, the longing. She played with his tie, kissed his throat, ran her hands along the back of his big bald head, squirming in his lap until she could feel him hardening, then she slid a hand down and undid his zipper, stroking the sensuous, knobby tube of flesh that popped out.

"No," he said, shaking his head, tearing her away from him. "Now's not the time."

She slapped him hard and hopped off his lap.

"That's it," she growled. "I *know* you're cheating on me now. When have you ever turned me down? You're probably afraid you can't keep it up because you just screwed that whore, whoever she is!"

"It's not true," he said, but he was lying and they both knew it. "Look," he said after a silence, "if I ever did cheat on you it wouldn't be because I loved another."

"Oh, don't you give that men-have-urges crap. Maybe I have urges, too. Maybe I've acted on them! What do you think of that?"

"Please don't say that. If I ever found out you were cheating on me . . ."

"Yes? You'd do what, exactly? The same thing I'm doing now that you're cheating on me? I'd like to see it. So go on, explain why you're breaking my heart."

"It's not like you think."

"Oh, so you admit it!"

"No! Calm down. It's the future I'm thinking of. If ever I did something . . . behind your back . . . it would only be because I loved you, because I'm trying to ensure our future together. It's part of what I was trying to explain . . . It's complicated—"

"You're a liar! You don't really love me, do you? Do you! Well, you'll regret this, I swear to God!"

"Kristen, baby, don't do anything foolish. Promise me!"

"Oh, and I'm expected to keep *my* promises? Ha!"

She stormed out of the room, hearing him call after her but not caring one fucking fig, brushed furiously past his soldiers and guards in her stolid march to the elevator. Reaching in her purse—such a little girl's purse, she realized suddenly—she whipped out the phone and ordered her limo to pick her up, and by the time she was outside, it was there.

"Take me to the albino's," she ordered.

The limo stopped in front of Jean-Pierre's eight-story hovel and Kristen hopped out, entering the building. *It oughta be torn down,* she thought. *Put out of its misery.*

As she stepped into the main hall, she noticed a horrible deathly stench in here and could see many dried-up trails of blood. Something horrible had happened here, it was obvious. A few of the albino's vagrant minions hung about, but there weren't as many of them as usual, and some looked to be nursing serious wounds. And, Christ, it smelled awful.

She found him in the Hooked Room, in a corner, slumped over in a little ball, pulling his knees into himself. He was naked, covered in blood and crying. It was clear to Kristen that he'd recently run through the gauntlet of the hooks and chains and various blades, trying to drive away his obsessive thoughts.

Crouching beside him, she laid a hand on his shoulder. Though he must have known she was there, he jumped.

"Go away."

"No." She grabbed him under the armpit and tried to pull him to his feet, but he wouldn't budge. She collapsed on the bloody floor with the effort. "What is it, baby? Why've you done this to yourself?"

"They've all left me," he muttered, his green eyes cloudy and wet and far away. "Or they will soon, even Byron. He can't resist that bitch. And Danielle, gone with Ruegger unless I kill them both . . . And Veliswa, I never thought she'd leave me, of all people. We've been lovers for a hundred years. Met in Paris, actually. I even think on some level she loves me. How foolish . . ."

Kristen slapped him, hard, and a vague clarity returned to his eyes.

"You're rambling, Jean-Pierre. Stand up. Come on, let's go for a nice cappuccino." She grabbed him again and lifted, and this time he rose, slowly, his bare back sliding against the rough wall.

"They're all gone to me," he said.

What could've caused this?

Ever since she'd realized Vistrot was cheating on her, she'd been having an affair with Jean-Pierre, whom she'd known forever in conjunction with the Titan. It was a sisterly love she felt toward the albino, but their affair was enough to relieve her frustrations. At least she was honest with him, and he went along with their little arrangement for his own reasons. Probably her youthfulness reminded him of Danielle (although Kristen was actually older, at least time-wise), but it could be something else.

But this . . .

She'd seen him just the other day and he'd been fine. Something traumatic must have happened. He never let his feelings show when he was around others; only when alone with himself did the facade shudder, and he must have been alone with himself for far too long for him to be in this state. He hadn't even straightened up when she'd come into the room, and that was all too uncharacteristic.

"I'm not gone," she whispered, and embraced him. "I'll always be here for you." She kissed his nearly hairless chest and tugged at his one silver nipple-ring gently.

The corners of his mouth slid up just a little. Thinking that maybe a little of the old two-headed-beast would make him feel better, she sank to her knees before him and started stroking his member.

"No." He pushed her away. "Sex isn't the answer to everything, Kristen. You're so immature sometimes, you really are. Some wounds are too deep."

She stood up and slapped him again. "Never push me unless I want you to!" Still, she was pleased that he seemed more his old self. "Ah, my poor, passionate, tragic Frenchman . . . what am I going to do with you?"

"Is that why you want me? Because I'm tragic? If I got over Danielle, would you still love me?"

"Of course. But, wait . . . you love me?"

He moved to a counter and lit a Pall Mall. How regal he looked, standing there, naked, covered in blood, but unbent and strong.

"To what end?" he said. "The feelings aren't there, not in that way. You love Vistrot and I Danielle. I'll say the same thing I said to Veliswa: you're like a sister to me. I'd never let any harm come to you."

She sighed, lit a cigarette herself, a Virginia Slim. It seemed that he felt the same way about her as she did towards him. At least he was being honest. But, ah, how she wanted someone to really, truly love her. Vistrot did to an extent. But no matter what he said, his work was his first priority and always would be. In her dreams sometimes she imagined herself eloping with the albino, but this was just a schoolgirl fantasy, just grasping at straws because they were the only things that were real.

"Are you reading my thoughts?" she asked.

"I would never do that."

"So what do we do now, Jean-Pierre?"

"You started whatever it is between us because of what's going on between you and the Titan. If I rejected you now your dissatisfaction would remain; you'd only find a new outlet. So I won't turn you away, and . . . now that you're the only one left for me . . ." He shook himself, clearly trying to avoid slipping back to the way he'd been when she arrived. That state seemed so close, as if he'd collapse at any moment. "I don't have the strength to turn you away. If either one of us leaves the other, it will be you."

"I'll never leave you, Jean-Pierre. Never. I may go back to Vistrot, I may stop sleeping with you . . . but I'll always be here for you as a friend."

He smiled. "Never say always."

"How about that cappuccino?"

His smile became more seductive, and as he walked over toward her, she felt an electric thrill pass through her. He pressed himself against her, and their lips locked. She threw her arms about his sweaty, bloody torso, feeling herself grow wet instantly.

"No," she murmured, her eyes catching the hooks and chains. "Not here . . ."

He led her into his bedroom. A stark testament to self-abnegation, at least it was devoid of blades and had a large mattress, if not a real bed. He lay her down on it, tore off her clothes and ravished her. She so loved to be ravished; Vistrot was much too gentle a lover.

Halfway through it, Jean-Pierre began to cry again, and she could see the shame and self-hatred in his face even as the sweat dripped from his brow. At first she was deeply annoyed. Then, as if his misery were contagious, she realized her own great unhappiness and began to cry as well. They resumed fucking savagely, this new emotion only fueling their lust. At the climactic moment, they came together, a first for them.

Afterwards, while they were smoking and staring out the great dirty windows of the apartment, he said, "Don't tell anyone about this."

She kissed his shoulder and smiled. "Of course. We wouldn't want anyone to know our secret, would we?"

"What would that be?"

"That you do have a soul."

"That again."

"You aren't the void that people think you are—that *you* think you are."

He sniffed. "If we're going to be poetic, we must be truthful. I have no soul. What I am is a void that knows that it's a void and wants to be something more."

"I saw it back there . . . when I looked into those eyes of yours . . . It's there, my pale one, like it or not." Suddenly she felt very vulnerable naked and returned to the mattress to throw a sheet over her shoulders. Still, there was something eating at her.

"What's wrong?" he said.

She lit another cigarette, fidgeting. "I don't . . . I don't know if I should tell you. Really, it's ironic, betraying Vistrot to illuminate the fact that he betrayed you . . ."

"What are you talking about?"

She sighed. She felt so close to him now that she couldn't keep it back. "He lied to you, Jean-Pierre, although I'm not quite sure what it means. I overheard a phone conversation. He was talking to someone named Junger, I think."

This got his attention.

Continuing, she said, "He said something about how he lied to you, but it was a necessary lie. He said that there was no general contract out on Ruegger and Danielle, that yours was the only death-squad sent to kill them and that Junger wasn't supposed to kill them, that his was a different purpose entirely, or something to that effect. Maybe I'm just reading too much into what he said. I wasn't really listening, but I heard your name so I paid attention. What does it mean? Does it make any sense to you?"

He frowned, and it was clear that he was thinking hard. "No. I don't know what it means, but don't ask him about it. Never let him grow suspicious."

"Of course not."

"Thank you for telling me this. *Now* I know you do love me."

"You're my brother, right?"

It wasn't long before she left, shrugging on the remains of her clothes and calling back her limo. She sat in its cool, leather-bound confines and felt the tension drain from her. If only she could bottle whatever it was that Jean-Pierre did for her . . .

She wasn't going home, which was her apartment, but back to the Titanic. Of course, Vistrot had put out the rumor that he was frequenting many buildings, never staying in the same place twice in order to avoid the Scouring, and he'd even fabricated some evidence to support this, because he said the best way to hide was to convince *others* that you were hiding. The fact of the matter was he hadn't left that building in six weeks. He'd warned her not to leave it, either—but, especially during the daytime, there was little he could do to stop her, except to have her forcefully detained, and he would never do that.

If she couldn't get him out of the building, maybe she could bring a little pleasure to him while he was there. She would have to shower thoroughly first, of course. That vampire sense of smell didn't fool around.

She called ahead and arranged for a romantic meal to be prepared for them this evening. Something Italian, the chef's choice. He was having an affair, she was certain, but she still loved him and knew that he loved her too, so why not make the most of it?

Of course, if she had known with whom he was having the affair, and why, it would have made all the difference in the world.

Chapter 13

In his War Room, Roche Sarnova sipped his bourbon and listened to his advisors describe how he was losing the war. A big map on the wall outlined different parts of London. A red star indicated the suspected location of Subaire, his nemesis. He, the officers and the other members of the Dark Council had been over the same material now several times, and he listened with one ear. Mainly he sipped on his bourbon.

It was the first week of January and the war was going badly. His enemies had established a successful stronghold in London, where most of the fighting took place. The enemy just sat there and waited for Sarnova to send in more troops, and when they learned of one of his secret bases, they had it destroyed. There were rumors that his enemies were gathering their forces, preparing an attack on the Castle. Even Sarnova was growing apprehensive, but he told himself to be steady. He'd ruled the immortal world for three thousand years and he'd not relinquish it now.

Back then he'd used his powers and his title to bring the immortal elements together, to make peace among them, and he'd been successful. For centuries he'd ruled in tranquility, letting the borders of his domain expand naturally as the humans themselves explored new regions, spreading to all corners of the world.

Unfortunately, this exploration had brought about the decentralization of power; his empire, always hidden from human knowledge, had become unwieldy and the different elements had started to unravel once again. He couldn't control them all. Many had become nomadic and still others had begun to build empires of their own, despite his best efforts to crush them. Then they had grown arrogant and had tried to band together to destroy him, but they were too weak and he'd easily won. It had been simple to gather them back into his fold. Order was needed. Togetherness. Unity.

The seeds of rebellion had been sown, however, and over the centuries more and more of his following had deserted him to establish themselves elsewhere. They had discovered the New World long before Columbus had been born and there they fled, and there they prospered.

Sarnova (who'd gone by a different name then) was ignorant of this new development for a long time—how could he have foreseen the discovery of a new continent?—but when humans began to explore this virgin land he'd sent his forces over there only to be beaten back by the immortals already there.

He'd concentrated on fortifying his position as the most powerful shade in the Old World, had moved from his long-established headquarters in northern Africa to the regions of Eastern Europe so that he could more easily conquer the many immortals that had gathered there, away from his Egyptian stronghold. And conquer them he did, at a terrible price. He'd lost his headquarters in Africa because he'd had to concentrate so many troops in Europe, leaving Egypt unguarded. What misery that had been, losing his home, and too weak to reclaim it.

Over the years he'd struggled to make the Carpathians his new home, had renewed his forces, had re-established his empire and would soon emerge yet again as the strongest immortal in the world. And, now that he was ready to make the boldest move of all—this!

His idea was too revolutionary, too radical, too sudden. His brashness had ripped the Dark Council in half, perhaps destroyed it forever. They were cowards afraid of change. He wanted progress and they were willing to make war to stop him. It pained him, their lack of vision, their eager conservatism. Didn't they see how glorious the future could be?

At least he had Francois to console him. Deep down, though, Sarnova felt that even the Ambassador was afraid of his new ideas, was hoping that the war would end and the Dark Council be reunified, but that no real progress would develop. Did no one understand him? It had come to the point where he was beginning to doubt his own plans.

He sighed, finished his bourbon and cleared his throat. The others in the War Room turned.

"Is that all?" he said. "Are you quite finished? I see by your faces that you wish I would make peace with them. No, the war will go on until our enemy gives in. Don't you see? Progress is always difficult. Only afterwards do even its facilitators fully appreciate it. You will, gentlemen, mark my words. *The new world order is almost upon us!*"

He rose, feeling the sweat on his brow, and looked each of his followers in the eye. "Thank you for your diligence. Now please excuse me. Do what you must to ensure the fulfillment of the vision."

He stalked out of the room, waving away his guards. Privacy was crucial to the meeting he would now attend. He moved swiftly down to the catacombs, where he slowed his pace to collect his thoughts. He'd an idea of what this secret meeting would be about, but the implications of that were too hideous.

Most of these crypts and vaults had been moved long ago from their original locations in Egypt. Inside them rested the bodies of ancient rulers and shades who'd been important figures in immortal history. A few were representatives of Sarnova's line.

His predecessors, those that had carried the mantle of Dark Lord before him, where not his genetic ancestors but a line of warriors. Rulers. At some point in every ruler's life he or she must choose a successor, someone to carry on the tradition and the mantle. The successor would not necessarily be chosen because the ruler was dying or in peril but often because the ruler was tired of his or her responsibilities and wished to roam the world. Sarnova felt no such inclination and wasn't prepared to name a successor until he did. *If that's what they want to talk about . . .*

He walked through a stone archway and into a tomb, where he made his way to one of the walls and depressed a panel. A wall swung back. He stepped through into the hidden room.

The *Sangro Sankts* waited for him. Four of them, hunched around a large stone table with a lantern blazing from its center. The flickering light caught the group strangely, and for a moment Sarnova thought he'd stepped into a dream.

He accepted his seat at the head of the table, which they had reserved for him out of tradition and courtesy (although they were much more powerful than himself), and addressed them: "Good to see you again, my friends. I see there are two of you missing."

"We have always been here to protect and support your line," one said, "but, even so, we were shocked to hear your plan. Two of our number decided not to come out of protest. For that, we apologize." He smiled, but it was a strained, tense gesture. "It's good to see you again, too, Roche."

Sarnova nodded. "There's something you're not telling me."

"What do you desire to know?" said another.

"I was attacked a month ago. My assailant was carrying the blood of a kavasari in her veins. Where did that come from?"

"Are you accusing one of us?"

"I accuse no one, but there aren't many of you in the world—half of you are represented here—so it's more than likely that one of you, or one of the two absentees, was responsible."

Silence. Then the first speaker said, "If—*if*—one of us was responsible, our intention wouldn't have been to kill you, but to make you aware of our displeasure. Your new decision goes against everything we're meant to uphold, and you should've realized that before announcing it to the Dark Council."

Sarnova laughed. "Your feelings were hurt, is that it? That I'd act alone. That's why you did it."

"We didn't say we did it," said a third. "None of us here gave the blood to Victoria Lisaund—and yes, we know all about it—believe me. We're loyal to you, no matter how foolish your actions may be."

"Will you vouch for the loyalty of the two absentees?"

"No."

"And there's nothing else you'd care to reveal before we get to the matter at hand?"

"No."

"Well, then. Why did you summon me?"

"A successor must be chosen. You're losing the war. On the off chance that you die, someone must replace you."

I knew it. "Surely Francois Mauchlery would be adequate."

"He is not a leader, and he does not desire to be one. Besides, that's not the way things are done; it must be someone relatively young, someone fresh that you can mold."

"You'd have me mold him despite the fact that I'm foolish?"

"As much as we abhor your movement, we recognize that your new ideas signify strength and vitality."

"Why do you fear my death? Would not you protect me as you're sworn to do?"

"Certainly we would protect you within bounds. But we are not to use our powers to interfere with history in the making. We're to remain in the shadows, always."

"You're as bound in superstition as you always were! You cling to it because it gives you purpose, yet you would, *admit* it, interfere with our affairs if it served your sense of morality. Did you not stand by as one of your number provided a potential assassin with kavasari blood?"

"You use our lack of action against us."

"Of course I do. How dare you cling to your purpose, your sacred duties to me, when you'd sit by and watch me die simply because you have no vision."

"We do not call it vision. We call it sacrilege."

"I'm sure you do." Roche ran a sweaty hand through his black hair. *Losing my cool will only serve them. They need to be reminded of their roots.*

"Allow me to refresh your memories," he said. "You once ruled all immortals, but your greed drew you into war against each other, and your followers saw their opportunity and rebelled, your power never to be reclaimed again. Afterward your kind warred each other into virtual extinction. You drifted without purpose or ambition, and there was only one of your number that was strong. One! He fell in love with a lesser shade, a great vampire warrior, and summoned you to protect her and her line. He realized your weakness and shrouded your purpose with myth and religious overtones, providing the necessary stipulation, which you loved. You leapt at the chance to have meaning—*to have a purpose!*—so you upheld the stipulation and protected her, as best you could, but eventually she was overthrown and destroyed.

"Weak of mind as you were, now without guidance or purpose, you chose to kill her assassin and then, instead of taking control of her empire yourselves you elected her successor and established the tradition which continues until today. The line of the Dark Lords. You move in the shadows as you've said, protecting me when it suits you, counseling me sometimes in important decisions but otherwise doing nothing but clinging to your ancient mythology. Now you hide behind that ancient stipulation so that you can sit back and *again* do nothing. You sicken me. How do you justify your actions?"

"We will not justify ourselves to you, Roche," said the second one, angry. "None of us were alive back then—we only carry on the traditions of our own predecessors, thank you. And that little stipulation that you sneer at is very dear to our purpose, our reason for being. It's even grown to eclipse our duties of protection."

"So I've noticed."

"You must *also* carry on the traditions … by appointing a successor."

"And the stipulation?"

"We cannot uphold it truthfully and let you live at the same time, not while you continue with your present course of action."

"Is that a threat?"

"No," said the first. "We have no desire to rule in your place or to kill you. For the love of dusk, Roche! You act as if we're not friends, as if we're hostile to you. Trust in us, please. We will try to uphold the stipulation in our own way."

"By blocking my advancements. By causing me to lose the war. Bastards!"

"It is the only way to let you live."

"I pity you." Sarnova lit a cigar. "I'm sorry for that, but you have no vision. You still cling to your purpose, and *it* is what eclipses everything else—not its technicalities, but its very existence. You would let it stand in the way of progress."

"It's our duty. Are you ready to discuss your successor?"

Later, when he was done, he gathered his cluster of guards and went off in search of Francois, whom he found in one of the living areas, watching the night through great glass panes. Drinking a glass of port, Francois turned at Sarnova's entrance.

"May I get you a drink?"

"Please," Roche said, sinking into a chair. He waited until he'd taken his first sip before he spoke again. "They're here."

"They?" Francois nodded. "*They.* What did they want?"

"To appoint my successor, naturally."

"Who'd they have in mind?"

Roche laughed. "My own Secretary of War, the little upstart."

"Damn it all."

The reaction was stronger than Roche had anticipated. "What is it?"

Mauchlery lowered himself into a chair. "There's a spy in our midst."

Dryly, Sarnova said, "One?"

"No, this is serious. It's why we've been losing so badly; the enemy knows when and where we're to attack. It's costing us several soldiers a day."

"And this spy. . ."

"Could well be the Secretary of War. It sounds awful, but there is a growing mound of evidence to support it."

"What do you suggest?"

"Take him off the assignment and lock him up until a deeper investigation can commence."

"Have it done." Sarnova leaned his head back in the chair. If he wasn't careful, he would fall asleep. "I'd love to see the look on their faces when they hear I've had my own successor imprisoned. It's almost worth going down there to tell them. Ah, but I'm so tired . . . Francois, are you as exhausted as I am?"

"I'm afraid so, Roche. The stress is terrible. But we must stay strong so that the others will take heart."

"Of course. Tell me, does the Scouring continue?"

"Indomitably."

"Great," Roche said, but he couldn't decide whether his voice sounded sarcastic or sincere. Well, it didn't matter. Francois would know.

Chapter 14

Harry Lavaca had intended to get drunk in peace, but it was not to happen. He slid the pistol with the silver bullets in it into his shoulder holster (it was only five in the afternoon and werewolves would be out) and walked down a few blocks to a local pub he sometimes frequented. Lots of oak and brass, bright colors, festive music, and a curtain of shiny beads hung behind the bar where the bartenders and bar-backs would occasionally duck into to snag something they were out of up front. Very pleasant, all and all, and Harry was feeling good by the time he'd gotten to the bottom of his first martini. He figured he'd be feeling *very* good after another three or four.

The gun dug into his ribs, and he shifted its weight. Maybe it was egotistical to think that he was being hunted at all times. *Maybe next time I'll leave it at home.*

Someone patted him on the shoulder. At first glance Harry thought the man was in his sixties, as he had lots of gray in his hair and mustache, and lines around his eyes. He had a deep weariness in him, but a fortitude as well. Harry looked closer. The man couldn't be more than fifty, he realized. Despite his fine suit and cufflinks, fear clung to him.

"My name is Martin Ascott. May I buy you a drink? I see you're almost out."

Harry rattled his glass. A bartender came.

"I'd like two martinis," Harry said. Then, to Ascott: "You?"

"I quit a long time ago. Please, may we take a booth? I've something very serious to discuss with you."

Harry waited for his drinks and then went with the man to the only corner booth available.

"You know me, but I don't know you," he said.

"I hope you won't get upset, but I've had you heavily researched," Ascott said. "I know you have dealings with the occult and that sort of thing. I know that you're acquainted with a, ah, vampire . . ." He stared at Harry for a long moment as if to gauge his reaction. Harry only sipped his martini. "Yes, well, you know a vampire named Danielle, don't you?"

Harry shrugged. "Not well. I know her boyfriend much better. If your game is to have her killed—sorry, Jack. I'm broke but not that broke. She's a nice girl, for a bloodmonger."

"Look." Ascott dropped his voice even further. "My name isn't really Ascott. I had it changed years ago."

"Keep talking."

"My real name is Malcolm Verger . . . "

Harry raised his eyebrows. Said nothing. *Can it really be?*

". . . and nineteen years ago I raped Danielle, mutilated her and left her for dead." He waited for Harry's reaction, but when Harry gave none he continued, somewhat apologetically: "I was very . . . evil . . . back then. I've changed. I nearly died of a heroin overdose ten years ago, and since then I've been clean. I changed my entire life . . . After the Gutter Angel killed a few of my old friends, her rapists, I knew she was saving me for last, so I moved, had plastic surgery, changed my name, but now I know it won't make any difference. Jason Locke, the last one she killed, also had his name changed, but she found him anyway. Don't you see, I'm the only one left. I'm next. I have a wife now. Two kids who depend on me."

"How did you make your money?"

"I made a good living in the drug trade, but then I got out of it and used the money to buy a chain of street-side food stands. I've got some money in stocks and bonds. I do okay."

"What do you want of me?"

"Protection. You must try to contact her, explain that I've become a decent person, try to persuade her . . . and you must come live with me so if she comes you'll be there. You could be just the thing that makes her spare me. You can have whatever you want, money unlimited."

Harry finished his second martini and started on his third. "Don't patronize me, Ascott. All the money in the world couldn't buy me if I didn't like the cause."

"But my kids, my wife . . ."

"Look, I'll come to your house, I'll see if you're the wonderful family man you claim to be, and if I like you I'll try to help. That's as far as it goes. No promises."

"Of course. You don't know how much this means to me. Come, I feel vulnerable out here in the open. What if I went into a public restroom and she was there, waiting for me?"

"Don't worry about it. She's out of town for the moment. That's not to say she couldn't sweep back in any time, but for now you're safe."

Ascott leaned back. "Thank you for telling me this. I can see that you're an honest man."

"Kiss my ass, you son of a bitch. You're a fucking piece of shit for what you did."

"I . . . I know."

Harry drummed his fingers on the table. "Do you have liquor at your house?"

"My wife drinks occasionally, yes."

"But not much. Well, we'll have to make a run by the liquor store. You're buying. All right, let's go." Harry set his empty glass down, starting to feel better. "Before we go over to your place, I need to pick up some things at my apartment, leave a note for visitors, that sort of thing." He moved towards the door. Ascott trailed behind. "Ah, but there's one thing I forgot."

"What's that?"

Harry belted him across the face. When Ascott didn't go down, Harry struck him again, then grabbed Ascott by the hair and slammed the sod's face down onto his knee. If Harry hadn't been tipsy, he was sure he'd have broken the bastard's nose.

"That's for … Danielle," he panted.

Hands dragged him away, and he put up no resistance. Ascott followed him outside, a hand over his face. The man said nothing. Together, they made their way back to Harry's apartment. When he opened the door, Harry immediately felt an uninvited presence.

A thin, black-haired woman with violet eyes lounged on his couch, smoking a Black Death cigarette in a cigarette holder. Harry instantly recognized her as an immortal and, thinking that she was a werewolf (the sun had just set— surely no other shade could be up and about at this time of night), he ripped out his gun.

"Silver bullets," he warned.

"La dee da." She rose. Several inches Harry's senior, she extended a hand, and he eyed it warily. "I'm Sophia."

He glanced at Ascott, who seemed hopelessly confused. Did the man realize he was looking at an immortal?

"Please, wait outside," Harry told him. Ascott obeyed, and Harry turned back to the woman. "Who are you?"

"Sophia, Veliswa's daughter, if you've heard of her."

"I know of her."

"Well, she came to me a few days ago in L.A., told me she and some friends needed my help. Understand, my mother's never asked anything of me before, so I was rather surprised. Having no pressing business in L.A., how could I refuse?"

"Get to the point."

"Please, lower the gun, Harry. Let's sit down and have a drink together. Have any Cristol?"

He chuckled but lowered the gun. "Afraid not, princess. How do you feel about a beer?"

"I'd feel great about a beer."

He fetched them each a drink. "You play chess?"

"Yes, but I'm not one to play games with inanimate objects. I prefer flesh and blood."

She meant it, too, he could tell. He slid into a chair near the couch, not too close to her. "So what is it you've come to see me about?" he said.

"I don't know him well, but the Vampire Ruegger is apparently very dear to my mother's heart, and he's in danger from Vistrot. I've come here to infiltrate Vistrot's organization and find out more about why Ruegger and Danielle are wanted dead."

"A charitable aim." Looking her up and down, he added, "Surely you didn't come here for purely unselfish motives."

"I think you misjudge me, Harry. Why must a self-assertive woman be seen as heartless?"

"Please."

She smiled. "I like to use people, Harry—bad people. It gives me satisfaction to see them squirm, and even more to destroy them. This situation gives me a chance to get close to Vistrot, a most worthy target. So, you see, I'm doing it for sport. To me, this will be like bringing down a lion among lions. You understand?"

"I suppose. But why won't he know what you're up to? Surely he'll investigate you and find out Veliswa's your mother. The jig will be up."

"I like you, Harry."

"My heart overflows."

"Now you're the one being cold. Can't we be friends?"

He sipped his beer. "Be sincere and maybe you'll grow on me."

"I'll try."

"Good. Now why won't Vistrot know you're Veliswa's daughter?"

"I was born ninety years ago in Paris, long before she moved to New York. She existed largely in the mortal societies back then and didn't want her friends to think she was just another silly girl getting pregnant out of wedlock, so she moved into the French countryside and raised me there until I was sixteen. Of course, I didn't look sixteen, because we ghensivs age slowly.

"When we moved back to Paris, Veliswa had been virtually forgotten. Of course, before she'd had me, she went by a different name. She changed it again when we moved back. No one knew she was the same woman. She hadn't aged a day; that's why she had to alter her identity, to avoid suspicion. Anyway, she pretended I was her niece— she didn't like the idea of people thinking she was a mother; not very sexy, she thought—and we lived there for a while until I hit puberty and matured more rapidly—at a human rate, you might say. That's why we moved back to the city when we did, so that I would blend in.

"She was eager to go to New York—she had a lover there—but I was just physically old enough to be accepted generally as a sexual being among the mortal society and I wanted to stay. Hell, it was Paris! I remained there while she moved to the Big Apple, where she's lived under various names ever since. After some time, I got the urge to move on, as well. I set out west to the new city of Las Vegas, then on to L.A."

Harry had finished his beer and moved to get another. "So what you're getting to is . . . "

"It was never admitted publicly that I was Veliswa's child, not even to other shades. Besides, we both changed names every few decades and back in those early years all our acquaintances were mortal, and none of them are around any more, so even if Vistrot tried to do a thorough check, he wouldn't find out that I was her daughter or even knew her. To the best of his knowledge, I appeared in Las Vegas out of nowhere. I have no history."

"Surely you and your mother kept in touch."

"Not very often. Every now and then she'd fly out to L.A., but what rich New York socialite doesn't fly out to L.A. once in a while?"

"There's something you're not telling me."

"If that's true, then I'm keeping it from you for a reason. Respect it."

He paced, then turned to her. "How do I fit into the picture?"

"Well, I'm going over to one of Vistrot's buildings tonight. I've already contacted his people and arranged a meeting. I'll need some outside help, some support in case something goes wrong, or at least a place to crash if I get discovered. Veliswa didn't want me to confide or accept help from any of her friends. They're good people, she says, but unreliable and terrible gossips. And none of them are particularly close to Ruegger or Danielle. She wanted me to get help from someone who knows them and likes them, would want to be of service, but still has good contacts. She said that Ruegger suggested you. Will you help?"

He stared up at the painting of Marcela, wondering if she would guide him through this. He was just ready to make a clean break from this wretched city. Did he really want to tempt fate by becoming involved in something as complex and sinister as this probably would turn out to be? His eyes settled on his Chess Table, to the board he and

Ruegger had been playing on last week. There was the toppled king where he hadn't bothered to re-set the board.

"I'll help," Harry said. "What can I do?"

"Not much, for now. You're supposed to find out who began the rumor that the Balaklava were chasing Ruegger and Danielle to the ends of the Earth—something like that, anyway—and, if you can, why Vistrot had that man of his killed not too long ago."

Harry called in Ascott, made him write down his number, address, and instructions on how to get to his house. When Harry handed the piece of paper to Sophia, she scanned it and looked up, smiling doubtfully.

"The Hamptons?"

Harry glanced at Ascott. "The Hamptons?"

Ascott seemed embarrassed. "This is New York. People like French fries."

"Right," Harry said. "Did I mention you're taking me to a liquor store?"

* * *

As Sophia was led to the lowest sub-level of Vistrot's building, she had to stop her jaw from hanging open. She'd never seen so many immortals in all her life. At last she was led into his office, and she could almost feel the suffocating weight of the entire building—all that concrete and steel—poised over her head. There was only one chair in the room and that was occupied, so she stood, forcing herself to remain calm.

Vistrot ran his eyes over her. Apparently liking what he saw, he gestured for her to step forward.

"So you're a ghensiv, is that right?"

"It's what I consider myself to be," she said.

"But from what I've determined, and I've had your past looked into, of course—you can walk about during the daytime?"

"Yes."

"How is that possible?"

"My father was a werewolf." She instantly regretted the comment, but Vistrot just nodded. Why *should* he be interested in who her parents were?

"Well, this is good," he said. "It gives you an advantage over other candidates for this function—and your cross-breeding might allow you access to other abilities as well. Can you shapeshift?"

"It does not come easily for me ... but yes."

"Excellent. How old are you?"

"Ninety-three."

He puffed on his cigar. "I suppose that's old enough, though it would be better if you were older. Ah, well. No one's perfect."

She said nothing, but she was wondering just what he was wanting of her.

He adopted a formal tone. "So: you want to join my organization?"

"Yes." The trick of this meeting, she felt, would be to come off as competent yet sensual. Despite Vistrot's bulk, it was not hard to find him attractive. "Do you have a position for me?"

He smiled. "So that's it, is it? Well, sorry, I'm taken, and I've done more damage there than I should've already."

She felt a flash of emotion, registering it as crestfallen, then rejected it instantly.

"You misinterpret my statement," she said.

"Did I?" He studied her for a long moment, evidently trying to size her up but failing. He shook his head. "So why do you wish to sign up?"

"The obvious reason. I mean no flattery, but you're the strongest shade in the world, save for Roche Sarnova, and I hear he's losing his war."

"So you wish to be on the A-team?"

"It's the only way to be."

He nodded cautiously. He seemed to be warming up to her, but couldn't quite get a grip on her. She would have to make an effort at being more readable.

"Have you ever killed someone you didn't need to feed on?" he said.

"Many times."

"Have you ever killed a shade?"

"Yes."

"Ever killed one that was not threatening you somehow?"

"No."

He steepled his fingers. "Look, I won't lie to you. I normally don't accept people into my fold who are just off the street, but there's something about you I find intriguing. Of course, you'll have to work your way up, just like anyone else, you understand."

"Naturally."

"First you must prove your loyalty to me by killing a shade."

"It's a reasonable request."

"It's more than that. It's an initiation; you need to earn my trust and respect. There is a complication—see, I haven't much time. I've reason to believe that my primary death-squad is falling apart, and I can't allow that to happen. I placed my own man in it when it was first banded together, but I have yet more reason to believe that he's trying to become independent and take the rest of the crew with him, save for its leader, a man named Jean-Pierre: the albino. You've heard of him?"

"Indeed."

"Well, Jean-Pierre is very dear to me. He's been doing jobs for me for sixty years or more, but he's having a bad time. His team was assigned to kill Ruegger and Danielle. The Marshals."

"Why do you want them dead, or may I ask?" God, could it be this easy?

"You may not. Jean-Pierre himself doesn't know, but that's none of your concern. Soldiers are not to reason why. Anyway, he's having trouble with the idea of killing Danielle—they had a fling once—and this is all the more reason why he needs to kill her. I need a mole in the team, to make sure they're doing things according to my wishes, and, like I've said, my current mole has designs of his own. I need to put someone else on the inside, someone new, someone fresh, to hold the crew together. Especially, you must be sympathetic to Jean-Pierre. That's another thing you've got going for you; you're attractive."

"It's served me on occasion. Are you saying I should sleep with this man?"

"No explicit instructions on that one, but be friendly. If you two have chemistry, that would be great. The important thing is to keep his mental condition primed. The team could break up, and while that would be a shame, I could easily put together another one provided I had the leadership of the albino to depend on. Now will you agree to be my inside man, or woman, as a test of loyalty, until the odd flock is hunted down? Then we can find a more appropriate position for you, unless, of course, you grow to like being on the team."

"I would accept the position with honor. In L.A., we hear that your death-squads are treated like rock stars."

He laughed. "There's some truth to that, but that's only because they do good work. Now, that's agreed." He wrote something down on a piece of paper and handed it to her. Their fingers almost touched. "That's the address you're expected to be at tomorrow at noon exactly. They're very punctual; don't be late. It's important for both of us that you make a good first impression. Don't act arrogant."

"Of course."

"Do you have a place to stay in town?"

"I'm at a little flea-bag motel right now. It'll do."

"I'll make arrangements for you somewhere nice. As you say, you'll be treated like a rock star . . . which makes me think of something . . . " He was silent a moment, then made a decision. "Cloire, one of the crew—their technical specialist—is the lead singer in a band. It's playing tonight at St. Lucifer's. It might be good for you to go there, ingratiate yourself with any member of the team that happens to be there before things really get into motion. Camaraderie is very important for the crew to function."

"I had no plans tonight."

"Good. Regarding your accommodations—I'll arrange a suitable place for you to stay on your return. For the present, you'll be out of town for awhile; Ruegger and Danielle are in Las Vegas, according to my sources. Another good reason for your presence on the team. So bring whatever you need to the meeting tomorrow. I don't know how long you'll be gone."

"Until Ruegger and Danielle are dead."

"Yes, you'll do," he said. "You'll do just fine."

Chapter 15

Byron sipped on a long-necked Corona and smoked a Camel as he watched the show from the second floor balcony, far removed from the mosh pit. Cloire was prancing around on stage, snarling and growling into the microphone while the band and the back-up singers provided atmosphere. The style of the band hovered somewhere between death-metal, punk and goth.

Vistrot had created the band for Cloire several years ago when she'd shown an interest in singing, and Peyote Dawn played several times a month here at St. Lucifer's, which Vistrot owned. After a while, she'd begun to draw in decent crowds and eventually became something of a success. The room tonight was crowded, the empty space near the ceiling filled with a blue thunderhead of cigarette smoke.

Lights flashed, music swelled and Cloire began to sing. She didn't have what one would call a pretty voice, but it was raucous and edgy, with a wide range and surprisingly filled with emotion. As Byron listened, he could feel the hairs stick up on the back of his neck. Pride surged through him.

I do love her, damn it. No matter what she said herself, he was convinced that on some level she felt the same. They'd lived together for years, and though she slept around every now and then just to prove she could, she was basically faithful to him.

He glanced at Kiernevar beside him, scowling deeply, dressed to the nines in a tailored suit. Byron was the one to look after him, and after her initial repulsion, Cloire had not complained, which was further proof to the Australian that she cared for him.

"What do you think?" he asked.

Kiernevar had made a little mental progress toward sanity. Apparently being cared for, talked to and restrained frequently for misbehavior was having some effect. A psychiatrist had even prescribed a drug, which he was to take three times a day.

Kiernevar looked alertly at Byron, then back at Cloire, but said nothing, and the Australian didn't press him.

Someone slid into the seat next to him: Loirot, smiling, in his typical Armani suit, which seemed incongruent amid the crowd, as did Kiernevar's. But with Kiernevar the suit was progress, while with Loirot it was simply irritating.

"So you decided to come?" Byron said.

Loirot shrugged. "How could I not? It's her release party, after all. I think even Jean-Pierre might show up."

"You talked to him?"

"Yeah, but—"

"How's he doing? He looked pretty bad last time I saw him."

"Not great, but better. He took losing Danielle for a second time pretty good, all things considered. That's not the big news."

"There's news?"

"Two things. First, Vistrot called Jean-Pierre and told him we're going back after the odd flock—they're in Vegas—and we leave tomorrow. Second, and more interesting—we're getting a new member to the team."

"You're kidding. Well, tell me about him."

"Her. Name's Sophia. They call her the Ice Queen. I don't know much about her, except she comes from L.A."

"Interesting. But why?"

"Who knows what goes on in Vistrot's head? Jean-Pierre said something about fresh blood, but he was vague. If you ask me, with the addition of Norman Bates over here the team is too large already."

"I'm inclined to agree, though I'd rather keep Kiernevar than Kilian."

"The same goes for me, of course. You know how I feel about that prick. But Kilian has a point, along with Cloire: Jean-Pierre may be losing it."

"Jean-Pierre," murmured Kiernevar.

The other two turned to look at him. Byron was thankful; it saved him from having to speak ill of the albino.

"Go on," he urged Kiernevar. "Tell us how you feel. Do you like Cloire's music?"

". . . no"

Byron tried to prod him with a few more questions, but Kiernevar remained silent.

"He may come round yet," said Loirot.

"He just needs time."

"Sure. Anyway, this new girl, Sophia, may be coming here tonight to meet us."

Byron sipped his beer, mulled it over, then decided to make it more entertaining. "Let's make a game of it."

"How?"

"Let's see . . . how about if one of us spots her before she comes over—say the first one to do it—gets a thousand bucks from the other." Money meant very little to them. There was so much of it to be had at their fingertips that even the smallest bet had to be substantial, just out of principle.

"I'm game," said Loirot.

They shook on it, then turned their attention to the show. Cloire was singing a ballad and the lights had dimmed. During the most emotional part of the song, her eyes fell on Byron and she winked. Byron nearly blushed.

It was Loirot who spotted Sophia first.

"Enter the dragon," he muttered.

Byron looked up and around, then caught sight of her. "Exit a grand."

Sophia entered, a small opened package in her hands, consulting a few pictures. She saw them and came over. She wore a sleek, glossy black outfit, zippered up the middle, with pants and sleeves, which only accentuated how long and graceful she was, and she walked in fashionable combat boots. Her black hair was tied back and her violet eyes nearly stabbed into Bryon they were so sharp. All and all, very interesting.

As she approached the table, Byron and Loirot stood.

"You must be Sophia," Byron said.

She smiled, seductive. "And you're Byron, and you're Loirot. Vistrot gave me pictures of all of you so I'd know who to approach and a little note—" (she held up the package, sat it down on the table) "—written by him, so you'd know I was legit." She stuck out her hand.

"What's this?" He looked at the hand and embraced her. Clearly, she was surprised. Loirot embraced her, too.

She put a hand to her face. "I wasn't expecting you to be so friendly. This is New York, after all. You've got a reputation to uphold."

"We're like a family," Loirot explained, and offered her a chair. "No matter how much we bicker."

"Thank you," she said, accepting.

The others resumed sitting, and Sophia ordered a daiquiri from a passing waiter, which was delivered promptly. Studying Kiernevar, she said, "Good evening."

"Kiernevar."

"That's his name," Byron told her, surprised again to feel a certain pride, this time for the lunatic; he'd actually introduced himself, in his way.

"Is he a member of the team? Vistrot didn't mention him or give me his picture."

"I'm sure he's trying to forget Kiernevar ever existed," Byron said. "He was our latest addition to the team until you came—we picked him up about a week ago."

"Actually, it was Jean-Pierre who picked him," said Loirot. "We still haven't figured out why."

"The albino tends to romanticize certain things," Byron said. "Insanity is one of them. Really, we don't know why he did it any more than you do, so don't feel uncomfortable about it."

"Thanks. So you're saying Kiernevar's . . ."

"I believe the scientific term is batshit."

She studied Kiernevar, who was looking back at her. "Are you okay, Kiernevar?"

"Kiernevar," he repeated. "Squish squash."

"Right. Well, it's refreshing to meet a nut who's taciturn; in my experience, it's usually the reverse." She watched the stage. "She's good."

"She'll be glad to hear you say it," Loirot said.

"Flattery is a child's game, though it has its uses."

She seemed suddenly cold to Byron. Then again, what had Loirot said: the Ice Queen?

"So, you're from L.A.," he said. "What do you do there?"

"This and that. Not much of anything, really. That's why I came here."

"We're delighted to have you," said Loirot.

She hunched over to sip her daiquiri and her outfit squeezed her breasts in a most titillating manner. Byron stirred despite himself.

"Come here alone?" Loirot asked.

"Don't know a soul."

"Now you do." His voice was husky.

"Thanks."

Loirot was evidently expecting something more, but Sophia held her ground.

"So what do you two do when you're not offing people?" she said.

If there was an insult there, neither of them recognized it.

"I don't know," Byron said. "Whatever it is, we usually end up hung-over afterwards."

She laughed again, a pleasant sound. She raised her glass. "Let's make a toast. To our future together."

They all clinked glasses and drank.

"Would you like to come to Cloire's big CD release party after the show?" Loirot asked her.

"I'd be honored," she said. "Can't wait to meet Cloire."

"You'll get your chance," Byron told her. "The show's almost over."

Loirot grinned. "Wait till she gets a load of you."

Apprehension filled Byron. Cloire might just go berserk at having a new member—especially another female—and kill Sophia, or the other way around. He wasn't looking forward to going backstage, and could feel the tension in his gut.

Jean-Pierre approached. Sophia rose to meet him. For some reason, it was odd, Byron thought, seeing them staring at each other, trying to take the other's measure.

"Welcome to the party," the albino said, and gave a little bow to her before sitting down.

"Glad to be here."

To Byron, he said, "Don't suppose Kilian's going to show up, do you?"

"I'll bet you a grand he doesn't," the Australian said.

Jean-Pierre smiled. "Another time." He summoned a waiter and ordered champagne, which was an odd thing to have at a rock club, but then Vistrot always had to add a personal touch. "We'll dedicate this round to Cloire."

Byron nodded, and the Frenchman winked.

"Good to have you back, Jean-Pierre."

"Good to be back," the albino said. He reached for Sophia's hand, which was creeping toward her box of cigarettes. He brought her hand to his lips and kissed it. "And with such lovely company."

Loirot and Byron exchanged glances, their thought unsaid: *On the rebound, poor bastard.*

Sophia did a strange thing. She took Jean-Pierre's hand to her own lips and kissed it. "The same to you."

Byron thought he might get to like Sophia and could tell from the expression on Jean-Pierre's face that the albino felt the same. The next few weeks could be very interesting.

The crew settled in to watch the last few minutes of Cloire's performance, which ended with a roar, then stood to clap. They finished their drinks and made their way into the chaotic backstage areas to find Cloire in a make-up room removing the skoal from around her eyes. A zip-lock bag of hallucinogenic mushrooms loomed on the counter near her elbow.

She swiveled at the crew's approach. Immediately her gaze went to Sophia. "Who's this?"

"Sophia, a new member to our group," said Jean-Pierre.

"Oh, fuck, whitey, not another of your strays."

"She came to us through Vistrot."

"Jesus fucking Christ, we could stand to lose a few members already. Well, she'll have to go through Initiation or I quit this team right fucking now. We still haven't initiated this bloody bastard," she said, hiking a thumb at Kiernevar.

"Oh, she'll be initiated, don't worry. Now be civil, Cloire."

"Bite me, Jean-Pierre." To Sophia, she said, "So you're Vistrot's new mole."

"That's right, sister," said Sophia. Her stance widened, preparing for battle.

Cloire stepped back a foot, crouching a little as if she were about to lunge.

Sophia smiled. "Shall we piss for distance now?"

Cloire glared at her, then swept her gaze over the others. Suddenly, Cloire exploded in laughter, stepped forward and embraced Sophia roughly.

"Nice to see another cunt around here. Shit, can't wait till we get down to some good ol' fashioned girl-talk for a change. We'll do each other's fucking hair. Just don't make eyes at Byron here—he's mine." She patted Sophia on the back, then indicated her bag of shrooms. "You trip, Sofe?"

"I'm from L.A."

The crew ate the mushrooms there, then went back to the apartment that Byron and Cloire shared, where many revelers had already arrived—all friends and associates of Peyote Dawn. After an hour the hallucinogens began to kick in, and Sophia lived up to Byron's expectations as a hard-living, hard-drinking shade, blending right in. Cloire even invited her to spend the night—they'd pick up her clothes and stuff tomorrow on their way out of town—and she agreed.

Around four in the morning, Byron began to come down, so he and Cloire smoked a couple of joints, took some Valium and retired to their bedroom. Before climbing into bed, she picked up the phone and called someone.

"Martin Ascott," she repeated, writing it down, "Hamptons, huh? Okay, I've got it. Nice job tracking him down. I'll put your money in the mail tomorrow."

"What was that all about?" Byron said when she'd hung up.

"Nothing, just some insurance," Cloire said. "Just in case . . . "

He patted the bed beside him and she scooted beneath the sheets. As he reached over her to switch off the lamp, he whispered "I love you" in her ear, but she was breathing heavily, eyes closed. He sighed, kissed her forehead and turned out the light.

*　　*　　*

Sophia woke up on the couch around ten in the morning to the smell of eggs frying. And something else, something horrible, underneath. She rubbed her eyes, lit a cigarette, and moved to the kitchen, where Byron made breakfast.

"You like omelets?" he said.

"Nothing better. Where's Cloire?"

"Shower. She doesn't eat breakfast."

"Right. Any beer left?"

"Help yourself."

Ignoring the stench, she rooted around in the refrigerator and came up with a Shiner Bock. This was all so weird to her, this easy camaraderie, and she wasn't sure her acting talents were up to it. She was a loner, happiest in seclusion, but for the purposes of the assignment she had to be friendly.

The assignment itself was nothing like she'd hoped—there would be no grand seduction of Vistrot, no cloak-and-dagger intrigue—and the only reason she'd agreed to it was because of the direct involvement with Ruegger and Danielle. Maybe, if she couldn't find out why they were being hunted, she could thwart the hunt itself. At any rate, she'd come too far to go back now.

Maybe she could turn her seductress impulses in the direction of Jean-Pierre, who was friendly with Vistrot. He could provide the access she needed, but the thought of sleeping with the albino turned her cold.

If that was the only way. . .

She and Byron breakfasted together, and she made an effort to return the light conversation that he put forward. Really, he was what she would call a nice guy, if in a bearish sort of way. Strange that he should be an assassin. And stranger still that he would be involved with someone like Cloire, who was not what Sophia would call nice by any standards.

Cloire ambled in, dressed in a bathrobe with a towel about her head, sat down next to Byron and lit a cigarette.

"Nothing better than a post-shower smoke."

"Enjoy your omelet?" Byron asked Sophia.

"Super." Something stunk, she thought. Something really fucking stunk.

"Well, I try." He smiled and glanced up suddenly at a just-arriving Kiernevar, naked and covered in his own feces.

"Oh, for God's sakes," protested Cloire. "Byron, you idiot, you forgot to give him his pills, didn't you?"

"I guess I must have. Sorry." He turned to Sophia, who'd managed to keep her composure, and shrugged. "He does this sometimes, part of his insanity, I guess . . . I'm sorry if it offends you."

"I've seen worse," she assured him.

"Well, go wash the bastard off and give him his bleeding pill," said Cloire, and Byron disappeared with Kiernevar. "So, Sofe, how does all this strike you?"

"You mean Kiernevar?"

"Everything."

Sophia smiled. "I can't wait to hit Vegas."

"That's my girl. All quite a switch from L.A., I imagine."

They talked for a few minutes about the differences between L.A. and New York before Byron and a very clean Kiernevar reappeared.

The big Australian glanced at his watch. "Time to go, ladies."

They set out for Sophia's motel so that she could collect what belongings she wanted to bring with her to Vegas, then started towards Jean-Pierre's apartment for the noon meeting.

"Like his digs?" Cloire asked Sophia as they walked down the main hall.

"What happened here?" Sophia noted the trails of blood and injured vagrants.

Cloire laughed. "Jean-Pierre kidnapped Danielle and took her here, devil knows why. He wanted her to come back to him, I guess, but she didn't fall for it. See all these homeless bastards? Well, the albino's a powerful psychic and he can control all these wretches if he wants to. He couldn't kill dear Danielle himself, of course, so he sicced his little friends on her. Luckily for her, Ruegger came along and played hero. Fucking *pendejo*." She stuck a finger down her throat and made gagging sounds. "It was a stupid thing for Jean-Pierre to do; we could've killed 'em and been done with it, but no. To tell you the truth, I'm not sure that whitey's got it in him to kill her. Fucking schmuck. I guess that's why you're here."

"At least we get a paid vacation out of it."

"Yeah, I guess." She seemed to be considering something and glanced at Byron, who watched her worriedly. This only made her smile broader.

"I missing something?" Sophia said.

"Don't, Cloire," Byron warned, but Cloire just laughed.

She hesitated, then seemed to decide to go ahead and say it: "You want this team to be efficient, don't you,

Sophe? After all, you've got to report to Vistrot, so you have a stake in the team doing well, right?"

"I guess."

"So if the team was inefficient, you'd want to repair it?" Sophia could see it in her face. "You mean removing Jean-Pierre."

"Stop it!" said Byron.

Cloire patted his hand. "Don't worry, lover. I'm only thinking about the well-being of the crew."

"Well-being, my ass. I thought we'd all agreed to give him a second chance. Doesn't he deserve that much?"

"If that's what it takes to convince you. But will you come with me—break with him—if he fucks up again?" She paused, then seized on something. "Do you love him more than you love me?"

"What are you talking about? I just feel loyalty to him, and I love you only as much as you love me."

She grabbed his hand. "I *know*."

He looked at her, and his face was agony. "Are you saying that . . . ?" He shook his head. "Because if you're saying that—if you really mean it—then yeah, I'll break with him, if it comes to that."

She pulled him down and kissed him. "Then it's decided."

"I don't understand," said Sophia.

"Don't worry about it, Sofe," Cloire said. "There's no way you can make up your mind until you've seen us in action . . . until you've seen the fucking albino refuse to open the emergency coffin of the odd flock until nightfall so that he could keep his precious Danielle alive that much longer. Just keep your eyes open. Observe everything."

"Roger."

"And don't comment on Jean-Pierre's apartment. You know what they say about how only a fool would be his own attorney—well, the same thing applies to Jean-Pierre and interior decorating."

The quartet made its way upstairs to the boss's lair and Sophia saw what Cloire had been talking about. All those hooks and chains and sharp protrusions . . .

Jean-Pierre waited in an uncomfortable chair in the living room while Loirot paced restlessly.

"Kilian!" the albino shouted and a small, dour man in a nice suit stepped inside from his position on the fire escape. "This is Sophia. Sophia, Kilian."

Sophia kept her face impassive as she studied Kilian, and, as he watched her, he began to scowl.

"So this is my replacement?"

"I'm not a replacement for anyone," she said, "but piss me off and you'll need one."

He raised a hand to slap her. She brought a knee up to his groin faster than he could respond and, when he doubled over, struck him on the side of the head. He tumbled to the floor. She kicked him once in the stomach and then pressed her foot down on his chest.

"This settled?" she said.

"You've gotta love her, don't you?" Cloire said.

"Okay, Sophia, you've made your point," Jean-Pierre said. "Now cool down, both of you."

Sophia lifted her foot and stepped back, while Kilian stood and brushed himself off.

"She'll have to go through Initiation," he demanded.

"Of course," said Jean-Pierre. "In fact, I have a treat for all of us. You see, it seems lately that loyalty's become something of an issue—"

Cloire groaned. "Oh, come off it, Frenchie. You're not suggesting we all go through Initiation again."

"That's it, exactly, only it's not a suggestion. We're doing it, like it or not."

"I think it's a good idea," said Byron.

"Thank you. Any other objections?"

"This is ridiculous," said Kilian.

Sophia cleared her throat. "Excuse me, but what is this Initiation exactly?"

The albino nodded to Loirot. "Explain."

Loirot sighed. "When we all banded together originally, we decided to share a bonding experience together. Basically, what it entails is this: we light some candles and some incense, draw some chalk patterns on the floor, drop some acid, meditate for awhile, then strip naked and drink each other's blood—everyone drinks from everyone else and allows him or herself to be drunk from, so that we all become intimate and share in each other's power—and we have an orgy. After that, we go for four solid days without feeding and at the end of those four days we all go hunting together, then share each other's blood again. Have I missed anything?"

"I think that about covers it," Jean-Pierre said.

"But why do you light the candles and the incense?" Sophia asked. "I thought we were all atheists here."

Jean-Pierre answered: "We're not praying to any divinities but to the natural forces and rhythms of the world, if there are any, to unify us and bond our life energies. It's really something we should start doing every year."

"It sounds like a bunch of mystical bullshit to me."

"Perhaps it is, to an extent, but it's the psychology of it all that counts. When we do it, we all become one with each other." He looked at Cloire. "It's very emotional, isn't it?"

"Fuck you, Paleface. You were in tears, too, if I remember. Weren't we all? Don't you dare single me out because I'm a woman. If that's what you think, then kiss my ass."

Kilian puckered his lips. She flew at him, but Jean-Pierre leapt from his chair and held her back. She wrenched herself free, breathing heavily, but made no more move toward Kilian.

Jean-Pierre lit a Pall Mall, looking each of his crew in the eye. Sophia was beginning to see why Vistrot considered him to be such a valued leader. He sucked a hit off the cigarette and smiled affectionately at everyone.

"This is exactly why we need to do this," he said. "Do you understand now?" He stared at Cloire pointedly, saw her sneer start to fade, went over, patted her on the shoulder and kissed her forehead. To Sophia's surprise, Cloire didn't pull away, though she became very stiff. Then he went over to Kilian and did the same. Grabbing Kilian's arm, he led the daydog over to Cloire and made them embrace. After their initial reluctance, they did, though it was a very brief contact.

"Now," said Jean-Pierre, "are you all with me . . . and, just as importantly, are you with each other?"

Byron nodded. The others followed his lead.

"Good, now let's all start setting up the candles."

They were shown several boxes, which held the necessary components to the ritual, and began arranging the ceremonial space. Jean-Pierre threw the blackout curtains over the windows so that they could feed during daytime, and Loirot broke out the LSD. After taking off their clothes, they all sat in the center of the chalk-and-candle pattern and dropped the acid. There were some nervous smiles from the group and Sophia could feel an excitement spreading up from her stomach and groin. They looked at each other pleasantly and reached for each other's hands. Then, feeling the presence and warmth of everyone else, they closed their eyes and began.

Chapter 16

"He's dead," the bartender said. "I'm sorry, but Hauswell's dead."

Ruegger glanced at Danielle, whose face was sober. They had been inquiring all over Las Vegas for Hauswell, and everyone had the same story. An assassin had murdered the city's most powerful resident.

"He can't be," Ruegger said. "The man hired to kill him is dead."

The bartender—a werewolf; this was an immortal dive, one of many—only shrugged. "Sorry, but they must've gotten another hired gun to do the deed."

Ruegger narrowed his eyes. "Where's the body?"

"Laslo's."

Ruegger looked away. It was the same answer he'd received before.

Danielle drew him away. "You're not going to get anything more out of that guy."

"But we killed Greggs."

She grimaced. "I don't know, babe."

"We've got to find out if Hauswell's really dead. I couldn't stand it if he was . . . I always wanted to return the favor, I guess."

"You've never really told me what happened between you. Were you and Hauswell . . . lovers?"

He smiled. "No. He saved my soul, maybe. At the very least, he saved me from myself."

"You mean, when you were evil, or whatever."

"There's no whatever about it, Dani. I don't believe in 'evil', but I was as bad as you can get. Hauswell pulled me out of it. Anyway, so we see if Laslo's really got his body and we go from there."

"Where's Laslo?"

"About seventy miles outside of town at a little private airfield Hauswell owns . . . or used to. But I warn you now, Laslo's elevator—the one that doesn't go all the way to the top in some people—it's in the basement, and if he thinks Hauswell's dead, he's probably gone completely insane; Hauswell saved his life about a hundred years ago and ever since Laslo's had an unhealthy fixation on him."

"That what you mean by insane?"

"No, you'll have to meet him to see what I mean. Seems God and the angels have a personal relationship with Laslo and he talks to them often—he frequently dresses like a priest and Hauswell humored him by building him a rather unusual mission. You'll see."

Somewhat nervously, she ran a finger across the thin silver adornments that pierced her left ear. "You can tell me, you know. I mean, about what happened, when you were . . . bad."

He stared at her for a long while. At last he shook his head.

"Some other time," he said.

She frowned.

* * *

When the sun set, they packed their bags and checked out of their hotel. Their new vehicle was a VW mini-bus with psychedelic flowers and peace signs painted on the outside and Mardi Gras beads hanging from the rearview mirror. A plastic Elvis jutted from the dashboard and a profusion of glow-in-the dark stars stared down from the ceiling, walls and floor of the rear interior, creating a small but brilliant universe when illuminated by blacklight—which they were.

Ruegger and Danielle tossed in their two suitcases and she climbed behind the wheel. She started the automobile with a dusty roar and headed east toward the desert that surrounded Las Vegas. Once clear of the city, Ruegger lit a cigarette, propped his feet up on the dashboard and turned on the radio; Aerosmith was singing "Sweet Emotion".

"So tell me about Laslo," she said. "Like what kind of shade is he?"

"A very rare one, what they call a *chalgid.*"

"Never heard of them."

"They've got the power to resurrect the dead. In fact, whatever force created them made it imperative that they *do* resurrect the dead. They're a kind of vampire, really; they need human blood to live, but this blood must first be passed through a corpse."

She made a face.

"Here's how it works," he said. "The chalgid resurrects a dead person by giving the dead one some of its blood, then the zombie—or whatever you want to call it—feeds off a human and goes back to its maker so that the chalgid drinks from its zombie."

"That's disgusting."

"The chalgid usually makes several zombies to carry out its needs. The more of its blood it gives to the zombies, the stronger they are; in fact, if the chalgid gives a zombie enough blood the zombie can become a chalgid itself. But this means the zombie then becomes powerful enough to be a threat to its maker, so this rarely happens. And if the chalgid doesn't give its zombies enough blood, they continue to decompose. Ideally, it gives the zombies just enough blood, every now and then, to erase the more visible effects of death and keep them from decomposing altogether. I should mention that the chalgid has a strong psychic connection to his minions and can even control them sometimes, unless the zombies have got enough of their master's blood to make them powerful enough to resist its mindpull. At any rate, the chalgid usually uses enough of its powers to instill a certain loyalty in its undead subjects."

"So how many zombies does Laslo keep?"

"Last time I saw him, which was about twenty-five years ago, he had four at his disposal."

"How strong could they be? I mean, if Laslo turned out to be unfriendly, could they hurt us?"

"Probably. One advantage they've got is the zombies aren't afraid of the sun, even though their master is. Typically they go and gather blood during daytime and return at night to feed him."

She thought about it. "So how do they get the blood? After all, they're in the middle of the desert."

He shrugged. "Hitchhikers and passers-through, I guess. Or they go to a neighboring town."

"How do you kill them?"

"Destroy their brain and you destroy their immediate psychic connection with their master. He can resurrect and restore them later, but it takes them out for the time being."

"Are they ... discriminate about who they feed from?"

"You mean, are they worthy of a visit from the Marshals?"

"Well?"

He frowned. "It would be a bad idea to kill someone we're trying to get information out of."

"Didn't stop you with Greggs."

He paused. "First let's see how bad they are. We can plan on delivering justice later."

"Fine. So how did Laslo come to be at this airport of Hauswell's, and why'd Hauswell build one out here in the first place?"

"Back in the fifties he built it for commercial purposes, so he'd have a place that he could import his drugs to directly. Never made much money on it, though; overhead was too high. And once the police caught wind of it, they gave him hell. Other mob bosses bribed them more than Hauswell could compete with; this was before he grew as powerful as he is today. Or was. Then, in the late sixties, a rival boss sent some of his thugs to torch the place. Burned most of the buildings and planted explosives along the runway. The airport's personnel made their final stand in the hangar and were able to hold out until the thugs were gone.

"Hauswell decided it wasn't worth it to keep the airport running in the same capacity it had been, so he dismissed the staff and rebuilt the runway so he could keep the airport running, if only on a private, non-commercial basis. He loves to fly around the world, you know. I remember he was always so excited whenever a new model plane came on the scene. He kept his personal jets there. And it was a perfect place to stick Laslo. Hauswell wanted Laslo to move out here with his zombies, but Laslo wouldn't have it because he said it was ungodly.

"So, when he got rich enough, Hauswell built a new hangar—a large one and out of stone this time. Built a three-story church on top of it. Made the church to look like a mission, out of stone like the hangar, with a bell tower, too. Spent hundreds of thousands of dollars setting it up just right so the mission would have enough support not to fall down on top of the hangar. It amused Hauswell to have God watching over his planes. He maintained the place as a private airport and Laslo's stayed there ever since. There's even a little cemetery out back full of mortals and immortals who've died in Hauswell's service and Laslo tends to it on occasion. That's where he gets his zombies if he needs a new one."

"Money can buy anything, can't it?" she said. "And Hauswell's an eccentric bastard."

"He's nothing compared to Laslo."

"Can't wait to meet him. So you really think Hauswell might have some useful information if he's still alive?"

"According to Greggs, yes. Hauswell was investigating the Scouring before he vanished, remember. Something about a mysterious third party trying to figure out how powerful he was, something like that. By now he's bound to have tracked that person down. He may know more, too. He may know the secret behind it all. Anyway, it's the only move we've got so far. If Hauswell *doesn't* know anything I was thinking ..."

"Yes?"

"We could ask Kharker. No one knows more about immortal affairs than he does."

She looked sideways at him. "You still love him, don't you?"

He sighed and lit another cigarette. "I know he kills innocents, but does that really make him, in your terms, evil?"

"Yes." Her voice was ice.

* * *

About forty minutes later they saw a hitchhiker just up the road, and Danielle said, "What do you think?"

"Pick him up and if he pulls a knife or a gun on us we have a sip."

They were both starving for blood.

"I concur."

They pulled to the side of the road, and the hitchhiker approached. Carrying a cheap-looking bottle of whisky in one hand, dirty long brown hair fell down his back, a ratty biker's jacket hung over an indescribably dirty shirt, and skin-tight black pants stretched down to his boots. As he approached, his face became more visible; his eyes were quite red and there was something gangrenous about his features. He flashed a peace sign and threw open the rear door before climbing in. Ruegger wrinkled his nose at the stench.

"Where to, mates?" the man said.

Ruegger spun around just in time to see him draw out a blade from his waistband. Ruegger shot him twice in the chest. The noise startled Danielle, who jumped in shock. The man looked down at his wounds, swore and took a big gulp of his whiskey.

"Danielle," Ruegger said casually, "meet one of Laslo's zombies."

The man winked at Danielle out of a blood-shot eye. "I prefer the term bloodfinder, m'self." To Ruegger: "How'd you know, mate—I mean before ye shot me?"

"I've smelled a lot of corpses in my day, son, and I could smell you a mile off. What's your name?"

"Tommy O'Connel. And forgive the stench, friends— Laslo ain't got any runnin' water at that friggin' place, not t'mention me own frailments. Is that where you two fine an' upstanding citizens're headin'?"

"Afraid so, Tommy," said Danielle.

He returned the blade to his waistband and made an effort to straighten himself up. He offered his bottle to Ruegger, but Ruegger declined.

"How do you come to know Lord Laslo?" Tommy inquired.

"From Hauswell."

"Oh, I've met him. On several occasions when the good man stopped by to say hi t'Laslo. He used to be m'boss, you know."

"Is that a fact?"

"Yes, indeed, my good sir."

"Have you seen him lately?"

"Oh, sure, sure. Got his corpse in the hangar."

Ruegger's heart sank.

Danielle saved the moment. "If you've got Hauswell's corpse, why not resurrect him?"

"Ah, simple. See, the sick sods who killed 'im took 'is head—for a trophy, I guess. Can't resurrect no one without a head, unless you're doin' it for amusement. Laslo's done it before, I've watched 'im. They corpses just flop around like dyin' fishes an' sometimes 'e c'n get'em to walk and stuff, though I 'spect that's just some of them ol' spoonbender techniques the Lord's got. Not my kind of man, the Lord, but 'e treats me well enough. Guess yer sundogs or somethin', right?"

"Something," Ruegger said sadly—he'd heard the rumor about Hauswell's decapitation before but had forced himself not to believe it—feeling Danielle's hand on his own. "I'll take some of that whiskey now."

Tommy handed it over. "Want I should give you directions to Laslo's?"

Ruegger fell back in his chair and stared blankly forward as the self-styled bloodfinder guided Danielle to Laslo's mission. He just couldn't believe Hauswell was really dead. So many things left unsaid, so many debts left unpaid, and at the end they weren't much more than casual acquaintances . . . *I should've tried harder*, thought Ruegger. *I should've tried much, much harder. All the time in the world and it's still left incomplete* . . . He took a swig from the bottle and swore under his breath.

At Tommy's direction, Danielle turned the mini-bus onto a poorly-maintained private road, pausing while Tommy pushed open the gate, then wound her way up to what was left of the airfield. There was the twisted maze of runways stretching off to the left, where the ruins of many buildings lay wasted, and off to the right, incongruously large and tall among all the bleak flatness, rose the stone hangar and the three-story mission on top of it. Or, more properly, part of it. It was one great big stone nightmare, complete with ominous tower.

The bell tower soared like a battlement in the center of the mission's roof, which was unusual; in most cases, the bell tower was located in a corner of the mission, whereas this one seemed to run through the center of the building itself. Ruegger could see that the roof of the bell tower had been torn off and the bell itself was missing. Most strange of all, stairs made of scaffolding material led up to the top of the tower from the roof of the mission and, where the roof of the bell tower used to be, a type of fragile wooden platform, almost like a diving board, stuck out, as if someone were about to jump into the well itself. Very curious.

"What's all that?" Danielle asked Tommy, seeing it too.

"Not s'pose to say, lassy. Sorry an' all, but me mouth is closed."

Climbing out, Ruegger noticed that all the windows of the hangar had been boarded up and the hangar door (the only thing not made of stone on the exterior of the building) was sealed.

"I need to go in the hangar," Ruegger said. "I need to see Hauswell's body."

"'fraid not, mate. No outsiders're allowed inside. Been closed up like that for nigh on twenty years. Hauswell'd taken to using the old hangar 'fore he got whacked."

"Then I want to see Laslo."

"Sorry there, again, pal o' mine, but yer uninvited guests an' the Lord'll come to see ya when 'e chooses. Nothin' I c'n do about it."

Ruegger felt himself grow cold. There was something very strange about this place, something haunted. He hoped they could just find Hauswell's corpse and get the hell out of here. Something bad was going to happen in this place.

"So what now?" Danielle said. "We sleep in the bus till Laslo decides to say hi?"

"Nonsense," said Tommy. "I'll show ya both to a room in the mission . . . Yer married, ain't ye?"

"Yeah, sure."

"Don't see no weddin' rings on yer fingers. Best not have relations while ya stay here or Laslo won't like it, an' you wanna get on the Lord's good side, trust me. I've seen folks who've learnt the hard way an' it ain't purtty, on that ya c'n be most certain." He hitched a thumb toward the mini-bus. "Best get yer bags. I ain't no bell-boy. You might be stayin' awhile."

Ruegger and Danielle glanced uneasily at each other and retrieved their two suitcases. He could see that Danielle was getting spooked and didn't blame her.

"Where are the other bloodfinders?" he asked.

"Oh, don't worry, mate . . . they're around. Follow me, if you'd be so kind."

Tommy ushered the vampires to the far side of the monolith, to a stone staircase that snaked up into the mission's vestibule on the first floor above the hangar. Once inside, Ruegger found it to be a narrow, angular room devoid of warmth.

"Wanna visit the chapel?" Tommy asked. "Have a chance to wash yerselves of yer sins? Laslo doesn't like the sin and that's a fact. Best to burn it off now 'fore 'e does, and this is m'good nature speakin' to ya."

"No, thanks," said Ruegger. "Just show us our room."

"You ain't atheists, is ya? The Lord doesn't like the ungodly ones." He yanked up his T-shirt to reveal a rotted torso marred by countless giant welts in cruciform shape: burn marks left by a brand. "I was without God once 'fore

Laslo showed me th'true an' righteous path. God is with that one, He is, and the angels sit on 'is shoulder."

"I'm sure they do. Where's that room?"

Tommy showed them past a large dining hall with stained-glass windows, down a series of corridors until they reached a staircase, which they took to the second floor, then down a narrow hall. Finally Tommy opened a dirty wooden door, which creaked as it swung wide.

"This'll be yer room, lass, an' the one down there'll be the mister's."

"Separate rooms?" she said.

"To ensure that this place remains without sin, y'understand. 'course, if ye were interested, Laslo could marry ye both in holy union an' you could carry out God's good work in the bedroom at yer leisure. I've seen 'im marry before, I have—burns the sin outta the newlyweds before they c'n be joined with God's blessin'. Beautiful, just beautiful."

"Thanks, but no," Ruegger said. He was becoming used to the strange, frenzied stillness of the place, but there was some sound, just under the silence, some horrible noise like screaming . . .

"Now, if that'll be all, I'll be off." Tommy crept back the way he'd come.

Danielle laughed nervously, then whispered, "I think we should just get the fuck out of here, Rueg, Hauswell or no Hauswell. You with me?"

Ruegger lit a cigarette, took her hand and led her into the room, which was small and sparse, a narrow bed there, a cramped desk here, and the only window shattered; the fragments left gleamed of stained glass. Above it hung a large iron shutter—open now—to block out the sun.

"We've got to find out if Hauswell's really dead. If he's not, we need to know what he found out. Either that or Liberty takes over the world."

"Baby, I want to get the hell away from here. Whatever we find out from Hauswell can't be worth what's going to happen here."

"Nothing's going to happen." He moved to the window and saw the cemetery not too far away, but there was something strange about it. The air outside blew suddenly cold, and dark clouds massed above.

"Looks like the storm's followed us," he said.

"Raining?"

"About to." He turned to look at her. "What?" She was staring at him strangely.

She bit her lip, then let out a breath.

"Nothing," she said.

*   *   *

Rain drummed against the windows. Danielle fidgeted. They'd been waiting for too long. A sudden impulse grabbed her. "Ruegger," she said.

"What is it?" he said, sounding wary.

She sucked up her courage. "Your story," she said.

"My what?"

"Your past. I want to know. I *demand* to know."

"Danielle, please. Now isn't the time—"

"It never is. It never *will* be." Fuming, she said, "Now is the *perfect* time. We're waiting on Laslo, we've got nothing better to do, we're in a spooky fucking castle and there's a storm. What better atmosphere could you want?"

He stared at her.

"I . . . don't know," he said.

She lit a cigarette, rebellious. "Start talking," she said.

"But . . . I—"

"I said start talking."

He blinked. He looked away in thought for a long moment, seeming to wrestle with something, then nodded. "You've waited long enough."

She almost melted, but made herself be tough. "I have."

"Where ... where should I begin?"

Finally. "At the beginning."

And, wonderingly, he began.

Chapter 17

Ruegger's family had moved to Vienna from Germany when he was ten. It was a large family, and he was the youngest of six children; as such, he'd pretty much raised himself, his parents cold and distant to him, having exhausted their supply of tenderness on the offspring who'd come before. Ruegger's father Henri had brought his parents with him from Germany, and they were harsher and more parochial than Henri himself, who was in every fiber a tyrant. In all fairness, he was considered a rebel by having married a Spaniard.

The family lived in the most upscale and conservative pocket of town they could find. They were aristocrats from old. Their estate was large and sprawling, complete with the catacombs of the family that had lived there before. In many ways, Vienna didn't suit them; its free-spirited and artistic ways offended them, so they mingled mostly with the moderately-politicked gentry of the area.

When Henri told his youngest son he was to be sent to boarding school, the young Ruegger disagreed. Henri would not be denied. Once in boarding school, Ruegger had tried to burn it down. His protest was duly noted by the school authorities on his way through the expulsion process.

Following, his family hired a private tutor for the boy, a governess. He liked her. In fact, he enjoyed learning in general, but he couldn't force himself to be idle. Wanderlust held him rapt at an early age. He ran away frequently, learning criminal behavior from friends on the street, but soon discovered a society of artists who accepted him and the good name his family brought.

By this time, his family had given up and all but cast him out. He didn't care. No love was lost between the Rueggers and their youngest son. The artists taught him poetry and literature, and it was in their company that he began writing. Under their tutelage, he also learned how to play chess, and he became well-known for his skill at the game. Only later did he come to see most of the artists as shallow and pretentious. They were disappointed when his family cut him off. Since the Ruegger family money solved a lot of their problems, they made their displeasure with the young poet abundantly clear.

One big exception proved to be Maria, a sincere poet with some talent. Seventeen when he met her, Ruegger fell in love from the start. She was an eighteen-year-old Spanish refugee, whose family had fled from the authorities in their home country after her father had killed a wealthy merchant for political reasons. The irony didn't escape Ruegger that, like his father, he'd fallen for a Spaniard.

Her intertwined innocence and cynicism attracted Ruegger. It hurt nothing that she was also voluptuous, with oily black hair and almond eyes. He couldn't understand what she saw in him, but she did. As they began courting, Ruegger's family became enraged at the low breeding of Maria's heritage and her family's lack of material assets, and they threatened to disown him. He invited them to do so.

Maria and Ruegger fell deeply in love, and eventually he asked her to marry him; she accepted. By this time, Ruegger was living almost exclusively among the poets in town—had rented a flat himself, in fact, and had very little contact with members of his family. The situation suited him fine, and Maria didn't seem at all disappointed that they wouldn't have the benefit of his family's money. Indeed, she was delighted at the romantic notion that she and Ruegger would have to make it together all on their own.

For awhile, they did. He honed his skill in vaudeville acts, always hoping to publish something, while she became an excellent professional dish-washer.

Their happiness didn't last. Perhaps due to all their romantic midnight cavortings, which had exposed them to rain more than once, Maria caught pneumonia and became desperately ill. Her family had no money for a doctor, and Ruegger's family refused aid—a fact which he would remember later.

He knelt by her deathbed day and night, tending on her every need, but to no avail. Winter had come, and though it was the kindest one in recent years, the cold was too much for her and she faded away, turning frail and skeletal, her dark skin now pale. Finally death claimed her, and Ruegger nearly died with her.

Some would say this was the beginning of his insanity.

He dressed her body in her nicest dress, stole a suit for himself along with a pair of tarnished silver rings, and slipped these on their wedding fingers so that they could be married in death if nothing else. He gathered her in his arms and crept onto his family's estate during the night, delving deep into the catacombs, where he walled Maria and himself up in a tiny chamber, with hardly air enough to breathe. Air which soon become unhealthy and fetid.

He stayed there with Maria, waiting for death, for three days and four nights before his family discovered the new brickwork and unearthed him.

Most said he'd probably gone insane during his days in the tomb, but the ones who spent the most time with him felt it was only after his release that madness took hold. Whichever, he was clearly sick, walking around his room talking to himself, throwing occasional violent fits and cutting himself with anything he could get his hands on. He blamed his family for Maria's death and vowed revenge. They sent him to an insane asylum, where he stayed for seven very unpleasant months before he found a way to escape.

Armed with thoughts of avenging Maria's death, he returned to his family's estate. Before giving in to his desire for vengeance, he kept the presence of mind to steal as much money and clothes as he could carry. Then he set fire to the house and ran off into the night.

He never found out if anyone had been harmed in the fire, but they had killed Maria through their own prejudices and he felt that they deserved whatever they got. Being raped and beaten and starved in the insane asylum didn't ease his feelings toward them. May their souls burn as bright as their house, he remembered thinking, though he cringed to remember it now. Two weeks later, he woke up to find his mind suddenly clear, sane again, and he was alone in an alien city, hung-over and sleeping in a ratty inn.

He became a wanderer. Times were different then and people were more hospitable to charming young vagrants. Ruegger always managed to work a certain spell on people, frequently finding lodgings with gullible families but street-smart enough not to rely on this.

Often, to occupy his time, he played chess. It was in this way that he met Ludwig:

"I was playing chess by myself on a stone bench near a fountain when he came up and plopped down opposite me and challenged me to a game," Ruegger said. "He was this tall, skinny thing who hadn't bathed in weeks, with wild hair and expensive clothes. I never found out why he'd left his home, but he had. Naturally, being the stubborn sort Ludwig is . . . was . . . it took him two hours to concede, but by then we'd grown to like one another, so we took up together, rogue chess-playing poets with enough stolen money to keep up minimal appearances and sustenance. For awhile, anyway."

They became well-known characters and often people would gather round to watch them play. When they ventured outside of Austria and discovered that they were unknown in other places, they turned their obscurity to their advantage when someone would challenge them to a game. Mostly these challengers went away disappointed, but it got so that Ruegger and Ludwig made a sort of living off of placing money on the games, and this sustained them until they got to Paris.

They'd bounced around Europe for so long that it was only a matter of time before they wound up there sooner or later; it was just a question of timing. They arrived starving and destitute, not even speaking much French. They were forced to learn quickly.

Ludwig had always been fascinated by Ruegger's poetry, so when they met a group of spirited, impoverished philosophers, Ludwig sent out some of his friend's material. In retaliation, Ruegger distributed some of Ludwig's weird epics to the populace, and they were both surprised when their literature was well-received. Of course, they learned soon enough that the young philosophers they'd encountered were anarchists—revolutionaries. To them, the fact that the newcomers' poems made no sense was a good thing. It showed a desire for change.

The revolutionaries dubbed Ludwig and Ruegger the "odd flock" (a phrase out of one of Ruegger's poems), and the two stayed on.

This was during the early stages of the Revolution, when most of the revolutionaries ended up dead and rotting of gangrene on the barricades. Gangrene tends to take the romance out of most things, Ruegger learned, and it was at this time that he discovered his natural violent tendencies. He killed better than he wrote, it seemed, even if his heart rested with the latter. Soon his fame spread among his peers for his suicidal antics on the front lines. Meanwhile, Ludwig rose in the ranks of the revolutionary leaders, becoming something of a commander, a strategist, which suited him wonderfully.

It ended one day when Ruegger was leading an assault on a corrupt police station. The revolutionaries were ambushed and slaughtered without mercy. A traitor had given them away. The survivors were forced back to one of their secret encampments, just about to be overrun. Ruegger, dying with two bullets in his stomach, gathered the remnants of his men and told them that he was going to make his last stand there. In a touching gesture, they agreed to stay with him.

Amid the stench of gunpowder, gangrene, burning flesh and hair, the anarchists loaded their weapons and waited for the final assault. When it came, it was swift and brutal. Half of Ruegger's men were cut down within the first minute, and he was struck twice in the chest and a few times along his limbs. He crumpled in a wet heap at the bottom of the barricade.

One thought chased at him as he lay there dying: he had to find Ludwig, make sure Ludwig knew that he was passing over. But Ruegger was too weak and there was no time. He was using his own blood to write a good-bye letter when one of the revolutionaries easily hefted him off the ground and sped him off into an abandoned alley.

Gunshots echoed off the streets nearby. The revolutionary patted Ruegger with a gloved hand on the cheek and smiled. It was a woman, a girl really, no more than seventeen, perhaps, but though she looked several years Ruegger's junior, she gave off a presence and had such command of herself that he felt she was much older, and of course she was. Approaching her 200th birthday, in fact. She had cloudy, pale green eyes and deep dark brown hair shot through with streaks of soot and ash.

"She told me that she'd read my poetry, had watched me from afar—watched me smoke my cigars, or mull over some stratagem, or laugh with the other anarchists at some small joke when the tension got too high. She said I should live forever, and that she would do that for me under the condition that I use my gifts to continue the fight for freedom."

He'd started to drift into unconsciousness, but the revolutionary pulled out a knife and nicked his throat to keep him awake. She made him promise, and he did. She drained him of what blood he had to give, then gave him her own, making him a vampire. He later found out that her name was Amelia.

Ruegger returned to Ludwig at once and offered him immortality, but Ludwig refused. At first. As Ruegger and Amelia became lovers, she introduced him (and by extension Ludwig) to the various covens and rogues in the area. The original odd flock met many of her immortal friends and acquaintances, and Ludwig discovered the morbines—an immortal race that fed off of brain fluid—and was delighted. He called them the "intellectual's vampire", and, since he was just as well-known as Ruegger, the morbines were honored to make him one of them. They seemed to consider it good publicity.

After another year of fighting, Ruegger grew disgusted with his mortal and immortal comrades, finding that they were every bit as corrupt as those they hated. Reluctantly, Amelia agreed. Together they left for the New World, leaving Ludwig behind in France. They begged him to go with them, but he refused, saying he must continue the fight.

Ruegger and Amelia spent nearly a hundred years together, and she taught him everything she knew, starting off with the basics: first how to choose his victims (only evil-doers), then how to amass one's personal fortune by taking money and properties (including stocks and bonds) off one's victims. It was a lesson many shades never mastered.

Other lessons followed—small-scale telepathy and telekinesis. Meanwhile they explored the New World from the frigid tip of present-day North America to the warmer tip of South America. They hired natives to build them an estate in the wilds of Canada. Occasionally war would break out somewhere in the world, and Ruegger and Amelia would go to fight for the side that they considered just, if there was such a side, then return to their exploration of the earth. They were deeply in love.

This, too, came to an end when they moved to New York. They had lived in the seething cityscape for about a year until one night when they decided to hunt separately. After his excursion, Ruegger ventured to their apartment to find Amelia lying lifeless on their bed, a dark immortal standing above her, her blood dripping from his lips.

It was a kavasari.

Ruegger charged the creature, a man, but the kavasari knocked him aside, a smile on his lips. Ruegger didn't stop. He kept charging Amelia's killer, and the kavasari kept throwing him back. Eventually, after he'd beaten Ruegger to the ground one final time, the kavasari took up Amelia in his arms and vanished out the window. Ruegger tried to follow but could not. Despair filled him. Amelia was dead.

Devastated, he sunk into depths of despair he hadn't known since Maria's death. In fact, this time his insanity completely consumed him, lasting for close to seventy years. It was a colder sort of insanity, the sort that would be hard for anyone to detect; to all others, he appeared rational. Around the time Amelia died, the Civil War was breaking out and Ruegger fled the claustrophobic city of New York for the more lush land of the South, where he started a cotton plantation in Louisiana with his fortune and bought several hundred slaves. He was not to return to New York for a long, long time; to him, it became a haunted place, a place of misery.

To him, the war represented the old ways versus the new. The traditional rural life against the industrial age. These were concepts that he could relate to, even though his love of life had completely disappeared. Before Amelia's death, he had killed slave-owners, and now he was one. Life grew to be an evil thing to him, and he set about its destruction coldly.

The war called to him, and he couldn't resist the temptation to break open the bones of those that lived in the northern world that so disgusted him, the world that had killed Amelia. He purchased the title of colonel from the Confederacy and became, once more, a leader of men. He was relentless and cruel, driving his soldiers savagely into the jaws of death again and again, but leading them out successfully. His men hated and feared him, but the Confederate generals loved him. They promoted him to their rank. He agreed, under the condition that he could still lead his soldiers into battle.

At this point they began to call him the Demon of the Mississippi, as the river was his stomping ground. To this day, a portrait of him (bearded and in Confederate uniform) lies embedded in one out of every four Civil War textbooks in the country.

Of course, others were aware of the delicate skin condition that prevented him from seeing daylight and understood his need to keep indoors during that time. Ultimately this little eccentricity became common knowledge, and the Union used it against him, leading their assaults during daylight and killing enough of his men to make his nocturnal counter-assaults ineffective.

To make matters worse, a few Union shades realized what he was and made several attempts on his life. After surviving the first, he immortalized a small group of his die-hard loyalists (there were only a few), and they protected him.

When the war ended, he retreated back south a burnt-out, hateful creature, only to find his plantation in ruins. The slaves had risen against their overseers and set the mansion aflame. The overseers hung by their necks from the towering oak trees surrounding the estate. The slaves had hung them by their bull-whips.

In a rare display of emotion, he danced around their bodies and collapsed laughing.

He had no idea where to go, so he disappeared into the never-ending Louisiana swamplands, where he lived alone, a savage. He actually enjoyed the solitude. But, as fate would have it, his reputation had intrigued a werewolf called Lord Kharker.

Kharker searched the swamps for months before finding Ruegger, who had become something of an elemental, an extension of the swamp itself. Kharker took Ruegger under his wing, teaching the one who was now often referred to as the Darkling the finer points of evil through a seemingly endless series of wars and debaucheries. They loved each other in the way that only they could, appreciating one another's darkness, yes, but it wasn't that simple. They understood that beneath all that they were still warm, affectionate beings, capable of emotion and caring. They relished and embraced their blackness, because they understood that that was their nature.

This was what Kharker taught him: to be evil (if there was such a thing), because that's what he was. But it wasn't *all* of what he was. Kharker tried to instill in him the zest for life that the Hunter had. In this, he failed. Ruegger could never be at peace with his darkness as Kharker was with his.

It all culminated in World War Two, the war Ruegger thought of as that which had taken his soul, if he had one left. The Hunter and the Darkling were indiscriminate. To them, war was a playground. Everyone on the field was prey. The two would attack soldiers, civilians, anyone. For fun, they even assassinated a few people with high rank, just to stir things up. It didn't matter which side, just as long as there were no witnesses left. With Kharker beside him, Ruegger committed unimaginable deeds, atrocities so dark he couldn't even name them.

Infrequently, but sometimes, they'd hunt separately. On one such night in Germany, Ruegger woke up in a cave surrounded by bodies, not knowing how he had gotten there and crying out for Amelia. It all came back to him in a rush, and he left the cave hating himself, determined to go out and slaughter a whole slew of humans to prove to himself one last time that he was really and truly evil. Then he would lie down, smoke a cigarette, and watch the sun come up.

Later, he would understand. After seventy years, the ice simply broke. The walls he'd erected between himself and emotion dissolved in a blaze; he'd killed one person too many. But what were his options? He couldn't continue on as if he hadn't reached a defining moment, and he couldn't suddenly reverse sides and fight for justice with the weight of his crimes poised above his head.

The Vampire Hauswell found him first. Hauswell saved him, if not the soldiers he'd destroyed. Hauswell, a staunch German who'd been living in America until the war, had come over to Germany to kill off the evil elements of his native country so that he could still be proud of his homeland. Ruegger never learned how Hauswell knew of him or found him, but the vampire did, and he brought

Ruegger back to the light. He convinced Ruegger not to kill himself, that there could be life for him yet in redemption. After Hauswell's arrival, Ruegger understood that he could never go back to Kharker, never surrender again to evil. As much as he loved his mentor and friend, Ruegger knew he could never see Kharker again.

After the war was over, Ruegger returned with Hauswell to Las Vegas, where Hauswell was rising in the ranks of the criminal underworld. He was a kind man, in his way, but not to be trifled with, and Ruegger learned much under his tutelage. Hauswell became a different sort of mentor to Ruegger, not goodly, exactly, but noble. Ruegger had to figure out how to be goodly himself. Breaking people's knees when they didn't pay up didn't quite qualify, in his opinion. For all Hauswell's virtues—for instance, his refusal to feed on the innocent—he was a ruthless businessman.

Soon, Ruegger knew he had to return to New York, if only to stare his demon in the eye. To conquer it.

Once he'd done this, New York became a sort of base of operations for him, somewhere to stay between his many road-bound odysseys. He only fed now on the unjust. Sometimes he even fed on other immortals who had preyed on humans indiscriminately. Slowly, he began to develop a new sort of reputation. He became an avenger. He became the boogeyman that unrighteous shades feared.

This went on for decades until he found Danielle, and except for the months Danielle had spent with Jean-Pierre at Lord Kharker's, they'd been together ever since.

* * *

Ruegger, though dry-eyed immediately after the telling, soon broke down with violent sobs. Danielle embraced him. She didn't exactly know how to respond. He'd been evil (she had no problem using the word), she knew that. She had already forgiven him for it, in fact. He'd never apologized for it, and she hadn't asked him to. It's simply who he was. Or had been.

The strange thing, to Danielle, was that in telling the story he made himself out to be more vile than he had been. Kharker had told her enough to give her an accurate picture of his days as the Darkling, and it was not the portrait he painted himself. Not that she believed Kharker, who had *admired* Ruegger's evil, but she would sooner believe the Hunter than Ruegger, who couldn't be objective about it. The way Kharker told it, Ruegger very simply hated life and wanted to stamp it all out. He had been quite cold and methodical about it. Without emotion. A reaper.

One day emotion had returned to him, and he'd lost the driving force behind his attempted genocide. And never apologized for it. Until now.

"I killed hundreds, thousands . . . " he said through his tears. "I deserve death a million times over."

"No," she said, stern. "No! Don't you see, you've changed. You're not with Kharker anymore. You've turned your back on all that. You're with me now, and we've never killed an innocent—have we?"

"No, never. I could never kill an innocent again, not even if my life were in danger. But don't you see, I go insane after I lose someone I love. If you were to ever—"

"No, stop it! You didn't go insane after Ludwig died. Besides, no one's going to kill me. But if they did . . . Well, consider this. You'd respect my last wish, wouldn't you?"

"Of course."

"Then as my last wish I command you never to kill an innocent. Do you hear me?"

"Yes, but—"

"No, never! Now swear, damn you."

"I swear it." He tore off his shirt, pressed his thumbnail over his heart and carved a bleeding X in his chest. "Cross my heart."

She kissed the wound, took his blood into her mouth and swallowed. Tearing off her own shirt, she threw her legs around him and straddled him, then pressed herself tight against him, kissing his face and licking his tears away.

"I love you, Ruegger. Always."

"I love you, too," he said.

Their lips met, and everything after was a blur.

Afterward, rain pounded the remains of the window, and Danielle knew that Laslo would not be happy; they had just defiled this room. *Thank God.*

"Let's go outside," she said. "I don't care about the rain. I can't stand this place. Mount Vapor never made me claustrophobic, but this place does. Let's dance in the rain and perform some ungodly rituals."

She led the way out, down the corridors and the twisting staircase and through the angular vestibule until a light rain fell on them. They picked their way down to the still-dry earth and toward a little rise, where the cemetery was, crested the hill and came to the burial ground, surrounded by a dilapidated wrought-iron fence. A large black archway, leaning to the right and with a twisted gate, allowed access to the holy ground.

"Damn it all," Ruegger breathed.

Danielle stared. All the graves—and there were no more than fifty—had been unearthed.

"What does it mean?" she said.

"It means that Laslo's resurrected them all."

Chapter 18

"Groovy," said Cloire, eyeing the penthouse, and her voice was only half-mocking. One day after Initiation, the death-squad had just arrived in Las Vegas.

Jean-Pierre nodded. Things had been going pretty well, he had to admit. There was still some tension among the crew, but it had lessened dramatically since the Initiation, and Sophia was part of the reason. Instead of focusing on themselves so much, the others could concentrate on getting to know her and, when they did start to bicker, she made an effort to come between them, acting in an almost motherly capacity. She was no mother, though. She could be as cold and brutal as any member of the crew. Because of this, she'd earned their respect.

The truth was that Jean-Pierre was impressed. Not only was she all the things he admired in a warrior, but she was sensual, as well. In his effort to detach himself from Danielle, Sophia might just be the thing he needed. And every time he'd made some small advancement on her, she'd returned it, which built his confidence.

It seemed childish, this little game, but he was determined that if he and Sophia were going to become involved, it wouldn't be on the sideline basis that Kristen and Veliswa had fallen into. Moreover, it wouldn't be of the obsessive nature as his love for Danielle. No, if this happened at all, it would be mature and, as such, it must progress at a mature pace. But did mature necessarily mean slow?

There were enough rooms in the penthouse suite for all of them, and after exploring their new surrounds the crew began to unpack. It was one of the nicer casino/hotels along the Strand, and the owner reputedly had connections with the mob.

After throwing his one suitcase on his bed, Jean-Pierre moved into the living area and broke out a Pall Mall.

The others drifted in. "I think we should hit the casino," Loirot said.

"Well, you would," said Cloire. "But hell, we're in Vegas, why not? Ruegger and Danielle can wait a few hours. As Sofe said a few days ago, it's a paid vacation. What d'you think, Jean-Pierre?"

He shrugged, thinking it would be good for them. "Let's do it."

Smiling, Cloire turned to Sophia. "You ever been to Vegas, Sofe?"

"Used to live here, a long time ago, back in the mob's heyday. It's nothing like it was."

"I'm fleshstarved," said Kilian. "Are we still going to uphold the tradition of the four-day fast? It seems ridiculous under the circumstances. Without food, we'll be weak, so what happens if we run across the odd flock?"

"If we find them, we'll feed," said Jean-Pierre. "If not, we'll uphold the fast and the second stage of the Initiation immediately afterwards. Everyone okay with that?"

They nodded, and he led the way downstairs to the casino. After trading in some cash for chips, Loirot went off to play baccarat, while Cloire and Byron found a roulette table and Kilian decided on a nice game of blackjack. Kiernevar migrated to the slot machines.

Suddenly Jean-Pierre was aware that he was alone with Sophia and that she was very near him, almost brushing his side. He remembered last night during Initiation when they'd all begun the ritual orgy, and he'd thought at the time—while he and Sophia were coupling—that they were especially close somehow. Something about the genuine nature of her smile. *Although* . . . She'd seemed reluctant to become intimate with him at first. Perhaps he'd imagined it. Still, standing so close to her, his mind flashed on that smile of last night, when she'd writhed above him in thoughtless abandon, and how that smile had warmed his heart.

Their hands touched. "Shall we play craps?" she said.

"Together?"

"I'll blow on your dice."

They wandered over to the craps table.

"Do I scare you?" she said.

"Of course not."

"Your hand is trembling."

Fool, he thought. *Suck it up. I can be every bit as cold as she is.*

It was this coldness in her that he liked, this impenetrable inner strength that reminded him of the way he'd been back in the days before Danielle. Even then he'd felt incomplete, though. Sophia was different. She accepted her nature, which was so close to the albino's own, but unlike him was complete in herself. Perhaps her inner strength would awaken its counterpart in him.

"It's nothing," he said. "Just need a cigarette." He fumbled getting one out. She lit it for him, and he liked the way she moved. "Thanks."

They began to play. Of course, it was easy for a shade to win at these kind of games, what with their telekinetic and telepathic abilities, but this took the fun out of it, and what did money mean to them? They played it straight, no tricks. True to her word, Sophia blew on his dice.

When she whispered in his ear thirty minutes later, "Wanna go upstairs?", he nodded, and she put her arm through his and let him lead her away from the table. They'd been losing in craps and didn't bother to retrieve the last of their chips. To the contrary, they went straight up to the penthouse. He took her into his bedroom, knocking the suitcase off his bed.

"You *are* frightened," she said, drawing him towards her. "Never made love to a woman you could respect?"

He studied her, but her face was gentle, not mocking.

"I—" he started.

She placed a finger to his lips, then kissed him, pressing herself against him. She did a slow pivot, not breaking the embrace, then pushed him roughly down on the bed.

"You just need to relax," she said, and her voice was so silky that he found himself giving in to the power of suggestion. She ran her hands up and down his body, then unfastened his belt with her teeth.

"Just relax . . . and have a little fun. Fun is allowed, you know."

Their lips met again. He gave in. Soon they were naked and rolling around on the bed. For some reason he found himself unable to go through with it, though, and before he'd gone very far he broke away, panting. He placed a hand over his eyes.

"What is it?"

He sighed. "What are we doing?"

"What do you mean?"

He stood up and started pacing. "Sofe, you're very good. I don't know why you're really here, but I know you're acting. You play the seductress very well. That's not what I want."

She stared up at him. "I acted too fast, didn't I? Is that what gave me away?" When he didn't respond, she said, "That wasn't really acting, Jean-Pierre. That was instinct. You and I, I guess we were meant to find each other."

"What are you talking about? Have we met before?"

"No. And I didn't come up here for a one-nighter. I wanted to begin something. Maybe I did it wrong, but it wasn't an act."

Who was she? Why had she tried to seduce him so quickly? Probably the Titan had set her up to it, in order that Jean-Pierre should get over Danielle. Perhaps some real emotion had gradually entered into it, though. He wanted to believe it.

"If you came here because you actually felt something," he said, "it wouldn't be right, not now."

"Then when? When Danielle is dead?"

"Especially not then. Then nothing could be resolved."

"Then where does that leave us?" She slid up against him, his back to her front, and kissed his neck.

"No," he said. "Just put your arms around me." She did. "Do it like you mean it."

"I do."

"You don't even know me."

"Then you don't believe in love at first sight?"

"Don't be absurd."

She paused. "Sometimes there's a connection between two people that happens instantly, and it's best to make the most of it before their differences tear them apart."

"So this connection—you feel it towards me?"

She squeezed him around the middle. "I do. I think you feel the same toward me."

He lit a cigarette and moved to the window, where he looked down on the neon city.

She came to stand beside him, her arm around his waist in a strangely familiar gesture. He offered her the cigarette and she took it, expelling the smoke with a cool smile.

"What do you say to finding a coffee shop?" she asked.

"No."

"What then?"

"I say we find a bar."

*   *   *

After the graveyard, Ruegger and Danielle explored the land beyond the airfield. Small hills rose up, covered by stunted-looking shrubs and ugly grass. The night was cool, and the air became fresher the further they got from the mission/hangar.

"I'm hungry," Danielle said.

"Me too. Should've eaten before we left Vegas."

The vampires made their way up the embankment, becoming slippery in the rain, toward the airfield and past the vacant cemetery. As they were descending the last hill, Ruegger started as lightning flashed. A lone figure stood on the mission's roof. The man seemed tall, but it was hard to tell from here, and he was utterly naked, his face raised to the heavens. He mounted the scaffolding toward the platform on top of the bell tower.

Ruegger gestured, and Danielle looked as another blast of lightning cut down, illuminating the glistening, storm-swept roof, but the figure was gone.

"What is it?" Danielle said.

"I think I saw Laslo, but I don't know. Whoever he was, he was on the roof near the bell tower. Then not. I think he went *into* the tower." Chills ran up his spine. Had Laslo been watching them? Was he watching now? Did he know that they'd been joined in ungodly union not long ago? Had he seen *that*?

"Let's go inside," Ruegger said.

The moment they entered the mission's vestibule, Ruegger was hit by a wretched stench.

"Do you hear something?" Danielle said.

He paused to listen. He could hear a strange, rhythmic noise . . . but it was something he'd heard before.

"Let's see what it is," she said, and her voice was a whisper.

They crept down a narrow hall, hearing the noise grow louder, then turned down another, and finally came upon the chapel.

"Fuck," Ruegger said.

The zombies were here, at least thirty of them, kneeling in the pews, chanting softly, steadily in Latin. They wore ratty gray monk-robes with hoods thrown over their heads, concealing their faces. The leader of the congregation was not Laslo but one of his bloodfinders, a man Ruegger recognized, had even played poker with a few times; Singer, he was called.

A tall man with a scarred face and a severe widow's peak, Singer had been a werewolf who worked for Hauswell before being murdered in a gangland war. Now he was Laslo's right-hand man and, to prove his devotion to God he'd had a cross burned into the smooth flesh of his forehead—smooth because he was an immortal and immortal corpses do not rot easily. In fact, Singer just might still possess the ability to shapeshift.

His eyes were closed, and he was leading the chant. A large cross stood behind Singer, suspended by wires, and a naked man hung where Christ should be, nailed at the hands and feet to the wooden beams, his blood dripping to the floor. Covered in a slick bloody grime, the man was tall and gaunt with salt-and-pepper hair and big glossy black eyes set back in his head, giving them a hooded appearance. His flesh was the color of ash.

"Laslo," whispered Ruegger. Laslo, taking the place of Christ! He must have only just gotten into position, as he'd been at the tower moments ago, Ruegger was sure of it.

Danielle pulled him away. "Why don't we plant some bombs and blow this place up?" she said. "We're supposed to fight evil where we can, and this . . . this is . . . "

"Evil?"

She shook her head. "I don't know. But to feed all these bastards they've gotta kill a lot of humans, don't they?"

"That follows." He caught a whiff of something else, more zombies somewhere close by. He set off in that direction, Danielle just behind.

They came upon a large wooden door, set in a little alcove. Half a dozen zombies grouped in front of it like a pack of wolves. One of them was Tommy O'Connel. The zombie smiled when he saw the odd flock and stepped forward, a shotgun in his hands.

"How d'you do, mates?"

"What's going on here?" Ruegger said.

"Nothin' much. We'd all be attendin' th'Midnight Mass if ya'll weren't stayin' with us. But we aren't an' we're here instead. Least we don't haveta don those fool robes."

"Where's this door go?" Danielle asked.

"Oh, that. This here's the door to th'hangar, but don't you be gettin' eager. We're here to prevent you two nice folks from goin' down there an' if you make a fuss I'll call the other brothers in Mass an' you'll git more'n ya bargained fer."

"What's down there?"

"If you were to know, we wouldn't be guardin' th'door, now would we?" With a quick snap, he chambered a round. "Now clear out 'fore I git meself worked into a tither."

"How do we get to the roof from here?" Ruegger said.

"Ya don't."

"We're going to the roof."

"Can't have that, now. An' if ya try for the door to it, you'll find some more brothers waitin' for ya. Now ya'll go on, say yer prayers an' retire. Feel restless an' ya might wanna try out th'library on the third floor." He leveled the shotgun at them. "Ya'll go now, an' God bless."

The odd flock moved away, down a series of stark rat-tunnels. Danielle paused, studying a large round bulge in the wall.

"What do you bet this is the bell tower shaft?" she said.

"Probably is."

"Why does it run straight through the building like this?"

"I guess Hauswell thought it would be more aesthetically pleasing if the tower was located in the center of the mission, and he always did like his secret passages. But the way I remember the mission, there was access to the bell tower on every floor and stairs that ran in a spiral along the inside wall leading up to the bell from the first story. It looks as if Laslo had the entrance to it on this floor walled up. Probably did the same for the other floors."

"Baby, I think it leads to the hangar. I bet if we broke through this wall we'd find it goes straight down. Why don't we? It'll get this mystery over with."

"Let's wait till sunrise when most of the zombies'll be out fetching blood for Laslo."

"But the sun—"

"Don't worry. All the windows have iron shutters, which they close during the day so that Laslo can walk around."

"What about the bell tower itself? It's open at the top and the sun can come right in."

His frown deepened. "Then we wait for first dark."

"I want to go now."

He debated. Really, there was no point in putting it off, other than his reluctance to endanger Danielle. Then again, every moment they were here was one of danger.

"Fine," he said. "Let's do it."

As quietly as possible, they began to break through the stone, setting the pieces on the floor so they could replace them later. The repair wouldn't pass an inspection, but that was the chance they took. Once they'd removed enough stones to create a hole big enough to slip through, Ruegger stuck his head into the bell tower and was immediately assaulted by a terrible reek. He knew that smell, knew it very well.

"You sure you want to do this?" he said.

"I'm sure."

He began to crawl into the bell tower head-first, looking for the staircase he remembered, but it had been removed. In fact, there was nothing here—no bell, no floors, just an empty hole above where the roof should be (and where a half-moon now hung instead, partially obscured by clouds that flung rain down on him) and a bottomless pit below. A pit that stunk horribly. Something down there *glistened* ...

Hands seized his leg.

"What the—?"

They yanked him back out of the hole. For a moment, he thought it had been Danielle pulling him out for some reason, but, then he saw Tommy and a dozen other zombies standing over him, their weapons drawn. Ruegger lowered his hands and stood slowly.

"Sorry, babe," Danielle said. Two zombies held her. "They came up on me too fast."

Tommy smiled, revealing corroded teeth. "Thought ya might be up to somethin'. An' here ya are, causin' trouble an' makin' me in my condition comb these damn halls an' wear meself out. A shame and a sin, neither of which're likely to go unpunished 'round here. Now come peaceably an' mebbe the Lord'll be gentle with ye."

"Mind if I have a smoke?" Ruegger said.

"Be quick about it, man. I ain't overbrimmin' with patience, y'know."

Ruegger thrust his hands into his jacket and came up with two enormous Colt .45s, which he fired directly into the zombies. Tommy's head exploded.

Danielle broke free of her captors and fired, too.

The zombies surged forward. Several flung Ruegger back against the wall, but still he kept shooting. One fell, then another, their rotting bodies unable to keep up the pretense of life.

They were overwhelming Danielle.

"Go!" he said. "Into the hole!"

"I can't leave you!"

"Go! I'll be right after you."

She resisted another moment, but they were all over her. She leapt into the hole and was gone.

When he ran out of bullets, he turned to the opening, gritted his teeth and flung himself in. A few dry hands scraped at his feet, but not fast enough. He plunged down, and down, and he had enough time to register a light patter of rain on his face and the vile stench of whatever he was approaching coming up fast. He passed through the spot where the lowest floor should be—but was not—and next he was flying through the empty space of the hangar . . .

He landed with a gruesome *plop*. For a moment he thought he was drowning. Fighting his way through the wretched liquid substance he'd fallen into, he clawed past a forest of dismembered body parts floating in the goo. A severed arm, a decomposing head, there the remains of some poor man's torso, the putrid flesh and the bones underneath, a free-floating liver . . .

Ruegger broke the surface, gasping, not for breath but in shock. He realized he was covered by a slick, bloody grime, the same grime that Laslo had been covered with. The zombie overlord had gone for a swim before crucifying himself. Ruegger reached for purchase, found the edge of the basin and hoisted himself up out of the pool, then fell to the cement floor of the hangar. It was a good drop, and he winced in pain as he cracked the cement.

Danielle, spitting and cursing, helped him up. She'd already emerged from the slime.

"Fucking great," she said, shaking her gore-coated hands.

He fumbled for his guns but couldn't find them. *Shit.* He'd lost them in the pit, and he wasn't going back in there, not for all the mushrooms in Morocco. He patted himself down, finding the weapons that hadn't been dislodged and examining them. The goop in the pool had clogged most of them up. Snarling, he hurled the pistols to the floor.

"What now?" Danielle said.

"The bell tower must have been cleared so Laslo can jump through it to this pool," Ruegger said. "The platform on top's nothing more than a diving board."

"Jesus."

Backing into something in his effort to distance himself from the pool, he knocked an object over with a metallic bang. Turning, he noticed a cluster of metal barrels. The one he'd turned over was leaking some oily substance—an anticoagulant for the pool so the blood there wouldn't clot. Damn, but Laslo was a sick bastard. And, if Ruegger had his way, a very dead one.

"Holy *God*," Danielle said, and such was the horror in her voice that Ruegger felt the hairs rise on the back of his neck.

He turned, and suddenly he saw it all, the whole hangar . . .

Hastily, the walls rose in his head, putting distance between himself and the reality of the situation. Despite that, he sank to his knees and retched.

The pale moonlight shooting down the bell tower cast the scene in an appropriately gray hue. Giant chains hung from the ceiling, hooks on the end of them that, one and all, were pierced through the Achilles tendons of humans, most of which looked dead and all of which were naked. Wall to wall corpses, and along the walls life-size crosses. *Occupied* crosses.

Ruegger and Danielle approached a woman who hung upside-down from a hooked chain and saw that she was in fact still alive … in a manner of speaking. Most of the bodies seemed decayed, some no more than skeletons with a little skin left, but horribly, some of them were moving, though surely most of their brains were so rotted that they weren't really human anymore—

Get a grip, old son. You've seen worse. WHERE, for gods' sakes? No, this is just about as bad as it gets. I knew he was insane, but even so how can Laslo justify this?

"Come … here …" the woman wheezed.

Cautiously, Ruegger and Danielle obeyed. As he drew nearer, he could see that the woman was past death, along with the rest of the hangar's occupants, but she was perhaps the freshest one.

"Hang on," he said, grimacing at the choice of words.

He leapt up for purchase on the chain, finding that his hands were so greasy they almost didn't stay on. As delicately as he could, he removed the hook from the woman's tendon, grabbed her ankle and hopped to the floor. He eased her to the ground, where she lay panting.

"Poor thing," Danielle said.

Ruegger removed his grime-coated jacket and laid it over the woman's wasted frame. She coughed her thanks, and he nodded, trying not to show his horror.

Laslo and the zombies would be on them soon. While the woman recovered, Ruegger scanned the room. There were the stairs that led up to the door that Tommy O'Connel and his gang must have been guarding. Ruegger knew it would burst open any moment.

Where was Hauswell?

The woman smiled weakly, but she was obviously scared, probably frightened that Ruegger would hurt her or that she would have to return to the hook, like living meat in a meat freezer.

"Laslo did this to you?" he asked.

"They call him the Lord . . ." Her voice filled with mocking rage. "He calls himself the Son of God."

"How did you get here?"

For a long moment he didn't think she would answer. Then, in a creaking and painful voice, she told her story:

"My husband and I were taking our son to Vegas for his birthday ... and we stopped for a hitchhiker, oh we were so stupid. He tore us up—he killed my boy, he was *dead!*—and nearly killed me. I passed out ... woke up hanging in this ... *place*. They left me to rot, my husband was gone, and then *I* was dead, no water no nothing, and I woke up and was still here ... and the Son of God was standing over me . . . he can make the dead rise, just like a god, but he's no god he's the devil and he or his demons killed everyone here and he keeps them alive so he can . . . he can . . . he can cut holes in them and put his . . . and put his . . ." She couldn't go on.

Ruegger didn't need her to.

"Sick *fuck*," said Danielle.

"But why?" Ruegger asked the woman.

"He says he must cleanse our sin ... through the fire of his seed. Sometimes he'll let one of us die and tear his victim apart afterwards ... just to raise them again and watch them struggle to move ... and he laughs. Oh, he *laughs* . . ." She looked up at Ruegger and her eyes were wide; she'd felt his strength. "Oh, my God! You're one of them!" She screamed and struggled out of his grasp, scrambling backwards, but not far.

"No," he said. "I'm here to help you." But she was no longer listening. She was shaking her head and muttering, transported into a wave of terror.

The zombies would be here any second, Ruegger knew. Where was Hauswell?

His eyes were drawn upwards to the ceiling, where he saw a cross hanging high in the air, and on that cross was the headless body of a sixtiesh white male ...

Danielle followed his gaze. "I'm so sorry, honey."

"No," he said. "Wait. I don't think ... "

"What?"

He breathed out in a sudden rush of relief. "That body's *decomposing*."

The door burst open. A horde of zombies—the whole congregation—swarmed down, blades and guns in their hands. Ruegger reached for a long knife, really more of a dagger.

"Give 'em hell," Danielle said, pulling out a blade of her own.

The zombies flew at them. Ruegger tore into the creatures with teeth and knife. He jammed the blade into his attackers until one of them sunk to the floor, the knife in its skull. Too far away for him to reach. He fought on with teeth and fist. A splash of corpseblood sprayed his mouth, and he nearly retched.

They surged all around him and Danielle. Ruegger swiveled, turned, punched, kicked. He heard his enemies' bones breaking. Soaked with blood from head to toe, he fought on.

"Danielle," he gasped. "Danielle!"

He could no longer see her.

"Ruegger ... "

There were too many of them. Escape was impossible.

He heard growls approach. Singer. In beast form. As the werewolf joined the fight, Ruegger realized his time had come.

A voice, Laslo's: "Come to God, my son."

Ruegger tried to answer, but one of the deaders rammed a dagger through his throat, and blackness overcame him.

Chapter 19

When Sophia woke up in the morning, sunlight streamed in through the window and she glanced at the clock on the bedside counter. Nine-thirty. Early enough.

She sat up in bed—Jean-Pierre's bed—and noticed him still asleep beside her. He was such an angelic sleeper. This was the first time in a long time she'd woken up next to a man that 1) she hadn't had sex with and 2) she had no plans to destroy. Oddly self-conscious, she ran her hand through his pale blond hair.

Last night had been good. Healthy, in its own twisted way. They'd danced and gotten drunk together. Even talked. She had let her guard down, *and wasn't sorry about it.*

She even felt a little guilty about her attempt to seduce him. It was her natural instinct, though, maybe the natural instinct of all ghensivs; when she saw a weakness in a man, she honed in on it and used it to her best advantage, or what she thought would be her best advantage at the time. Sometimes she was wrong.

She reprimanded herself for her emotional outlook. Emotion made one weak. And yet he looked so beautiful lying there ...

She rose and lit a Black Death. She would wait and see. If she felt anything real towards him, she'd make an effort to own up to those feelings instead of turning away from them as usual. Of course, part of her cringed at the whole notion. *Gods, girl. You can't do this. He's ...*

She banished the thought. They were immortals and above such concerns.

She showered and dressed, and by that time he was up as well. While he showered, she found the kitchen and brewed some coffee. She saw that Kilian was already up. Cloire marched into the room, two cigarettes in her mouth, and smiled.

"Mornin', Sofe."

"Mornin', Cloire. Wanna cup?"

"Hellfire and fuck yeah. Byron and I finished off four liters of tequila last night. He puked on me in the middle of the night and the sad thing is I couldn't blame him."

The morning progressed, and by ten-thirty everyone was dressed and ready to go. Since they'd rented a van at the airport last night, the first priority of the day was to find some sympathetic criminals and purchase hardware, as, having taken a commercial flight to Las Vegas, the death-squad had had to leave their guns back home. Unfortunate but easy to rectify, which they did quickly and were on to the second objective by noon. It was a nice day outside and the team was in good spirits.

The second objective was to find Ruegger and Danielle, which meant interrogating anyone that might've come in contact with them in the past week. Ruegger and Danielle were certain to be looking for Hauswell, even though the rumors of his death were now common knowledge. As the day went on, the death-squad talked to many minor underworld figures, who would be the best sources of information on Hauswell, and by five o'clock it became clear that the underworld was really and truly in turmoil. Hauswell's absence had left a hole that many were trying to fill. In fact, they were warring over the position, without success. All Hauswell's former lieutenants and rivals were at each other's throats.

No one seemed very powerful. No one, that is, except for an enigmatic figure few seemed to have met in person, a shade named Karl Barnaby. Apparently he'd just arrived on the scene, and it was rumored that he was very wealthy and powerful. Though he was a newcomer, he was quickly making Las Vegas his territory. Mystery surrounded him, but no one the death-squad talked to proved helpful in solving it.

They did find out a critical piece of information, which was repeated over and over again in rumor: Hauswell's body was at Laslo's. That, Jean-Pierre was certain, was where Ruegger and Danielle would go. The others agreed, but Kilian had something to say:

"I don't think Hauswell's dead. I think he planted the rumor of his death himself to make going underground easier."

Surprisingly, Jean-Pierre agreed. "Hauswell's too crafty to die."

"So what do we do about it?"

"I've an idea."

Jean-Pierre took them to a particular casino/hotel operated by one of Hauswell's former lieutenants. If the death-squad had learned anything today, it was that the underworld was so weak here that the name Vistrot carried great weight and, while they probably would've been killed within a few hours of entering the city had Hauswell still been in power, they were at the present time feared as emissaries of Vistrot. Vistrot had the power to wipe all these insignificant players off the board at a whim if he was willing to devote the man-power.

Jean-Pierre parked the van and the crew followed him inside, where he demanded to see the operator of the establishment. After some mindpulling, he got his way. The death-squad stormed into the office, closing the door behind them. The operator, a morbine named Stacey, had been expecting them and had a small army of shades behind his desk, all armed, just in case.

"We're looking for Hauswell," Jean-Pierre said.

"He's dead," said Stacey. "Or haven't you heard?"

The albino laughed. "He's not dead; it was just a trick to evade the Scouring."

"As far as I know, he's quite dead."

"Then who killed him?"

"He was Scoured, I suppose."

"Yes, but as we've all come to know, the Scouring usually works through local hit-teams. That's how it killed Lord Chang in Hong Kong yesterday, or haven't you heard? That's how it killed Hernandez in Columbia two weeks ago. And that's how it would have killed Hauswell. Since we've been here, we've heard many rumors and many false braggarts, tales of several squads who take credit for the killing. It seems to be becoming common knowledge that the body at Laslo's mission is missing a head—so if it really is the body of Hauswell, the team that killed him took his head as a trophy. But none of the braggarts have the head. *So who has it?*"

Of course, much of what he said wasn't quite true; the death-squad hadn't been in town long enough to gather all this information. Jean-Pierre was simply making the necessary leaps based on the assumption that Hauswell was still alive. The bluff worked.

Stacey swallowed. "I . . . don't know. Now please get out of here."

The albino turned to his crew. "Do it." They all withdrew their weapons. The small army behind Stacey raised theirs as well, but Jean-Pierre held up his hand. "Not yet," he cautioned. "Stacey, do you see that all our guns are silenced?"

"Yes."

"Yours are not. We can shoot you all night without making a sound—no cops will come and no awkward questions for you to answer. If your men return fire, it makes a big loud sound and the poor tourists in their rooms are certain to call the boys in blue. And the boys in blue will alert the mob. Other bosses will find out about it. You'll look weak. You're at a disadvantage, Stacey. We have nothing to lose and you do. Trust me, we will shoot until every last bone in you is shredded, and I'll personally throw what's left of you out for the sun to enjoy, and if you return fire you're fucked. In addition to that, if so much as one of your rounds hits any one of my crew, you'll have the wrath of Vistrot down on you tomorrow."

Sweat popped out on Stacey's brow. He took a sip of his gin and tonic. "What do you want to know?"

"Tell me where Hauswell is."

"His carcass is at Laslo's . . . "

"Incorrect answer. Now my team is going to fire at you for approximately ten seconds. Then I'll ask the same question: if Hauswell's not alive, where is his head?"

"No, wait—"

The death-squad fired, knocking Stacey from his chair and sending his blood across the desk. After ten seconds, they stopped and Jean-Pierre asked the question again—with the same results. This repeated itself several times until Stacey was in tatters, but the results did not change. The location of the head was not known.

Satisfied, Jean-Pierre nodded to his crew and they left. He'd gotten the answers he expected; without the head, Hauswell's death could not be verified and therefore there was a very good chance he was still alive. Which meant that if the death-squad could not reacquire the odd flock at Laslo's mission, all they would have to do was find Hauswell and wait for Ruegger and Danielle to show up.

days, this is still the conclusion to our second Initiation. We all must kill. Surely you see that."

"What do you say, Sophia?" Jean-Pierre said. "Would you kill him to prove your loyalty to us?"

"I kill only for personal or financial reasons," she said, "and I very rarely have to kill someone. You do what you need to do in order to stay alive and so do I. There's no reason why I should go beyond that to prove my loyalty to you. In fact, I think you should show your loyalty to me by respecting that."

The albino nodded. "That's her decision. Everyone okay with it?"

"I'm not," said Kilian. "It's not fair to the rest of us."

"Ditto," said Cloire. To the others: "Are you with me?" Reluctantly, Loirot and Byron nodded, but Kiernevar just stared at them. She turned to the ghensiv. "Sofe, we could be friends, but if you refuse to do this thing, it'll create a rift between us. What do you care if some piddling mortal lives or dies?"

"It's not necessary," Sophia stated. "If I killed him, I'd be a wastrel. I don't see how that would be proving my loyalty to you."

"Goddamnit, don't you see? This changes everything!"

Sophia shook her head sadly. "I won't do it."

"Then, by God, *I will!*" Shaking with anger, Cloire moved over to the man, who was quite petrified, and punched through his chest. Wordlessly, she ripped out his heart and held it up for Sophia's inspection, then flung it to the floor. She didn't even feed from the man.

"Does that make you happy, Sofe?"

"No."

Jean-Pierre walked over to Sofia and put a bloody arm around her shoulder. "Okay, show's over," he said. "Everyone shower and let's get on with it."

"This isn't done," Cloire said.

"It is for now," he said.

Sophia, feeling Jean-Pierre's strength around her, watched as the others shuffled away.

"It'll be okay, you'll see," Jean-Pierre said, and though she knew he couldn't be right, she was glad just the same that he stayed with her until the others had showered before moving off himself.

*   *   *

The death-squad turned off the highway onto the private road, bounced down its winding path, passing a strange big yellow van (but not stopping to inspect it, though very shortly Jean-Pierre would realize it belonged to none other than Junger and Jagoda), then pulled up to the mission/hangar to park near the odd flock's Volkswagen. Though Jean-Pierre wasn't entirely positive it was their quarry's vehicle, it didn't go with the environment.

He saw Cloire smile with satisfaction as she climbed down from the van.

"A perfect night for mayhem," she said, hands outstretched to catch the cool wind.

Sophia glanced up at the half-moon, looking troubled, though Jean-Pierre couldn't guess at what. There was certainly enough to be troubled about.

Cupping his hands, he lit a Pall Mall, and the others gathered around him.

"Okay, here's the deal," he said, looking at Cloire and Loirot. "You two walk the perimeter, find a way into the hangar and come back, fast."

"You mean you're actually going to kill Danielle?" Cloire turned to the others. "Guys, I think we should make our leader here personally kill that bitch. He's already shown a weakness for Sofe, so maybe he's finally over his little Gutter Angel—but we should make him prove it."

"I agree," Kilian said.

"I don't know . . ." said Byron, and Cloire slapped him. "Shut up, Aussie. Loirot, you with me?"

Loirot nodded, carefully keeping his eyes away from Jean-Pierre. "I guess."

"Normie?" she asked Kiernevar.

"Kiernev—"

"Oh, I don't wanna hear it. If you wanna see your maker squirm, just nod." He nodded. "Good, that's settled. Sofe?"

Sophia returned Cloire's glare. Could friendship really turn to hatred this fast? Jean-Pierre wondered. "You seem very worried about Jean-Pierre's loyalty," the ghensiv said. "It's called displaced aggression. In other words, you're the one with the loyalty problems."

"You're goddamned right," Cloire said. "Jean-Pierre, will you kill Danielle?"

For a long moment, he said nothing, then: "Cloire, if you and Loirot don't do as I've said—scout the perimeter, if you need me to repeat myself—I swear by the Night that I will, here and now, take off your fucking heads."

"That's my boy." She and Loirot sauntered off.

"Now are there any other loyalty problems here?" asked Jean-Pierre.

Kilian's eyes narrowed. "Just don't fuck up."

"Forget about Danielle," advised Loirot, trying to be friendly. "She's white-trash."

Jean-Pierre sneered. "I would see you dead before her, if I had a choice in the matter. Byron, can I trust in you?"

"Of course." The Australian looked offended, but deep down, the albino felt, he would decide in favor of Cloire.

"And Sophia?"

She nodded silently. Jesus, was she the only one he could really count on? And he'd known the others, except Kiernevar, for decades!

Cloire and Loirot came back at a trot.

"What did you find?"

"On the other side, there's a stairway that leads up to the mission—all the other entrances are sealed up," Loirot said.

"Well, that won't do. If we go up that way, we risk the odd flock being in the hangar and escaping. We can't afford to divide ourselves. The only thing to do is to blast into the hangar itself—we'll chase them up to the top and deal with them there."

"And if they jump off the roof?" Cloire said.

"Then we jump, too—remember, we've just fed and will probably be stronger than they will."

"I don't like it. The blast will make too much noise. In fact, you know what I think? I think you just want to alert Danielle so she can run away."

"He's right," Sophia said. "Going from bottom to top is the most strategically sound idea in this situation."

"Oh, and we're supposed to trust you?"

"Yes."

Cloire snorted. "Fine, but if this thing goes sour, I'm through, Jean-Pierre. The team will have one less member."

Loirot and Kilian agreed.

Jean-Pierre headed back to the van. "Let's get it over with, then."

They broke out the hardware—grenades, automatic weapons, a variety of pistols. He knew Laslo was a chalgid and probably had some zombies at his disposal, though surely not more than half a dozen or so, and if Laslo was friendly toward Ruegger and Danielle, that meant the death-squad had to be prepared.

After arming themselves, Jean-Pierre said, "Remember: if you come across any zombies, aim for the head, just like in the movies."

As they started in the direction of the hangar, he lobbed several grenades at the great wooden door. The death-squad barely broke stride as the explosives went off, blowing a hole. Almost casually, they strode inside … but then their resolve broke. *Holy hell, what happened here?*

As he crunched over the debris the explosion had made, Jean-Pierre became aware of walking on top of long wooden beams—crosses—and beneath them—nailed to them—bodies. Bodies being ground into the concrete floor as the crew made its way into the hangar.

"Fuck!" Cloire said.

Through the smoke Jean-Pierre saw the forest of living skeletons and bodies, and along the walls crucifixes. He tread on a dried gooey substance. Damn it all, he was walking on the dried-up liquids these bodies had released on dying.

He noticed a large group of hooded monks, just visible through the swaying forest, clustered near one wall, around a cross with someone on it—

Danielle!

His heart thumped.

At that moment, the monks (zombies, he realized) saw him too. The deaders' heads had snapped in his team's direction at the explosion. Now, in unison, the things turned from Danielle and ran, howling, toward the death-squad.

"How can there be so *many*?" Loirot said.

Most of them were armed, Jean-Pierre saw. And there was Laslo, the sick puppy, wearing a priest's get-up and reaching for a rifle—

The door leading into the mission burst in. Jean-Pierre turned to see another group of zombies descending a flight of stairs. At their head was Singer, a man the albino recognized. With a start, Jean-Pierre realized he himself could join their ranks if he wasn't careful.

He turned to his crew. As always, they looked up to the task, even Kiernevar and Sophia.

"Form a barricade," he said.

He fired at some of the chains that the bodies were suspended from, breaking the metal links and causing several corpses to fall to the ground, striking it hard. With the quickness of an immortal, he arranged the bodies (some of which stirred slightly) into a little mound, then squatted behind it, setting his various guns out on the floor around him for easy reaching.

Turning, he saw that some of the other members of his crew had done the same. Pride surged through him, and he felt the sting of sadness at the possibility of losing them. It all depended on whether or not he was willing to kill Danielle.

The zombies charged. He paused to light a cigarette, possibly his last, then raised his automatic rifle, took aim, and fired.

*   *   *

From his perch on the wall, Ruegger had a clear view of the action. He was high enough to stare down at an angle on the rotting forest of flesh and the demons that warred among it. Those that were down there would have their sight obscured by the bodies, but not him—if he cared to look. Mainly he watched Danielle, battered and bruised and crucified. *Crucified.*

How could he have gotten her into this? She'd been right when she had said they should leave.

Suddenly he wished that Hauswell hadn't saved him all those years ago, had let him go off on his merry way to hell where he surely belonged. But then what about Danielle? Hadn't he, in some small way, saved her from a drug overdose or a suicide attempt at some point? Maybe that simply his ego speaking. Well, he would atone for his sins now. Either the death-squad would get him or they would join him here on these crosses to die, slowly and painfully—then be resurrected as a slave to Laslo.

Closing his eyes, he tried channeling his power, but the mindthrust wouldn't come. He was simply too weak, drained of blood.

Suddenly, he saw something, something that chilled him to the core: Junger and Jagoda walked through the hole the death-squad had created, unfolded two lawn chairs and sat down in satisfaction, each holding a long-necked beer. Jagoda produced an enormous joint, lit it, and they began taking hits.

Junger saw him, pointed him out to Jagoda, and they both smiled and raised their beers to the Darkling in a toast. Bullets whizzed about them, even striking them, but they took no notice, and the combatants took no further notice of them.

Chapter 20

Zombies rushed at Jean-Pierre, firing what weapons they had, their rounds slamming into the flesh of the corpses in his mound, some into Jean-Pierre himself. He fired back, aiming for their heads. Three crumpled to the floor. He swore. He'd delivered five good brain-shots, meaning that at least two of the remaining five had been immortals in life and still retained some of their power.

Just before they came over the barricade, he grabbed a Magnum .357 semi-automatic and a large knife from off the ground.

One leapt for him. He swung with the blade, slicing through its neck, feeling the spray of its deathly juices. He hacked again, cutting off its head and kicking the corpse out of his way to put five rounds into the face of one of the zombie-shades.

The others fell on him. One started to eat into his stomach and he broke its skull open with his elbow. It still lived.

He stabbed his blade into the chest of one of the others (to no avail) and lost it there. Feeling their hands on him—digging into his back, his groin, his throat, his belly—he twisted and writhed, emptying his gun uselessly and then unable to reach his other weapons.

DAMNIT, I will NOT die like this.

A gun fired nearby. One of the zombies fell off him, deader than ever. Jean-Pierre grabbed another creature, this one a zombie-shade, by the throat. He could hear the last one wheezing and grunting a few paces away.

Once freed from the constraints of the other undead, he tore into the zombie-shade, decapitating and dismembering it.

Gasping, he turned in time to see Sophia finish off the other one, knocking it to the ground and stomping on its skull. She was completely covered in putrid zombie-grime, and he knew that he must be, too.

"Thanks," he wheezed.

"No problem. They only sent three after me."

A volley of bullets tore into both of them. Crouching back behind the mound of corpses, they exchanged nervous looks.

"Are you going to kill Danielle?" she asked, a few bullets whining over the top of her head. The zombies seemed to be holding off on another all-out assault for the moment.

"I don't know," he said.

"If you kill her, you'll never be able to get her out of your mind. Only by letting her live can you deal with your feelings for her."

A bullet struck a corpse near Jean-Pierre's head, spraying his hair with blood. "Now isn't the time for this!"

"It's the *last* time."

She was right, of course. "What about my crew? Vistrot?"

"You've hit what they call a defining moment, Jean-Pierre."

The rounds of an AK-47 slammed into his disintegrating mound of the living dead, and he figured the time for conversation was about up. Still, he hesitated.

"They'll abandon me," he said.

"*I* won't."

She was serious.

Glancing over the mound, he saw that the zombies were employing his own technique—taking down the bodies from the hooks and building mounds to hide behind. Their mounds, however, stretched longer and higher, making Jean-Pierre think of his days in the First World War. Trenches and razor-coil ...

He searched through the forest of bodies until he saw Byron and Cloire. They'd finished killing off the zombies that had attacked them in the first wave and were looking for him, too.

"What now, Frenchie?" Cloire shouted when she found him.

"Take down more bodies. Extend your mound and I'll come over."

As they obeyed, Loirot darted out from his own shelter and dove behind Cloire's, receiving a barrage of bullets for his trouble. Together, Kilian and Kiernevar rose from behind their barricade. Firing from the hip, they sprinted to Cloire and Byron.

A *de facto* cease-fire fell among the two sides as they fortified their barricades. Several zombies broke open the heads of some of the more dead ones and worked on fastening the skulls to their own heads, making gruesome helmets to prevent brain-shots. When the mound Cloire and the rest had been working on became large enough for the albino's tastes, he grabbed Sophia's hand.

"We're going to make a run for it," he said. "Keep your head down and your gun up. On three: one, two, THREE!"

They broke cover and ran to the others' mound. He felt rounds tearing into him but didn't pause. He and Sophia ducked behind the mound, gasping.

"You're out of shape, Jean-Pierre," Cloire said.

He stuck his head over the mound, feeling a few slugs slamming into his forehead but ignoring them, and saw again through the swaying bodies the long, low barricade the opposition had erected. The zombies apparently realized how vulnerable they were to head-shots and were staying undercover. Accordingly, they showed no signs of sending out another wave, and why should they? They could just sit and fortify their position indefinitely, waiting for the werewolves to attack or go away. Every minute the werewolves didn't strike, the zombies' position grew stronger. He turned to the crew.

"What's the plan?" Byron said.

"Kill Laslo. He's controlling the zombies. Singer, too, because he looks just ripe enough to be becoming a young chalgid himself." Jean-Pierre popped his head up again briefly. "Laslo and Singer are at opposite ends of the mound. Laslo's closest to the door that leads up into the mission to the left. It'll take at least four shades to kill the bastard, and that's being optimistic. So Cloire, Kiernevar, Kilian, and Byron—when the time comes, you chase him up into the mission, kill off his escort and do him in. Loirot, Sophia and I will try to take out Singer and any others that get in our way. First, we make a run for their mound, divide them up into two groups and then you four scare Laslo up into the mission. You do your thing, while we three stay down here and do ours."

"Sounds half-assed to me," said Kilian.

"Can you think of anything better? All right then, get your grenades ready. Throw them right before we hit the barricade. Throw them all. Okay, on three: one, two, THREE!"

They sprinted toward Laslo's wall of flesh, shooting even as rounds tore into them. They threw their grenades seconds before breasting the barricade. The explosions rocked the zombies, destroying many and creating large gaps in their mound.

Once over the barricade, the crew fired with abandon, scattering zombies in every direction. One fired into Jean-

Pierre's chest. He shot just beneath its bone-helmet, right into the forehead, and it dropped like a stone.

"Blasphemers!" Laslo shouted. "Heretics!"

Snarling, the chalgid gathered a small contingent and made his way toward the stairwell, disappearing into the mission. Cloire and the other three followed.

A long burst tore into Jean-Pierre. He ducked behind what once had been the barricade of his enemy and which was now vacant of them; they were playing it very conservatively, which would make it that much more difficult to eradicate them. Loirot and Sophia crouched as well. Shifting a leg of one of the mound-corpses to create a window, the albino chanced a quick peek at the opposition.

The remaining zombies—about twenty—had taken cover behind the several smaller mounds that the death-squad had made. Since there were only three of the crew left, it would be next to impossible to flush the zombies from their hiding places—positions which even now were being fortified—because the mounds were scattered and the death-squad couldn't afford to divide up their forces. Jean-Pierre couldn't even see Singer, so no point in making a run to kill the man. Plus, no more grenades. They would have to wait for Cloire and the others to kill Laslo and break the psychic hold over the deaders.

However . . .

Turning, Jean-Pierre saw that the crucified Danielle wasn't very far away, about fifty feet to his left and behind; he would still have the cover of the rotting barricade for several yards and then the swaying bodies would obscure the zombies' line of fire.

Loirot saw his look. "Are you going to do her, Jean-Pierre, or has Cloire been right all along?"

The albino shot him.

Loirot swore. "What'd you do that for?"

To Sophia, Jean-Pierre said, "Help me get her down from there."

They moved off at a brisk crouch to the wall where Ruegger and Danielle hung, surely dying. Jean-Pierre glanced over his shoulder, trying to determine his vulnerability to enemy fire, and saw that it was as he'd hoped. He couldn't see the zombies because of all the hanging bodies, and if he couldn't see them, they couldn't shoot him.

Danielle was still unconscious, and it pained Jean-Pierre to see the wounds in her hands and ankles where Laslo's minions had driven their nails. He glanced away, feeling hatred rise in him, and his eyes fell on Ruegger.

The Darkling observed him coolly.

Neither spoke. Jean-Pierre bowed his head in acknowledgement of his enemy, and Ruegger returned the gesture, as much as he could; he seemed terribly weak. Strangely, his attention turned to Sophia.

"Sophia ..."

"It's me," she said. "I'm here."

"Here," the albino said, ignoring the exchange. There would be time for explanations later. With the ghensiv's help, he lowered Danielle's cross to the ground, letting it down as gently as possible. As he started to remove the razor wire around her wrists, Sophia held him back. He flashed an angry look at her.

She indicated Ruegger. "No. Let him."

Puzzled, the albino glared at the Darkling, who had eyes only for Danielle. Jean-Pierre understood. It would be selfish for him to play Danielle's hero. Then again ... hold that up to the ultimate ironic pleasure of Jean-Pierre, at last, *being* her savior, and it was pretty much a toss-up as far as he could see.

Heads, tails.

"Goddamnit," he grunted.

With Sophia's help, he lowered the Darkling's cross. They released him, removing first the chains and then the thick, heavy nails; Ruegger gritted his teeth and sweated, but he made no sound. When he was free, he lay there, too weak to move, and Sophia helped him to his feet, where he swayed. Like Danielle, all his major arteries had been slashed, and he had been grievously wounded beforehand. Jean-Pierre was surprised he could even stand.

When he was stable, Ruegger nodded to his benefactors. "Thank you."

Silently, almost in awe, they nodded back.

Without another word, the tall, lean vampire knelt beside Danielle and extricated her from the cross, carefully pulling out the nails from her wrists and feet. The pain evidently registered somewhere in her unconscious, and her eyelids fluttered. She let out a soft moan, and her eyes snapped open. When she saw Ruegger, a tired smile swept her face and was gone. She flung her arms about him and held him tightly, so tightly, and as she closed her eyes again tears spilled over and ran down her soiled cheeks.

Jean-Pierre glanced sideways at Sophia. She nodded.

Running a hand through Danielle's tangled hair, Ruegger kissed her forehead right on the cross-shaped brand and eased her back. Still one more nail to go. The one through her feet. She released him while he went about the painful business of freeing her, but after that first moan she made no other sound. Finally, he helped her stand, but they didn't break the contact, just stood there feeling each other and breathing.

Danielle noticed Jean-Pierre, but she didn't seem to know what to make of him, and she didn't seem to recognize Sophia, or perhaps she was simply dazed. In any case, the battle had stopped for the moment, neither side wanting to go on the offensive, and the four had a few seconds of peace.

"Danielle . . ." began Jean-Pierre, then stopped. What was there to say?

"You remember Sophia," Ruegger said to Danielle.

"Oh," she said. "Of course. The Ice Queen."

"Good to see—" Sophia started.

With shocking strength, Ruegger belted Jean-Pierre across the face. Jean-Pierre reeled back, then placed his hands over his bloody nose.

"That's for trying to kill Danielle at your apartment," Ruegger said.

"I suppose I deserved that."

Ruegger offered his hand, as if to shake. "And this is for saving us."

The albino stared at it. The hand stayed out there, and after a minute Jean-Pierre accepted it.

"Thank you," said the Darkling, and for a moment, just an instant, Jean-Pierre could see what Kharker saw in him.

Gunfire erupted. Somewhere Loirot issued a scream. A moment later the man himself staggered toward them through the bodies, bleeding badly, his arm almost severed. When he reached them, the sight of the four of them standing there rendered him speechless for moment.

"What is it?" Jean-Pierre said.

"Singer," Loirot gasped, finding his voice and glancing quickly, nervously, over his shoulder, "He and his zombies are attacking."

On cue, the zombies appeared, a band of about fifteen. They formed a ring about the odd flock and what remained of the death-squad.

Singer stepped forward, smiling. His canines had grown quite long, and there was something bestial in his face. "May the Lord take your sinning souls—because if He doesn't, the Devil surely will."

That was when something strange happened.

*   *   *

Byron was beginning to think they wouldn't find Laslo. This didn't disturb him.

Laslo's death would be difficult to arrange, but it was also irrelevant; Byron was perfectly aware that the albino had sent them on this mission just to have a few moments with Danielle. What would be the outcome of those moments? Byron was relatively sure that Jean-Pierre wouldn't kill her and that this lack of action would break the squad apart. If so, what would Byron do?

To be truthful, he knew the answer, as much as he might wish he didn't. He was going to miss Jean-Pierre. He only hoped that in all her anger, Cloire would refrain from killing the albino, or getting him to help her do it. That was one thing he couldn't do; if Cloire asked him to do that, no matter how he felt about her, he would refuse, and that would probably put an end to their relationship, as well. If only he could just hear her say that she loved him, just once, before that happened ...

They found Laslo in the chapel, praying. When he heard Byron and the other three enter, he wheeled about and without hesitation began shooting, a wild grin across his face. His dark eyes shone brightly. He was loving all this, thought Byron, and suddenly found that he wouldn't mind killing the bastard, after all.

Zombies sprung up to either side of the chapel's doorway and descended on the death-squad, forcing them back out into the hall. Byron shot one through the head, then another. Several fell, but then the bloodfinders were too close. One wrenched Byron's gun from his hands. He twisted its head off, but he had no time to leap for the gun. More deaders pressed in tight.

Hand-to-hand combat broke out. After crushing one of the fetid things in his big arms, Byron punched another through the chest, where his hand stuck. Seizing the opportunity, the zombie sent its fingers toward his eyes.

Cloire knocked the thing's head in with the butt of a rifle she'd managed to hang onto, then left him to struggle with getting the corpse off his arm while a third deader jumped on her back and tried to strangle her from behind. Two zombies had pinned Kilian up against a wall while another beat at his face.

Laslo emerged from the chapel. With a few zombies trailing behind, he started off down the hall, Kiernevar the only crew member free to chase after him. The two lunatics disappeared from sight.

Byron shook the thing off his hand and helped Cloire remove the zombie from her back. That done, they liberated a badly-beaten Kilian and dealt with the deaders remaining. They followed the sounds of gunfire and cackling down a series of halls until they reached a staircase, which they ascended to the top floor.

Up ahead, the laughter continued, only now it was Kiernevar who made the sound. He was just disappearing through a small arched doorway when they rounded the last bend. They entered it to find a narrow staircase. Not pausing, they ascended the single flight to the roof. A blast of cold wind raised goose-bumps along Byron's spine as he stepped outside.

At first he couldn't spot Kiernevar or Laslo, only hear their cackling and hooting, but then he saw the bodies of several zombies lying dead and broken on the roof. Kiernevar was chasing the psychotic priest up some scaffolding to the beheaded bell tower. Wind whipped madly around them, fluttering their hair and clothes.

Laslo turned on the brink of the abyss, firing his last bullets into the Lord of the Flies before they collided, struggling on the edge of a well that Byron couldn't see so much as sense. Illuminated against the stars, the two madmen locked their hands about each others' throats. It was amazing to Byron that Kiernevar was still alive, that Laslo's age wasn't enough to slay the young werewolf easily. But for some reason the two lunatics were deadlocked, struggling like two bulls, neither gaining ground, just smiling maniacally at each other even as their fingers sank tighter into each other's throats.

The two lunatics teetered, then went over into the well, both still intent on throttling the other. So focused were they that, even as they plummeted, they didn't make a sound, not even a chitter, but simply disappeared from the lip of the bell tower as if they'd never existed.

"Shit," said Cloire.

She ran up the scaffolding and peered down into the well. Byron joined her, but could see little.

"Shall we?" he said.

Cloire smiled faintly. "If Kiernevar wants to get himself killed, that's his problem. Let's go back down to the hangar the old-fashioned way."

The three loped downstairs through the cold stone corridors to the hangar. They passed the swaying bodies and empty barricades until they heard a strange *wet* sound and followed it to find a very odd scene indeed. The scattered remains of the zombies, along with Jean-Pierre, Sophia, Loirot and the odd flock (!), were standing around a large pit, or pool, located directly below an opening in the ceiling.

The surface of the gooey substance, though too high to be seen by those below, could be heard to thrash and bubble. Laslo and Kiernevar fought in there—an epic battle between two truly demented immortals. The pool bucked, the corpse-filled sludge (Byron could smell the reek of death) boiled, and the observers looked on with awe.

Finally, the waters stilled. A calm grew over the hangar.

A hand gripped the rim of the pool and a head rose over the edge: Laslo's. He was bloody and beaten, more ashen than ever, his glossy black eyes faded by battle. His expression deathly, he gave a sickly, twitching smile.

There was something wrong, something in his hair. There fingers curled tightly, gripping the roots.

Kiernevar rose from the putrid water, holding Laslo's decapitated head in his hand, located the stairs and followed them to the concrete floor. Dripping, bits of flesh and decaying matter plastering him, a manic grin spread across his features.

How was this possible? How could a werewolf so young destroy a chalgid so old? Few assembled were ever to know, but everyone was eager to conjecture about it. Perhaps Kiernevar's innate strength—the quality which had prompted Jean-Pierre to immortalize him in the first place—was simply stronger than Laslo's.

With Laslo's passing, a shudder worked its way through the assembled zombies. No more were they bound by a psychic hold; they were free, although without his blood and powers of resurrection they would probably die within a few days or weeks—unless Singer had absorbed enough of Laslo's blood over the years to make a true chalgid out of him. In that case, he would become their new leader. In any event, several of them began tearing off their monk-robes and a few even spit on them. One said, "Praise Satan," and the others chuckled.

Kiernevar started to toss the head to them, but Ruegger stopped him. With some formality, the vampire approached him and held out his hands. Kiernevar stared at him, then, wonderingly, handed the head over. He watched on intently as Ruegger whispered something to the head, then bent his ear to Laslo's lips to hear the ragged answer. Ruegger nodded, satisfied, then handed the head back to Kiernevar. Though obviously confused, Kiernevar accepted, and immediately did what he had been about to do.

Like a pack of wolves, the zombies tore the head apart. Their new-found freedom was almost intoxicating to watch.

Cloire would have none of it; Jean-Pierre had released Ruegger and Danielle and that was all she saw. Picking a shotgun from off the ground, she marched over to where the albino, Sophia, Loirot and the odd flock stood. Taking aim at Danielle, Cloire fired. The vampiress crumpled.

Jean-Pierre had the Magnum in his hand instantly and emptied its clip into Cloire before Danielle had been on the ground long enough to settle. Cloire staggered backward. Before she collapsed, she got off another twelve-gauge round, hitting the albino in the chest and sending him to the floor.

Byron helped her up. Jean-Pierre rose, too, and slapped another magazine into his gun.

"You let them *live*, you bastard!" seethed Cloire, picking up some shells from the ground and reloading the shotgun. "Kill her now, Jean-Pierre, or I swear I'll do it for you."

Ruegger knelt over Danielle, holding her in his arms. It wouldn't be long now, Byron saw: she was dying, and quickly. All the blood in the world wouldn't be able to save her after another few minutes, and Ruegger certainly didn't have enough to save her. Someone here would have to do it, and fast.

"Don't touch her, Cloire," Jean-Pierre said. "As my last act as your leader, I command you to let her live."

She arched her eyebrows at Kilian. "You with me?"

"Hell," he said, "I'm second-in-command. Are you willing to elect me as your new leader?"

"For now let's just say we're equal partners. Deal?"

"Deal."

"Kiernevar, you ugly bastard, you'll probably have made a name for yourself now, after having killed Laslo. You with us?"

"Kiernevar," he chirped, but there was clarity in his eyes. "After, albino gone?"

"That's right, shit-for-brains."

"Kiernevar is with you."

"I made you," hissed Jean-Pierre, "and I will unmake you."

"Empty threats," said Cloire. Then, to Loirot: "What of it, you bastard? You in?"

Loirot stepped away from the albino. "I'm in, goddamnit."

She faced Byron. Softly, she said, "You with me, lover?"

He hesitated. God, but what would it accomplish if he stayed with Jean-Pierre? He'd only lose Cloire. Really, his decision was inevitable.

"Do you love me?" he asked her.

"Shit," she said. "Is that what it all comes down to?"

"Yes."

"All right then, *damnit* . . . I do."

He nodded. "Will we still work for Vistrot?"

"If he'll have us."

Byron forced himself to look at Jean-Pierre, who gazed back at him with a strange . . . empathy.

"It's okay," the albino said. "I understand. Do what you have to do."

Surprising him, Byron felt tears burn behind his eyes. He straightened. "Okay," he told Cloire.

"And what about you, Sofe?" Cloire said. "We were friends for a short time, and we can be friends again. Jean-Pierre has nothing for you. Look at him, he's pathetic. Come, just think of all the great times we'll have. All you have to do is—just—say—*yes*."

Sophia stepped forward, but it was to the side of Jean-Pierre that she went. She grabbed his hand and squeezed it.

"*He's* not pathetic," she said.

"Fine. We don't need you. Step out of the way, both of you, and let us finish the job. Remember that I'm only sparing you two out of courtesy and that I'll revoke the privilege if you piss me off. Now stand down!"

Jean-Pierre raised the .357 and Sophia brought up her own pistol, a 9mm Beretta. Together, they positioned themselves in front of Ruegger and Danielle, blocking off the death-squad's line of fire. This was an irrevocable action and they both seemed to know it; a glance passed between them, and Byron didn't miss it.

"Okay, you bastards," said Cloire. "Prepare to die."

Violence would have certainly erupted, but it was at this time that help came from a very unlikely source. Booming laughter broke the tension and the Balaklava emerged from the nearby forest of swaying bodies. They chuckled and clapped their hands, and Jagoda put fingers in his mouth and whistled.

"Very good, very good," called Junger, the bald, tattooed one with the tusks. "You've all put on a marvelous show, very dramatic."

"*Very* dramatic," concurred Jagoda.

"But now it must end, because little Danielle is dying and that's not part of the plan, though it would be worse if it were Ruegger . . . but enough of this. All of you, lower your weapons or we will do it for you."

They lowered their weapons. The Balaklava were much stronger than all present, and not even Cloire wanted to fight them. Jagoda walked past Sophia and the albino to crouch next to Danielle.

Ruegger's eyes burned, but he didn't object as the bearded one sliced open his wrist and put it to Danielle's mouth. At first, she resisted, but she wasn't in every sense of the word conscious; her eyes were open, but Byron doubted she could actually see. The Balaklava's blood touched her tongue and she swallowed reflexively, growing more vital with each sip.

"That should do it," Jagoda said, and started to draw his arm away, but Ruegger grabbed it.

"What did you mean my death would be worse than hers?"

The Bone-Crusher smiled. "I can't give all the secrets away, my boy, or else it would be no fun. Besides, and whether you believe me or not, I don't know. Not completely, anyway—but find Hauswell and you'll get some answers. Trust me."

"That's the last thing I'll ever do."

Jagoda pulled his arm back. "That's the thanks I get for saving your woman?"

Ruegger's face was utterly and completely without humor. In fact, it seemed to make Jagoda uncomfortable.

"You will die, Jagoda, and your friend with you—this is a promise, a vow, and I've never been known to break a vow."

"You don't scare me, vampire. I'm more powerful than you could ever be."

"It won't matter," Ruegger whispered, and now he did smile, a tiny, grim smile that only made his bloody face more severe. His eyes were cold and black, and he held Danielle carefully in his arms as if to shield her from the world itself.

"It won't matter," he repeated.

He removed the albino's jacket from her shoulders and tossed it to Jean-Pierre, then lifted Danielle gently and carried her past the zombies, the werewolves, the Balaklava and the ghensiv, through the swaying forest of flesh and through the breach that the death-squad had created on entering. Bloody and naked as infants, they passed through the hole and left the hangar behind.

*   *   *

"So," Danielle said, glancing at Ruegger from the passenger seat of their car, when she had roused somewhat. "What did you find out from Laslo?"

Ruegger grimaced. "Hauswell's in Lereba."

"Morocco?"

"The one and only."

"We weren't far from there just a few weeks ago. I guess he wasn't there then, though. Why *is* he there?"

"In hiding from the Scouring. Laslo was covering for him."

"Shit." Danielle frowned. "So I guess we're off to Africa."

"So it seems."

"Damn. I could really use a break, Rueg."

"I know, babe. I know."

Chapter 21

Sophia watched as Cloire and Kilian prepared their crew to leave, though first they salvaged what weapons they could from the corpses. Jean-Pierre and Sophia stood side-by-side, watching and smoking. It amazed her that any sort of peace had been declared, but so it seemed. For all her anger, Cloire made no move against them now that things had been settled. Junger and Jagoda, meanwhile, discussed something with Singer and a few other zombies. Although they were anxious to return to New York, the Balaklava seemed to see artistic possibilities with the hangar and wanted to buy it from the bloodfinders, who were quite willing to make a deal. The bodies that still moved were disposed of, quickly and mercifully.

When the death-squad had gathered all the salvageable guns and was ready to leave, Cloire approached Jean-Pierre and Sophia. "I should shoot you both just for good measure."

"Then why don't you?" said Sophia.

Cloire raised her shotgun, but Byron, coming up behind her, said, "Time to go."

She blew a kiss at Sophia and the albino. "'Bye, kids, and have a nice walk back to town."

"No," said Byron, "they're coming with us."

"Fuck off. Now isn't the time to discover you've got a pair."

"Goddamnit, Cloire, Jean-Pierre's been with us too long to treat him this way. The least we owe him is a trip back to town. After that, we can declare all debts paid."

She nodded reluctantly. "Okay, you two, shut up and come with us. But, Frenchie, remember what By said—after this, all debts are paid. Don't come looking to me for a handout. Maybe in a few decades you can join us again, but that's it, and even then you won't be our leader. As for you, Sofe . . . well, bitch, may you live in interesting times."

She marched back to the exit, Jean-Pierre and Sophia following her at a more reserved pace. Sophia reached out for his hand and he took it.

The drive back to Las Vegas was silent, tense, and seemingly endless. When it was over, the occupants of the van climbed out and made their way up to the penthouse they'd rented. After packing their bags, Jean-Pierre and Sophia decided against making a farewell speech, left quickly and took an elevator down to the Strand, where it was cool and dry. Sophia felt dizzy. Events had been moving too fast.

"What now?" she said.

"I could use a drink."

"Best plan I've heard all day."

They found themselves a bar, sat down at a booth near a window and ordered a few beers. She leaned back, closed her eyes and sighed. Suddenly, she felt very tired, but it was good to be here, alone again with Jean-Pierre.

"Sophia," he said slowly, letting his words sink in, "I'm not known for my impetuous actions, but our relationship seems to be progressing rapidly."

She opened her eyes. He seemed sincere, despite the businesslike nature of his tone.

"It does," she said, feeling the heat from his hand.

"What I'm proposing . . . well, why don't we stay here, together, for a few days, before we return to New York. See if we can't make something out of this?"

What in hell is going on? she thought. *Love? Really?*

She studied his moist green eyes, which reflected the brilliant neon of the Strand, and saw that there were tears there. God, he was so open! And, more than anything else, she could respect this, because it was something she wasn't yet strong enough to be. Accepting his proposal would bring her that much closer.

She removed her hand from his and busied herself by lighting a Black Death.

There was, of course, that other issue between them, that issue which bound them no matter what, an issue which would make any union between them rather unconventional. It was this issue that finally decided her.

Immediately she found herself laughing *(Can't wait to tell Mom!)* and reached for his hand. "I will, Jean-Pierre. God help me, but I will. You must do one thing for me, though."

"Yes?"

"I could never be with an evil man. I must teach you how to be good. Not that I'm on particularly good terms with *good*, but ... do you accept?"

He blinked at her. "A defining moment, you said." When she didn't reply, he ran a hand through his hair.

She waited, tense. Would he actually forgo the dark path?

Finally, he straightened. "So be it. For you, Sophia, I accept. But teaching me will not be easy."

* * *

Leaving the airport, Ruegger and Danielle rode a taxi into the heart of Lereba. Excitement coursed through him, and Danielle seemed to feed on it.

The city blazed, bright and colorful. Capital of immortal activity in Africa, Lereba played home to the two dominant races of immortal here: the abunka, like the assassin Jarvick, and the karula. The karula tended to be Arab-looking and, unlike abunka, they fed exclusively on humans, on whatever bodily tissue or fluid was convenient and tasty at the time. Relations between the two races were always tense, but their coexistence was made easier by the fact that one race lived largely below ground and one above.

The narrow streets twisted and turned in labyrinthine corridors, and the taxi was often halted by the people and their mounts swarming the streets. Clay buildings towered to either side. Spicy scents of local cuisine drifted out from open windows.

"It's beautiful," Danielle said.

Ruegger watched her. The cross on her forehead was completely gone, erasing all physical evidence of their time in Nevada, but there was something that was too quiet about her, too composed. She showed little of her usual spark or enthusiasm, which worried him.

"Yes," he said, "it is."

"What's wrong?"

"Just wondering where the hell we're going to find Hauswell in this madhouse. He could've already left by now. Laslo wasn't in any condition to tell me how long he'd been here."

She patted his hand. "Maybe Saskia will know."

"Maybe."

"If he doesn't, then at least he can provide a place for us to stay while we ask around, right? Everything will be okay, don't worry."

The taxi dropped them off a block short of Saskia's hotel, and they enjoyed the chance to walk among the townspeople. Ruegger hoped their energy would be contagious. Upon entering the hotel's lobby, the odd flock immediately noticed the many guards in attendance—at least five of them immortal. Though the guards were discreet, their presence was unnerving.

The lobby, like most of Moroccan buildings, radiated heat, as the clay absorbed the warmth of the sun and retained it for long periods. A few fans stirred the air, and with the buzzing clientele and the friendly nature of the place, the effect was warm and pleasant. The odd flock moved through a small archway and a curtain of beads into a heavily-shadowed room that appeared to be a sort of nightclub, filled with several different kinds of smoke, sat down at the bar and ordered a beer. They sipped their drinks, getting comfortable, listening to a small native band that played on a raised stage in the corner. A few local businessmen of respectable ages sat nearby, celebrating something. They smoked marijuana but didn't drink, not uncommon in the region.

Ruegger asked the bartender to send a courier to inform Saskia they were here. The bartender obliged, and in a few minutes Saskia came through another archway spanned by beads. The karula looked more severe than usual, his thick black beard braided formally and wearing a brown robe and head scarf, as if in mourning. Three immortal bodyguards hovered about him.

"Well, well," he said, putting on a smile. "So my favorite nomads have returned!"

He embraced them both, exchanging greetings. Saskia bid his guardians relax and plopped down at the bar, ordering a bottle of vodka and a shot glass.

"I wasn't sure you'd make it back here, my friends," he said. "We hear rumors about your Balaklava and your Jean-Pierre. We heard what you did to Triboli. He was quite well-known around these parts."

"We were hoping you might know something about the hit Jarvick was carrying out."

Saskia shrugged. "Well, I can tell you that he had vague connections with Roche Sarnova's people."

"You think Sarnova wants us dead?" Danielle said.

Saskia chuckled. "That seems unlikely, but it's all I know. I'm sure you've more than a few enemies lying around, but you'd know them better than I. Would you consider Lord Kharker an enemy?"

Ruegger shifted uncomfortably. "No. At least, I wouldn't have phrased it that way."

"Well, I know that Lord Kharker and Roche Sarnova are friends, which leads to the connection with Jarvick."

"What are you saying?"

Saskia downed a shot without a chaser and said, "Probably nothing. I didn't mean to upset you. Please, let's not discuss this anymore."

"So what's with the guards?" Danielle asked. "And why are you dressed that way? What's wrong?"

Saskia made a face. He started rolling a joint. "Care to join me? This is prime stuff."

"Sure."

"It's been a bloody awful last few weeks," the karula said while he worked. "Lyrenk and Testopha were killed within a few hours of each other, twenty-five nights ago. Since then, it's been war."

The news jolted Ruegger. "I'm sorry."

"I don't get it," Danielle said. "Who were they?"

"Lyrenk and Testopha were the leaders of the karula and the abunka here for over three hundred years," Ruegger said. "They kept the two races at peace."

"Without them, who knows what will happen?" Saskia said.

"Hell," Danielle said.

Ruegger lowered his voice. "Who killed them?"

"The abunka claim that we killed Testopha and they retaliated by assassinating Lyrenk," Saskia said. "But it's all very shady, very mysterious. No one knows for sure what happened. There's a rumor that someone from the outside had Testopha killed to ignite a war. Maybe, maybe not, but either way, war's what's happened, though so far it's been small-scale stuff, an assassination here and there. But sooner or later . . ." He licked the joint shut and lit it.

"You think there will be actual war?" Ruegger asked. "Fighting in the streets?"

"I'm afraid so; at this point, it seems inevitable. The abunka and my kind have hated each other for thousands of years—our gods versus theirs, and both sides claim that this is their homeland. The usual. I've always taken a stand against that crap, being friendly to the abunka when I can, but it's only the renegades—like Jarvick—that will deal with me. They've rejected their gods, for the most part, and I've rejected mine. We have no quarrel, but it's all the others, the traditionalists, that are out for blood. Figuratively, of course." He passed Danielle the bomb.

She sucked in a long toke, then a sip of her beer. "Maybe they'll kill each other off," she said. "And the only ones left standing will be the enlightened ones."

Saskia smiled sadly. "That's my dream, too, kid. But it seems that I'm in some danger, and not just from the sand-rats."

"You're afraid of karula, too?" Ruegger said.

Saskia nodded. "I think my free-spirited ways have gotten me in trouble. My peers don't appreciate my rejection of their values ... and the fact that I deal with abunka. And the abunka know I'm a valued leader and representative of my kind, at the same time my kind wish I weren't. So, you see, it's looking pretty grim for your humble friend either way, don't you think?"

"Why don't you just get out of here?" Danielle said, passing the joint to Ruegger. He declined.

"This is my home. I've been thinking of abandoning it, though, at least until things calm down. I've thought of relocating to Iraq for a time." He shrugged again. "Looks like we're both being hunted, doesn't it?"

"Nothing makes sense," Ruegger muttered, knocked back a vodka shot and passed the shot glass to Danielle.

Saskia looked contemplative. "Chaos is breaking out all over the world. Immortals are being slaughtered every night, every hour. The Scouring, they call it, but no one knows what's really going on, or what tomorrow might bring to light. By the way, I am sorry about the loss of your friend, Ludwig. I never met him, but he always sounded like an interesting character."

"Thank you. You wouldn't happen to've heard anything about Hauswell, would you?"

"I heard he was dead, but I'm sure you know that already."

"If he wasn't dead, and were in town, where would he be?"

"There's only one place I can think of: the territory of the renegade abunka." Saskia stood. "Well, my friends, I'm afraid that I've got things to do, but you're always welcome to come chat and smoke with me. I think you'll be quite safe in Lereba as long as you stay here; I've some clout, you know, and no one would dare harm one of my guests. Would you like your old room?"

"That would be great."

"Is there anything else I can do for you while you're here?"

"We could use some hardware," Ruegger said. "I feel naked without a few guns on me."

"Of course. I'll send a man around tonight." Smiling affectionately, he embraced them both and departed.

Watching him go, Danielle said, "I'm more confused now than I was before. What the hell's going on?"

* * *

"What about that one?" Jean-Pierre asked, pointing out the dirty window of the truck towards a man standing on the street corner.

"*No,*" said Sophia. "They must be *evil.* That guy's just selling 'shrooms."

Every day he was getting better, or thought he was, but this just wasn't something he was used to thinking about. All the same, he knew he had to. *A defining moment.* Besides that, Sophia had made it plain that she would not stay with his old amoral self. Now, days after the showdown at Laslo's, he had bought a used Bronco and, together, they were trying to pick out a victim to feed from. They'd been at it for hours.

"Well, then you choose one," he said. "Show me how it's done."

She squinted at the crowded street. At long last she admitted, "To tell you the truth, I've never really done this. A ghensiv doesn't have to."

"Then how'd you expect me to tell which one of these people is evil?"

"I don't know. You're supposed to be a powerful psychic."

"You said reading their minds was an invasion of privacy."

She let out a breath. "I take it back, for the moment. Better to invade their privacy than kill them if they're innocent."

While he was probing the brains of the passers-by, he mused, "How do Ruegger and Danielle do it?"

"Heard they ousted lowlifes from prison sometimes, killers and rapists—then feed from them. But mainly, I think they just use their contacts. They pay people all around the world to keep tabs on bad guys for them. Plus, they kill a lot of shades and drink their blood."

They didn't find anybody purely evil that night. Instead, they returned to their hotel room and made love, then called up room service and ate until they couldn't move. Next evening they camped out again, looking for bad guys. The cycle repeated itself several times, and to him that was a good thing. No more roaming around, executing Vistrot's enemies, maintaining order in the criminal underworld. Still, it was frustrating. Going hungry wasn't the glamorous life he'd pictured. He missed the crew and the constant rush of adrenaline.

He was learning, though. Sophia taught him to be patient and to bide his time. Her calm was contagious. If this was being in a constructive relationship, he could live with that. When another few nights passed without food, he told her the situation was unfair. Every day he sustained her—sometimes several times—yet she expected him to starve.

"What's your point?" she said.

"Maybe I'll let you go without for a couple days and see how well you do."

"I'll bet you can't."

"Bet I can," he said.

"Care to make it interesting?" When he said yes, she asked, "What're the stakes?"

"If you hold out longer than I do, we'll go on like this. If I resist you, you help me fill my belly unless you want to go without as well."

They shook on it. After two nights of nothing but heavy petting, she grew more strident in her efforts at helping him feed. To make up for lost time, he sustained her as often as he could.

Days passed. Then a week. Then two.

After the second week had gone by, and he and Sophia were closer than ever, he announced his plan. They were sharing an omelet in the last Ma and Pa restaurant in Vegas when Jean-Pierre told her how he felt, and what he felt they ought to do about it.

"While in Vegas . . ."

"You can't be serious," she said.

Jean-Pierre, the albino, retired world-famous assassin, slipped out of the booth and dropped to one knee.

*   *   *

In Los Angeles, at Sophia's home in Beverly Hills, Veliswa was enjoying the moonlight out by the pool and stroking the three-legged cat when the phone rang. She smiled when she heard her daughter's voice.

"Yes, yes, the cat's fine. How about Ruegger and Danielle?"

"Safe for now," said Sophia.

"I'm so glad you've been able to keep an eye on them. So what bizarre circumstance compelled you to call your poor mother?"

When Sophia told her, Veliswa dropped the phone. "Jesus H. Christ!"

She waited for the tears to come. After all the affection she'd wasted on that bastard, he'd married her daughter! She couldn't believe it. But the tears didn't come. In fact, after a minute she found herself laughing so hard that the cat ran off.

"Does he know?" she said.

"No. He has no idea."

Chapter 22

The first thing Ruegger noticed when he woke up was that the maid was late again. A body lay near the door, where it had been left last night, a dry host to flies to be taken out during the day while the vampires slept—but this was the second night in a row a body was still there when he woke.

He nudged Danielle, immersed in a silken sea of reddish sheets. She murmured something, then slowly rolled over and propped herself up against the adobe wall the bed was shoved against. Though naked beneath the sheets, she didn't cover herself. She smiled sleepily.

"Hey."

He smiled back. "Hey."

He kissed her sweaty throat, playing his fingers through her hair. He rose, rooted briefly through a wad of scattered clothes on the floor, produced a couple of cigarettes—not cloves, thank the gods—and lit them both one. Smoking, she threw off the covers and climbed out of bed as well, obviously relishing the warm clay against her bare feet. She wrapped herself loosely in a rouge sheet and moved to the window, hidden now behind a curtain. Ruegger felt it, too: the pulse of the young dusk outside, its crackling energies lush and unrestrained.

Danielle found a pack of incense, shook a few dry brown stalks into her hand and plunged the sharpened tips into the bloodless chest of the dead man, a former child peddler and murderer they'd stalked last night, then lit her clove from the incense flame, blowing her first lungful out to tame the fire and taking a moment to study the hot glow of the burning tip.

"I'll never get over having to kill people to live," she said. "At least we're able to take down some bad guys, though."

"Indeed."

Ruegger slipped into a pair of white silk pants, stepped over to the wall near the balcony and hit a button that made the blackout curtains swoosh to the side, letting in the strong light from outside. He blinked, knowing that the sun hadn't been down for even five minutes. But it was night now. Moving onto the balcony, he leaned over the balustrade to peer at the bustling robed merchants and brightly decorated camels that banged through the narrow street. Danielle joined him. Together they watched the exotic frenzy, letting the spices and scents of the city tickle their noses.

"I love Morocco," she sighed. "Too bad we can't stay here much longer."

Ruegger arched his eyebrows, thinking of the telegram they'd gotten last night. Hauswell had contacted them; he was indeed staying with the renegade abunka in the southeastern part of town, though apparently he was using a false name and few there knew him. He'd gotten wind of the vampires' questions and sent for them. They'd been in Lereba five days trying to find him, unsure which branch of the renegade abunka to look into or if he was really with them at all.

"It's almost over," Danielle said.

Ruegger kissed her forehead. "Let's just hope that what he has to say was worth what we went through to hear it." What he was really thinking was that it was a shame they had to leave, because he felt that another few weeks here could bring her back to her old self. Already she seemed in better spirits. But they couldn't risk the chance that the death-squad would reacquire them here, especially now that Jean-Pierre wouldn't be able to protect them. And Ruegger sure didn't want to meet up with the Balaklava again.

She reached for his hand, then leaned out over the balcony on tip-toe, allowing the wind to tease her dark hair.

"We'll have to come back soon, though," she said.

"We will."

"Umm," she murmured, still studying the street, but something in her face had changed. She raised a hand lamely and waved at someone down below, then turned to Ruegger. "I think we've outstayed our welcome, babe."

"How?"

Then he saw them too. They weren't hard to spot. Out of all the hundreds of people below, they were the only ones standing bone still and staring up at the hotel. Six tall, thin black men who wore desert-blue robes, they carried machetes at their sides. Ceremonial designs had peen painted on their faces, supposedly giving them strength to walk above ground.

"Great," said Ruegger.

He guided Danielle inside and closed the door. His eyes darted into the corner, where their suitcases lay open on a little table. Courtesy of their host, they'd been able to purchase a wide variety of weapons not normally available in the States, and Ruegger was looking forward to trying them out. As was his custom, he had devoted an entire suitcase to his firearms.

"We've got to warn Saskia," he said.

"Lead the way."

Carrying their luggage, Ruegger and Danielle fought their way through the busy halls, flailing against the current—what the hell was going on?—to reach Saskia's suite on the top story, two floors above. Saskia's soldiers ranged everywhere here, some storming about, some grouped in pairs, guns ready. This was Saskia's domain; everything that happened on this floor related directly to his criminal interests. Usually it was busier here than the other three stories, but obviously Ruegger and Danielle weren't the only ones who'd foreseen bad tidings.

Guards stopped them.

"Take us to Saskia," Ruegger said.

The guards hesitated, then one said, "Come." The guards led them down a hall into Saskia's office. At the little bar against one wall, Saskia bolted down vodka shots by himself while his guards waited listlessly, one keeping watch at the windows.

Saskia glanced up, coughing as if the vodka had gone down wrong. "Well, this is it, my friends. They've finally decided to have it out with me."

"So you're getting drunk?" Ruegger said.

"Don't tell anyone. I'm not Muslim, but it pays to put on the act around here. Anyway, I'm just waiting for my ride. The helicopter should be here any minute. Have you ever seen my helipad?"

"We've landed on it before." It was on the roof.

"Ah, that's right. Well, would you like to come with me? Though I honestly doubt the abunka will bother you much—if they killed you it would look as if they are indiscriminate in their wrath, and they want to give the appearance of a holy war. Arrogant bastards."

"Thanks, but we'd only weigh you down. As you said, we'll manage."

"You're evacuating the hotel?" Danielle said.

"Yes, tourists and personal guests alike, all encouraged to leave," Saskia said. "The least I can do for loyal patrons. Besides, this place probably won't be standing in the morning." He cocked his head and called to one of his guards, the one near the window: "Do I hear our ride?"

The man nodded, his gaze on the object of inquiry. "Should be here in a minute."

Saskia lifted the vodka bottle toward Ruegger. "Would you like to do one last shot with me?"

Ruegger obliged. After Ruegger had swallowed, Danielle downed a shot herself. By that time, the helicopter had drawn near and prepared to land. Ruegger could hear it through the ceiling.

Saskia's eyes turned up. "Guess my ride's h—"

The explosion shook the chamber. The aircraft fell to the clay roof of the hotel, missing the helipad but smashing through the ceiling to settle between floors, caught in the ragged hole it had made upon impact. Ruegger didn't witness it, but he soon saw the proof as Saskia and the vampires ran into the hallway and watched what was left of the helicopter burn. Smoke filled the hall.

"Hells," coughed Saskia. "This is worse than you know."

Danielle wiped soot from her face. "What do you mean?"

Saskia drew them back into this office. "It means that the abunka have decided to use modern technology. Never before would they have shot an aircraft down; they would've tried to win without mechanical devices, using only machetes and the like. This is very bad." He collapsed onto a stool. "Well, let's not make this too dramatic. Not all is lost." He stood suddenly and called his men to him. Before addressing them, he turned to his guests. "I can give you five minutes before I come down. It looks like we're going to have to blast ourselves out the old-fashioned way, but I couldn't live with myself if I endangered you. So please, go now, and I hope to see you again soon, under better circumstances."

Ruegger didn't like leaving his friend in such an emergency, but he knew that Saskia could take care of himself, and the last thing Danielle needed was another battle. Just the same ...

"I can't leave you," he said.

"Go. I swear, if you stay—yes, believe it—I'll kill myself. My honor demands nothing less. I could not risk the lives of my friends without need and go on. Only by leaving will you give me a chance at victory."

Ruegger nodded, unsure how much this was true but suspecting it might be, and they said their farewells.

"Good luck," Saskia called out behind them.

The vampires emerged into the lobby amid colorful anarchy of the exodus. They stumbled outside, where it only seemed to be more crowded. The stench of camel dung was prevalent, and Danielle lit up a clove. They reached a taxi, its dented metal still smelling of the sun, and hopped in. The engine leapt to life, Ruegger said a few words to the driver, and they set off, the little white car seeming to ricochet from point to point. The lines on the road were little more than decoration.

Not far away, in the direction of Saskia's, gunfire erupted amid a maelstrom of explosions. Ruegger tensed.

"We had to leave him," Danielle assured him. "It was the only way. Besides, if we'd died back there we couldn't stop what's going to happen. If we don't find Ludwig's killer ..."

"I know."

She glanced back. "I think we're being followed."

"Never a dull moment."

They held hands while the strange dusty city clanked by, letting the spices and street sounds lull them as they made their way to a hellchild carnival on the eve of war.

* * *

The taxi let them out in the lower-east side of town, located on the rise of a hill—the highest in the city—a wild area where corrupt oil millionaires and eccentric foreigners came to stay, enjoying their most depraved fantasies for pocket change. The pocket change being considerable, of course, so that certain undead elements thrived here amid massive adobe villas and Salvatore Dali-influenced bordellos, the desert and its dark-skinned demons waiting just beyond. And below.

Ruegger and Danielle leapt up the steps of a clay mansion painted a pastel red. Torches blazed on the porch, casting shadows across the pillars and the giant statue of a winged lion above the door, flame licking at its teeth and burning from its eyes.

The vampires stepped through the open door, hearing the cacophony of African tribal rock blasting its way out from the bowels of the mansion. As they made their way inside, they noticed the colored lights, the blacklit posters, the torches, and the pulsating projections thrown upon the walls in twisting gothic patterns. Aside from some glowing televisions and hip artistic couches, there was little furniture other than the bars. It was all very Western, which probably seemed exotic to the natives. The smell of opium, hash, sweat and sex flooded the halls, getting thicker the further down the vampires went.

They moved through the secret door, down the secret steps, and into an immense underground cavern of a basement. Pillars stood everywhere, as did torches. All manner of beings rubbed elbows here, from black-winged shades to glowering, suited mortals, from abunka to karula. Different pockets of the room performed different functions, from the crowded bar to the mosh pit to the moaning tangle of the orgy.

Ruegger and Danielle found a certain hallway—one of the many—and followed it until it became a sandy corridor snaking off into the busy darkness, wooden boards holding it up. Here is where the territory of this branch of the renegade abunka really began, and it was a joyous place where the more open-minded mingled and partied. Mortals came too, intrigued by the sex, drugs, and the possibility of meeting the bizarre. They arrived in legions, and they were easy prey not only for their flesh but their money. The ones who didn't get swindled or killed had the possibility of finding themselves, and they spread the word.

A bare-chested, blue-painted man blew flame from his mouth while in the shadows a human male was being sucked off by what seemed to be an under-aged girl, but who was surely an older-than-she-looked ghensiv. Some insectile, red-skinned creatures with tails and moist exoskeletons were pleasuring each other in a confused cluster in the middle of the path, and Ruegger and Danielle were obliged to step over them. A sorcerer with the head of a dog did tricks for the audience while his assistant picked their pockets.

Once Ruegger and Danielle got lost among the maze of tunnels and found their corridor dead-ending into the upper portion of a gigantic atrium, where jandrows flew and swooped in great arcs, perching on comfortable landings that hung from the ceiling. Danielle found herself wondering if Maleasoel had ever been here.

Eventually they found themselves in another open chamber. A lavish sea-water aquarium lined one wall and speed metal crashed through the speakers. The mosh pit was larger and the perversions more wicked, but otherwise this room seemed very similar to the last. Mostly Americans gathered here, so it was more likely that they would find who they were looking for, or at least someone who knew where he was.

After forcing their way to the bar, they asked a bartender if she knew where Ciara was. The bartender could only spare a second, but she shouted an answer and turned back to the thirsty horde.

The vampires picked their way down another corridor, emerging into a smaller, dingier room, with jazz blooming from the speakers. They found Ciara reclining in a dark corner booth, opium smoke hovering over the table. Waiters and waitresses handed out menus designed for rarer pleasures. Ciara and a small group of baked friends lounged on the soft purple cushions, taking a breather before smoking some more.

Ciara was an abunka, long and black, dressed in a shimmering suit with a bright orange shirt beneath the dark jacket, and before him sat a small dusty jar filled with living fish. Part of the curse of the abunkan race was to crave the taste of fish from the sea, while at the same time knowing that salt water was toxic to them. Ciara seemed like a lot of New York jazz lounge cat mixed with a little Las Vegas snake-oil salesman. One of Ruegger's many contacts, he smiled as the vampires approached.

"Made it out alive?" he said in raspy African-tinted English.

"We made it," Ruegger said.

Ciara clapped his spindly hand on his knee, cufflinks glittering in the blue-ish light, and chuckled to himself. "You two look like you're still on honeymoon, you know. Warms the heart just to see you."

"We're not married," Danielle said.

Ciara's smile grew wider. "That sounded very pointed. I think that was a hint, my boy." When Ruegger didn't reply, Ciara said, "Touched a nerve, did I?" The abunka pursed his dark lips. Blue light bounced off the gold rings on his fingers and played winsomely about his face.

"Shades don't get married," Ruegger said.

"What of your dear departed friend Ludwig and his lovely bride?" asked Ciara, reaching into the jar in front of him with a pair of tongs and pulling out a squirming fish. He stuffed the fish's belly in his mouth and bit down gently, savoring the juices. Using what mindthrust he had, he stilled the fish's thrashings with a soothing, psychic finger.

"So what've you heard of Ludwig's death?" Ruegger said. "Anything new?"

Ciara smacked his lips, set the fish skeleton down in a small pile of its predecessors, and wiped at his mouth with a pink napkin. He nodded guiltily. "I'm afraid so."

"Well?"

Ciara rolled his eyes. "It was those two Balaklava, wasn't it—Junger and Jagoda—that killed him? Well, I happen to know that Testopha was killed by none other than the dynamic duo. Unfortunately, this knowledge comes too late to make reparations between the karula and the abunka. War often isn't something that can be stopped by something so trivial as truth."

Ruegger exchanged a glance with Danielle, and she felt just as surprised as he looked.

"Then Testopha wasn't Scoured," he said.

"Not unless the Balaklava work for the Scourer," Ciara said.

This was interesting, but it didn't jive with what they'd learned in Las Vegas.

"The Scouring doesn't usually work that way," Ruegger pointed out. "It works through local hit-teams."

"You speak of the Scouring as if it's a natural phenomenon, my boy, and I admit, it has the right proportions—relative to the Community, of course. At last count, I've heard that it's claimed over a hundred immortal lives, not to mention those killed in its rather chaotic aftermath. See, it always kills a crime lord, or someone in a position of power—every now and then a religious figure— which causes insanity afterwards as that position is battled or grieved over. It's my opinion that *that* is the intention of the Scouring, not the immediate death of its victim."

"You've given it some thought."

"I have . . . I have." Suddenly Ciara seemed weary. "Please tell me you're staying awhile." His face turned bitter then, shark-like anger rising to the placid surface. "If you go tonight, you might miss the city burning. Fucking fanatics, I don't understand it! I'm an abunka and I don't hate the karula, do I? No. We eat fish, have dark skin, live underground and they don't, but so fucking what?"

Ruegger nodded gently. "It's all connected to the Scouring somehow. Junger and Jagoda must be working for the one who's been pulling the strings. The Scourer. We know they're working for Vistrot, but I don't see him as the Scourer. Anything else, maybe, but that just doesn't seem like him. Why would he want to eradicate crime and religion? Junger and Jagoda must be working for someone else, as well. Do you have any idea who?"

Ciara licked his fingers, sucking with wet smacking sounds, then shook his head. "I have absolutely no idea, although I do know that the Balaklava were hired not too long ago to do some artwork for Roche Sarnova, which is the first contact that I know of that they've had with the outside world since their days in Jamaica. It'd seem possible that Sarnova could be their employer. But again, I don't know."

Carefully, Ruegger said, "Do you know anything of Hauswell?"

"He's dead, isn't he. Why, do you think that was just a ruse?"

"Could it be that he's here somewhere?"

Ciara looked at him steadily. "Anything's possible. He could be staying with us under an assumed name, I suppose, but I wouldn't know him if I saw him. In fact, you two are probably the only ones in this part of the world that *would* recognize him." He lowered his voice still further. "However, I will … make inquiries."

It would have to do, Danielle supposed. She knew that Ciara would pass the word to Hauswell. Now it was up to Hauswell to make contact.

The abunka nodded, seeing the vampires' understanding. "Well, I'm sure you'd like to get some rest and unpack. Please, come visit me later, if you have time." He snapped his fingers and a young boy stepped out of the shadows, bare-chested, with various-colored designs painted on his hairless torso. He was silent, but his eyes were sober. "Gabriel, would you please show my friends to a room?"

Gabriel glanced them over, cocked his head and marched off. Ruegger and Danielle hurried after. Gabriel led them through a tunnel that turned out to be a shortcut back up to the mansion. He showed them to a room and left in silence.

Ruegger looked out the window while Danielle shut the door and reclined on the bed.

"Very informative," she said. "Sad, all of it, but informative."

"What are you thinking?"

She shook her head and smiled. "Nothing, really. And everything. Strange to say this, after what we've been through, but this place is depraved. Despite that, I actually like the people here. It's the atmosphere. Drugs and sex and violence." She patted the bedside beside her. "Now you're the one that looks gloomy. Come here, love. Let me see if I can cheer you up."

* * *

Later, after they'd broken the bed in and were lying around on it smoking cigarettes, Danielle nudged him.

"What about that breakfast you promised me?"

He crossed to the window and looked down on the sprawling city. Danielle joined him. She could see a building on fire far away and thought it might be Saskia's, but she couldn't be certain. Several buildings burned.

"I'm hungry, too," he said.

They dressed and followed Gabriel's corridor down to the halls of the renegade abunka, and from there drifted over to the mosh pit, which was slowly becoming as much an orgy as the orgy, though the sex was a little more violent. The vampires stayed to watch the band for a bit, though they declined to dance.

What do mortals think of all this? Danielle wondered. If this was their only glimpse of the immortal community, they must think all shades were debauched. The shame was that, say, fifty percent of the shades here were decent folk like Ciara, who stood head and shoulders (morally) above most of the members of the Community. The thought saddened her.

"Here, I saw a food vendor just down the way," Ruegger said. "Breakfast, remember?"

They ordered beer and goat meat in a wrapper and sat down on a dining rug in a quiet corner of the area. She downed her beer quickly, trying to cool herself down, and drank the next one at a more leisurely pace. The goat wraps, as it turned out, weren't half bad.

"Still hungry?" he said.

He didn't mean for food, she knew.

"Insatiable."

After finishing their meal, they moved through the familiar din of the party, drifting until they found a little wooden stand not far from what looked like a theater of sorts, with hundreds, maybe thousands of seats planted along a slope with a stage at the bottom. Something was going on down there, but the vampires didn't pay much attention.

They stopped before the wooden stand, where a few mortals watched them. One smiled and yelled something in salesman-ese ("Come and enjoy yourselves, ladies and gentlemen—tonight may be the END OF THE WORLD!"), but the vampires were already there. The mortal who ran this booth made his living off selling intelligence, mainly catering to immortals who, like Ruegger and Danielle, preferred to feed only off the scum of humanity; the man had a small army of scouts infiltrate the hallways regularly on the look-out for tasty evildoers. The scouts would keep tabs on these villains' locations, selling this information to shades.

An hour later, after Ruegger and Danielle had fed properly on a murderer, they returned to the theater area and bought a pair of tickets. As it turned out, a circus side-show run by a shade named Maximillian was touring the world's seedier quarters; they had just come from Calcutta and tomorrow they would leave for New York. Apparently, the so-called freaks (a word they themselves used) belonged to a troupe called The Funhouse of the Forsaken. The odd flock bought some popcorn and settled in for the show.

Maximillian—a tall, skinny man with a wicked leer and a thin, curled mustache—acted the ringleader, and he presented a creature that looked to be a horribly obese two-headed man. A fellow in an outrageous tuxedo complete with tails emerged from the wings wheeling an array of knives and daggers on a small table.

He bound the two-headed man to a portable wall (painted psychedelic colors), then staggered back a great length, brandishing his knives wildly. The crowd cheered, and Danielle latched onto Ruegger's hand.

At first, the man in the tuxedo threw the knives in a ring around the two-headed man, but then one of the knives flew straight into the fellow's midsection, and blood (fake, surely) squirted out. The knife-wielder laughed, grabbed a double-sided dagger and charged toward the helpless captive. As he plunged the blade into his victim's midsection, the two-headed man seemed to come apart at the seams, revealing that he was in fact two men, Siamese twins who had been separated but could give the illusion of coming together again. The twins grabbed their tormentor, engulfing him, and he seemed to disappear into the portable wall amidst a geyser of more fake blood, leaving only his gaudy tux behind.

The twins cackled, freed themselves, and gave a bow to enthusiastic applause. As they departed the stage, Maximillian presented the next show. After another few acts, Ruegger and Danielle relinquished their seats to someone else and moved to another part of the carnival. Eventually, they found a jazz lounge far removed from the action, where they sat down at a nice table close to the musicians.

It wasn't long before Ruegger recognized a familiar figure sitting alone at a booth, drinking a Bloody Mary. Ruegger sat up bolt-straight. Danielle turned.

It was Hauswell.

Chapter 23

Two weeks after the showdown at Laslo's mission, Vistrot awoke from a peaceful sleep to the sound of a ringing phone; it was his most private of private lines and the only one that could have interrupted him in his bedroom. He snatched up the phone and demanded, "Yes, what is it?"

"It's Cloire, sweet-cheeks. Hope I didn't wake you."

"This better be good."

"Oh, baby, 'good' doesn't cover it."

"Did you kill Ruegger and Danielle or not?"

"Not as such."

He sighed. Cloire always had been a bitch and he'd never had much occasion to talk to her, but for some reason he liked her. If nothing else, she had spunk.

"Where have you been?" he said. "I sent you to Vegas two weeks ago and you haven't even checked in, yet. Where's Jean-Pierre?"

"Calm down, cue ball. We've been away testing loyalty. Trust me, it was needed."

"Explain. Quickly."

As she described the events that had taken place, he couldn't help but to notice the satisfaction in her voice.

"So you've broken with Jean-Pierre," he said when she was through, trying very hard to disguise his disappointment. He wasn't angry at Cloire; she had, in fact, done what she was supposed to do. If the albino couldn't hack it anymore, then he was better left out. But this changed things greatly.

"That's a fact," she said. "But we still work for you, big guy. Are your orders still to kill the odd flock?"

"No."

"What?"

Keeping his laughter in check, he said, "That's right, sweet-cheeks. You're not to kill them."

"Goddamn you, you fat bastard. You can't *do* this to me."

This time he couldn't keep it down. He laughed, long and hard, and he could hear Cloire growling on the other end, which just made it more enjoyable. Finally, when it was out of his system, he said, "You're still to pursue them, Cloire. You're to capture them, not kill them. Do you understand me?"

"The line's breaking up. I didn't catch that last part. You said kill them?"

"Don't irritate me, Cloire. If you have them killed, I'll have you hunted down, no matter where you are, and believe me, death will be the least of your worries." When she said nothing, he went on. "How do you intend to reacquire them?"

Some good humor returned to her voice, and he could hear the smile there. "I think you'll like this one . . . "

He did. When she was finished speaking, he had a new respect for her; she was quite the devious mind, wasn't she, and she knew very well how the human (or immortal) mind worked. Yes, her plan even smacked of genius.

"Do it," he said, and hung up.

Beside him, Kristen stirred. More and more, she had taken to leaving her apartment and spending the days with him, which he liked, although it made some clandestine matters more difficult.

Like a child, she was curled into the fetal position and her thumb was stuck cutely in her mouth. So innocent and so full of fire. Vistrot felt a strong paternal instinct toward her, which he knew she both liked and didn't; sometimes she said he behaved like an overbearing father and didn't see her as a grown woman. Sometimes he had to admit, if only to himself, that she was right. But he loved her.

Little did he realize then just how much that love would be tested in the days to follow.

* * *

Kristen woke up around three in the afternoon and dressed in silence, letting Vistrot sleep. After leaving him a note on her pillow, she departed, giving her driver instructions to take her to Jean-Pierre.

Upon entering his apartment, she was shocked at the changes she saw. All the chains had been taken down, as had most of the sharp objects that once sprouted from the walls, and an empty bottle of champagne stood on the kitchen counter. She moved into the bedroom to see the albino and some strange woman lying peacefully. The woman slept, but he didn't.

When he saw Kristen, he pulled on a pair of pants. Taking her arm, he led her from the bedroom and closed the door behind them.

"Who was that?" she asked, expecting him to say that it was another of his whores.

"That's Sophia," he said. "My wife."

"Your what!"

"Keep your voice down, Krissy."

"Sorry . . . but you're *married?*"

"Very much so."

"Christ, I didn't know the drugs in Las Vegas were that good. Honey, let me feel your forehead."

"Kriss, don't. I think I might just love her."

"Have you told her that?"

"Of course not."

"So you married someone that you don't love. Why?"

He sank into his uncomfortable wrought-iron chair, and she eased herself to the floor beside him. "She's completely changed my world, Kristen. I can't put it in words—but yes, I really do think I love her. She's so *strong*, so collected, and she's *moral*, for God's sakes; she's teaching me how to not kill innocents, to only feed off criminals and such." He smiled. He looked happier and more at peace with himself than Kristen had ever seen him. "I think she just may be my salvation."

The news stunned Kristen. It had only been a few weeks ago that he'd been a miserable wreck huddled in the corner, covered with tears and blood. How could he have come so far in so little time? She'd overheard Vistrot's conversation with Cloire and knew that Jean-Pierre was no longer the leader of his death-squad—a fact which she thought might have crushed him and which was the reason she'd come here today. But *married*?

"Baby. . ." she said hesitantly, "I'm going to tell you this because I don't think anyone else would dare: you're on the rebound—that's all this woman is. You lost both Danielle and your crew. You've turned to this Sophia for comfort . . . Although I'm glad to hear your choice in food has changed. I really am. That's wonderful."

"You don't understand," he said. "All this time I've been looking to Danielle for purpose, for definition—my tragedy was who I was. Sophia is teaching me how to *find* myself—how to live! Come, Krissy, I'd expected you, if no one else, to be happy for me."

She frowned. What he said was true: he did seem much improved. And surely this Sophia was responsible for the removal of the hooks and chains, and the glow that Jean-Pierre gave off ...

"Okay," she said and tried to give a genuine smile, though on the inside she felt shell-shocked. "I'm happy for you." She embraced him, giving him a peck on the cheek. "But where does that leave us?"

"We'll always be there for each other, Kristen. Nothing will change that. It simply won't be in a sexual way."

"So why are you two still in New York? Why aren't you off on honeymoon or something?"

"Sophia just joined Vistrot's organization. She was a part of the crew, but she stayed with me instead. So it's important for her to stay in town so that he can find another position for her; it would look bad if she just ran away with me. As for me . . . well, I suppose I need to find a new position as well."

"What will you do—head another death-squad?"

"I don't think I could ever do that again. I could never kill another innocent."

"She's changed you that much?" When he nodded, she said, "You're like a completely different person, Jean-Pierre. You really are."

"Do you still love me?"

"Of course, and I'm happy that you're finally over Danielle, but this is all very strange to me, baby. I can't believe you're married. Jesus, you're somebody's *husband!* Do you two have little cute names for each other and all that crap?"

"We're working on it."

She swayed. "I need a drink."

He fetched them both a beer. Before too long, she left, still in a daze, thinking of marriage and insanity. But somewhere inside her, an idea was growing.

* * *

Jean-Pierre returned to the bedroom, where he watched Sophia sleep; she could sense it. She smiled, her eyes still closed, and she said, "I can feel you watching me, you know."

"Shall I stop?"

"No, I like it." She opened her eyes and reached for a cigarette.

"Your eyes . . ." he said. "They remind me of something—something from a long time ago. I'd almost forgotten."

"What?"

"My mother. She had eyes just like yours."

She wondered if she should tell him. What would be his reaction? *Well*, she reasoned, *I'm going to have to tell him sooner or later. Why drag it out?*

She moved to the window, feeling the dying sunlight against her bare skin, soaking her in its warm rays like an olive in a martini. These past few days had been bliss, from their acid-laced wedding to their hallucinogenic road trip back up to New York, to tearing all the chains from his ceiling and thrashing around on his mattress in lustful abandon. That, she thought—removing all the hooks and chains—had really been a milestone.

Recognizing his discomfiture at her gentleness toward him, she had, over the last few days, been trying to make him understand that he possessed this same quality and that he should rejoice in it instead of rejecting it. They were both so similar in that way, having spent most of their lives denying and suppressing their emotions instead of thriving in them. She was now more certain than ever that this is where true strength came from, and he was slowly coming round to this conclusion, too.

The teachings weren't all one-way. She wouldn't have been able to teach him what she did if she hadn't had him to learn from in the first place. She saw the tenderness in him (which he hated and suppressed, but which she was still able to see) and learned how to express it herself, and then she taught him how to do the same. Though he considered her to be his redemption, he was really the redemption for the both of them.

Now it was time for the great unmasking, an event inevitable in any of her previous seductions (even pleasantly anticipated), but it was probably avoidable. Being honest with him wasn't going to be easy—in fact, what it amounted to was her declaration of love, though he might not see it as such—but it was just as well. After all, she was a masochist and a sadist. She gave as well as she received.

"Jean-Pierre," she said softly.

"Yes, darling?"

"I've something to tell you. Please, sit down." He came to the bed, puzzled, while she crossed to her discarded clothes and produced a cigar which she'd bought yesterday in preparation for this event. She handed it to him. He stared at it dumbly. No matter. It was a bad joke, anyway.

"What is it?" he asked.

She smiled. "First, tell me this: do you love me?"

"I . . . yes, I think so. I married you, didn't I?"

"Yes, but we never said the words."

He shook his head as if to clear away the cobwebs. "Do *you* love *me*?"

"You didn't answer my question, sweetheart. What have I been trying to teach you these last few days? Don't be afraid of what you feel. You were hurt once and, yes, you could be hurt again, but you're never truly going to live until you accept yourself, feelings and all. This means you must learn to express them when the timing's appropriate. Now's one of those times."

He looked at her for a long moment. "Yes," he said finally. "Sophia, I love you."

Her heart rose into her throat. Of course, no tears came to her eyes. Crying was something she'd never been able to do.

"Do you love me?" he said again.

"Yes," she replied honestly. "I love you."

His hugged her, and she rejoiced in the feeling of his hard body against her.

"Baby," she said, pushing him away gently, "what I have to say is this: I am the daughter of the Ghensiv Veliswa and the Werewolf Jean-Pierre."

He jerked away, and his green eyes grew dim.

"It's true," she said.

"My god," he murmured. "All this time, I've been sleeping with my *daughter*!"

"Does it really matter?"

For another long moment he said nothing. Then, standing abruptly, he lit a cigarette and started pacing. "Of course it does, Sophia. How can you—why did you—how come you didn't tell me before? And how could you *marry* me? Is this a joke?" He seemed to notice the cigar, which he still held absently in his hand, and threw it to the ground. "Christ, why didn't Veliswa ever tell me?"

"Because she loved you and knew that if you knew, you'd perceive some sort of emotional attachment and reject her. But you're strong enough now. Listen to me! I am your daughter, goddamnit, but it doesn't change a thing. If anything, it should strengthen our bound."

He mashed his eyes shut. "You're sick."

"How? How does this change anything? Answer me."

Shaking his head again, he said, "I don't know, but it does."

"We love each other, Jean-Pierre. Isn't that all that matters? Don't give in to societal conditioning."

"And if we have kids?"

"No immortal child has ever been born mentally or physically inhibited. The curse prevents it. Besides, what are the chances of us having a child? It's very rare, you know. Immortal tissues are highly reluctant to change. You know that."

He slumped down in a corner, his eyes looking in her direction but not directly at her. Slamming the back of his head against the wall, he balled his fists, inadvertently crushing his cigarette.

"Veliswa," he said. "Did she set you up to this?"

"She asked me to help out Ruegger and Danielle—and I tried. Becoming involved with you wasn't part of the bargain. It was an accident, but I'm glad it happened. I admit that you probably wouldn't have gotten as far with me if I hadn't known you were my father, but I did, so I gave you . . . us . . . a chance. And it changed everything, even how I perceived the world. You opened me up, Jean-Pierre, more than I can ever say. Now please, come here and tell me you love me."

His eyes met hers. He was composed once again. "Daughter," he said, and his voice was distant. "Kristen— the girl who was here just now—asked me if we had pet names for each other. I guess now we do."

She hesitated, still unsure of his reaction. "I love you."

He didn't look at her for a long moment, and her heart twisted violently. At last he reached out for her, and she nearly wept in release.

*   *   *

Roche Sarnova stared out the great windows of his study to the windswept mountains beyond, sipping on a glass of bourbon, as Francois Mauchlery entered the room.

"How did it go, Ambassador? Did the former Secretary of War confess?"

"Not at all. He still claims to be innocent. Loyal."

"Do you believe him?"

"No, but I don't think he's the only spy around, either."

Sarnova nodded. "That's what I've been told."

"Oh?"

"I've just spent five hours in the War Room, and none of what I learned was good news. Seems we're still losing the war, mainly due to security leaks and poor morale. It's finally started to hit me that we may actually lose."

"Don't tell me you're giving up, Roche. I won't believe it."

"As well you shouldn't, my friend. I'll die before I see my cause crushed."

"What are you going to do about morale?"

"Actually, I've had a thought on that subject. You see, if I am going to die, then I'll need a successor."

"Don't look to me," Francois said.

"Oh, I know you've no interest in such things. You've no reason to worry on that score. But I have another idea, one that will kill two birds with one stone. I think we should set up the Arena again."

"The Arena—of *Death*? Two shades trying to kill each other in an iron cage with a horde of spectators watching? That's barbaric, Roche—we haven't allowed the Arena in three hundred years."

"True, but I seem to remember that the public loved it, and that it boosted morale incredibly."

"You wish to use prisoners of war as in the old days?"

"No. This time it will be used to select my successor. We must either use visitors or our own people, preferably prime stock, but it will only be on a volunteer basis, so anyone may enter."

"This is absurd, Roche. Strength alone shouldn't determine your successor."

"But it is a necessary component. Have it set up so that at the end of the competition there will be eight finalists left. They will then engage each other in a series of chess matches—the winner gets the crown."

"But Roche . . ."

"Yes, Ambassador?"

Francois looked at him but said nothing.

"You don't like me to speak of my death, do you?" Roche said.

"I see no reason why you should die. If it comes to that, why don't you simply concede? We can bring the Dark Council back together and begin the mending process. Perhaps someday the world will be ready for your movement."

"No. We've been complacent with our role for far too long." Closing his eyes, he took a sip of bourbon and cleared his throat. "Ambassador, I know you have only good intentions at heart, but this is as it must be. Now please leave me for the moment so that you can attend to the arrangements we've discussed."

With obvious reluctance, the ambassador nodded and left. Sarnova returned to watch the night.

*   *   *

Several hours later and thousands of miles away, in the Hamptons, Harry Lavaca was also drinking in a study. However, he was sitting, not standing, and his drink was not bourbon but a homemade vodka martini.

Nearby the man who called himself Martin Ascott perched in his own chair sipping on a ginger ale. True to his word, he drank no alcohol. In the days Harry had spent living with him, he'd noted that, as advertised, Ascott was a decent family man, even if the money that he'd used for capital in the hot dog business had originally come from being a very successful heroin distributor. Still, drug money, especially the relatively small-scale stuff Ascott would've been involved in, would not be enough to buy an estate here. No, Ascott must have a good mind for legitimate business to have done as well as he had. In fact, and despite himself, Harry found that he could even get to like the man; Ascott was intelligent, soft-spoken, modest and gentle. Although he tried hard, Lavaca couldn't picture him as a rapist or a drug runner.

The two had been enjoying a companionable silence for several minutes before Ascott spoke: "Harry, I must tell you that I've enjoyed your being here. You know what Charlotte told me yesterday? She said that Michelle, our youngest, asked if she could call you Uncle Harry." He smiled. "I told Charlotte to tell her that that was just fine with me, but we ought to ask your permission first, of course. So what do you say?"

Grudgingly, Harry smiled. Ascott had raised some fine kids. "It's okay with me," he said. "But I don't know how much longer I can stay here and I wouldn't want to hurt little Michelle. She's precious."

"Please, we would love to have you stay on. Maybe permanently. And I don't say that just because I'm afraid of Danielle—although I am, terribly—but because, well, I've come to regard you as something of a friend. I like to think that you feel the same towards me."

"I suppose I do, Marty. If I did leave, I wouldn't hang you out to dry as far as Danielle is concerned. I've got contacts, friends of friends. I could find her, eventually, but most of these contacts I'd have to see in person. Some dislike telephones."

"Why on earth is that?"

"Shades have been around long before modern technology and many are resistant to it. I've been around them so long, I don't have a telephone, either."

Ascott considered that. "Harry, you know a great deal about these creatures, don't you?"

"I've gathered a lot of information over the years."

"Do you know how they came to be?"

"There are many stories, creation myths, but I can't say that I absolutely believe any of them."

"Tell me."

Harry wet his mouth. "Magic."

"Magic?"

"Oh, according to the myths, this old world of ours used to be full of mythical beings, from unicorns to dragons and other, more esoteric creatures. Spirits from other planes came to Earth regularly, and many worshipped them. They altered our reality, created the various immortal races. Cursed some, blessed others. But that's just a story, and of course it's a lot more involved than that. I don't actually believe in *dragons*." He smiled.

Ascott frowned. "Well, why not?"

"What do you mean?"

"If you accept the existence of vampires and werewolves, you accept the existence of the supernatural. Like you said, what is that but magic? Call it by a different name if you want, but it amounts to the same thing."

"Perhaps," Harry said. "But unicorns—"

The lights flickered out. A scream curled up from one of the lower floors (Michelle hated the dark), then silence fell. Only a glimmer of moonlight washed in through an open window, which also let in a current of cool air. This wind was the only sound.

"Is it the Gutter Angel?" Ascott whispered, and there was a trembling in his voice. "Is it Danielle?"

"Quiet." Harry made his way to the telephone: dead.

He pulled out his gun and pressed his back to the wall beside the door just as several dark figures leapt into the room and surrounded Ascott.

"Stop right there," commanded Lavaca. "These are silver bullets."

A petite woman, the only female of the group, laughed. "You've got the race right, but if you believe we're going to be afraid of some silver, you'll be disappointed. Who do you think you are, Harry Lavaca?"

"That's right, darlin'."

"Are you serious, old man?" asked one of the others. "You're the Slayer?"

"In the flesh."

Another raised his gun. "Not for long."

"Cut it out," said the woman. "He could be of use to us. He knows the odd flock."

"She's right," the largest shadow said; he had an Australian accent. "We'll take him with us."

"Who the hell are you people?" Harry said.

"I'm Cloire, and you can meet the others later. Funny, I'd always expected you to be taller."

"You're Cloire?" Harry nodded. "I've heard of you. A member of Jean-Pierre's death-squad."

"Not anymore."

"Knock it off, all of you!" roared Ascott, who seemed about to pass out. "Get out of my house, you demons! I'm not going anywhere with you."

The one Harry would come to know as Loirot lit a cigarette, the flare of his lighter very bright in the dark room. "I guess we go for the hard sell," he said, and reached a hand toward the man who'd once raped Danielle.

"Leave him be," said Harry. "You obviously didn't come here to kill him."

"Shut it, mortal."

Harry shot him in the heart. These were werewolves and it was the first time he'd really been able to try out his silver bullets. A waste of money, as it turned out. Loirot straightened out and glared at him; Harry could see it well enough, even in the dark.

"Let's get out of here before the maid runs to the neighbors' and calls the cops," the one Harry would learn to call Kilian said to Cloire.

"Don't you hurt my family," Ascott said, and for the first time Harry got a glimpse of his more brutal side. A vein throbbed in his forehead, and spittle sprayed from his lips. "Or I swear I'll hunt each and every one of you down and, before I kill you, I'll destroy every single thing that you love in this life."

"Be agreeable and no harm will come to your family," Cloire said. "Now clam up and come with us. You too, Harry."

Chapter 24

On the third day of apartment-shopping, Jean-Pierre and Sophia found what they were looking for: a nice little place in SoHo. With cash down, they could move in on Monday.

It was not to be.

The Funhouse of the Forsaken had arrived in New York, just in from Lereba, and were performing their second show, which Jean-Pierre and Sophia decided to attend. The freak show played to an eclectic audience and charged high prices even for Manhattan; a six-hundred and sixty-six dollar cover charge and an extra two hundred for backstage passes. It was an intimate audience with no more than a hundred seats arranged around small tables, as if at a comedy club. Sophia chose a table near the center of the room and the two ordered drinks from a waiter. She ordered a strawberry daiquiri and he a gin and tonic.

The show started with the snake-oil salesman, Maximillian, coming out onto the stage before the curtains and making a few purposefully bad jokes.

"He's the shade, right?" Sophia whispered to Jean-Pierre.

"That's the story. Supposedly he owns the troupe and gives the freaks—if you'll pardon the term—just enough blood to temporarily immortalize them—it also allows them to perform acts that they couldn't do otherwise."

"Does the audience know what he is?"

"Some of them, probably. Trust me, we're not the only shades here."

The audience laughed at some tasteless joke Maximillian had just delivered, and he gave an evil smile.

"I see you're a group to my liking." He rubbed his hands together. "Alas, it is not me you have come to see. In this world where so many of us are trapped in conformity, it is the majority who are imprisoned by their own ideals. Everyone seems to be alike in this world, so it's those that are different that are the truly free. We call them freaks, and oh! how we love to revile them, but somewhere in our minds there is part of us that sees their social liberation and yearns to join them—yearns for *release!* Tonight, ladies and gentlemen, I give you the opportunity to join them and for a few brief moments of eternity feel that release. Deliver yourselves into our embrace and let your minds float uninhibited by the jailhouse of convention. I now present to you, my good people, the Funhouse . . . *of the Forsaken!*"

He bowed and everyone applauded. Then, stepping backwards, he disappeared through the psychedelic curtains amid a burst of purple smoke and a barrage of surreal lights. Jean-Pierre was impressed. The showman had just insulted a roomful of people who had paid a high admission and gotten them to *clap* about it.

The curtains parted, revealing a dark dreamscape of props, smoke, and background. There were winding roads and tilted, pointy hills dotted with stunted trees, a cemetery with some nightmarish tombstones, and galaxies of wild, multi-colored stars above. It was arranged to resemble some Eastern European countryside—perhaps even that of Romania itself.

Haunting music swelled, the lighting grew more intense, and a score of actors dressed as peasants swept onto the stage and began to dance in what seemed to be a spooky folk-ritual celebrating something. Tittering back and forth and swirling across the stage, they raised their hands to the stars, then down to the ground again.

They stopped abruptly to see a sort of procession appearing around a hill. Six peasants held up a carriage-like bed, and lying on the bed there was a rather homely woman, grotesquely obese, but she smiled serenely and her eyes were warm. Dressed in a simple nightgown, she was playing a jaunty song on a fiddle. The six peasants set the carriage down and everyone gathered around, leaving an opening so that the audience could see what transpired.

A man dressed as a priest helped the woman out of her nightgown, while the peasants started chanting and then began to dance in a circle around the bed, still leaving room for the audience to observe the action. Other than being extremely fat, the woman had what seemed to be a long scar running up from her groin to her breastplate. As she started to croon in a low voice to the rhythm of the chanting, something in her abdomen seemed to buck; it appeared as though she was about to give birth. At the climactic moment of the chant, a head popped out of the scar running up her belly, which wasn't really a scar at all but an *opening*. With a little help from the peasants, a short figure emerged from the chasm of flesh and stepped to the ground, dripping fake blood.

The bearded dwarf wore a skin-tight shirt (that bore horizontal black-and-white stripes) and green trousers. Most unsettling, he boasted four perfectly-formed and mobile arms.

The priest raised his hands to the sky, howled, and ran off stage. The peasants performed a dance of fright and followed the example of their holy man. The woman, whose cavity had sealed as soon as the birth had been complete, stared at her child with panic, threw on her nightgown and began running away from the dwarf, who followed her with a smile.

He chased her through the hills and around the stage a few times (to the delight and laughter of the audience), then grew discouraged and sat down at the top of the hill the cemetery was located on. His mother returned to her bed, sobbing. The scene was tragic despite its comic undertones, but Jean-Pierre was settling into the spirit of the show.

A mime appeared. He was a tall man who looked rather ordinary except for the fact that he had no cartilage in his nose, just a stubby bone and two long black holes for nostrils, which lent his face the likeness of a skull—an image complemented by the thick white make-up and his big dark eyes. He studied the mother and child, tapping his foot thoughtfully. Then he grinned, snapped his fingers, and from the bed grabbed the fiddle, which he brought to the four-armed dwarf. The bearded "child" accepted it, turning up his ear as the mime bent down to whisper something to him. The dwarf smiled and took a bow to the fiddle, while the mime stepped courteously to the side.

As the dwarf began to play, swaying atop the cemetery hill, the mother watched him, the serenity returning to her face as the music moved her. Her son performed a little jig of affection and happiness, placing his free set of hands on his hips. The mime clapped along and joined in the jig.

The mother smiled, wiped the tears from her face and, after climbing down from the bed, went to her son and embraced him. The lighting grew warm and a rim of orange appeared above a hill, as if the sun were rising. In the glow of the brilliant dawn, the mother, son, and mime began to dance anew. Soon, the peasants returned to the stage, all smiling. The dwarf gave the fiddle to the mime and, taking his mother's arm, led her over to the bed, where she cradled him in her arms and kissed his forehead tenderly.

The six peasants who'd carried the bed onto the stage lifted it and led the way out, the rejoicing peasants just behind. The mime followed last, smiling, dancing and playing the instrument. He glanced once over his shoulder to give a kind wink at the audience before the actors all disappeared behind a green hill. The curtains closed.

Really, thought, Jean-Pierre, the act had been quite sweet and even strangely affecting. Along with the rest of the audience, he applauded loudly, then reached for Sophia's hand. She smiled at him. There was something else in her eyes, something particular that had touched her about the act. She turned back to watch the show, leaving him to wonder.

He reflected that they had grown extremely close over the last few days, their bond only strengthened now that they could openly call each other father and daughter. A thought had hit him yesterday and he'd suggested inviting Veliswa to dinner one night in a sort of family reunion. Sophia had smiled and said that they should wait until they'd moved into their new home.

There was only one thing that bothered him, and that was the urge he kept feeling. Strange thirsts welled up in him, and hungers. He craved violence. Casual brutality had been a part of him for too long.

For the first week he hadn't even noticed, had been perfectly satisfied with his more conservative eating habits, and his more villainous selection of victims had only seemed to add a little spice to his meals. It had finally hit him today that what he craved most in all the wide world was just to run through the streets tearing off the heads of passers-by and sucking out their brains. *NO!* his new-found conscience screamed, but it was too new a voice to override his bloodlust. He could actually feel his hands shaking at the thought of violence, as if he were trying to kick cigarettes again.

Was that it? Was it an addiction? And was it one he *wanted* to overcome? If anyone could help him, it was Sophia, but he hesitated to speak to her of it; despite everything, she was moral and unlikely to understand his predicament. Also, of course, she was half ghensiv—maybe more than half—and ghensivs didn't generally behave in patterns of violence. They must shed blood occasionally, but only occasionally.

He ordered a vodka gimlet and settled in for the rest of the show. Not all the acts were as gentle as the first had been—in fact, some were downright cruel—but they were all interesting and varied enough to hold his attention. Lord Kharker had instilled in him an appreciation of the finer things in life—smooth automobiles, fine wines, Cuban cigars, classical music—but the only one that had really stuck with him was the love of opera. When moved by a particular opera, the albino was able to forget himself for awhile. It was this same pleasant feeling that he rediscovered now, with some surprise, by watching the performances of the Funhouse of the Forsaken. He found he was looking forward to his visit backstage and hoped that Sophia shared that anticipation.

Eventually, the last act came. It concerned the fate of a spider and a woman. The woman appeared normal, with blond hair and wide blue eyes, but the spider was a long, thin man with arms where his legs should be and hands where his feet should be. He had three eyes and two sets of upper teeth, all of which were malformed. Despite this, he appeared quite dignified—stately, even.

The tale unfolded thusly: the woman was passing through a forest when she stumbled across a giant web, the centerpiece of the stage, suspended between two large trees. The spider had gotten tangled in his own web, so the girl ascended one of the trees until she drew close enough to liberate him. Pulling a saber from a sheath, she cut him free, but in doing so inadvertently tangled herself in the web.

Immediately the spider descended on her, intent on feeding.

She began to sing. A low, beautiful song rolled out, full of mourning and redemption. Moved, the spider released her. She kissed him and disappeared into the forest. The spider watched her go, then returned to the center of his web, where he waited. He danced around playing an accordion, calling to the gods to deliver him sustenance, but none came. The sun rose and set, the night grew dark, then the sun rose and set once more. The cycle repeated itself several times, and the spider grew so weak from starvation that he collapsed into the web.

Finally, the girl reappeared. Seeing him caught again, she set about freeing him, successfully staying clear of the web's entrapments. Once he was liberated, they began to dance, but suddenly the spider broke away from her, crying because he still had no food.

The girl offered herself to him. He resisted. Seeing that he would die without her sacrifice, the girl flung herself into the web, becoming firmly entangled. Immediately the spider freed her, but she just entangled herself again. The spider cried and watched her, then began to dance with tears in his eyes. Still, he refused to take her, and as he came to free her again, his body went rigid and a fixed expression swept his face. He collapsed beside her, having died of starvation because he wouldn't accept her sacrifice. Only now she was trapped in the web with no hope of release.

The sun rose slowly behind her, and silence lay over all. Suddenly there came a soft humming, which grew louder as another spider descended from above. Singing a happy tune, he cocooned the two lovers for future use—despite the low crooning of the girl—picked up the accordion and started to dance, silhouetted against the rising sun.

The curtains closed. Maximillian walked out on stage to enormous applause. He bowed, and after several moments a line of actors appeared behind him to accept the warm recognition of the audience. After a few final words

("Thank you for coming, my friends. Enjoy your differences and relish in them! Now good night!"), the troupe departed, some clutching flowers thrown by fans.

"That was lovely," said Sophia. "But sad."

"I thought so, too," he said.

They made their way backstage, Jean-Pierre aware of brushing the elbows of a few fellow shades along the way. For the most part, they saw who he was and nodded in deference. He could see them trying to figure out who Sophia was.

When the newlyweds reached Maximillian, he was swarmed with people trying to get autographs, learn his secrets, or, in a few cases, seduce him, but when he caught sight of Jean-Pierre he disengaged himself and made his way over. He ushered the couple into a more private area, away from the hubbub of the main rooms. He smiled and reached for Sophia's hand, then kissed it.

"You two lovely people must be the albino Jean-Pierre and his gorgeous bride Sophia. Please, call me Max."

"You know of us, Max?" she asked.

"Of course, of course. Especially your husband, the right arm of Vistrot himself."

"No more," said Jean-Pierre.

"Yes, I've heard that you no longer preside over your team, but fate unfolds in mysterious ways."

"There is no fate, Max."

"Be that as it may . . ." The snake-oil salesman grinned in friendly mischief. "Jean-Pierre, my good fellow, I have some interesting news for you, if you would like to know it."

"What's your game?"

"Oh, let's just say a favor."

The albino nodded impatiently. He had no intention of owing this hellish bastard a favor. "What is it?"

"Well, I was just in the wonderful city of Lereba, Morocco, and heard some rumors . . . about your little Gutter Angel, Danielle."

"She's in Lereba?"

"She was when I departed, as was her beau, the Darkling."

Jean-Pierre considered. It was useful information, and he was glad that Danielle was somewhere far away, although by no means was Lereba a safe place at the moment.

"You're going to have to do better than that if you want a favor out of me," he said.

"Then we're going to have to define the favor. Let's say I give you another tidbit and you give me some of your blood—word is that you've some of Kharker in you. I can see how that could be rather ... invigorating."

"That's reasonable. But this better be good."

"Oh, it is. How would you like to know who killed Testopha?"

"Wasn't he Scoured?"

"Indeed, my dear chap, he was—one of the very first ones, too."

"Fine."

Max pursed his lips. "It was your Balaklavian artists, Junger and Jagoda."

"That *is* interesting. But doesn't the Scouring usually work through local death-squads?"

"As I've said, this was one of the very first Scourings—perhaps a system had yet to be worked out back then. You fail to see the broader uses of using Junger and Jagoda. See, Testopha's death created great havoc in Lereba because it was thought that the karula killed him—and that situation couldn't have been achieved if a local death-squad was running around bragging about knocking off one of the greatest leaders in history. The killer would have to be an outsider."

"So you're saying his death was meant to cause the abunka-karula conflict?"

"Indeed. Now, how about that blood now? I'm sure we could find an empty room back here somewhere."

"I'm not in the mood. I'll return in a few days' time, don't worry. Technically, Sophia and I are still on honeymoon."

Silently, Max nodded. "I certainly wouldn't want to spoil your honeymoon, of course. I look forward to your visit." He withdrew a pen and scribbled something on the back of a business card, then handed it to Jean-Pierre. "Here's the address where you can reach me. We will make your appointment a comfortable one. Having been on tour so long, we've collected a large variety of the world's best wines. Perhaps when you come by—"

"Yes, perhaps. Well, thanks again and good bye." Jean-Pierre led Sophia away. He had the feeling that if Max was angered, he could become a very dangerous man. The albino could just imagine that, after a few days went by and he did not call upon the Funhouse, the Funhouse might just come to him . . . and that would most certainly spoil the honeymoon.

The couple happened upon a cluster of Funhouse performers, arranged in a line, happily chatting with their fans and posing together for pictures. There was the dwarf with the four arms (whose name they learned to be Claude) sitting in a chair in the center of the line, looking relaxed and composed. He seemed to hold a high position among his peers, perhaps even that of leader.

The large, obese woman with the empty abdominal cavity slouched at his side, and they were holding hands in a loverly fashion. Not too far away stood the skeletal mime, standing side by side with the blond girl in the web. To their left was a man with two tails holding hands with another man with one head but three faces. And there sat the two large Siamese twins, who could give the illusion of coming together, posing for a picture with the spider-man, who smoked a French cigarette. A woman with four breasts but no ears whispered to an androgynous figure with no eyes but two perfectly formed mouths.

As he studied the freaks, Jean-Pierre realized how symmetrical, even beautiful, some of their aberrations were. He supposed that most of them had undergone plastic surgery to give a more even appearance to their deformities. Or perhaps Maximillian's blood had enhanced their aesthetic appeal; the curse was known to do such things on occasion. Nonetheless, they were fascinating to behold.

As the night continued, he was able to meet several of the freaks themselves, who weren't overly deferent to his status as an immortal but were gregarious and friendly just the same. Eventually, Sophia tugged on his sleeve.

"I'm ready to go if you are," she said. "And ... I have something to tell you."

They returned to his apartment. Over the last few days, they'd purchased some furnishings to the suite—nothing too elaborate, because, after all, they were about to move— just a few chairs (with cushions, which was a major change), a couch, stereo, television, and several various odds-and-ends.

Sophia had placed the cigar that she'd bought to announce herself as the albino's child in a drawer. She retrieved it now and tossed it to him. Catching it, he stared at her dumbly, then saw her begin to smile.

"You're kidding," he said.

She moved over to him, pressed her body against his, and gave him a long, passionate kiss.

"I'm not," she said. "At all."

"But such a thing is so *rare* ... and with us, the way we are ..."

"The curse will preserve it. There will be no deformities. Of that I'm sure."

"And you're sure. Positive."

"Absolutely."

He stared at the cigar, shoved it in his mouth and lit it. Taking the smoke in, he thought briefly of Kharker, but his mind was far too preoccupied to consider his old friend long. Slowly, he smiled, staring into the violet eyes of his bride.

"I can't believe it," he muttered. "We're going to have a baby."

* * *

The series of events that quickly spun out of control and led to such violent upheaval began the next day. It was late Saturday afternoon and Kristen was playing on the great white Steinway Vistrot had bought for her years ago, when she decided to pay him a visit.

It would be a very important visit. She dressed in a seductive-but-mature little dress and called for her limousine, which took her directly to her lover's base of operations. She marched down to the appropriate sub-level and made her way to the end of the main hall where his private office was located, but neither of the two guards (both of whom she'd known for years) opened the door for her.

"He's not in," one explained. "I believe he's in his quarters getting some rest. He said he didn't want to be disturbed."

She smiled and held up the bottle of Cristol she'd brought along. "Well, I'm going to him anyway. We have something to celebrate—I'm going to ask him to marry me! If Jean-Pierre can do it, so can I. It's gone on like this for too bloody long."

The guards glanced at each other.

"Better let him sleep, dear," cautioned the second one.

"Bullshit." She stalked away from them until she found her way into one of the secondary halls, where Vistrot's sleeping quarters were. Two more guards stood before it; they stiffened at her approach.

"He's sleeping," one said.

"So I've heard, Leroy. But today's a special day. Wake him up!"

She tore past them. Since they weren't about to manhandle the boss's girl, they had no choice but to let her by. As it turned out, this was an unfortunate decision. She threw open the door and strode into the room victoriously, bottle raised high, then stopped and gasped in horror.

Vistrot laid naked on the bed, an equally unclad woman straddling him. She had auburn hair and wispy green eyes, and her wrist was to his mouth; he was drinking her blood. Stranger still, his wrist was to her mouth as well—she was drinking *his* blood! For a moment, Kristen thought the woman was some sort of victim of Vistrot's and was surprised; she'd never seen him feed before. But no, the woman appeared very willing—in fact, it almost seemed as though *she* were the dominant one. But that couldn't be, could it?

Instantly, Vistrot ceased his movements and turned in shock to Kristen. In less than a second, his expression transformed from lustful to dismayed. The woman on top of him seemed quite unperturbed. She hopped off her mount, tearing her wrist away from Vistrot, who'd been biting down on it absently. He lurched up, his body beet-red while his face was very pale, then with an effort rose to his feet and yanked on a pair of pants.

"Kristen," he said, "this isn't—"

"Isn't what!" She grabbed the bottle of Cristol by the neck and launched it at him. Despite his considerable bulk, he dodged it ably, and it shattered against the wall behind him. "God *damn* you, you cheating bastard! And I was going to ask you to *marry* me! You fucking pig, I can't believe you."

"Kristen, baby, I swear—"

"Swear *what*, exactly?" She grinned bitterly. "Well, if you think you're the only one who can hurt someone else, you're wrong! Oh, Auggie, you're *so* wrong! I knew you were cheating on me, you lying turd, so I returned the favor!"

"Come on, Krissy . . . Krissy, honey, don't talk like that."

"Oh, but I did." She watched with satisfaction the hurt in his eyes. "And you know what else? It wasn't with just some *bum*—it was with your own Jean-Pierre!"

"Krissy, *no!*" Vistrot's face had gone from shocked to traumatized. There was almost no expression left there at all. Behind that, though, a seething rage grew, and Kristen was well aware of it.

"*He* said he loved me, what do you think of that!"

"Take it back, Krissy," he warned, his voice all too quiet. "If you don't, I swear—"

"Oh, and now you swear *again!* But it's all right when *you* cheat, isn't it? Well, isn't it! Fuck you, Michael Augustine Vistrot—and the ulcer-ridden elephant you lumbered in on!" She glared at him one last time. "You bastard, I hope it was worth it. And as God as my witness I never want to see you again."

She stormed out of the room.

Vistrot glowered at his guards, who'd watched the whole scene with mounting dread. He smiled at their fear.

"I'll deal with you later, men. Now get me Junger and Jagoda!"

* * *

Lying beside him as he slept, Sophia ran her fingers through the albino's pale blond hair and thought about their life together. This was not only *her* father, but the father of their future child. He would be its father and grandfather at the same time. She'd made him a daddy twice over and a granddaddy once in less than a week. It was splendidly perverted, and she loved it.

During their time together, she'd learned so much from him about the arts of tenderness—but she had her doubts. Serious doubts. He was still much better at displaying his emotions than she, and he was finally beginning to appreciate it. She, on the other hand, was beginning to think that perhaps she wasn't cut out for being emotionally healthy; it just didn't come naturally. Still, she couldn't see leaving him, and maybe in time she could learn even more from him. Could it ever be enough?

Of course, there was that other business of Ruegger and Danielle. Sophia had selfishly abandoned the quest to save them in the deserts of Nevada so that she could pursue her own love life and self-fulfillment. Now it struck her that perhaps her skills would be best suited to furthering the quest instead of apartment-shopping with Jean-Pierre. Well, time would tell.

Abruptly a fusillade of knocking sounded from the front door. Jean-Pierre snapped awake beside her. Tossing on some clothes, they answered the summons. Kristen burst in, sobbing, and threw herself around Jean-Pierre.

"What is it, Krissy?"

"Oh, Jean-Pierre," she moaned. "I've done something terrible, so terrible."

"What, honey? What?"

She backed away from him and wiped at her eyes, then hastily lit a Virginia Slim.

"I told him about us," she said. "I caught him with his whore and I blabbed! I'm so stupid, so horribly stupid. I should be shot, shouldn't I?"

"No, of course not."

"Yes, I should. I really should. Say you forgive me, my beautiful pale one, and I'll feel better."

"It's done. I forgive you."

"No, you shouldn't. I don't deserve it. Don't you realize what he'll do?"

"What could he possibly do? He deserved what he got and he knows it. You know he'll never hurt you."

"It's not me I'm worried about." She took a deep breath before going on, then looked meaningfully back and forth between Jean-Pierre and Sophia. "You've got to go, both of you. Far, far away, somewhere he can never find you."

"That's no use, Krissy. If he wanted, he could find us anywhere."

"Jean-Pierre, don't say that! He's not one to take things passively. He'll do something rash, I know he will. Now pack up and go! Here, I'll help you."

He laid a hand on each of her young shoulders. "Calm down, girl. What's done is done and there's no use hiding. I knew what I was getting into when we first started sleeping together, and I'm not afraid to face the consequences."

"Then I'm afraid *for* you. Don't you get it? There's no point in acting noble now. Just run! If you run, it will be an act to appease him. He doesn't want to kill you and that'll give him an excuse not to. Don't argue with me, Jean-Pierre. I know him better than anyone alive."

"We're not going anywhere, Krissy. But here, you stay with us tonight, okay? And for however long you need to."

Clearly, she was not lulled into any sense of security, but she gave in under the albino's ministrations, and Sophia helped. Around four in the morning, Sophia awoke with a start. Something was wrong. Beside her, the albino lurched up. Two large black figures seized hold of her and tore her, naked, from bed. Her first thoughts were that they smelled foul and that she missed being in Jean-Pierre's arms, and then one of them struck her over the head and she was out.

*   *   *

Peeking around the doorway, Kristen marveled as Jean-Pierre leapt to his feet. She knew Junger and Jagoda were much stronger than he was and either one of them would've been more than sufficient to rip him limb from limb.

"Release her," he commanded.

Kristen gasped. He was so brave!

"Vistrot has a message for you," said Jagoda. "He says that since you took from him the only thing he loved in this life, he would take your bride in her place."

"He'll never live to lay a finger on her, the bastard."

Junger laughed. "You misunderstand. *We're* to dispose of her. Consider it a professional courtesy that we don't kill her in front of you. After this, you and Vistrot will be even." He turned to his comrade. "Brother, don't you love New York?"

"It's beautiful," agreed the bearded one. He peered at Kristen in the doorway. "Vistrot says you're free to return."

"Fat chance!" she said.

"He says no harm will come to you."

"Tell him to fuck himself!"

Jagoda winked. "With pleasure, little one."

He and Junger left through the front door, Sophia slung over the bald one's shoulder. After they were gone, Jean-Pierre collapsed on the floor and Kristen knelt beside him.

"I'm so, so sorry, Jean-Pierre. You'll never forgive me, I know, and I wouldn't deserve it if you did. Here, would you feel better if you hit me?"

He cupped his hands over his face. He limbs shook.

"No," he said. "I don't want to hit you, for God's sakes. It's you that doesn't understand. Kristen ... Krissy, honey . . . she was pregnant."

"My god. I didn't think that could *happen*."

In that moment, something snapped in him, Kristen could feel it. It was as if all the knowledge Sophia had given him, all the morality—with her abduction, it was gone. Vaporized. The old Jean-Pierre had reemerged.

Fury possessing him, he started smashing things. It didn't matter what it was, he thrust his fists and his feet into it, cracking and splintering, ripping and tearing—destroying blindly, until there was nothing left big enough to smash. Then he moved into the living room. By the time he was through, the entire apartment was broken apart, the walls fractured, the floor littered with gaping holes, the furniture shredded, the ceilings caving in.

Then he started on the hall.

At first Kristen cried, hating herself, but then the anger blossomed outward. She kicked at what was left of the toaster because it was the nearest thing to her. As she listened to Jean-Pierre's sounds of destruction from beyond the suite, she realized that Vistrot's revenge had been a mistake, a grave miscalculation. His act had been irrevocable, and now it was war.

*   *   *

Claude, the four-armed dwarf, had to step over sleeping performers on his way to the door. It had taken three penthouse suites to accommodate all of them, but ever since that initial challenge it had been a non-stop party.

Pretty much everyone here was in a fitful, drunken stupor except Claude and several friends, including Max, and that's only because they were snorting the last of an eight-ball. When he finally got to the door and flung it open, he saw a very severe Jean-Pierre with a grim-faced blond girl at his side.

"You're here to see Max."

"That's right," said Jean-Pierre.

Claude led them through the living room into the oversized den, where Maximillian and a few others—one or two of them groupies—were still carrying on the festivities. The troupe had put on a good show tonight and were hoping to spend another few weeks in New York. That would all change shortly.

Max glanced up at Jean-Pierre, then, smiling, rose to meet him.

"So glad you could make it, my dear fellow. And who's this lovely creature?"

"My name's Kristen," she said coldly.

Max studied the albino, and Claude saw what Max saw: something about the werewolf had changed. He was more composed, more confident. It looked, to Claude, as if Jean-Pierre had made up his mind about something. And, having done so, he seemed even deadlier than before.

"So, my friend," said Max, wary, "are you ready to give a little blood?"

"No. But if you're willing to do something for me, you'll be able to taste blood far richer than my own—blood that has been building strength since 500 B.C. It will make you immeasurably more powerful than you are. Of course, I'll need the complete cooperation of your troupe."

Max frowned. "Whose blood would this be?"

"Vistrot," Jean-Pierre said. "The Titan."

*　*　*

When Sophia finally woke up, she couldn't open her eyes at first because of the soreness and dried blood. She smelled something horrible, some slaughterhouse stench. The bruises and abrasions she'd suffered under the hands of the Balaklava burned. Worse, from the throbbing between her legs she realized that they'd raped her while she'd been unconscious. *Fucking bastards. Let them try to do that when I'm awake!*

She forced her eyes open only to find herself inside of a giant belly. Human bones had been fused together to create much larger ones, which arced over the chamber and down both sides like the ribs of an enormous animal. A vertebral column ran along the top and walls of flesh composed the top and sides, in which the ribs were embedded. Though it was surely some illusion, the flesh appeared to be alive, as if it was in fact the abdominal wall of some beast. Perhaps the Balaklava had dribbled some of their blood on their gruesome artistry to give it life, or perhaps the illusion was created by one of their voodoo tricks.

The belly stretched, cavernous, overhead, with a height of maybe a hundred and fifty feet at its greatest, and tapering off at either end, where brightly-colored black men with dreadlocks carried guns. Apparently Junger and Jagoda had brought along some of their followers from Jamaica and were using the humans as guards for their prisoners. Prisoners there were, perhaps fifty of them—all perilously mortal—engaged in various boredom-induced activities. Sophia noted that each and every one of them, man and woman alike, was beautiful. This is why the Balaklava had let them live, she supposed. Then it was surely the reason that she, too, had been spared so far. Where were her hosts, anyway?

She sat up, joints aching. The prisoners nearest her, two young men resting their haunches on upside-down buckets and playing a game of checkers, noticed her.

"Well, will you look at that? She's up."

"How do you feel, miss?"

She placed a hand to her pounding head and smiled, going for points. "Fine. How long have you two been down here?"

"About a week, I guess. To tell you the truth, I've kinda lost track of time. Easy to do in this place."

"At least they haven't eaten us yet," the other put in. "That's just because we give good head, though."

Sophia nodded unsentimentally. "And by 'they', you mean . . ."

"Junger and Jagoda, the dark gods. That's what the Rastas call 'em—that or the Balaklava."

"The Rastafarians are the guards?"

"Sure, if that's how you wanna say it. Wardens, more like. Executioners when we 'misbehave'. That's what we call them, anyway. If they were actually Rastafarians, things would be a lot cooler down here."

She surveyed the scattered prisoners. "There are enough of you to make a break for it when Junger and Jagoda go out for food. What stops you?"

The second pointed towards the belly's entrance. "Beyond that is the Labyrinth. No one knows the way through 'cept Junger and Jagoda and their people. And in case any of us were inclined to give it a go ..." He gestured. In a corner, about ten feet from a cluster of the Rastas, rose a mound of gnawed corpses and bones. Lying there as if it were a throne, a massive tiger lazily chewed on a fresh human skull.

"That's Kalanda, the Balaklavas' pet. Pretty, isn't she? They say she's got enough of their blood to make her one of them."

"Kalanda's a shade?"

"You got it, miss. Not only that, but smart, too. They say she's got a mind connection to the gods and that they can watch us through her."

"You know I'm one of them, don't you—an immortal?"

The young men exchanged glances. "It won't make a difference, miss."

Chapter 25

A week earlier ...

Hauswell smiled as the odd flock approached, gesturing for them to take a seat, which they did.

"Ciara told me you were here," he said. "I was hoping you would find me."

Looking at his old friend, Ruegger found himself at a loss for words. "It's good to see you again."

"You, too, my friend. And Danielle, you look as sumptuous as always. How did the sled race go?"

"Sophia won again."

Hauswell stirred his drink. "A shame about Ludwig."

"Yes. We've come a long way to find out why he died."

"I'm guessing it had something to do with his army hanging in the balance. Second largest army in the whole Community, you know."

Quietly, Ruegger said, "I was under the impression you knew more than that."

Hauswell shifted his eyes, indicating the crowd. "Later," he said.

They talked about Ludwig, and old times, getting used to each other once again, falling back into the rhythm. For her part, Danielle was largely quiet.

When the pleasantries had been put behind them, she said, "But why . . . why did you fake your own death? If it's the Scouring you're trying to avoid—well, I'm sure the Scourer knows that he hasn't killed you. So the one person—or group of persons—that you're trying to fool isn't fooled."

Hauswell smiled. "That's true, although I think even the Scourer will be a little confused, because surely he did hire someone to kill me, and there are many death-squads that claim to have done me in. So it's more than likely that the Scourer will be uncertain whether or not I'm in the ground. In any case, my 'death' did manage to stir up quite a bit of confusion, and hopefully my trail was lost in it. But . . . well, that's not the only reason I led others to believe I was taken out."

"Why then?"

"I wanted to see what would happen. Whenever someone like me is Scoured, chaos erupts; I wanted to study this. In the time that I've been 'dead', I've researched the phenomenon in great depth. The pattern is largely the same. In most cases, a crime lord is killed and all hell breaks loose in the aftermath. All the lieutenants of the deceased clamor for the throne, *but it's rare that any of the lieutenants ever get the throne.*

"The only circumstance in which one of them does claim it is through an enormous infusion of money and resources—someone *helps* them to build a power base large enough to enable them to rule. It's either this or an outside party—in my case, a shade named Karl Barnaby—comes from nowhere to take the crown for himself. Interesting, isn't it?"

"So you're saying that these ascendants to the throne were given a boost by someone."

"Exactly. And it would follow that they would then owe loyalty to this person. In my research, I've found out who this person is." He spoke in a coarse, strained whispered. "I know who's behind the Scouring."

Ruegger and Danielle waited with baited breath.

Hauswell smiled mischievously. "Ah, but I can't tell you here and now. Someone could be listening. I don't mind if you know because your lives are on the line, too. But I don't want an outsider to benefit from information that I've sacrificed so much—my entire kingdom, for the gods' sakes—to gather. I've really said too much already."

Danielle ordered another drink, this time a margarita. "But what's happening here in Lereba? We know that the Balaklava killed Testopha, but we don't know why. Is it part of the Scouring?"

"Very much. See, there are two patterns to the Scouring. One is the killing of a criminal boss—this is the most prevalent pattern—and the second is the exploitation of a tense situation, such as that one here between the karula and the abunka. The interesting thing to this pattern is that the tension that the Scouring exploits is inevitably caused by religious differences. That's what I've come to study."

"The karula and the abunka have been at each other's throats since the death of their leaders, and I believe it will all come to a head tonight. You have impeccable timing, I must say. But, if you want to observe the phenomenon yourselves, stay here awhile. Mark my words, after a few days of fighting, when everything is in ruins, out of nowhere there will come a leader with a powerful gathering and a new fortune that will seize control of the city. If Testopha was really Scoured, and if the Balaklava work for the Scourer, that's what will happen."

"So the Scouring either kills a crime lord or a powerful religious figure," Danielle said. "Chaos breaks out, a lot of people die, and then an agent of the Scouring steps in and takes over."

"Precisely."

"Ludwig doesn't fit the profile."

"Therefore he wasn't Scoured. I think it's significant in more ways than one that the targets of the Scouring represent crime and religion. Ruegger, doesn't this strike you as interesting?"

"What are you implying?" Ruegger said.

"Well, the fact that you despise religion is well known. You put up with some elements of crime as long as they suit your purposes, but . . ."

"You think I have something to do with the Scouring? You've already said that you know who it is, and if that's true, then you know I've nothing to do with it."

Hauswell looked doubtful. "Maybe. Ruegger, back when I saved you in Germany all those years ago, did you think I did it simply out of the goodness of my heart?"

"Of course. If not, why?"

"It's true that my goodwill was partly the reason—in fact, I was actually *selected* because of my goodwill."

"Hauswell, what the hell are you saying?"

Hauswell stared at Ruegger silently, then shook his head. "You really don't know, do you? Well, now is not the time or place to tell you. Here, why don't you two accompany me upstairs so that we can watch the city burn?"

"You certainly know how to show a girl a good time," Danielle said.

They returned upstairs to the mansion, where the odd flock trailed Hauswell to his suite. The German retrieved a bottle of fine bubbly from the mini-refrigerator and three glasses from a cabinet, and they moved to the balcony. The city below lay in darkness cut by a smattering of fires, which seemed to be spreading. Tendrils of smoke blotted out the stars. Far away, the rattle of gunfire drifted from a tangle of narrow streets. A cool breeze gusted up from the city, carrying with it occasional warm spots.

"Beautiful, isn't it?" Hauswell said, pouring the drinks. "Ruegger, you look upset. What's wrong, my dear boy?"

"Thank you for sharing your information with us. We've . . . been through a lot . . . to see you and to hear what you have to say. But before I listen any further, I want to know why you let Laslo live. You must've known how far gone he was. And if you lie to me, I will kill you."

Hauswell nodded slowly. His face was suddenly weary.

"I'd heard about his death, and I've mourned him. Before he passed, what did he do?"

"He crucified us. And many others."

"Damn. I knew he was far gone, but I never knew just how much. When he locked me out of the hangar, I didn't put up a fight. I guess I didn't want to know."

"He killed hundreds, maybe thousands."

Hauswell's hands shook as he sipped his champagne. "I swear to you, I didn't know. But, Ruegger, you were pretty far gone yourself once, and I helped you out. Eventually you came around. I had hoped that, in time, Laslo would come around, as well, although he refused all my offers at getting him help and counseling. What else could I have done? Kill him? What if I'd killed you all those years ago? If I had, you would never have had a chance to redeem yourself. Redeem yourself you did, admirably, and the world is a better place for it. I just couldn't kill him before he had that same opportunity. Do you understand?"

"Yes, but I don't know if I can forgive."

"Try."

Suddenly Ruegger remembered how he'd felt when he believed Hauswell to be dead. Of things unsaid, unresolved.

"Hauswell, no matter what your reasons were for doing it, I want to thank you for saving me all those years ago," he said.

The German looked surprised. He smiled. "You're most welcome."

"And I . . . I forgive you for not killing Laslo. I know you were only trying to do what you thought right. It couldn't have been an easy decision."

"It wasn't. Now it's my turn to thank you. It means a great deal to me to hear you say such things. Now, I'll tell you all I know about the Scouring."

Ruegger sipped his drink, strangely at peace. The fires of the city were reflected in Hauswell's eyes, curiously a little moist. Ruegger held Danielle's hand, and together the trio watched the city burn.

Hauswell began to speak.

*　　*　　*

"Remember when I met you in Liberty and told you that someone was investigating my total resources? Well, I continued my search for the person behind it and at last was successful. However, in the process, I alerted this person, and now she wants me dead before I can spread the news of her identity."

"She?" said Ruegger.

"That's right. Before the Scouring began, she wanted to determine how powerful I was. I believe she'd planned to start the Scouring soon and was looking for a partner— someone that could provide her with what contacts she lacked. She investigated me to see if I fit the bill and, for whatever reason, decided not to go with me."

"Would you have gone along with it?"

"Of course not, which is perhaps the reason she went with someone else. Or perhaps it was that I wasn't powerful enough."

"Who'd she decide to go with?" asked Danielle.

"My former greatest competitor—Vistrot."

Danielle exchanged a glance with Ruegger. "So this woman and Vistrot are the forces behind the Scouring."

"Yes. This I've learned through weeks of hellish research. In the early days of the Scouring, Vistrot used Junger and Jagoda to perform several of the killings, including that of Testopha. I presume he did this to cloud the issue, because people have recently tended to associate the Balaklava with Roche Sarnova. Don't misunderstand me; I'm not saying Vistrot intentionally framed Sarnova—not in that instance—but he surely did it to create general confusion in the event that the identities of the murderers became known to the public.

"After the first few killings, Vistrot and his accomplice decided to play it safe by hiring local death-squads to perform the wet work. They hired the teams through a series of front companies, and it took me a long time to sort through them until I found out the truth of the matter."

"What's the purpose of the Scouring?"

"To rid the immortal world of crime and religion, I suppose."

"Then why did this woman seek help from the greatest criminal alive? It takes a thief to catch one?"

"Who knows? I still think she sought out Vistrot because of his contacts and his power base. Perhaps it appealed to her sense of irony. Besides, who else could she have turned to but a major crime lord? But we'll get to that in a minute. It all makes perfect sense."

"So once they've cleansed—excuse me, scoured—the world of crime and religion, then what? Vistrot gets to be the head honcho from then on and the woman disappears into the nether from whence she came?"

"I don't know. As we've discussed, after every Scouring's resultant chaos, a lone figure emerges to take over the area, like Karl Barnaby of Las Vegas. A great deal of my investigations have dealt with finding a commonality among these doomsday princes, as I call them, and the only thing I've come up with is Vistrot. That's where his contacts come into play; he has to be able to control these folk, so they have to be people that have worked well for him before. After he Scours, he sets someone up in each area that's loyal to him. These doomsday princes are one of the main things the woman needed him for."

"What about Ludwig?" Ruegger asked. "Where does he fit into the picture?"

"Think of it this way: Roche Sarnova could be a serious impediment to the Scouring. So if you wanted Sarnova out of the way, how would you go about killing him if you didn't want to use your own soldiers?—and it *would* take an army."

Ruegger nodded. "So you're saying that Vistrot and the woman had Ludwig killed—using the Balaklava, who are thought to work for Sarnova—to incite the wrath of his widow and the Libertarians so that they would attack the Dark Lord in retaliation."

"It probably would've worked, too, hadn't someone stepped forward to take responsibility for Ludwig's murder."

Ruegger leaned closer. "We heard you know who ordered the hit. In fact, that's why we came to find you."

"I figured as much. You won't like the answer, though."

"Who?" Ruegger breathed. "Who ordered Ludwig's murder?"

Hauswell paused. "Kharker," he said. "Lord Kharker has taken responsibility for it."

Ruegger stared at him. "But that ... that can't be."

Danielle squeezed his hand, but he barely felt it. "Why would Kharker have had Ludwig killed?"

"An excellent question," Hauswell said. "When I first became aware of this information—only known to a few very high-ranking shades—I assumed he had some motive. Revenge of some sort, possibly. Or perhaps it has something to do with you, Ruegger. Jealousy, maybe. Who knows?"

"I don't believe it," Ruegger said. "I think Kharker's covering for Sarnova. Vistrot and this unnamed woman had set the Libertarians up to attack him, so Kharker took credit for Ludwig's death in an attempt to divert them."

"Possibly," Hauswell said.

"Then why haven't Ludwig's followers killed Kharker?" Danielle said.

The old German smiled. "He is in the middle of the Congo, Danielle."

"That accounts for some of it, but you're missing something," Ruegger said.

"What's that?"

"I don't know. I suppose we'll have to make a trip to the Congo to find out." He lowered his voice. "Crime and religion, eh, Hauswell? Who's the woman who started this whole thing?"

Hauswell took a nervous sip. "My dear fellow, make an effort of restraint when I tell you."

"I'm restrained."

"Okay, then. Here it is: Vistrot's accomplice is none other than Amelia."

Ruegger's face grew ashen. He sat back, blinking rapidly. "You're sure?"

"Quite certain. Amelia, your long-lost love, is in cahoots with Vistrot. She, my dear chap, is the one who came to me all those years ago and prodded me to save you from yourself during the Second World War. I suppose she chose me because I'd done a similar thing in saving Laslo. But don't get me wrong, Ruegger—I was glad to help you."

Ruegger stared. "Why didn't you tell me, you bastard?"

"Please, let's not get nasty. I wasn't so sure you didn't already know, and in any event she told me to keep quiet about it."

Ruegger shook his head. "But she's dead. I saw her . . . "

"You saw a kavasari taking her blood. I assume he changed her into what he was."

"Then why has she never contacted me?"

"Calm down." Hauswell lit a cigarette and passed it to Ruegger. "I suppose the reason for that is that the kavasari are very secretive. We know of their existence, but when have you ever heard of an individual of that race? And who can blame them? They must kill shades to live—so what shade wouldn't want to exact a measure of protection by performing a preventative strike? Besides, I've often heard it rumored that they belong to an ancient religious order that shuns publicity. She probably realized she could never be with you in the same way again and wanted you to get on with your life. She only revealed herself to me because she knew it would be a one-time meeting. With you ... especially in the condition you were in ..."

Slowly, Ruegger's composure returned. "I'm sorry for my outburst."

"Nonsense. Under the circumstances, I feel you've behaved quite appropriately. But you see why I implied that you might be connected to the Scouring?"

"You thought I knew of Amelia."

"I suspected it was possible, especially with the emphasis on eradicating religion—I suppose during your time together, you must have rubbed off on her."

"Maybe. I think Amelia developed her own line of reasoning independent of me, though." He looked at Danielle, who had gone very quiet. "You alright with this?"

She didn't respond at first, but then she nodded. "It makes sense, doesn't it?"

"What?"

"The reason why the Balaklava have been terrorizing us. Vistrot wanted them on our backs—on your back—so that he'd have some leverage if Amelia turned against him. He was blackmailing her with our lives. And torture. Because he couldn't hope to overpower a kavasari himself."

Ruegger's brows drew together. "Then the Titan sent Jean-Pierre's death-squad for the same reason, knowing that the albino wouldn't kill *you*."

Hauswell nodded. "I see that you two have come to the same conclusions I did, although much quicker, I must say."

Ruegger inhaled gratefully on the cigarette. "So that solves the question of the Scouring—at least, some of it— but what of the War of the Dark Council? Do you know anything about that, Hauswell? It seems awfully convenient that it began around the same time as the Scouring."

"To be honest, I know absolutely nothing about the war. My concentration has been on the Scouring. If I had to guess, I'd say that Amelia began *that* when she did because the war would've created a helpful distraction, taking some of the focus off of her own activities."

Danielle drained the last of her brandy. "It's all starting to fall into place now, but there's some major pieces missing."

"We need to find out more about the war and Kharker's involvement in all this," Ruegger said. "Why he claimed credit for killing Ludwig."

She rose to fix herself another glass. After taking a long sip, she said, "I haven't seen Kharker since my days with Jean-Pierre."

"I haven't either," Ruegger said. "And before that, not since World War Two."

"Are you two really planning another trip?" Hauswell said. "You're mad! It will be dangerous."

"It's the only way to stop all this," Danielle said. "Find the heart of the knot and unravel of it." Darkly, she added, "Or just cut it in two."

Ruegger grimaced. "To the Congo it is."

Chapter 26

"It's almost over, you know," Amelia said.

"What's that, dear?" Vistrot asked. The two lay in bed.

"The Scouring of course. Just a few more deaths and it will be complete."

He nodded, feeling a certain pride for the murderous phenomenon he and this strange being had created. What would happen now that it was over? He found himself hoping that Amelia would stay with him, then immediately chastised himself. *What about Kristen?* Still, he was quite taken with the kavasari. She was everything that Kristen was not—voluptuous, mature, and welling over with power—and it had seemed only natural that they strike up an intimate acquaintance to parallel or strengthen their business relationship.

Not only that, but he wanted her blood—the strongest blood an immortal could know—and, being a kavasari, she hadn't turned down a free meal.

He wanted to be what she was. He wanted to feel that power and know that it was his own. She'd said that she wouldn't allow this, that a certain number of kavasari had to be maintained in order to conserve the status-quo, just as the number of lesser immortals could not be allowed to go beyond a certain point. The exceeding of this limit was one of the several reasons she cited for having begun the Scouring in the first place, and she would be damned if she contributed to the over-population of the Community.

Nevertheless, what Vistrot wanted …

"When it is over, Amelia my darling, will you stay with me in order for us to rule the world together?"

"We've discussed all this before," she said. "Maybe I'll stay and maybe I won't. It depends on how good a job you do. But in no way will I be subordinated to you. The lords you've installed in the various power vacuums must serve me with the same diligence that they serve you."

"You know they will. I've taken great pains to ensure that they think of you with the proper respect. If I were to leave, they would be yours to command. After all, you are a kavasari and could eat any of them for lunch if you so desired."

Instantly he regretted the comment; he was already quite afraid that she would turn on him when everything was over, when their Kingdom had been established. He did not need to be planting thoughts in her head.

"Augustine," she said softly, running a hand over his chest, "there's one more thing you need to do for me."

"Anything."

She smiled, but not warmly. "You must kill Kristen."

He started. "Never!"

"Now now. I'm a jealous woman and if I were to stay on after the Scouring, I would naturally want to be your one and only. Not only that, but you need to prove your loyalty to me. You've hounded me with the threat of killing Ruegger for so long that I feel you've been taking undue advantage of my one weakness; this is not the act of someone I can place great trust in, is it? If you do this for me, if you kill Kristen, then I'll be pleased. I will trust, respect—and love you."

He stared at her. "You love me?"

Running her fingers across his bald head, she leaned over and kissed him. "How could I not? And don't you love me, too, just a little?"

Feeling her lips against his face and her fingers sliding ever further south, he snarled, "Yes. Yes, devil help me, I do. But Kristen . . ."

"Do it and we can rule together. I give you one week. If you fail me, I can never trust you again, and why would I want to keep someone I can't trust alive? Do this and things will be wonderful and beautiful always. But if you cringe from your duty, I will have to deal with you—permanently—and Kristen, too."

* * *

Vistrot left Amelia to return to work. Of course, he had enough of both money and employees to ensure a peaceful, luxurious life without the everyday hassle of business, if that was what he desired, but he found the concept of idleness unsettling.

As he took station behind his desk, he found his mind swallowed by thoughts of Kristen. Even though they'd been apart only a short time, he missed her. She was so sweet and pure and vital, and he had wronged her through his liaison with Amelia. Of course, this didn't entitle Kristen to cheat on him, and certainly not with Jean-Pierre. How could he possibly justify her death, though? Amelia had no right to ask him to arrange such a thing. If he were to kill Kristen, he would be destroying everything sweet and pure that remained in himself, if he hadn't done so already. What was he to do?

The phone rang. Slowly, distracted, he picked it up.

"Vistrot?" It was Jean-Pierre.

The Titan snapped to attention. "It's good of you to call, my friend. Are you ready to come back into the fold?"

"We need to talk, Vistrot. Alone."

"I'll schedule an appointment."

"You don't understand; I want to meet with you on my terms, not yours. You must leave your building and come to *me*."

"Out of the question, son."

"Then I'm out of the fold permanently. You'll never see my face again. Not unless you're willing to come to me. Tonight."

"It's not to happen, my friend. How am I to know that you aren't planning some cheap retaliation for the murder of your bride?"

"All the pain I could inflict upon you, if I had from this moment until the sun exploded, could never bring back Sophia or replace the soul that you stole from me with her passing."

"All melodrama aside, you should know that I regret her loss sincerely. She showed promise. Her passing, as you call it, was necessary to achieve the proper understanding between us. You're one of my top officers—you *know* that, damn it. I look on you with a fondness unlike any other. For you of all shades to show me such disrespect … What action I took was required to reestablish the foundation of our relationship."

Jean-Pierre laughed. "Who are you trying to convince, you fat bastard? If you're trying to sway the ears of God, you're wasting your breath."

The Titan reined in his anger. "Your tone's uncalled for, boy. It provides me with the sort of reason I really do not require in order to refuse your invitation. If you keep up this disobedience, I'll find some way to reprimand you—and it will not be pleasant, I *assure* you. Now—is Kristen with you?"

"She is. I suggest you send your love to her while you've still got the chance."

"Put her on, please. We'll talk after you've had time to reconsider your attitude."

Shortly, Kristen came on.

"What is it, Auggie?"

His heart swelled. The anger he felt toward Jean-Pierre disappeared with her first syllable. God, how he wished she was here!

"Dear . . . " he started. "Baby, how are you?"

"What you did to Sophia was unforgivable. Did you know that she was pregnant?"

He considered that a moment, at the end of which he felt a little pity for Jean-Pierre. Perhaps killing Sophia had been a touch rash, after all.

"Here, why don't you come back home?" he said. "I miss you, darling. There's no reason why we shouldn't be together."

"I miss you too, Auggie, but I'm with Jean-Pierre now. Unless you come to him, you'll never see either of us again."

"This is insane."

"You brought it on yourself, Auggie. If you wanna see me ever again, come to the Funhouse of the Forsaken tonight. Otherwise, this is good-bye."

"The freak show—?"

"That's right," answered Jean-Pierre. "Purchase backstage passes and we'll meet you after the show."

"Jean-Pierre, you . . ." Vistrot made a fist and forced all of his anger into it. It trembled with rage, then grew still. "Fine. I'll come tonight, but if I don't show up for work tomorrow, you'll receive a very special visit indeed from Junger and Jagoda. Their faces will be the last you see, and that is not a fate I would wish upon you, however necessary it may become. Do I make myself clear?"

"Perfectly."

The line went dead.

* * *

The rest of the day passed with such infuriating slowness that by the time evening came Vistrot was oddly looking forward to the Funhouse show. Nonetheless, he had no illusions about Jean-Pierre's intentions, but surely if Kristen were with him she would temper the albino's fury. He made quick arrangements with Junger and Jagoda, then set out for the Funhouse of the Forsaken, a small army of guards in tow.

The performance was sold out, but they'd been expecting him and even gave him a choice table close to the stage. His guards, however, were made to stand in the rear of the room. During the show, Vistrot fidgeted, unable to try to enjoy himself while Jean-Pierre was scheming to do him in. More troubling, what was Kristen's place in all this? After the performance, Vistrot shoved his way backstage, where a man met him. He had no lips but his teeth had all been filed to sharp points. Grinning his horrible grin, the lipless man led the Titan into a backroom.

Surrounded by misshapen performers and illuminated by a single harsh bulb, the albino waited in the center of the room smoking a Pall-Mall. This was the old Jean-Pierre, full of cold venom, unbound by such niceties as love. For some reason, Vistrot was reminded of his meeting with Sophia. She and the albino bore the same menacing postures, grim expressions and disinterested eyes.

"Where's Kristen?"

Jean-Pierre bared his teeth. They were sharp. "If you wish to see her, come with me. Leave your guards behind." He held up a finger, silencing Vistrot's next words. "If you say something stupid like 'Out of the question, son', then I'm going to turn my back on you right now. As promised, you'll never see Kristen or myself again—unless, of course, there is a hell."

The Titan nodded to his guards, who, prepared for this eventuality, left him.

"Alright," Vistrot said. "Let's get this over with."

"Not quite, Titan. We've been friends for a long time. I know your tricks." Jean-Pierre turned to one of the freaks, who handed him a large robe. "This is what you're going to put on. Strip."

"I will not."

"My word is law, vampire. The reward of following the law is that you'll see Kristen."

Vistrot shed his clothes and threw on the robe. At the albino's order, the bundle of garments that up to a moment ago had hung from the Titan were searched thoroughly until a performer found what he was looking for. After a slight ripping noise, he brought a small black object to Jean-Pierre.

"What is it?" one of the freaks asked.

The albino held it up to the light as if it were a diamond. "It gives off a radio signal, so if Vistrot doesn't show up for work tomorrow some soon-to-be-dead Jamaicans can track him down with yet another device that receives the signal this one gives off. Where was it?"

"Sewn into the lapel."

Nodding absently, Jean-Pierre held out his hand, and another small box was placed there; after tearing it open, he threw a sheet of pills at Vistrot.

The Titan looked down at the pills in his hand. "Laxatives."

"That's right," said Jean-Pierre, as much to his following as to Vistrot. "See, the device we found was only a decoy; the Titan would've swallowed another, just in case the first was found. He knew I'd look for it. The laxatives will wash out the second one. Then we can take him to see his beloved."

A sudden twinge of fear ran through Vistrot. "Does this mean I won't be showing up for work tomorrow?"

"It depends upon how cooperative you are."

Vistrot knew this was probably a lie, but what choice did he have but to make himself believe it? He could leave this room and return to the safety of his guards, but then he would never see Kristen or Jean-Pierre again. Tearing open the sheet of pills, he dropped several of the laxatives into his hand and swallowed them dry.

Jean-Pierre led him out back to a small procession of limousines, which the performers were climbing into; his proved to be an old black 40's-style Rolls-Royce, a model, he knew, which happened to be a particular favorite of the albino's. After a series of intricate twists and turns (to make sure there was no one shadowing their movements), Vistrot was driven to a large if run-down motel. A hearse parked out front of their room.

"A hearse?" he asked.

"There's a coffin inside," Jean-Pierre said. "We'll stay in this room until the laxatives kick in—by which time the sun will most likely be up—throw you in the coffin and take you to our final destination, where we'll release you into Kristen's arms."

"What are you going to do with me?"

"Again, it depends upon your level of cooperation. I happen to have stumbled across some rather odd tidbits of information which incriminate you greatly—in what, I'm not sure; that's what you're here for. For instance, I know that the Balaklava were never intended to kill Ruegger and Danielle—and further, that Junger and Jagoda were responsible for the death of Testopha, the great abunka leader in Lereba. Both raise some rather interesting questions that I feel compelled to answer. Not only that, but I'm under the impression that the retrieval of this information will afford me some modicum of revenge."

"You're going to torture me."

"Naturally."

"If I cooperate—answer your questions in full—will you still feel compelled to do this?"

"Need you ask? You still have Sophia's death to atone for—and many more besides. But ... on the occasion that you satisfy my curiosity completely and without resistance, I *might* refrain from killing you. Then again, I might not."

They entered the apartment, where many of the freaks were already in attendance to make certain that Vistrot remained harmless. Presumably, the rest of their number had gone on to prepare the "final destination".

They made room for Vistrot on a couch, where he settled down to watch television while the pills worked to flush the small radio device from his system. The others ordered a pizza and smoked some indica (they offered him some, but he declined; he'd never been one to give his mind over to chemicals and he wouldn't start now, even if this was to be his last night on earth), watching some late-night marathon of horror movies.

As the hours ticked by, Vistrot was given plenty of time to dwell on his fate and to organize his final thoughts, concluding with the realization that he truly did not want to die—not now, not ever. Just the same, he found to his surprise that he could not look forward to his glorious, post-Scouring days if Kristen were not there with him. Yet Amelia had promised to kill her if he didn't. Kristen's days were numbered regardless. Would it not be better and more humane for him to perform the act?

By the time *Vampire Circus* flashed on the screen, he'd yet to decide, but it was at this hour (after black-out curtains had already been placed over the windows, signaling that the sun was up) that the laxatives began to jump-start his intestines, and he relocated to the restroom. To his annoyance, Jean-Pierre kept the door open; apparently, the albino thought Vistrot might be desperate enough to salvage the radio device from his own waste and ingest it again. Which was unfortunate, because Vistrot would have done exactly that.

After the device was expunged, Vistrot was made to lie in the coffin, which the performers carried, at some pains, into the back of the hearse. The coffin was large, but he was a big man, and claustrophobia set in.

Though it was difficult to judge time in the thing, Vistrot estimated it was close to an hour before the hearse pulled to a stop and the black box was carried a short distance, then set down. His captors levered its top open. With a little help, Vistrot climbed from the narrow tomb and stepped to the concrete floor of an immense, dingy, and largely empty warehouse, its windows spray-painted and boarded-over. He registered his surroundings in the flash before Kristen was on him, her arms about his middle.

"Auggie!"

"Baby!"

He embraced her, tight. They kissed passionately, and joy filled him. At last!

When she was done, she turned to Jean-Pierre. "I want some time alone with him, J.P."

"You'll get it—afterwards."

"After what?" Vistrot said.

The hands of humans strengthened through decades of sipping immortal blood seized him from behind and dragged him to a section of floor that had been readied for him. Thick titanium chains trailed from large stakes driven through the concrete, and nearby gleamed an assortment of long sharp instruments perfect for driving through one's body.

"This isn't necessary," he said. "It was never my intention to keep anything from you, Jean-Pierre. You would've found out soon enough. After it was all over, you were to be my first officer. That's one reason you were sent to kill Danielle—if you could do that, then I could completely trust you. If you couldn't, that was fine, too, because just the threat of it was enough to put a certain business associate in her place. Please, Jean-Pierre, I won't stoop to begging, but this isn't necessary."

The albino lifted one of the instruments—it looked like some sort of demonic fireplace poker—and tested its sharpness. Still quite dull, Vistrot saw with mounting dread.

Jean-Pierre smiled. "Vistrot, you stole from me my single chance at redemption; not only have you killed the one person I loved—and who loved me in return—but you've damned my soul, if ever I had one and if there is a place for it to go. Without her, I'm lost in darkness. Of course, if you're not on the wrong end of it, darkness can be amusing."

He indicated the floor with his poker, and the sideshow performers began to chain Vistrot to the ground. Kristen protested, but they ignored her. Vistrot's robe was torn away, which left him naked, and the coldness of the concrete made his balls contract. Next they threw the chains around his limbs and torso.

Jean-Pierre hovered dispassionately above. *Dear Lord, boy, what have I done to you?*

Shifting his glance from the Titan's face to the tip of the poker, the albino's face finally registered emotion. It twisted into a mask of utter hatred. Raising the poker high over his head, he stabbed it down with a howl.

* * *

After a few hours in Stomach Prison—as, among other less endearing terms, she'd come to call it—Sophia grew accustomed to its rhythms.

The Rastas, intolerant of any rebellious behavior, fed the rebels to the always-hungry Kalanda, who prowled the living cave intermittently to keep the prisoners in line.

Sophia watched Kalanda and the Rastas closely, observing their patterns of movement and behavior. She frequently tried tapping into the Rastas' minds.

After doing this a few times successfully, but briefly, she decided to make a more thorough attempt, so with great concentration she focused on one man in particular and extended her mind into his. She began exploring, in the process learning much about the Balaklava and their personal histories as observed by this mortal, who had seen and heard a great deal (and despite his youthful appearance was over a hundred years old, due to frequent infusions of Balaklavian blood).

Unfortunately, Junger and Jagoda also kept a constant finger in the minds of their soldiers and discovered Sophia's presence. They stormed into Stomach Prison and beat her severely, and—though she taunted them with the concept of rape—they were quite aware of her ghensiv half and contented themselves with beating her again.

After that, she kept her mental wanderings brief.

*   *   *

Around noon, Jean-Pierre allowed himself a breather from torturing the Titan, for which Kristen was grateful. For the last few hours, his revenge had a musical accompaniment; there had been some instruments lying around the Funhouse's penthouse, and it seemed that a baker's dozen of the semi-mortal mutants had formed a band. When a longer version of the show was performed, they would play several selections for the audience.

"Play for me," Jean-Pierre bid them, and they had gathered their instruments and obeyed.

Their sound, which was somewhere between Romanian folk, rock, and jazz, made Kristen shudder, but Jean-Pierre seemed to delight in savaging Vistrot to the jouncing beat.

The Titan writhed, looking less like Kristen's beloved Auggie and more like a pincushion of flesh with every passing moment. It broke Kristen's heart to see, and she tried not to watch.

During his breather, Jean-Pierre lit a Pall-Mall and went out the warehouse's backdoor, which opened onto an alley. Kristen followed, striking up a Virginia Slim.

"It's gone on long enough," she said. "Don't you think you should release him?"

"No."

The sounds of the band drifted out, seeming to mix with the swirl of smoke and the slight drizzle.

"I think you were right when you said no amount of pain you could give him would do you any good," she said. Looking at him, though, she was uncertain. In some bizarre way, he actually seemed to be enjoying this—*This is him*, she thought. *I think I'm seeing him for the first time. Please, baby, prove me wrong.* When he didn't answer, she said, "You going to kill him?"

"That would take the fun out of it, wouldn't it?."

She could feel her shoulders collapsing a little, her breath tightening. If she didn't watch it, she might start to cry. He had said it was *fun*. A minute passed in silence and he seemed to sense her misery. Suddenly coming to her aid, he wrapped his arms about her. She started to pull away but stopped herself.

"I'm sorry, honey," he said. "For everything."

"Please ... end this. I know you hurt, but this isn't the answer."

"Justice is messy."

"This isn't justice."

"I'm exacting vengeance on the murderer of my wife and child. There can be nothing more just."

She examined him sadly. "Then would you do me a favor?"

"Tell me."

"Give him some hope, at least. You're not even asking him questions like you said you would, just torturing him senselessly. Please, if you love me, if you love yourself—if even a part of you is still human—ask him what you want to know. He'll tell you, Jean-Pierre, not because you're hurting him, but because—once—you were friends. Please don't torture him pointlessly; if nothing else, interrogate him. Otherwise you're just an animal." She fumbled with a cigarette, averting her eyes. "Tell me you will, Jean-Pierre."

He tilted up her chin with one hand, flipped his silver Zippo with the other, and said, his green eyes sincere, "I will."

He moved back inside. As the door opened, the music swelled. Funhouse music.

Kristen stared at the sky for a long time, let the cigarette burn down to her fingers, then opened the door to hear the sound of the Titan screaming. Cringing, she stepped in out of the rain.

*   *   *

At nine o'clock that evening, when Vistrot was supposed to have phoned Junger and Jagoda to call off the attack on Jean-Pierre and the search-and-retrieval of the Titan himself, the two Balaklava were driving around Manhattan searching for their next series of victims and/or muses. When he didn't call, they examined their electronic homing device to pinpoint his location, but he was nowhere to be found. Both of his emitters must have been destroyed.

"Bummer," said Junger.

"He was a prick anyway."

"Without him, we may never find out what all the excitement was about. Of course, he probably wouldn't have told us willingly. But we could've been persuasive."

Jagoda smiled. "Perhaps the odd flock will turn up something. Unlikely, but it's all we've got now."

"No, brother. We know all we need to."

They did. Within a month, they prophesied, the world oyster would be theirs. For now, though, they must continue to curry favor with the Titan, even if it meant saving his sorry bloated hide.

The first logical place for acquiring Vistrot was at Jean-Pierre's apartment. After entering the eight-story hovel, they found something strange: none of the albino's mortal minions were present, though their recent presence was undeniable; their smell had baked into the walls. In any case, their absence signaled that something was amiss, but what?

Junger and Jagoda made their way to the top floor, where they quickly found the albino's room. Pausing before twisting the knob, the bald one turned to Jagoda and, seeing the bearded one shrug, flung open the door.

The explosion actually destroyed the top three floors of the building. Flames caught hold and slowly consumed the whole structure.

* * *

From his vantage point atop an opposite building, Jean-Pierre turned to Kristen.

"Good work, baby," she said.

"Thank you." To Maximillian, he said, "Let's go make sure they're dead."

"Think there'll be anything left?"

"For their sake, let's hope not."

Max rounded up the score of performers and, at the albino's lead, marshaled them across the street, where a large crowd was already gathering. Fire trucks wailed close by. To prevent recognition, Jean-Pierre had had to select the performers that looked the most externally normal. Even so, all wore masks and costumes to conceal their identities; at Max's demand, the troupe must not be implicated in any of this. Even Max himself wore a disguise, leaving Jean-Pierre the sole member exposed. He didn't want to be hampered in case he needed to defend himself.

They poked through the ruins, quickly and efficiently, ignoring the policemen and firemen that urged them to leave. The performers found no trace of the Balaklava.

Jean-Pierre felt a surge of disappointment; the bastards had been vaporized. *They deserved a much slower death.* If they hadn't been so powerful, he would've had them put through the same treatment as Vistrot, but, alas, it was not to be.

More police vehicles arrived.

The troupe had brought along firearms, but the guns proved unnecessary. Jean-Pierre was able to lead the troupe out the back way and, without violent incident, down a few blocks to where vans waited for them in an alley. They sped off, their destination the cemetery in which the Balaklava had lived during their final days in New York long ago. Under the questioning that Kristen had recommended, Vistrot had given up the location.

"You really think she'll be alive?" Max asked as he peeled off his disguise.

Not looking at the snake-oil salesman, Jean-Pierre checked a pistol to make sure it was loaded.

"She'd better," he said.

Chapter 27

Sophia scanned the minds of the Rastas on an almost hourly basis. When they were informed of the departure of their lords, they gave no outward sign, but she was easily able to access the information. After learning of Junger's and Jagoda's withdrawal, she whispered softly to one of the prisoners, who spread the word.

The Rastas often made a habit of sending a couple of their number to wander through the scattered ranks of captives just to instill a little fear in the condemned ones, and Sophia waited for such an occasion before launching the attack: divide and conquer.

As the two Jamaicans drew near, she summoned her powers of psychic dominance, which were greater than her mother's but far inferior to her father's. Controlling the semi-mortals was not easy, but she grimaced and pushed harder—broke through.

Throw down your weapons and disrobe, she instructed them, and they obeyed.

The other Rastas, sensing she was the culprit, turned their guns on her, but too late. At her signal, the prisoners had slowly crept to either end of the Stomach and at the disrobing of the first two Jamaicans launched themselves on the others.

Like crabs beneath a wave, the Rastas fell under the hands of their prisoners. Several died on both sides. The Rastas lay bleeding on the ground, along with several wounded and dying prisoners, while the majority of the freed men made their way to the Labyrinth beyond the Stomach.

Kalanda woke.

The large tigress opened her eyes, surveyed the scene and leapt from her bloody throne with a roar.

"Shit," said Sophia.

Kalanda set her sights on Sophia, who stood alone in the center of the living cave—and charged.

Sophia scooped up one of the Rastas' submachine guns and fired. The bullets tore into the tigress, shredding her beautiful coat into bloody streaks and drilling into her face. They didn't even seem to slow her down.

She'll kill me, Sophia realized. If, that was, Sophia was human-shaped.

She *was*, after all, the daughter of a werewolf.

Throwing down the rifle, she let the gifts of her father storm her bloodstream for the first time in years, and before she could consciously comprehend what was happening she'd transformed into a hairy demon and was flying through the air at Kalanda.

They collided in the air with a thunderclap and meshed into a web of tangled limbs, talons and teeth before they even hit the floor. Hair and blood flew in every direction. Bone cracked.

Sophia would have been killed in seconds save for the damage that the gun had done to Kalanda's mouth. Splintered teeth and bone protruded from the wreckage, making it difficult for the great beast to use her most awesome weapon. Kalanda raked her claws down Sophia's side, and Sophia screamed. Growling, she locked her jaws around the tigress's shoulder and bore down with all her strength.

*   *   *

Jean-Pierre and the vans arrived on the scene to find a group of mortals emerging from the crypt. "Where's Sophia?" he demanded. "Tall, with long dark hair and violet eyes."

"She died," one man said, panting. "Brought down by the tigress Kalanda. Sacrificed herself for us all."

Jean-Pierre pushed toward the ruined tomb and took the stairs down to the crypt. As soon as his eyes adjusted to the darkness, he saw hands gripping a broken tile, and a mortal pulled himself out from the abyss.

Jean-Pierre swallowed a gulp of air and threw himself into the pit. His landing was cushioned by four feet of thick mud. Struggling out of the muck, he marched past the boulders and waited. Vistrot had told him that the Balaklava guarded the entrance to their prison with a labyrinth, making it difficult for any prisoners that managed to escape to actually get free. Jean-Pierre didn't have the luxury of time to navigate the damned thing, so he decided to let the humans do it for him.

A man emerged from one of the tunnels. Just what the albino had been looking for. Jean-Pierre stalked into the tunnel and followed it till it branched off. Yet another mortal appeared in one of the forks. Using these stragglers as his breadcrumbs, Jean-Pierre navigated the Labyrinth until he emerged into a great open chamber that looked like nothing so much as a massive abdominal cavity. Even the walls were fashioned from pink tissue.

In the middle of the room sprawled Sophia, nestled in the embrace of a tiger. Cautiously, he advanced. Neither of the combatants stirred. Were they unconscious? If Sophia were dead ...

Sophia's chest heaved.

Pulse quickening, Jean-Pierre ran to her and carefully extracted her from the embrace of the beast. The tiger shifted, but did not wake.

"Sophia, darling, I'm here."

Her eyelids fluttered but didn't open. With a sinking feeling, he realized that she was dying. Not wasting a moment, he carried her in his arms back through the winding corridors of the Labyrinth, his heart beating faster, faster. He had to get her out of here.

Suddenly, rounding the corner ahead of him—*Dear God!*

Jagoda stepped forward, burned and bloody. He cradled his brother, Junger, in his arms. The tusked one was little more than a blackened skeleton, his motionless mouth open in an expression of agony. Apparently, Junger had sheltered his comrade from the blast—and now, without a doubt, Junger was dead.

Tear-stricken, Jagoda glanced up at the albino. He studied the butchered Sophia in the albino's arms.

For a long moment, neither the werewolf nor the Balaklava said a word.

Then, in a raw voice, Jagoda said, "It looks as though we're even, albino. One for one."

Jean-Pierre nodded, hoping that that wasn't the case.

Warily, the albino and the Balaklava approached each other, one leaving the Labyrinth and one seeking sanctuary in it. As they passed, their eyes locked. Then tears erupted from the Bone Crusher's face. Silently, he spun about and retreated back into the darkness of his home.

*   *   *

I'm going to get to see my sugar, Kristen thought as the warehouse hove into view.

She'd gone with the albino to watch the destruction of his old building and hopefully the deaths of the Balaklava, but before Jean-Pierre and the troupe entered the flaming ruin to assure themselves of their victory, he'd sent her back to the warehouse, claiming that if Junger and Jagoda were still alive, things could get dangerous. Plus, of course, there was always the chance of a confrontation with the police, and he didn't want her hit by a stray bullet.

The albino's dismissal had stung at first, until he'd pointed out that now she could have some time alone with Vistrot.

She noticed a delivery vehicle outside of the warehouse: Chinese food. It pulled away as the taxi dropped her off. Entering the decrepit building, she found what was left of the troupe playing, of all things, a game of Bingo. Claude was the leader. Off to the side lay Vistrot, massive and naked and bleeding; unconscious, chained to the floor and run through with all manner of blades and stabbing instruments, he looked perfectly pitiful, reduced from the most powerful crime lord in the world to a soon-to-be cadaver.

After Jean-Pierre had impaled him with that first hellish poker, Kristen had instantly forgiven the Titan, and whether or not this represented some weakness in her she didn't care. In any case, she knew that Vistrot's usefulness to the albino had come to an end. Without the need for duress, he had willfully confessed all Jean-Pierre had wanted to know and more. It had come as a shock to her that of all things Vistrot was the Scourer, along with that kavasari female Amelia, whom he'd been sleeping with.

Strangely, this had appeased Kristen; his liaison with Amelia had been more a business relationship than anything else, and whatever personal feelings he had for her were secondary.

Now it had come time for Kristen to spend some time with him, alone, before he was to be executed. The execution would not come before he'd been drained by that awful leech Maximillian, though.

Kristen approached Claude. "It's time," she said.

He rolled his eyes at the troupe and they streamed out through the rear of the building; even here, they were worried about being recognized.

Taking a little white box of fried rice, she knelt beside the great man.

"Hey, baby."

At her voice, his bruised eyes opened. A weak smile played about his face, and he managed to croak, "Krissy . . ."

"We're alone, Auggie."

"I'm surprised ... Jean-Pierre kept his word."

"Brought you somethin'." Using a pair of chop-sticks, she shoveled a small amount of rice into his mouth.

It took a long time for him to chew and swallow—he choked several times—but he managed.

"Thanks, angel. My last meal, eh?" Seeing the pained look on her face, he added, "It's okay. I deserve it, you know. All the crimes I've committed, all the crimes I would've committed . . . I just wish I had one last chance to redeem myself."

She stroked his big bald head. The thought of giving him a last blow job crossed her mind, but three different lances had been driven through his scrotum.

"I love you," she said. It was the only thing she knew to tell him. Slowly, she began to cry.

"And I love you," he said. "Could you . . . could you lower your hair to my hand . . . I want to feel it once more . . ."

Letting her tears fall unashamedly, she let him caress her hair. He moaned. When she looked up, tears hovered in his eyes, as well.

"Could you . . . could you bring your head to my chest?"

Bursting into fresh sobs, she gingerly wrapped her arms about him and, navigating carefully between the spears, laid her head on his chest. They stayed that way for a long time before he said, "Tell Jean-Pierre I'm sorry I killed Sophia. If I could change it, I would."

A sudden anger gripped her. She rose back to her kneeling position and wiped at her tears. "I won't let this happen to you."

"There's no way . . . Jean-Pierre won't change. And these spears he drove through the concrete itself. You can't move them."

She held his hand, squeezed it. "I can take your blood."

His eyes widened. "You'd need a lot, baby. You . . . you would become what I am . . . and you've always said you didn't want that. No . . . no, Krissy, I won't let you do it. I'm not worth damnation."

"I'll be the judge of that." She smiled sadly. "And, dear . . .you have very little choice in the matter."

She bent down to his wrist and bit into the big vein there; it spurted some, then she had her mouth around it and nearly gagged before she became accustomed to the flow. The blood was warm, coppery, sort of salty, kind of bitter. As it pooled in her stomach, she began to get a strange high off it. *It's immortalizing me*, she realized. It welled up from her belly into her veins and circulated throughout her body; her skin burned with it wonderfully and her eyes blazed. She felt like she could move a mountain. After a time, she heard him say, "Enough, baby . . . I don't ... have any more."

When she pulled back from the wound, only a few drops trickled from it. Vistrot looked even closer to death than before. Thrusting her arm before his mouth, she said, "Now it's your turn."

Without argument, he bit into the proffered wrist and began ingesting her blood. To Kristen, it was a very singular, rather unwelcome feeling, although there was a certain high that came from this as well. She soon grew lightheaded.

When Vistrot stopped swallowing, she stood up and steadied herself, then started tearing the chains out of the floor. She was so *strong*. Once that was done, she took a firm grip on one of the spears and gave it a hard yank, pulling it roughly from its concrete bed. Its angular head made it impossible to pull back through Vistrot without causing him severe pain, so her task would be to free all the spears from the concrete and then to roll him over onto his side so that she could pull the spear shafts out through his back.

The task took a whole of fifteen minutes, and that was only because of the delicate nature of the last part of the operation. Vistrot cried out in pain only once. When it was over, she helped him to his feet, then searched through the overnight bags of the troupe until she found some oversized clown garments. Not only could he fit into them, but they would disguise his injuries, as well. With her assistance, he dressed.

He wrapped his arms about her and held her close, and long.

"How do you feel?" he said.

"Strange . . . but I'm the one who should be asking you that, Auggie: how do *you* feel?"

Weakly, he smiled. "Let's just say that I'm not going to be retaining any water for some time."

Despite herself, that made her grin a little. "Let's go home."

They left the warehouse and hot-wired one of the vans out front, which Kristen drove to the Titan's building. Though they didn't talk much, they frequently held hands. Eventually they reached the Titanic, parked, and made their way down to the proper sub-basement, then to his bedroom, where he called a doctor, who was to arrive within half an hour. While Vistrot showered and dressed, she flung herself on the bed and tried to pinpoint Amelia's scent. Did the kavasari wear perfume? Did Vistrot like sleeping with a woman who was mature, voluptuous? She'd have to confront him with these questions and more before her mind would be at peace, but now was not the time.

When he emerged from the dressing room, she patted the bed. He flopped down beside her, shaking the bed.

Unbidden, he said, "I'm sorry for Amelia. I was weak and selfish, but that's no excuse."

She sniffed. "I'm sorry for Jean-Pierre. What about him, now—are you going to . . . take revenge?"

He fell silent for a moment. "No. Really, I deserved what he did to me. I'll consider us even; let's just hope that he will, too." He held her small hands in his. "Kristen, I really respect what you did, standing up to me like that, but I couldn't bear it if you cheated on me again."

"It runs both ways, Auggie."

"Of course . . . but that's not what I meant."

She felt something cross her face; seeing it, he visibly grew excited, too.

"Don't tease me," she said, somewhat nervously. "And I don't want you to tell me later that it was just one of those in-the-heat-of-the-moment things."

"Believe me, it's not. I've been thinking of this for a long, long time."

Seeing her eyes grow bright and her breathing grow shallow, he rose from the bed and knelt beside her, her hands still in his. His face red and his fingers trembling faintly, he said, "Kristen, will you . . ." He coughed. "Kristen, will you marry me?"

She smiled and threw her arms about him. It was all the answer he required.

* * *

"Where are they?" Max raged at Claude, who had one pair of arms folded across his small chest, was defiantly scratching his balls with one of the hands from the second pair and smoking a cigarette with the other.

"Up my ass," said Claude. "Where do you think they are?" He spun to the albino. "You told me to give them some time alone and that's what I did—don't think I'm owning up to any culpability. It's really not my problem."

The albino let his eyes rove the scattered freaks and could not find fault with any of them; as Claude had said, it wasn't their mistake. Max was still admonishing the dwarf, but Jean-Pierre cut in.

"Max, it's a shame you didn't get your goddamned blood, but don't take it out on them. Don't blame yourself, either; I accept full responsibility. At the appropriate time, I will administer my punishment. Unfortunately, Vistrot knows who you are, and, as he's still living, I'd suggest going underground for awhile. From what he told us, I don't think you'll have to worry about him for long."

"What do you mean?" Max said.

"Just what I told you." Jean-Pierre glanced over to Sophia, comatose in a nearby chair. He'd given her his blood, which would sustain her until she was able to procure sustenance on her own. But what to do with her? Where he was going, she couldn't follow.

"Max," he said. "I want to repay you for what you've done, but now is not the time. There's somewhere I must go to sort things out. I'll make a deal with you; you look after Sophia for awhile, as collateral, and I'll come back for her. Soon. Then all debts will be paid in full."

Slowly, Max nodded. "It's a deal."

To the troupe, Jean-Pierre said, "Thank you all for your cooperation. We'll meet again soon. Count on it."

With that, he turned to leave.

"Wait," said Max.

"What?"

The snake-oil salesman hesitated, but his eyes were sincere. "Jean-Pierre, my friend . . . you have no place to go, do you? And you—you are a freak, aren't you? An albino, more or less. Well . . ." He gestured to the others. "We're all freaks here, Jean-Pierre. We could be your home, your family. Why not stay with us?"

Jean-Pierre closed his eyes. Really, why not indeed?

* * *

"When the albino was interrogating you, you didn't say anything about how you were supposed to kill Kristen, did you?" Amelia interrupted.

It was the night after Vistrot's escape. Amelia had come to visit the Titan's office. She wanted to know the details of his absence, and he filled her in on recent events.

"Of course not," he said. "For a long time, she was in the room."

"That's a shame. I'm sure he would've gotten a kick out of it. Anyway—continue."

When he told her of how Kristen had freed him, she smiled. He was almost able to convince himself that it was a sweet smile.

"So I take it you haven't killed her."

"No, and I don't intend to. In fact, I asked her to marry me, and she said yes."

"That was quite contrary to our agreement."

"I won't apologize, Amelia. You'd no right to ask me to do that."

"I wasn't asking, dear. Now isn't the time for foolish valor. Now is the time for proving our loyalties to each other, and you've more to prove than I do, goddamnit. I sought *you* out, not the other way around. Need I remind you that if you won't kill her, I'll do you both?"

"You're bluffing. Not only am I sure of that, but to be on the safe side I've given instructions to Cloire, who will have rounded up both Ruegger and Danielle shortly, that if I die, she should kill them both. Which won't be a problem for her, if that's what you're thinking—in fact, I believe Cloire's been looking forward to the job."

Amelia's face went still. "You've hung that over my head for too long, Titan. It's given you some leverage, I admit, but now I realize that if I'm to stay true to my vision—a beautiful world, free of crime and superstition— that I may have to sacrifice certain nonessentials. If it's your desire to kill the odd flock, I won't stop you. But you'll kill Kristen regardless."

He felt genuinely unnerved. "Christ . . . how can you have such little heart? My love of Kristen won't affect anything! She doesn't need to die."

"No, but *you* need to kill her, for the same reason you sent Jean-Pierre to kill Danielle: to rid yourself of that baggage and to prove your loyalty. The albino faltered; are you as weak as he?"

Vistrot stared. "Is that what this is? You're making me do this to Krissy in order to punish me for sending Jean-Pierre to kill the Gutter Angel. That's it, isn't it? A taste of my own medicine, and at the expense of the most innocent person involved in the whole affair."

"That just makes it all the sweeter, doesn't it? Even if she doesn't deserve it, you do."

"That's perverse."

"Perhaps. But, then, Vistrot, you're a perverse man. You're just lucky that I'm equal to it. So: now that you understand why I'm making you do it, I expect Kristen to be dead by tomorrow—and trust me, her death at your hands will be much more pleasant than at my own."

She blew him a kiss and left the room.

*　　*　　*

That night, as he watched Kristen sleep, Vistrot thought of all their times together and all of their times to come. He couldn't wait to see how bright her face would become on their honeymoon to Hawaii—hell, it would only *start* in Hawaii.

They could go around the world endlessly, buying a beach house there, a lodge in the mountains there, a flat in Paris . . . he could make her so happy, and now they had all eternity to spend together. . . How could he wrap his gigantic hands around her delicate, milky-white neck and squeeze the life out of her? He tried to imagine what advice she would give on the matter and for the briefest of moments thought of waking her, but no, that would be madness. God, Amelia was so . . . so evil, wasn't she? How could Ruegger have been her lover all those years? Of course, the Darkling had more than ably demonstrated his own talent at sin, hadn't he?

So had Vistrot, if truth be told, all for the sake of his business, his empire. Kristen had often accused him of loving his business more than he loved her, and of course he'd denied it, but they both knew that there was a certain truth in what she said. By killing her, he'd only be proving her right. Even during the years he hadn't been sleeping around, he'd always had a mistress, and her name was Power.

Could he ever expect to leave his business behind and dote every waking moment on Kristen? How preposterous. After all, he was on the verge of a power so great, so global, that he could not possibly turn his back on it now, could he? Shed his burdens and go gallivanting around the world with the one person he truly loved—

What a . . . what a joke . . . what a cosmic fucking … *joke* it had all turned out to be, wasn't it? *Go on, convince yourself that what you're doing is right so that you can strangle her and be done with it, then go on to be King of the World—now that would be grand, wouldn't it?*

He put his hands over his face and cried silently for a long time, but not silently enough.

Kristen opened her eyes. Groggily, she said, "What is it, baby? Bad dream?"

"Yeah," he replied. "Bad dream."

"Here, want me to make you some milk or coffee?"

"No . . . no, that's okay. Kristen, you know I love you, right?"

"Of course, baby." She smiled. "You've only said that a thousand times today, although you know I couldn't hear it enough. And you know I love you, too. Here, want me to hold you while you fall asleep?"

He smiled sadly, wiped away his tears and stroked her hair. "No, that's okay. I just need to think for a little while. You go on back to sleep. Sweet dreams, darling."

She patted his hand and closed her eyes, her head resting gently on the silk pillow. Soon she was fast asleep. He watched her for two straight hours, wrestling with himself. Finally, he breathed a great sigh, placed his large hands around her smooth, creamy neck, and *squeezed.*

**THE END
OF VOLUME ONE**

AUTHOR'S NOTE:

Thank you for reading. You might want to check out my website at jackconnerbooks.com. *The Living Night: Volume Two* is now available.